LOST PRINCESS
JACE'S STORY

Saving Planets, Book 1

AWARD WINNING AUTHOR
KATHLEEN GARNSEY

Publishing Coordinator & Book Designer – Sharon Kizziah-Holmes

Paperback-Press
an imprint of Paperback Press, LLC
Springfield, Missouri

ISBN -13: 978-1-970560-24-4

Dedication

I would like to dedicate this book to a friend of over thirty-eight years, Sharon Kizziah-Holmes. We have been through a lot together, and I cherish our friendship dearly. She is the best at what she does, creating books and covers, and writing as well. We have learned our craft of writing together, and I have loved having her with me on that journey. Thank you my friend for always being there for me.

Acknowledgments

I would like to thank my friends in 'Writer's of the Purple Page, Sharon, Tierney, Susan, Shirley, Conetta and Lois for their support and encouragement. They are all the greatest!

Chapter One

Jace tapped his foot on the floor of the transport lobby while he waited for his contact. Whoever made this appointment with the office refused to leave a name. Could this case truly be so clandestine? It didn't matter; they'd pay for his time no matter what. He and his two brothers ran the most prestigious secret force on planet Lorton. They took pride in the fact their business ran like silkus and remained successful.

The lobby was a busy place with people rushing in every direction imaginable to catch their particular transport. He kept his eye on those who looked a bit lost. His client obviously knew what he looked like, yet he had no idea who might show up in front of him. He noticed a woman wearing a long flowing gown, with a head covering to match. Unfortunately, he could not see her face, so it must be her.

Sure enough, she made her way across the open space in front of him and stepped up to the bench he sat on and took a seat beside him, a safe distance away. She acted totally out of place, and looked the part. The style of her attire seemed above average although the quality of the fabric gave her away. She appeared dressed in far more expensive clothing than any average citizen could afford. Plus, it took a lot of credits to hire his firm. This woman obviously did not travel on public transportation.

"You are one of the Bryton Brothers?"

She did not lean toward him and remained looking straight ahead, so he did the same. "I am. How may I help you?" Slowly, he turned a bit and saw her remove a folder from her carry bag and lay it on the bench between them. She used extreme care not to be noticed or seen, which opened a myriad of questions.

"For you. Everything you need is in the folder. I have nothing more that will help. I can't be seen here. Please do this job. I need your help. Do not contact me, it's too dangerous."

Before he could utter a reply, she stood and walked away from him. One glance told him she headed straight for the exit door, well on her way out. He surveyed the area carefully, but saw no one on her trail. In fact, no people were within eyeshot at the moment to witness anything. Good. The woman planned well and he wished he could compliment her, and ask all the questions lingering in his mind.

Jace picked up the folder, rose up off the bench, then walked in the opposite direction the woman took. If her actions were any indication of how worried she felt about being seen, he'd play along. He certainly didn't want to do anything to endanger her or his firm. Still, he had no indication of what she wanted, or who she was. In fact, he hadn't expected a woman at all. Surprise.

The longer route to his transport craft should throw off any onlookers in the area, should there be anyone watching. He'd play her game. She must have good reasons for her undercover, clandestine behavior. Most people didn't, even though they thought they did. He casually walked out into the waning sunlight.

It did not take long to reach his craft. Once in the captain's seat he proceeded with his vertical take-off. Carefully, very carefully since most driver-pilots in the area were the worst he'd ever seen, and he refused to put his craft in the repair shop again. He called them driver pilots since they never ventured very far, and never off Lorton. That made him chuckle. The worst drivers were usually older people who were more used to the old type of transportation.

Jace took the lull in traffic and quickly disappeared into the upper allotted flying atmosphere. Less crafts around him suited his nerves better, and at the moment, he felt nervous for some reason. He began to think he got paid to be nervous. At least he got paid. He hurried back to the office and landed on the roof of the parking garage.

When he opened the sliding doors a vertical lift attached to his craft and lowered it into the underground parking area attached to their home and office. He touched the button on the control panel of the craft and the door opened straight up and allowed him to easily stand and exit the smaller craft he took. When he reached the backdoor of their residence, it opened the instant he looked at it. He walked down the hall to the main room, then on to their work area.

"Light on." Once the overhead lights shone down on the table in front of him, he slid onto the stool and opened the folder. The woman he'd met obviously felt her case to be of the utmost importance, and anxiety rolled around in the pit of his stomach. He couldn't be more ready to see exactly what was in the folder.

The moment he pulled out the picture and saw the face staring at him, he froze. The Supreme Ruler of Lorton, Raulf and his life-mate, Marna, looked back at him. He took a deep breath. Anyone could have this picture. Then he saw the letter and began to read:

> To the Bryton Brothers:
>
> This job request may surprise you. I want you to locate Lania Sloten, whose name is officially Lania DeMorgan. Raulf DeMorgan had her drugged to completely remove her memory. He then then sent her off to who knows where, most likely another planet, in another galaxy. This is no joke. As I'm sure you heard, our Royal Ruler, Raulf DeMorgan, told the public Lania died from pregnancy complications. She did not. At least he had the decency not to kill her, which I hope will be his undoing when you return her to her rightful home.
>
> I have enclosed in this envelope everything I have which could possibly help you. I wish I knew where Raulf sent her, but I don't, and in the six annual-cycles she's been gone, I have not heard her name spoken here at the palace since her funeral.
>
> In case you haven't figured it out by now, I am Gale DeMorgan, The Ruler's sister. The reason I want to take my brother down, is

> because he is the meanest man I have ever known. He even treats his own family like dirt. There are a select few men who work closely at his side which he treats almost like humans, and they will do anything he pays them to do. Credits speak loudly; everyone knows they do.
>
> At the end of the file in the back pocket, you will find your payment. I tried to be generous, and if you succeed and return the prize, I will add to this amount. I hired your security firm because you are professional, and no one is to know I contacted you. If any of this information were to get out, you, your brothers, and I will all be dead. The stakes are high. The reward for success cannot be measured if we want to continue life on Lorton.
>
> My sincere thanks, Gale

Jace flipped to the back of the folder and pulled out an overstuffed envelope containing nothing except large-denomination-credit bills. A quick count put it around half-a-million credits. He'd never held this many real credits. He and his brothers earned this much on jobs before, although the way business always went, they never saw cash, the funds were always transferred. He couldn't deposit this all at once or he'd draw attention. A bad idea to be so obvious.

The wall safe located right behind him, opened when he stared at the lock. He quickly laid the unexpected payment inside, then secured it. No one except his brothers could possibly open it. Wait until they heard this story. He knew he'd need their help. They all worked their specialties, and he planned to make use of them all.

Chapter Two

Lania leaned against a tree and watched all the children play ball in the grassy meadow. She loved kids, so it made her job easier since she liked being in charge of all the pre-school children. Kids always kept her busy creating something to do, and they usually had an emergency of some sort to keep her running. Although she got tired at times, she gladly kept going. What choice did she have? With no memory of anything about her life, she knew nothing else to do. Besides, the kids were nice to her, their parents were not. The mean people here told her while returning from an air trip, her vehicle malfunctioned, and her landing turned into a very bad, fiery crash. At least that is what they said. The people insisted her crash ranked number one on the 'noisiest-crash-ever-heard' scale.

They still wondered how she survived. They told her she spent ninety-seven sun-cycles in the med-unit, nearly a lifetime in this age. Surviving death must have been a strange experience, one very difficult to digest. The odd part still remained, she did not remember a crash. She'd yet to find anyone to talk to who saw it happen. If it had been as bad as everyone said, it should remain imbedded in her mind forever, but it was not there.

Not one person on Extram knew her. They said she came from off-world. That did not help her since she could have come from anywhere in the universe. With no memory, and without knowing where she came from, she did not know where to begin learning about her past. The info-system here contained one small program, and no one would ever tell her anything about how it worked, or where they hid the device. They must have hidden it since she had never seen it. In fact, no one ever talked about the system or its location. They told her any information concerning her could only be found in the system located on her home planet, wherever she came from in the great unknown. Without a name, she would never learn anything. They also told her not one piece of information survived the fiery crash, only her.

Everything she knew fell into the category of instinctual, normal things, naturally ingrained in a person to remain alive. Like taking care of children seemed natural to her. As a woman she could have children, maybe not, but she knew how to care for them. She glanced at her wrist-piece and realized the sun-cycle would soon end. It did not take long to gather the little ones and begin their walk back to the settlement. A wrist-piece was the only thing they allowed her to have, and that was only to ensure their requirements of having the children in different places at certain times. So the wrist-piece served them, not her.

The kids played so hard they all happily merged into a line and walked quietly on the path through the bushes to go home. Luckily, the men kept the trail cleared since the jungle always remained completely impossible to navigate without one. She'd never seen so many plants. Then again, this might be normal everywhere for all she knew.

She'd learned not to ask questions since the people around her refused to answer anything. For some reason, they hated her. She'd see them talking to other people, yet when she wanted to be friendly, they turned their backs on her and walked away. In other words, they refused to speak to her, unless they were giving orders. Basically, she lived the life of a slave.

She must not know about proper behavior. No matter what she did, she got the same result, unable to make a friend. No one understood how difficult life was with no one to talk to or share things with. There had to be someone living here who had lost their memory and could possibly have sympathy for her feelings. She also wanted someone to answer her questions, and she had plenty. She needed to learn her identity and how to return to where she came from. Her life before may have been extremely boring, yet she still wanted it back.

For some reason, this sun-cycle proved to her, without a doubt, she did not belong here. Her mind screamed at her, 'past time to leave'. How exactly she could accomplish an escape remained a mystery. She owned nothing, not even a map. It didn't matter; life had to be better somewhere else, anywhere else.

A woman opened the door of the building they just reached and helped usher the children inside then slammed the heavy, wooden obstruction in her face. Typical, the same thing happened over and over everywhere she went, so their behavior no longer fazed her. It remained a mystery to her why every person here thought they needed to be so mean. What in the universe made everyone hate her so much? She tried to be nice to all the people here, yet it did no good at all. In fact, it usually made matters worse. Everything here seemed beyond strange.

Escape from this place appeared completely impossible. She only knew about the few areas where she took the kids in her care. She owned no tools, she owned nothing. Right now, it didn't matter what she did or did not have, she felt more than ready to leave, and the sooner the better. She hated being here. It equaled no life at all. A person did not need a memory to come to such a realization. Soon. She might be able to save a little food from each meal, and possibly sneak a bit out of the supply room a little at a time. Of course, if she saw her chance to run away, she'd take it in a flash.

Some people here thought she was plain stupid, possibly the reason they all treated her so badly. Without a memory she had to learn everything again, which was a painstakingly slow process. Since all remnants of her memory were gone, nothing seemed to matter to her anymore, except getting out of this place. Without a family or friends to think about and care for, what else was there? That was a question she constantly asked herself, without one chance of an answer. This was her problem to deal with, as she had been told numerous times.

Since she never saw anyone leave this place it seemed extremely strange to her. They may have everything they needed for life in general, but she never saw anything fancy here. For some reason she felt she knew what fancy looked like, even if fancy did not exist in this place. Maybe these people were happy here. She could not say the same. She felt more than ready to go down in their history books as the first woman to ever escape this miserable place.

The people here were past strange. Everywhere they went they walked. There were no vehicles of any kind, flying or otherwise. The housing units seemed all the same, rather small and dismal, all built somewhere around the shopping area. They all lived so close to each other that walking to see your neighbor was very easy. Of course, they kept her in a far corner where nobody ever went, except the guard or two they paid to kept an eye on her.

There was a place in the center of all the housing areas where, credit-takes, which they called shopping-businesses, which had establishments containing food, clothing, tools, about anything a person might want to purchase.

She knew flying crafts must exist somewhere since they told her she crashed one on the border of this place. That also meant she knew how to operate one of those crafts since she had been alone. All of her past was a mystery. To her, she should be able to remember flying here and crashing, yet all of that information and experience still remained a mystery. She was one giant mystery.

Jace felt relieved both his brothers were home from the trip they took for a client. He couldn't be more anxious to share the good news with them. The giant paycheck remained foremost in his mind, even if he had no idea about the actual case. It might be best to do it quickly, then allow them time to digest the assignment he'd accepted, or the one thrown at him. Dane and Holt were sitting at the table having lunch, so he walked over and joined them.

"Hey guys. How's it going?" He wanted to begin slowly. Their shock would happen soon enough.

"We're good, Bro," Dane said before he took another bite of food.

Holt looked up from his plate. "Same way we always are."

"Glad to hear it. You two have been gone for three sun-cycles. Hate to admit I missed you." Jace tapped the table with his finger. "I put something in the safe I need you both to go get. You need to see it at the same time, okay?"

"You're weird, Jace. You know you are." Dane laughed while he stood. "Come on, Holt, let's appease our overly-mysterious, crazy brother."

Jace watched them both walk to the safe. The moment the door swung open he heard both of them react to what they saw—not exactly a scream, but pretty close. You can bring it over to the table if you like. It's fun to look at."

"Please tell me you didn't rob a bank," Dane said while he sat on his chair.

"Are we all going to jail, Bro?" Holt shook his head while he sat down on his chair, the pile of credits in the center of the table.

"Wow, is about all I can say." Dane scratched his head.

Holt nodded. "I agree with Dane. This is hard to believe. Surely you have more information, right?"

Jace stared at his two brothers. "Surprised?" He laughed at the strange looks on his brothers faces.

"You know we're shocked by a stack of credits like that!" Dane laughed.

Holt stared at Jace. "Are you going to tell us where this stack of credits came from? Like who hired us and for what?"

Jace studied Holt and Dane for a moment while they touched the credits. "This may shock you, but we have been hired to find Lania DeMorgan, who this person swears is still alive. Her death was a lie, like all of Raulf's statements." He took a deep breath. "This person did not exactly give me a chance to turn the job down. An envelope was given to me and this person just walked away. I was not able to check it out until I arrived home. I was just like the both of you."

Jace could tell by the looks on his brother's faces that they were in a state of shock, same as he had been. Well?"

"It's a deep well for sure. What are your thoughts, Jace?" Dane asked. "You're the one who accepted the assignment and the very generous payment."

Holt shook his head. "Do you have any clue where we should begin?"

"Not yet. If we all work together, maybe we can come up with something. Or somewhere for me to go look"

Dane stood. "You know we can't stay long due to our other job. Hopefully long enough to get you started."

Jace smiled. "Okay then. Let's do it." All three of them walked over to their work area in front of the info-system to read what it sent to the air-screen. Holt had always been a true genius in this area, and Jace knew he would find something fast. At least he hoped so because he had no idea where to begin.

He couldn't be more relieved his brothers were here. Now he hoped Holt could work his magic and find the information he required before they had to leave. He stood behind Dane while he searched for leads in his own way. Holt explored every possible avenue that might show this woman leaving the planet six-annual cycles ago. It seemed to be a viable scenario, even if old info disappeared quickly. The date it occurred remained about the only thing they positively knew within a three sun-cycle time unit.

"So we need to check all the closest destinations for arrivals?"

Holt laughed. "I wish it were that simple, but you're close. I'll get started, but you know Dane and I have a job to attend to. Think you can handle this by yourself?"

"I'll have to. You leave me no choice. If you get back and I'm not here, check in with me."

Dane walked up behind Jace. "You're so sweet to worry about us."

"I might need help." He laughed, so Dane and Holt joined him. They were usually on the same wavelength. After all, being identical triplets gave them communication advantages other people never experienced.

Holt shook his head. "Help or not, we have to leave. Our transport vehicle is ready, and I want to wrap this up quickly, if possible. We're nearly done. Except to transport the last two clients to Delmora, then settle a couple of issues for them."

"Sounds good. Appreciate what help you've given me."

Dane slapped him on the back. "We're here for you."

"Yeah, except when you're not, like any moment now."

"It's hard to keep good men still. You know?"

Jace nodded.

Holt stood. "Jace, sit for a minute. I need to show you something." He waited for his brother to sit on the stool, then he pointed at the screen. "The computer will give you the percentages of flights based on location, etc. All you can do is sort through the results to see what best fits. The computer will do most all of the work for you. Concentrate on the intent behind it all."

"We're used to those angles." Dane patted Jace's shoulder.

"Intent?" Jace laughed. "Really?"

Holt nodded. "Like why they didn't kill her. Wouldn't it have been easier?"

Dane nodded. "It would have erased the threat of her showing up again. It seems careless to leave her alive."

"You're right, Bro." Jace studied the large screen. "So, what planet do you think they sent her to? Super far away? Close? Somewhere in between?"

Holt laughed. "You sure know how to cover the entire universe quickly. Yeah, one of those for sure. Motive is driven by time, necessity, and credits, so you need to decide which one of those drove the decision."

Dane scratched his head. "Do they need to bring her back at some time in the future? Does she know something important? Let's face it, this planet is in dire need of an energy adjustment, and we haven't experienced a real one since the princess went missing, or supposedly died. The stupid ass and his current life-mate, Marna, have only accomplished chaos. I still have problems with the idea he life-mated Lania's sister, but Raulf had to remain in power."

Jace shook his head and groaned. "I have no answers, yet I totally agree. I must bring the princess home if she's alive, but Raulf is not the person who wants her back."

"No need to get uppity now, bro." Holt checked his timepiece. Come on, Dane. We must leave now." He walked to the door, Dane stood and followed.

They both stopped at the door. Jace walked over to them while they put their jackets on. "You guys behave yourselves and come back safe."

Holt patted Jace on the back. "I think you're jealous you're not coming with us."

"Maybe a little." Jace laughed. "I'll be too busy to miss you guys. Besides, I must earn the half-million credits the client paid." He watched both brothers smile widely at him.

Holt lightly hit him in the back of the head like he did when teasing him. "Fine. Let's say I spend the half-million credits while you two are gone."

"What? Wow! Maybe we should stay with Jace! What do you think, Holt?" Dane asked.

Holt laughed. "He knows better than to spend a dime of those credits. If he does, we'll hunt him down and...let's say he knows better."

"My first job is to find the princess. Maybe she can fix the rising unrest here on Lorton before the entire planet explodes in violence!" Jace stared at Holt. "I hate to say it, but we all know truth when we hear it."

"Absolutely, and the unrest has grown worse every sun-cycle since she's been gone. Our credits are on you, bro. Go find her and bring her home!"

"Will do." After their brotherly hugs, Dane and Holt left. The door quietly slid closed behind them and Jace stood alone with his dilemma. Hopefully, the info-center would spit something out soon because he wanted to get started. He watched one of the smaller screens on the desktop while it searched every possible take-off and destination fitting the criteria. Then it stopped and his jaw dropped.

Extram. The info-screen showed it to be the one planet meeting all the criteria they'd asked the system to assimilate. It matched five out of six possible parameters. Everything he read seemed good. Relief spread through him. His destination was the planet Extram.

Jace parked in the large craft area on the tarmac of the main landing zone on planet Extram. It said 'Temporary Parking,' which seemed perfect to him since he didn't plan to be here long. Once he exited his craft and began to walk toward the terminal, he felt a very odd, different feeling surround him. Not really evil, simply unexplainably strange. Eerie summed it up. Hopefully he'd find the girl quickly and they could head back to Lorton. He was surprised by the amount of crafts parked in the lot, which meant the terminal would be crowded.

While he walked, he kept thinking he'd need a lot of luck to find this woman. The only reason he landed here in the first place was because the info-center readout ranked it the number one possible location to begin. Why? When he looked around the place, it seemed they had no traffic at all, yet there were all kinds of craft parked in the lot. Strange. Even more reason to hurry and take off.

The moment Jace stepped into the terminal shock rapidly flew through his body. There was not one person inside the very large building. Every terminal he'd ever been in had lots of people looking for something, like food, drink, information, or friends and relatives. Back to the strange, eerie feeling. He stepped up to the info-window.

Of course, not one person stood in line, since the entire area was completely empty. On a different and quite odd planet, you took note of everything, especially if it seemed out of the norm compared to what you knew. Everything became a clue to something, especially when you did not understand who owned all the crafts parked outside. He might have an idea if there were businesses or housing close by, but he'd seen nothing relating to people.

A pretty blonde lady stood behind the window, so he turned on his flirt mode. He always obtained more info from women when he threw his smiles at them, especially when they were alone, like the lady behind the window. "Hello, my name is Sami, and I've never been here before, so I have a few questions I hope you can answer." He gave her one of his sweetest smiles.

"I'll certainly try. Where ya from, Sami?"

"Pacatrla."

"Never heard of it before."

"Not in this galaxy." He leaned closer and smiled again. It must have worked since she leaned even closer to him.

"I'm Leta." She smiled. "I'm on the short list; in case ya wanted to know."

"Glad you told me. Happy to meet you, Leta." He followed suit and leaned even closer to the glass separating them. "If you didn't want to be found on this planet, where would you go to live?"

"I can think of one place so remote and strange; nobody ever wants to go there. The people are mean. They aren't liked by anyone, and they live in an out of reach area. It's not easy to get in or out of there. We have a difficult time finding people willing to make deliveries to them no matter how much they're paid."

"Sounds like an area I need to avoid." He gave her his come-on look. "Do you have maps here? I want you to circle the place we talked about so I can stay far away from it. I certainly don't need any trouble while I'm here."

Leta smiled. "It's your lucky sun-cycle, sweetie. A new load of maps arrived earlier this morn. Let me get one for you." He watched her saunter slowly across the inner office to where the maps hung on the wall. She took one down then returned to him. She pressed against the glass in the exact location she'd been in before. She gave him the familiar, kiss-me look, and he knew his luck held since she couldn't get out of her little glass cage.

The woman spread the map on the counter in front of her and studied it for a moment, then circled some small area on the other side of the planet. "I'd love to take you there, Sweet Thing." She smiled. "But they won't give me time off. I've never actually been there, but from what I hear, it's a really miserable place. Too hot and hard to breathe. It's a defimoon-cycle jungle to be sure." She smiled at Sami. "It's a good thing you plan to avoid it. Because you're so cute I'd show it to you from the far outside perimeter, but I'd never go in there. Too scary. Even with you to protect me."

"Glad you warned me." He looked up at her and winked. "We could have had fun together. I would have protected you. No matter what." Jace gave her one last enticing smile. How much for the map?"

"Five credits." She pushed the map through the small opening. "I bet we could have had a lot of fun together. You certainly look like a fun man to me, and very capable of protecting me."

"Thanks." She gave him a big smile and he couldn't miss her implied intent. He almost laughed since she did not want to go where he was going, she simply wanted him. Of course she was great for his male ego, but the woman was far from his type. He pulled ten credits from his pocket and handed it to her. She started to get change. "No darlin', keep it for yourself, for all your help. Thank you very much, sweet thing."

Quickly he turned, her chuckle still in the air while he headed for the exit. The moment he stepped outside the building, the same creepy, uneasy feeling hit him again, and he felt it seep through his entire body, indicating way past time to leave.

While walking to his parked craft, the picture of the woman he came here to find kept flashing across his mind's eye. He'd done nothing except study her picture the entire flight here. It took over ninety space-hours for the flight, so he knew her well. Her brown eyes in the picture seemed to look right through him, and her dark brown hair appeared, fairly straight, with a slight curl at the ends. Her locks hung past her shoulders in a perfect manner, and he wanted to reach out and touch the silky strands. The woman could not be more beautiful, no doubt about it.

He did love brunettes, especially when they looked perfect the way Lania did. It might prove interesting to see if she would be responsive to his request to go with him back to her home planet of Lorton. From the information he was given, Lania had lost her memory, so she had no idea where she came from. Losing one's memory must be extremely difficult, especially when she couldn't remember anything from birth until now.

In his research he learned about a possible cure for this particular type of poison. Who would think, or guess that a certain Lizzard's venom had the ability to erase someone's memory? And the same venom could possibly return the memory. Very interesting.

First, he needed to find the dark-haired vixen before he'd be able to address the problems ahead. He thought about the letter he worked from and couldn't remember anything about what to do with her, except to find her and bring her home. Gale said if he succeeded and returned the prize, she'd make it worth his while—whatever she meant. He'd do everything within his power to get her to Lorton.

Jace was nearly at his craft. This trip he used the largest craft they owned since he didn't know what kind of a journey he faced. Of course, his brothers had the slightly smaller version, but considering the distance, it was convenient, and safer to have a craft that could travel at the speeds this one did. Even at top speed it still took him over ninety space hours to get this far. It proved to be a long trip, and as his grandpa always said, 'better safe than sorry,' and the old man always spoke the truth.

He opened the hatch and entered his transport craft quickly. He needed to get away from the creepy feel of this place. Hopefully his final destination would be better, although he decided not to bet on it. He entered all the location coordinates from the map into his info-system and waited for it to settle. In a flash it told him it would take half a space-hour to arrive at his destination, and it also told him parking his craft might be difficult.

Couldn't anything be simple? The best scenario would be to land and park nearly a two sun-cycle or less, walk from where he wanted to go. At least he'd be close enough to make the trip, even if he didn't like the idea due to the problems attached. Anyone would be able to do damage to his craft, and it would be disastrous. Doing damage would be tough, yet if someone knew what they were doing, they could disable the entire craft. He worried too much, and worry seemed to be his worst habit, along with a lack of patience. Didn't matter, he had to leave his craft if he wanted to find this woman.

His auto-pilot told him to take over and find a landing place since he'd now arrived at his destination. He searched for a less obvious place to park. There wasn't one. He could only butt his craft up against the abundant foliage. A large tree limb hung over the center of the craft and helped keep it hidden, not great, yet better than nothing. The craft sat very secure once he locked it. No one had ever come close to his password yet, so he assumed it would remain secure. Besides, he did not see one single person out and about.

He grabbed his short, over-moon-cycle backpack, which always sat ready to go, no matter where he headed, within reason. Not the best food, a few nifty weapons and other miscellaneous goods were also contained in the bag. He then slipped Lania's picture in the bag even if he didn't need it, he'd have it. The way it looked he might be the only human in the jungle. He grabbed his bag, put the straps over his shoulders, picked up a machete from the large bottom drawer, then walked out of the craft, sealing the ramp closed behind him.

Jace entered the dense jungle foliage next to where he parked, and hacked away to clear a path. He still wished he'd been able to park closer. Closer to what? This situation looked impossible. Every man wished he could find a gorgeous woman out in the jungle in the middle of nowhere. Right. Sounded like a strange dream to him. He had no idea exactly where he was, or how close to the village, or town, or settlement, or whatever these people called their home. He still needed to be careful since he didn't know who might show up out of the blue to stop him.

Chapter Three

Lania looked three times before she slipped out the far back gate. There were times she could see a guard, and other times there would be no guard. The few pieces of food she saved to take with her easily fit in the small pocket of her well-worn skirt. She'd waited endlessly for this sun-cycle. Actually, the courage to leave had been her reason for waiting so long. She may have memories of being here, but they were memories she truly wanted to forget.

Once she closed the gate behind her, she stood in cut-back jungle foliage. Twenty more steps and she'd find freedom. She only took several steps, but quickly found herself in the thick of all the miserable sharp, large-leafed plants that concealed her and prevented anyone from spotting her. This heavy, jungle-growth had to turn into something else somewhere. She prayed it disappeared soon since it rapidly drained strength from her body.

She did not know her location now, or where she might be going. Nothing mattered except leaving this horrible place. The children were fine at the moment, and they were her only concern. The entire village she'd been living in proved totally unbearable under the conditions those cruel people created for her. Something must be wrong with her to be treated worse than a slave. Strange or not, her life here had turned impossible to deal with any longer. She'd seen a couple of slaves they brought in once for a short time, and they treated them far better than her. Enough was enough.

The large palmus leaves with sharp edges cut into her hands when she pushed them aside. She wished she had some kind of a blade to chop her way through. This just happened to be like everything else in her life here, miserable. She could not possibly have a blade, or gloves since they allowed her to own nothing. The future somewhere else had to be better, if she ever got out of the overgrown jungle alive.

Time dragged on slowly while she tried to walk, shoving greenery far enough away for her to pass. It seemed the vegetation became thicker and thicker with no end in sight. These rough jungle plants proved more difficult than she ever imagined while she made her way through the rough thorny leaves that drew more and more blood on her hands. Everywhere she took the children was on well-cut paths the men provided for their children. Nothing was too good for their children. Never for her. The babysitting job may now be over, however; she did not know if this would turn out better or worse than the life she left behind.

Where would she end up? No matter where she went, she knew one thing for sure, she would be in trouble with no credits to her name, whatever her real name might be. For all the work she'd done, she never received one credit for her trouble. Others were paid, she heard them talking about their credits, yet not one credit ever came her way.

She walked and shuffled along, pushing the prickly limbs and leaves away, her hands bleeding badly now, her skirt the only cloth to wipe the blood on, which enabled her to keep going. Time passed and she became overly tired and really needed to rest, but not possible here. Where could she could stop? At the moment she felt she may not live through the ordeal. Her biggest problem seemed to be a lack of protein. In fact, she could not remember the last time she ate anything.

The sound of animals closing in on her, following her like they were planning an attack, became louder and louder. She had seen the giant catis who could tear a person up with their claws and teeth. Other animals jumped from treetop to treetop until they landed on you like a tree limb. One more reason to get out of this place. A tree limb blocked a small path ahead, and she decided to use it to rest on for a moment while she caught her breath.

In the distance she heard a strange noise heading in her direction. It did not sound like an animal, more like someone cutting foliage like she wanted to do in order to pass through the area. She stood and moved toward the whacking sound. It should be safe since no one from her area ever went this far from the settlement, and if they did, they stayed on the one tiny path that continued in front of them. It could be a path out of here, but she had no idea where she actually was at the moment.

She pushed back more huge palm leaves, and when the way cleared her heart nearly stopped. Shock rattled through her battered body. Before her stood the most beautiful man she had ever seen. His features appeared perfect beneath his short, dark, sexy facial hair. He looked friendly, almost happy, especially with some of his hair hanging down wildly on his forehead. The back of his hair touched his collar and he looked amazing. He appeared clean-cut, muscular, well-proportioned with everything about him perfect.

Never before had the sight of a man made her stomach flutter, yet right now it felt like thousands of butterflies trying to get out. His shirt bulged where his, tight, well-formed muscles pressed against the fabric, and the sight drew her attention more than she wanted to admit. His muscles made him appear to be a perfect warrior, ready to win any fight. He was taller that all the men in the area and she felt sure he could win any battle. His face was more handsome than she had words for, while his body appeared tough and ready, a man not to make angry.

He stopped chopping the brush and simply stared at her. No way did this gorgeous man live here. From the moment she arrived in this miserable place, she never saw a man she would call handsome. She wanted to throw herself into his arms, even if the idea had 'inappropriate' written all over it. These were thoughts she'd never had before, at least not in recent memory. Although, with no strength left, it seemed like a great idea since he might help her out of here. He certainly appeared strong enough for the job.

"By the Gods, you're her! Lania. I don't believe I found you so easily! I suspected you might be somewhere around here. This is extraordinary! Lucky beyond belief."

"What name did you use for me?"

"Lania. You have a beautiful name."

She had never heard the name Lania before, and was not sure it should be called beautiful, yet the way the sun kissed the man's dark, shaggy hair and tanned skin, he certainly could be called beautiful. "And who might you be?"

"Oh, sorry. I became so shocked to find you, I forgot to introduce myself. I am Jace Bryton, and I've been sent to find you and return you to your home. I also know you have no memory, and I will try to help you retrieve it. No promises. However; I'll do my very best."

"I'm Lania?" Her legs began to shake, then she became dizzy and the landscape spun before her eyes. She felt an inevitable fall coming, something she hated to do in front of the handsome man. She so wanted to impress him and show him her strength, yet the situation simply fell out of her control. Her eyes closed and her legs gave way.

Jace lunged forward and caught Lania before she hit the ground. He pulled her unconscious body tight against his and held her still for a moment. She felt soft, yet strong at the same time, and so beautiful, words could not do her justice. Of course she was disheveled out here in the jungle, especially with her skirt all bloody. There was blood on her hands and face, yet it was Lania. The pictures of her he studied showed her real beauty, yet even in her miserable condition he saw her beauty hidden beneath all the blood and dirt.

He lifted her and cradled her body against his chest and began to walk back in the direction of his craft. Every place her body touched his made him feel as if he were on fire. Sweat beaded on his forehead while he marched through the leaf-ridden jungle. With each step he took, he felt more and more like he would never make it. Not because of how heavy she felt. In fact, she appeared and felt extremely underweight, only because she made him want her in an impossible way. He should not have such thoughts, especially about Lorton's Royal Princess, plus she was a woman he hadn't really met yet.

He pressed on at a faster pace in an effort to suppress a building desire for Lania. Of course she looked nothing like her picture right now. Her hair appeared dirty and very tangled, a clear reflection of her journey. Her face was also covered in dirt and blood, which did little to help her beauty. Yet still, he saw through all the mess to the gorgeous woman in his arms. What man wouldn't want a woman like Lania? Her perfect facial features still shone brightly through her tattered hair, dirt and blood. No matter how perfect she may be in her picture, the oppressive landscape created severe difficulties. He tried desperately to keep the sharp leaves from cutting her even though it remained nearly impossible while carrying her through this overgrown jungle. At least it seemed the rough leaves attacked her skirt more than her skin.

Then he came upon the last opening to endure and caught view of his ship under a tree on the other side, deep in the brush, or leaves, or whatever one wanted to call these jungle bushes and trees. Poor Lania needed some rest, and food. At least he hoped she only required food and rest. He'd know for sure once he took her to the med room. He hurried across the open grassy area and headed toward the slight bend where he'd parked.

It didn't take long to reach the craft. He set her feet down to allow him to tap his wrist-com so the ramp would lower. The door above opened, so he scooped Lania into his arms once again, hurried up the incline and inside the craft. The moment they arrived safely inside, the ramp automatically closed. Jace walked across the open area, laid Lania on the lounge, and secured the straps around her for takeoff. It would not be good for her to slide off and land on the floor, especially when he planned a quick, undetectable move. It wouldn't work on most planets, but this place would never know he'd been here.

He walked to the front and settled into his pilot's seat. It took a moment for the massive engines to reach full power. When they did, he slowly backed up into the clearing which was barely big enough for take-off. He pulled the throttle toward him and the craft lifted straight up, then he pushed the control forward for a fast take-off into the wide-open sky.

Once the craft completed all its take-off procedures and found the proper coordinates he'd set, it moved faster, and Jace could finally take the well-needed deep breaths he'd put off. He'd skirted the law before. With no idea what the laws on this planet might be, he still felt quite safe taking a chance at an unclaimed take-off out here in the middle of nowhere. He'd only met one blonde lady on the entire planet, other than Lania.

They reached the outer realm and he checked the controls he'd put on auto for the return flight to Lorton. At least he now had the time to take Lania to the med room, so he turned his seat, unbuckled, then stood and walked over to the gorgeous woman still lying unconscious on the lounge. She presented one amazing picture. Even dressed in blood-covered rags, no make-up, and hair not combed—she still had an amazing appeal that pulled him to her. What did they do to her? He hated to even imagine.

He released the safety straps around her, picked her up and had to carry her sidewise to maneuver his way down the narrow hall to the med unit. When he entered the small room, the table was directly in front of him, and he gently laid Lania down on her back. The exam ball knew what to do the minute he turned it on, so he relaxed a bit while he watched it hover slowly over her.

Sometimes the ball stayed in one place longer than he thought it should, and he'd worry because lingering usually meant problems. The machine amazed him since it was never wrong about the results and solved the worst physical mysteries he'd ever encountered.

Jace took a seat close to Lania's head, then leaned back to relax. What he'd been through did tire him out, and he needed a bit of a rest. One time-unit. He leaned his head against the back of the chair and closed his eyes. He knew Lania would let him know when she woke, especially since she couldn't get out of this room without him. He smiled and dozed off.

Lania opened her eyes and blinked several times. Nothing changed. She'd never seen this place before and felt quite lost with no idea where she laid. How did she get here? She turned her head and saw a man in a chair next to her, and it all rushed back. He found her in the jungle, and must have brought her here, wherever here may be.

She'd already forgotten his name. Figures. Her memory was gone anyway so why remember a stranger's name, especially when she'd been on the verge of passing out? At least she remembered some of what happened. She coughed loudly then cleared her throat, her way of putting an end to his sleep. It worked. He opened his eyes.

"Well, hello there. Are you feeling better?"

"May I sit up?"

"Of course."

He stood, slipped his hand under her back, and helped her sit up. She swung her legs off the table in order to remain upright and be comfortable. "I believe I'm okay now. I don't know what happened back there."

"When did you eat last?"

"I have no idea."

"Come, I'll escort you to the galley."

He reached out and she took his hand which was twice the size of hers and way stronger. The man could only be called super handsome. In fact, in all her time she could not think of another man who would be able to best him in the looks department. Granted, her memory may not be long, and was also quite limited, but something told her he could hold his own against the very best anywhere. Broad shoulders, muscled arms, a small waist, and long legs. Nothing about him looked weak. She loved his strength…a lot. At the moment, she would follow him anywhere.

He led her down a narrow hall until they arrived in an area that looked like some sort of kitchen, or whatever he called it. The sight before her seemed fantastic next to what she normally observed. The animals the people kept lived a better life than she experienced, which was not hard since they made sure she had nothing. She never saw anything like this in that miserable village. He let go of her hand, stepped over to a chair and put his hands on the back and held it for her.

"Please, Lania, have a seat."

She did what he requested without a second thought.

"What would you like to eat? I can get you anything you want. Just tell me."

"I'm sorry to say, I don't remember your name." He smiled at her and her heart melted. He looked so appealing, her stomach flipped in circles again—tickling her insides. How could she eat facing such a handsome man? Right now, it seemed difficult to even catch a breath.

"I'm Jace." He took a seat across the table from Lania. "I'm not surprised. You were not all there when I found you. I mean you were about ready to pass out, and..."

"I understand. No offense taken. If the truth be known, I haven't been all there for a very long time, a story I don't think anyone wants to hear."

"Don't worry. I plan to help you with your memory, Lania. Even I don't know the whole story yet, but I plan to help you find out. If you allow me to." Jace picked up a jar from the counter and handed it to Lania. "Wipe your hands on one of these. They are sterilizing wipes."

"Thank you." She took one out and used it to clean up, and constantly glanced into his eyes for proof of sincerity. She saw what she looked for, along with other things she dare not think about. "I would appreciate any help you can provide."

"Good." Jace leaned on the table and looked into her eyes. "First, you need to eat. What can I get for you?"

"My stomach does not feel well."

"Got it. I'll get you some nice hot cereal."

When the handsome man looked into her eyes, her stomach flipped over and over again, even though it seemed fairly sick. At least Jace made her feel better when she looked at him. Right now, she watched him press a few buttons, then he returned to the table with a spoon and a bowl with cereal, milk and sugar. She simply stared at it. The people where she came from ate this, even if they never served it to her. They never allowed her much at all.

"Is something wrong?"

"With my current memory, I have never eaten this before." He sat across from her and stared at her, his eyes full of questions. "The entire time I lived on Extram I have basically been a slave. They never paid me for any work, and I did nothing else. They barely allowed me any food. They mostly gave me a slice of bread and a scoop of water, once in a while a piece of meat, or a bowl of some kind of slop. I don't know what they called it." She looked up at him. "I called it terrible."

Jace reached out and put his hand on top of hers while she rested it on the table. His skin felt warm and all too nice, even if he only gave her kindness. This man seemed special. So very nice and thoughtful.

She knew nothing about men, but Jace made her feel comfortable, and was the first person she knew who gave her any positive, good attention at all.

“Lania, I’m very sorry for what you’ve been through. What you speak of is horrible and no way to live. I plan to rectify your lifestyle immediately, and together we’ll find who is responsible for your torture. It certainly seems like torture.”

“Thank you, Jace. I would like to know who did this to me, if that is possible. I also wonder why he, or they, wanted it to happen. If I knew, I might be able to help.” Lania shook her head. “I have no idea, so I suppose I’ll just eat this cereal.” She picked up the spoon, scooped some food on it and took a bite. Great stars it tasted good! After several more spoons full she looked up at Jace who still carefully watched her. “This is wonderful! They never gave me anything like this. I watched them eat it.” She nodded her head. “I love it.”

“I’m glad.”

When he smiled at her, she felt the tickle in her stomach again. He created strange effects in her she couldn’t explain, and she couldn’t stop reacting to him. Actually, she didn’t want to, she rather liked how it felt. In all her sun-cycles, memory aside, she never felt the kind of reactions Jace stirred within her. Damn. When she looked at him, she felt relieved she remembered no other men. She believed this man to be the best. She took the last bite of cereal then pushed the bowl to the center of the table.

“Would you like another?”

She shook her head. “I don’t usually put that much food in my stomach. Like I said, they never gave me much.”

“I believe you. You’re skin and bones. I need to take care of you and get you healthy.”

“I’m fine.” She smiled at him.

“Yeah, and you passed out because you’re fine.” Jace shook his head. “Lania, I know what I’m talking about and you’re not fine. You can be in a short time, but you must start eating. Especially protein. So, listen to me. You need to get your strength back. So, please, eat.”

“You’re right, I know, I only. . ..”

“Oh, Lania. You don’t remember feeling better, or being anything more than you are now.” Jace smiled. “I plan to fix those problems for you. One way or another, we’re going to get your memory back, and soon you’ll see how good life can be when you feel better.”

"I hope you're right." She looked into his deep blue eyes and studied his hair which was nearly shoulder-length, but only in the back. She did love to look at his black hair, which helped make him more handsome than any man should be. She knew he must have many women on his arm, why would he not? "Tell me, Jace, how do you plan to recover my memory? I haven't been able to, so how can you?"

"One thing at a time, My Lady."

"Wow. No one has ever called me My Lady before."

"I think they have. You just don't remember."

"I'm sick and tired of the 'I don't remember stuff'." She wanted to touch the dark hair curling slightly on his collar. She needed to get over him fast. Why would a man who looked like Jace want anything to do with her? He was hired to return her to Lorton and would probably disappear once they arrived, so it would be best for her to remain calm and enjoy her time with this man while she could.

"Lania, I plan to do everything in my power to rectify things for you."

"I don't know what you can do! If I can't remember, you can't make me!" Tears rolled from her eyes and down her cheeks. Jace rose from his chair and knelt on the floor next to her. He put one hand on her knee and one on her shoulder and it almost felt like a hug.

"My Lady, don't cry. You'll see, all will be well. I'll make sure everything is righted, no matter what it takes." He handed her a cloth.

She wiped tears then looked at his concerned expression. "I apologize for crying. I have a feeling I don't normally do so. At least I did not do it while living with those extremely mean people."

"I doubt you did it much before." Jace smiled. "You're a strong woman with a will that doesn't quit. I also believe you have a big heart. Allow me to help you."

"Why would you want, or need to?"

"I'd love to see you laugh and have a good time for a change. You deserve it."

"And how do you know things about me?"

"Trust me, I know more about you than you think, so I'll be able to help you regain some of what you lost. If I'm lucky, all of what you lost, if you want it back."

"Why wouldn't I want it back?"

"I'd rather you decide in good time. For now, we have a long ride. Let me show you to your room so you can get some rest." Jace checked his wrist device. "We still have well over eighty-eight space-units before we reach our destination, so you have plenty of time to sleep. I'll be doing the same so we'll be ready to work when we arrive."

"You're right. Lead the way, Captain."

"Captain, am I?" Jace laughed. "Don't let my brothers hear you say Captain. I'm sure they'd object. They don't like to give me credit for very much. At least not out loud. We get along great and work together very well. Give credit, not very often." He laughed again. "We joke around a lot, and rarely take each other seriously, unless we're working on a job."

"I think I understand. I don't remember if I have any siblings."

"You do. We'll get to your family in time." He helped Lania stand. Right now, I'll show you where you can take a bath, or a shower whenever you like."

"You're so thoughtful. Thank you." Dear stars, she could fall for him. Probably not a good idea. He held his hand out for her to take, and she accepted because it seemed to be his way of showing her down the hall of his craft. She followed him along the narrow walkway until he opened a small door and indicated for her to enter, so she did. Her mouth dropped open at the beautiful room containing every luxury she ever heard about, and more.

"This will be your room. If you need anything, you can reach me on the intercom. Push the button next to the bunk, or by the light over there. It will buzz me and I'll answer. In the drawer you'll find sleepwear, and there are towels in the lav through the door over there." He pointed to his left. "You can also find all the clothes you may want hanging in the closet over there." Jace pointed to the wall at the end of the room.

"Thank you so much. You're most thoughtful, Jace."

"Rest well, My Lady." He bowed at the waist then left her room.

Why did he keep calling her, 'My Lady'?

Chapter Four

Jace rubbed his eyes and groaned. Sleep evaded him this moon-cycle. He hadn't planned to be so besotted by Lania. The woman somehow planted herself under his skin and they'd barely met. He must be slipping badly since this never happened, and he'd met, and been with some very gorgeous women in the past. Lots of them. One in every crowd stood out, or so the saying went, yet he couldn't say why he felt the way he did about Lania, especially since she was very different from other women.

This strange feeling would pass once he got home and returned to a normal routine of work and seeing his brothers. Holt and Dane were finishing up the odds and ends of the current job they'd been on. He'd stayed home to keep things running at Bryton Security, which remained the only reason he went after Lania and left their office unattended.

One thing he knew for sure, Lania would be full of questions he would have to answer. To pass time on the way to find her, he'd worked on clips to show her that chronicled her entire life. After all, she'd lived in the spotlight of the government since the sun-cycle of her birth. Too bad she'd been born a female, since only men were allowed to become Supreme Rulers of Lorton. Those laws may need to be changed. For now, they both needed to take things one at a time.

Since the sun-cycle Lania named Raulf DeMorgan as her life-mate, her father, The Royal Ruler of Lorton, died suddenly. Then, the energy on Lorton changed dramatically for the worse. He never thought it possible, but Lorton's energy slipped miserably from a happy positive, to an angry negative scenario. It seemed strange, and no one knew how, or why it happened, except it remained Lorton's new normal. The entire atmosphere on Lorton needed to be fixed immediately if the planet's inhabitants were to survive.

Poor Lania did not have any idea what lay ahead for her. Once she legally made her presence known, she'd once again be life-mated to the evil ruler, Raulf. What would happen to her sister, Marna, Raulf's current life-mate, remained unknown. Something needed to change since Lorton's laws did not allow any man, or woman to legally have two life-mates. Even though the government declared Lania officially dead, her living presence would certainly void the death declaration.

This entire situation might explode the moment Lania returned alive and well. In fact, all of Lorton may well explode like a giant bomb—his thought since he'd like nothing better than to be rid of Raulf. Hopefully, Lania would know what to do with Raulf. It would be interesting to see what she did with her sister who life-mated Raulf. Did she take part in Lania's disappearance? To his knowledge, no one yet knew what happened to Lania, nor who might be guilty of the plot. Bryton Brothers' Security needed to solve all those questions.

Only the universe knew if they would be able to accomplish the job at hand. Sure, he'd been very well paid to fix an impossible problem. Nothing about bringing a woman back from the dead would be easy, especially when she belonged to the Royal Family. Bryton Brothers' Security accepted this unfeasible assignment. Actually, he alone accepted the paperwork from Gale. At the time though he knew nothing about the job she presented to him.

Another question remained unanswered, what lay behind Raulf's sister's motive? It appeared Gale truly hated her brother, why else would she pay Bryton Brothers so much to find Lania? And why would Lania's sister, Marna, turn on her? Could both of those scenarios be dead ends, or were they the answers? He'd learned long ago, there were no dead ends or accidents. Those ends and accidents always led somewhere, and he needed to know where.

It no longer mattered if he hadn't slept, the work ahead always began fast and continued the same way. Watching Lania learn about her past might be difficult since she did not experience the best past a person could have, especially one from the Royal

Family. Where did Raulf come from anyway? He seemed to simply show up and grab the ultimate power. How had the population allowed such a thing to happen? Jace knew Lania's public persona, like everyone else on planet Lorton, and she never appeared gullible.

Footsteps in the hall made him look up in time to see Lania walking toward him. She looked better now after her rest. In fact, she looked quite amazing, a thought he pushed to the back of his mind. "Hello. Feeling better?"

"I think so. I guess I needed some sleep."

"Obviously." He smiled at her. "You've been sleeping for," he checked his wrist-piece, "sixteen time-units."

"What a long time. Wow. I had no idea." She looked him in the eye. "Is it time to eat? I believe my appetite is returning."

"Absolutely. How about a nice mid-meal? Or do you prefer the first-meal?"

"I don't really care. Whatever you decide will be fine."

She turned and headed to the galley. Plenty of time remained for mid-meal since they were three time-units from landing. He followed her into the galley and ordered them both some food. She said whatever he wanted, and right now he decided on a meat-filled sandwich. He needed protein—and so did Lania. He saw both sandwiches drop down, ready to serve. He opened the slide window and pulled out both plates, carried them to the table, putting one in front of Lania.

"That is the biggest sandwich I've ever seen!"

"You have no memory. You may have seen a bigger one."

She laughed. "My sandwiches consisted of one piece of stale bread with nothing on it." Lania looked into Jace's eyes. "You may be right."

Jace laughed now. "I'm always right. Ask my brothers." Now he really laughed. "No, don't ask them. They'll tell you they're always right."

"How many brothers do you have?"

"Two. All three of us work together. We own and operate Bryton Brothers' Security. One other thing, we're identical triplets, so don't be shocked when you see them."

"I see. I suppose if I had a memory, I might have heard of you." She smiled at him. "Well, you know—especially if you three look alike."

"That we do." Jace nodded at Lania. "I plan to provide you with vids of everything concerning you to help you regain your memory. We, meaning Bryton Brothers' Security, work hard to keep a low profile because of the work we do. Many people have heard of us but don't recognize us. We like it that way, especially since there's a lot of undercover jobs required in our line of work. It's always easier if we don't have to wear a disguise."

"Your work sounds interesting. I want to ask who hired you to find me, but I doubt you'll tell me."

Jace chuckled. "You're absolutely right." He took another bite of his sandwich. "It wouldn't make any sense to you right now anyway." He shook his head. "Some things I don't understand." He looked straight at her. "I plan to get to the bottom of it all. For you." He looked straight at her. "For us both."

Lania nodded. "Great idea."

The way she looked at him made him feel as though he had to have her right now. Damn, the woman for being so gorgeous. She was perfect from the top of her head to the tips of her toes, and once she gained a few pounds he may not be able to keep his hands off of her. She looked really thin which confirmed what she'd told him was all true. They'd obviously fed her next to nothing. "Lania, it may take a little while." He tapped the table with his fingers. "I promise we will solve this strange plan surrounding you."

"To say I'm confused would be a huge understatement." She took a bite of her sandwich and chewed for a moment while Jace did the same. "I want to say how glad I am you saved me. If you had not found me, I would have either died in the jungle, or they would have found me and dragged me back." She looked him in the eye. "I decided it would be better to die than continue living the life they forced upon me."

"I can't believe they treated you so badly. Although I've heard about such cases, and people."

"Most of the time they refused to even talk to me. They only spoke to me when absolutely necessary, and I could never be in their space. I had to stay in my room, which was the smallest possible space, and the farthest away from everything in the settlement. Most of their closets were bigger than my room. It looked like a tiny prison cell I saw once on a trip they made me go on."

Jace nodded. "I hope you'll be happier now. Remember, it will take some time to reinstate you properly."

"I'm not sure what you mean." She chewed the bite she took. "I'll take you at your word."

He watched her eat. The woman ate so daintily, neat and precise, which completely fit her personality. They'd both finished their lunch, and he realized how nice it felt to spend time with Lania. She drew him in, chewed him up, then let him go, just like lunch, and he enjoyed every moment. He hoped his brothers didn't notice his growing attraction to her. If they did, they'd tease him until he begged for mercy. His brothers were the biggest teasers he'd ever known. They were either fun or painful. Either way he expected it.

Jace finished his lunch then wiped his hands on the clean-sheet. "Lania, if you want to shower or change clothes feel free to do so. We'll be landing at my home in about two space-hours. I don't know if my brothers will be there or not. I just want you to feel free to help yourself to whatever you want or need."

"Thank you. I believe I will." She pushed her empty plate to the center of the table then stood.

"Help yourself. You have two time-units before we arrive, so take your time."

"Thank you. You're very kind. I'm not used to people like you, you know."

He stood, walked over to her and put his hands on her shoulders. "Truthfully, I'd never treat you any other way." She trembled beneath his touch. "I will never lie to you either." She stared up at him.

"Thank you, Jace. I appreciate you and your honesty. More than you know."

"You're very welcome." He pulled his hands back, the heat from her body fresh on his fingers. He wanted her. What he wanted didn't matter, only the job he'd been hired to complete. It might take serious effort on his part to refrain from giving her the attention he wanted. He'd do his best to behave himself and remain professional.

Lania found the hair dryer and a brush. She knew what to do with them since she had used them on some of the children, but never on herself, until now. It had turned into a true luxury on this trip with Jace. She so wanted to forget that awful life. Could he possibly deliver her memory, something so extremely necessary?

Why couldn't he just tell her about her life? Instead, he wanted her to watch vids. How many times could she have been in the news? She thought only the rich and famous were in the news enough times for him to create so many vids, not the ordinary. Where did he come up with the idea of making a vid? It felt like a vague memory even though those parts of her were missing.

She shook her head and finished drying her hair. Maybe he thought vids would wake up her memories. It did not matter; she would watch them to please Jace. Simply looking at the man pleased her, and she certainly wanted to please the man who saved her life.

After she put the dryer away, she went to the closet to check out the clean clothes. She still couldn't believe how many clothes Jace had for whoever needed them. Every kind of attire any person might want. Clothes for women or men hung neatly on the long, closet rack. Jace was super prepared. She picked clothes to wear on the trip but did not have a clue regarding what women wore on Lorton, her destination.

She found what would be called formal wear where she came from, so she eliminated those dresses. She narrowed her choice down between a dress, and a pant suit. In all the limited memory she possessed, not one time did she remember wearing a pair of pants, so she picked the most ordinary long dress she could find, hoping it did not seem too special. Never in her memory did she have so many choices.

A brief search of the drawers toward the bottom of the closet held undergarments of all sizes and colors, again for men and women. She took out what she needed and slipped on the fancy undergarments. Then she put on the dress, and it fit much better than she expected. The pretty shade of lavender, with a bit of lace at the top should make it presentable in most situations. She should have asked Jace what to wear, instead she decided simply to ask if she looked good enough to fit in with the other women on the planet.

The mirror on the closet door told her most everything she needed to know. She looked more than presentable, although she could not be positive since there was no one to compare herself to. The women where she came from never wore anything as nice as the dress she put on. Those strange women might consider the dress she wore to be stunning, appropriate for a wedding, or a formal affair only. One last glance through the numerous dresses proved she'd picked the least fancy one hanging there, so it must be acceptable. At least the color of the dress made her freshly washed dark hair look good.

Now she needed to face Jace. She closed the closet door and pushed the button so the exit door slid open. It would not take her long to get used to this type of lifestyle, even on a craft, or an airship, or whatever Jace called it. Wait, she forgot shoes. She opened the door again, rushed to the closet, then tried on several pairs of heels until she found a pair that fit pretty well. In recent times she lived with a lack of shoes, sometimes strapping animal skins to the bottom of her feet, so this truly was an experience to wear such wonderful attire.

She returned to the door to leave when she saw Jace standing in the open doorway. He looked her over from head to foot, then smiled. "Do I look silly?" He did not speak, only smiled "Well, say something please. Am I presentable? Do I look like the other women on the planet we're going to?"

"You look incredible, My Lady. And yes, you chose a common dress for the women of Lorton."

"Really? You're not just trying to appease me, are you? Can I trust you to be honest with me? I'm worried I won't fit in, like where I came from. I never fit with those strange people." She felt tears escape and roll down her cheeks. Jace closed the short distance between them and pulled her against his chest. He held her tight and it made her feel so good, warm and protected. More tears escaped. "I'm sorry I'm getting your shirt wet."

"You're fine. Cry if you need to. I'm sure you're full of emotions you don't understand, which is very normal. You've been through a lot. Now you're free and headed home." He tilted her chin up with his finger and looked into her eyes. "It is your home, and I'll take you there when you're ready. And I'll stay with you and protect you. You're not alone in this. You can trust me."

Jace softly kissed her on the lips, then released her, turned and headed for the door. Then he paused and held out his hand for her to take, and she gladly accepted. He led her down the hall and into the cockpit of the craft. He assisted her to sit in the co-pilot's seat, then he took the captain's seat.

"Put on your seat-strap. We're landing soon. Now, don't panic. We're going to my office, and no one will be there except us. It may be a few sun-cycles before my brothers return from their job. You'll like them, I'm sure." He looked at her in the seat next to him. "Even I like them." He laughed.

"You're funny. Did you know?" She laughed for the first time in a long time and it felt good. "I really don't remember the last time I laughed."

"Laughter is good. You shouldn't be serious all the time, it's far too stressful, and none of us need more stress. So, relax and follow my lead."

"Will anyone see us?"

"No. We have full view of the outside, however; the glass is specially treated so no one can see inside. It's a costly extra, but it's very handy, even necessary at times. Especially when I'm far from home, or with my brothers. Either way, sometimes you don't want others to know you're alone and vulnerable. "

"Sounds logical." She stared at all the controls he toyed with, turning some on and some off. "I'm glad you know what you're doing. I sure don't."

"Now you're being funny, and I'm glad." He stared at her. "You're so beautiful."

Lania looked away and focused on the controls in front of her. She didn't know what to say about his comment. She felt embarrassed. "Thank you for the compliment."

"You're welcome. Actually, it is more a statement of fact." Jace smiled. "It is also my compliment." He shook his head. "You mean to tell me no other man has ever told you how beautiful you are?"

She stared at him and tried to think of the right answer. "I can't remember." They both laughed at her comment, even if she only made a statement of fact, based on what she currently knew.

"You know, I enjoy spending time with you and talking. Where I came from, no one ever talked to me. Not the men or the women. They talked at me, not to me, if you know what I mean."

"I do. I still have a hard time believing they were so horrible."

"They made my life miserable. Which is why I finally ran away. I'm sure they know I'm gone by now." She looked at Jace. "Luckily, they'll never find me. Not one person there has any type of vessel like yours, so they have no way to chase me down and drag me back. I'm still determined never to return. Ever."

"I don't blame you. I'd be the same way." Jace looked at Lania. "Did they keep you under guard?"

"In a way. Someone always kept an eye on me, although they were not very good at their job. I watched them, studied them, because in the back of my mind, I always planned an escape. The man watching my room just before my escape, did nothing but drink. So, I simply waited until he wandered away to use the lav before I made my brave move and left. I managed to slip out the back gated area where I always took the children, then I ran for it. I never saw anyone coming after me. So, the stupid guard watching me probably still has no idea I left. He became too busy getting rid of all the alcohol he drank." Lania nodded. "He needed to make room for more."

Jace smiled back at her and nodded along with her. "You are the only person I saw, and believe me, I consciously looked and waited for someone to stop us, although no one did." Jace flipped several switches then turned his attention back to Lania. "I know they made you work all the time."

"I ran the child school." She took a deep breath. "I kept track of all the little kids during the sun-cycle, until their parents came for them. At times I'd watch kids till late in the moon-cycle. Their parents were out having fun and never gave a thought to how many time-units I worked. It got really bad at times, yet I could do nothing. I could not complain either since they did not allow me to speak to them for any reason. They did not care if I lived or died, although, if I died, they would be without a babysitter."

"And all at your expense. Wow. What a place. What took you so long to escape?"

"I don't know. At first, with no memory, and not knowing what their sun-cycle activities included, or were like, I waited. I also did not know my identity, and still do not. Plus, I did not know normal treatment from abuse. They enjoyed abusing me, for sure. And they were very good at it. Lots of practice, all on me."

"I'm sorry for what you went through. We'll get to the bottom of this, rest assured, and we'll get satisfaction when we imprison them."

Chapter Five

Jace's heart broke for Lania. How could those strange people have treated such a beautiful woman worse than an animal, especially when she hadn't done anything wrong? Could it have been her natural beauty that angered them? Had all this been part of the evil dictator's plan? Raulf must have given instructions to make her so miserable she'd want to kill herself. Again, why? Living in such a horrible, primitive, unfriendly place should have been punishment enough. From what Lania told him, they lived their life with little, or no technology, which verified one reason why they were so primitive.

He could not picture in his mind the abuse she'd taken. How she'd been able to deal with such treatment every sun-cycle remained a mystery to him. He'd have killed someone. Of course, as a man, with enough strength to do the job, he'd find that option easy. Even with no memory, Lania remained a true lady, and she'd never hurt anyone. She'd been in the public eye enough times for most people to know about her kind personality. She only showed kindness and gentility, she gave of herself to others, and never needed or asked for a reward.

Hanging everything on Raulf would be his greatest pleasure, and the most logical choice. He'd like nothing better than to see that evil man locked in solitary confinement for the rest of his miserable life. Every person who lived on Lorton knew about Raulf, and hated Raulf. One fact remained; an existing ruler had never been replaced, unless they were very old and willingly turned their reign over to their firstborn male—an extremely rare event that may have happened once long ago. Throwing Raulf out of reign stood next to impossible. First of all, Raulf had no firstborn male son, he had no children at all. Raulf did not belong in the ruling position, no matter what.

He remembered the first moment he caught a glance of Lania. Her appearance and facial features told him exactly how she felt; lost, confused, and abused. Hopefully her recent memories disappeared faster than they came, and her past returned and allowed her the freedom she desired and needed to make changes in the government. He vowed to do everything within his power to ensure her memory returned. Whatever it took, he'd do everything possible to help her. She more than deserved his help.

He really needed her help to solve the mystery that surrounded the Royal Family and Raulf DeMorgan. What had Lania noticed? Who had she confided in? Every person had someone they told their secrets to, and he needed to talk to him, or her. Her best friend? Her sister? Whoever it may be might possibly have a few answers which could lead to new information and answer a lot of questions. One step at a time. He usually did get ahead of himself. First, he must absolutely find a way to return Lania's memory, whatever that may entail.

Finding a medical genius to restore everything Lania lost may prove to be the most difficult task ever. Hopefully their secret doctor could do the job, he was excellent at his profession. He'd find out soon enough. In the meantime, with all the vids he'd put together, it should provide her with a start on her past. He had no idea if the vids, or medication of some type, or some other treatment would work, but something better do the trick. She needed to remember her name for real, what happened to her, and who to hold responsible.

They finally arrived at the edge of Lorton's atmosphere. Where the planet authorities scanned every craft. The Bryton Brothers purchased a special registry pass through the Lorton government like many businesses, which granted special clearance for entrances and exits without applying and paying for permits every time. The pass made their trips abroad easy and actually saved credits and lots of time-units, so the special pass proved well worth the credits.

Without warning, four ships suddenly flew around them and he glanced at Lania, who looked scared to death. "We're in

Lorton's atmosphere now and have entered the traffic area. Don't be afraid. I've flown this area more times than I care to count."

"I'm glad you told me. I'm not used to this. I never saw any air traffic where I came from."

"Understood. However, most planets have more air traffic than they can handle. Where you came from, there was one universal port, and I landed there. I went inside and bought a map from a strange lady behind a counter. Anyway, the map led me to you. I still can't believe the only check-in port for the entire planet was empty. I fully understand why you never saw air-traffic. They basically had none." Jace smiled at Lania. "Please, don't be sorry for anything. I'll take care of you, I promise, and I never break a promise."

"I shall hold you to your words, and your promises, Jace Bryton."

"You sound upset. Did I say something, or...?"

"No, it's not you. Everything is just hitting me in the face right now. There's so much to take in. Look!" Lania pointed straight ahead.

"That, My Lady, is the Royal Palace with all of its trimmings. It is...well you'll see soon enough."

"Can't wait. I should have stayed in the galley where I couldn't see all of this confusion around us."

"You're welcome to go into the main living area behind us. Just strap in since we'll be landing soon."

"Landing where?"

"At Bryton Security complex here on planet Lorton. It's where we, the Bryton Brothers, live and work. You'll see. Our complex is quite large. Plenty of room for you."

"Good to know."

Jace nearly laughed when Lania fastened her seat strap, crossed her arms in front of her and closed her eyes. Poor woman. She must be completely distraught and lost right now. He hoped he'd be able to put her at ease soon. He turned the craft to the east, then a short bit to the north and they finally arrived home. In hover mode, he landed on the roof of the building, where it opened up, and the lift lowered the craft down into the underground parking area.

He and his brothers felt the pricey lift system a good precaution to keep all their crafts out of sight, and the hidden parking garage had plenty of room. Most of all it prevented damage to their crafts in any way since they remained hidden. His large craft now rested safely, close to their three small crafts. His brothers now flew the other large craft to finish up with their clients. Hopefully they'd be home soon.

Lania's eyes opened wide, and an even greater shocked expression took over her face. "Are you all right?" She only nodded at him. "We're here. Safe and sound, for now." Jace released his safety-belt then stood and offered her his hand. She started to get up, but had forgotten her belt. He held back a chuckle while he unfastened her strap. helped her stand, then walked her to the back exit where he pressed the open button which laid the exit ramp down to the ground.

He still held her hand, but felt her entire body shaking. Only one thing would bring her nerves back close to normal, a drink of his favorite wine, which always calmed a woman down, and most men. He helped her walk the sloping ramp slowly since she might faint, or fall. Finally at the bottom she looked up at him then gave him a big hug, her cheek against his chest. "What did I do to deserve this?"

"For all you've done for me. I so appreciate everything." She looked up. "I appreciate you."

"Thank you, My Lady. Happy to be at your service."

Lania smiled at Jace.

No way could he bring himself to pass up this opportunity. He bent his head, pressed his lips to hers, kissing her softly, and gently. Then he deepened the kiss, and it told him a lot about the woman in his arms. The way she kissed him, told him he was the first man to ever really kiss her, based on her movements and reactions. He simply sensed it in her—something he could not prove, yet he felt it deeply in every part of his body. How could it be possible to be the first when she'd life-mated evil Raulf? He ended the kiss. Maybe she just did not remember. "I'm sorry if…"

Lania placed her fingers on his lips. "You did nothing wrong. I expected you to kiss me. I wanted you to. I...."

“No need to explain. I understand. Come on, let’s go inside where we can get a drink and relax. Space travel always makes me tired. He looked her in the eye. “How about you?”

“I believe you’re right. Again.”

“Be sure you tell my brothers when you see them. Like I said, they always think they’re right and I’m wrong.” He laughed while he walked Lania to the door. He looked into the lock-pad, the door complied and slid into the wall. Jace assisted her inside, then the door auto-closed behind them. He took Lania’s hand and guided her down the hall and into his home. When they reached the main living area he heard her gasp, then she covered her mouth with her free hand. He had no idea what may be wrong. “Are you okay?”

“I’m fine. I can’t explain how all this beauty makes me feel. I’m so privileged to be here with you. It’s...well....”

“Come. You need to sit down.” He walked her to the divan and helped her sit at the end, close to the chair he would take. “I’ll be right back.” Out the corner of his eye he saw her watching him walk across the room, then through the galley door. He ordered two glasses of wine from the serving unit. He opened the slide window, removed the glasses of wine, then returned to Lania and held a glass out to her. “Here you go. This will calm your nerves.”

“What is it?”

“Sweet, dark-berry wine. You’ll like it. Take little sips.” He watched her expression after she took her first sip, and it went from displeasure to I like it quite fast. “Well?”

“Very good.”

“I told you to trust me, remember?”

“I do. I wasn’t sure. I have no memory of drinking wine.”

“I’ve seen you drink it before. You’ll see for yourself on the vid I’ve prepared for you.”

“You seem to know me quite well. Have we met in the past?”

“We’ve been at some of the same events, but never personally met or spoke to each other. I wish we had.”

“It might make things easier.” She gasped. “I can’t believe I said that since I have no memory.” Lania looked across the room and her eyes widened. “What is all that?” She pointed to her left.

“It’s the info-center where our base info-unit rests, and all the vid-displays are visible.” He stood, then walked over and turned the system on. When the entire wall lit up with a beautiful picture of Lorton's most popular ocean view, Lania's face went from shock, to surprise, and ended in admiration. Or so it seemed. "What do you think?"

"I'm too amazed to decide. It's phenomenal. I don't...sorry."

"No need to apologize. I'd say the same thing if I didn't understand the system. Your memory has been removed which is why you don't know more. Be patient." He returned to the sitting area and took the chair beside the divan where she sat, looking more beautiful than he'd seen her look before, if that were even possible. "Are you tired?"

"Actually, I'm very rested. Why?"

"Then you might want to begin the vid tour of your life. I finished your early sun-cycles, so you can begin now, and by the time you're done with the first part, I'll have the rest ready for you."

"Where do you want me?"

"I'll bring the three-dimensional mask to you and you can lay here on the divan where you're comfortable. Are you okay here?"

"Very comfy, and what you want me to do sounds interesting. I'm ready whenever you are."

"Be right back then." He returned to the vid-center, found the mask, inserted the tiny chip that contained all the information, then returned to Lania. "Here is the control for the vid. Hit this button to play at a normal pace. Press here to slow it down. Press here to pause, and here to stop. This is rewind, so you can go back to whatever you want to see again. You'll probably hit play and simply watch to the end. You can always watch it again and again if you like." He helped her put the mask on. "I'll press play now," He stepped back. "I'll leave the control with you."

"Thanks. I'll be fine."

Chapter Six

Jace started Lania on the most recent vids he'd completed, then took a seat across from her where he watched her reactions while she lay on the divan. Several times her whole body stiffened in a way he'd never seen anyone do before. Then at times she'd lay completely relaxed. There was a lot of emotional scenes in the vid which might explain her reactions, but she'd tell him in time. He needed patience, the one thing he usually fell short on. He'd try to be good for her sake.

He hoped to spur her memory by letting her watch the vids. He'd do anything to help her memory return to normal. He did like the sight of Lania lying prone on his divan. She looked vulnerable and so very beautiful. His fingers itched to caress her skin, and he wanted nothing more than to kiss her again. This time he hoped she'd kiss him back. He may need to teach her how to kiss, which could prove quite fun. Obviously, his patience issue just popped up again. He tipped his head back against the chair and decided to take a little nap, or at least relax for a bit.

"No!" Lania screamed.

Jace bounded out of his chair, rushed to the divan and knelt by her side. "Are you all right?

Lania pulled the mask off. "Pause this, please."

He took the controller from her and hit the pause button. "What caused such an angry response?"

"The evil man, or so you call him. I call him the idiot I life-mated."

"Have you learned yet why you life-mated him?"

"Not yet, but he is infuriating. Watching the vid told me I can't stand to be in the same room with him. I don't even know where he came from. I thought the vid might clarify that, but it hasn't so far. It seems like he showed up out of nowhere, and I was forced to life-mate him."

"It never seemed clear to anyone how, or why you two came together. Nobody likes Raulf. Most people, including myself, wish for his early demise."

"Based on the vid I watched, I agree completely." Lania sighed. "Well, since I've regained my composure, I'll finish the vid. Then we'll have some talking to do."

"I'll be here. Put the mask on and I'll click the button for you." He got her going again, then returned to his chair and waited. He hoped the long vid might inspire her memory. He knew everything in the presentation well since he created it, plus he lived it along with every citizen of Lorton. Lania was one smart lady, so if anyone could catch on quickly, it would be her.

Her memory played an essential part in Lorton's survival, and he knew Bryton Brothers' Security would help her regain all the necessary facts. He also knew she contained some strange chemical in her based on the med-machine readout. He needed a doctor he could trust, and he knew the man to call. The one and only medical expert he and his brothers used. This particular doctor catered to people like him and his brothers who did work requiring the utmost secrecy. Brighton Security truly loved their special arrangement with Doctor Ghostrom, who never revealed anything to anyone regarding their visits. Time to make an appointment.

Lania shook Jace's shoulder again. This time he woke up and found her looking at him. "I know you need your rest, but we need to talk."

"Sorry. Didn't know I fell asleep."

"Why don't you get us some wine like before, and we'll sit at the table. Don't want you falling asleep again." She giggled at him when he frowned at her. Jace became so cute when he pretended to be mad and made a face that caused him to appear even more handsome. The thought of his kiss raced through her mind, and now it became the only thing she wanted. She really made quite a mess of his first attempt, and she still felt it was her first real kiss by any man. The vids even verified that—she saw none, not even with her supposed life-mate, Raulf.

For some reason, she sincerely believed evil Raulf never touched her in any kind of intimacy. Instinct screamed those kinds of messages to her. Of course, the vid never showed whether they were intimate or not. She hated being around the evil man and sensed she might kill him if he tried to have sex with her. He would only want sex since he had no knowledge regarding the meaning of love—he was too evil to ever know how to *love*. She did not need a memory to understand his intent, or hers. To the best of her ability, she sensed nothing ever happened between them in an intimate manner, a strong feeling that went throughout her entire body.

Jace set a glass of wine on the table in front of her, and she sat down to take a drink. "I may need more than one of these. She held the glass up for him to see.

"I have plenty. Drink all you like." He took the seat across from her. "So, what do you want to discuss?"

"You're drinking coffa?"

"Yeah. I need to wake up and stay awake. Now, what got you so upset?"

"Do you know why I life-mated Raulf? My father did not even approve of him. I saw that written all over his face!"

"I wish I had answers for you, but I don't. I doubt anyone does. When you life-mated Raulf, the entire planet went into shock, and not in a good way. No one on Lorton wanted to celebrate your ceremony."

"Obviously, based on your vid. Every guest looked forced to attend, including me. Even my father looked angry at the so-called celebration. Just watching your vid, I felt he did not want anything to do with Raulf, nor did he want the man around me. I also sensed he could not stop the life-mating, no matter what. Then only a few sun-cycles later, my father mysteriously dies. The brand-new coroner claimed it to be a heart attack. For some reason I do not believe his assessment either."

Jace tapped the table then looked into her eyes. “I’m so sorry, Lania. Every person who watched the ceremony, and you could say every person on Lorton saw it since it appeared on planet-wide viewing.” He stared at Lania a moment. “I know what you just saw. I’m so sorry that happened to you. All we can do now is figure out the who and why, so we can fix it somehow.” He tipped his head. “I mean fix the things we’re able to fix, of course.”

“Understood. First off, you’re telling me I am a princess? Yet I have no control, only that idiot, Raulf?”

“Correct. Lotron’s laws are clear, only men have the ability to rule.”

“Great. Now, let me get another thing straight. The entire population of Lorton believes me dead, and supposedly, so does Raulf and my sister? Plus, my sister is now life-mated to the evil man, and he is still in charge? Also, the people of Lorton have become very unhappy with life here, and it appears unrest is growing everywhere. Am I correct?”

Jace nodded. “Absolutely correct.” He groaned. “I guess my vid was clearer than I realized. I’m glad you understood it so well. Everything on the vid is only part of what is missing in your memory. My goal was to try to prod your memories and hope the vid could unlock something real in your mind.”

She looked straight at Jace. “So, savior of mine, where do we start?”

“I made an appointment with a very discreet doctor for next sun-cycle. Very early by the way. He is the private physician my brothers and I use. He’s a qualified med-expert. We trust him and have a longstanding agreement with him. So, you can be sure no one will find out about you. We do not want your presence known until we’re ready. For now, you stay dead. Okay?

“When do I make an appearance?”

“I think we’ll both know when the time comes. Patience.”

“Easier said than done, you know.” She took a sip of wine. “I’ll try.”

“I ask no more.” Jace smiled. “I realize where you’re coming from, and all the reasons you’re in a hurry, but caution must be practiced, or circumstances could turn bad very fast.”

“I understand. I do.”

Jace reached across the table and took Lania's hand in his. "My job is to keep you safe, and you know I will do my job. You can make it easy, or hard, your choice, but safe you will be."

"I'm very happy you are my guardian and protector. I trust you." His hand on hers felt warm and comforting, and she gave it a little squeeze which caused him to smile broadly. His magnetism radiated through her, and she knew his handsome face just became imprinted on her mind for the rest of her life. Whether they had much time together or not, she decided to relish every precious moment she spent with Jace.

"Thank you. I appreciate your trust. I will not disappoint you."

He released her hand and she felt an immediate loss. She could not understand how, why, or when her feelings for Jace had become so strong. He made her feel alive, wanted and important. Even if Jace happened to be the only man she ever had, she would be happy to relish all her growing feelings for him.

Maybe if her entire memory returned, she would have knowledge of other men, and whether she possibly experienced any feelings for them. Any feelings for a man should stand out to her. Although so far, according to the vid, her father proved to be the only exception for strong feelings for another being--especially a man.

Jace checked his wrist-piece. "We'd better turn in for the moon-cycle. Your appointment is at sun-cycle, time-unit four."

"Four in the sun-cycle? Dear stars. What doctor works so early?"

"Our doctor does to keep our visits unseen. We must do the unheard-of times to accomplish such visits."

"What about the doctor to the Royal Family? Wouldn't he know me better than anyone?"

"Possibly, but he also knows your identity and believes you dead. Even if he promised to keep our secret, I don't trust him. And there is no way we would ever be able to make our way into the Royal Palace and back out without being seen."

"Do you know the Palace doctor?" She truly wondered.

"No, I don't know him. He's new, but does take care of your life-mate Raulf, your sister, Marna, and most every member of The High Council." Jace rubbed his forehead with his fingers. "Lania, we can't trust anyone unless we're positive they're safe, and right now, no one in the Royal Palace is truly safe for us."

She nodded. "I think I understand. Obviously, you're better at this type of thing than I am, so I believe you." He looked frustrated, and she knew her questions caused his reaction. All of a sudden, she felt like she knew everything and nothing at the same time. "I'm sorry, Jace. I didn't mean to question you, mistrust you, or cause you frustration." He looked up at her, his gorgeous deep-blue eyes staring into hers. He sent the same strange tingle through her entire body. His gaze penetrated her to the point she felt invisible. What this man did to her seemed very thought provoking. She wondered if he even heard what she said. "Did you hear me, Jace? I'm sorry I..."

"No, I'm the one who's sorry I upset you. You didn't frustrate me, I'm just tired. I think I need some sleep. It will be an early sun-cycle."

"You're right. How about a glass of wine I can take to my room? It will put me to sleep for sure."

Chapter Seven

Lania sat next to Jace and waited for the doctor to arrive. Jace had let them into the office through the secret entrance. He even had his own key, allowing them interior access. It did not take long for Jace to get them into the exam room on the right, which contained every piece of equipment a doctor could possibly use.

From the looks of it, the doctor spared no expense setting up this private exam room. Jace told her on the way here, the doctor saw several other exclusive clients. He also said the Brytons were his longest standing secret patients. In fact, according to Mr. Expert, the Brytons took credit for beginning this segment of the doctor's practice. He claimed it to be a very lucrative addition.

Jace seemed nervous himself. This appointment held great importance to them both. She needed her memory back, and fast. He held the readout from his craft's med-lab that he took while they flew to Lorton. She did not remember anything about it since she lay unconscious on the table. She hoped it might save some time for everyone and prevent her from going through the experience again.

The door opened and the doctor stepped inside, the door shutting behind him. "Good sun-cycle, Doctor Ghostrom," Jace greeted.

The good doctor's jaw dropped wide open and a shocked look crossed his face. Since everyone believed her dead, she had to be the reason for the doctor's reaction. She could only offer him an appreciative smile. He was an older man, yet quite handsome for his age, white hair, white facial hair and nearly as tall as Jace, who was considered very tall. She did not fear him since his appearance remained very welcoming. He was not what she expected at all.

Jace looked the doctor in the eye. "You're correct. Lania is not dead. The reports were obviously wrong."

"My Lady." The doctor shook his head while he bowed to her, then straightened. "I cannot believe my eyes! You truly are alive." He touched her cheek with his hand. "What can I do for you?"

"My memory is gone. Someone must have given me an injection when I lay unconscious, because I woke up suddenly when a very long needle was roughly pulled out of the back of my neck. I do not know who did it since I immediately passed out. I then woke up on a very strange planet, many galaxies away from Lorton. And so, my new existence began."

Jace held a paper out toward the doctor. "Here is the readout from my ship's exam-cam when I found her. It might help and save some time."

They both watched the doctor scroll down the long page. He finished reading the paper then went over to his computer and typed something. A moment later he turned and faced them.

"You're not going to believe this, but the particular poison My Lady was given, originated from the Lizzardious Eraseomus, a very rare lizzard who lives in the mountains far above us. Most people have never seen one, nor will they. These creatures are extremely rare and dangerous. They are the largest breed of Lizzard known anywhere, and the most poisonous. And I mean they are extremely larger than every known variety of Lizzard you have ever seen or learned about. In fact, they're larger than about all the animals in the forest—just a comparison for you. They will attack, bite, kill and eat anything, or anyone who comes near them."

"So, how did someone get this poison?"

"My guess is with some kind of a trap. Then they had to carefully milk the venom. This Lizzard is dangerous, make no mistake. Lizzard is the nicest thing to call this creature. Now, in order to return Lania's memory, I must have venom from that exact breed of Lizzard. Don't ask me how to get it, just get it. Once I give her a measured dose by injection, her memory will return. And from what the computer indicates, it should return immediately."

Jace sighed and shook his head. "I'll see what I can do. When I have it, I'll contact you. Thanks for meeting with us."

"Wait. I have one more thing to address." The doctor took Lania's hand, turned it over, pressed on the skin of her forearm, then let go. "You are very dehydrated and malnourished. Do not dismiss these two symptoms. I assume you're already working on the situation, correct?"

"Yes, Doctor. Jace is making me eat and drink all I can. I am working on it."

"Good. I want you to stay around and be healthy. You're in good hands, My Lady."

"I am glad to hear you say so, Doctor."

"I've known this man a very long time, and you could not find a better man if you tried. He's good at what he does. If I trust him, you can trust him." The doctor stepped toward the door and opened it. "I shall begin my research so I'll be ready when you return with the venom. Here, Jace." He handed Jace a piece of paper.

"Thank you. I'm sure I'd have forgotten by the time I needed it."

"Good luck to you both. See you soon." He opened the door and left the room.

Jace took Lania's hand and walked her outside, then up the steps to the parking area. Once on the small tarmac, he assisted her to his small craft. She knew he would take his bigger ship, but the location of the office here did not necessitate or accommodate a large craft. At least that is what Jace said on the way here. He also called it 'a bug' since it flew extremely quiet and had no engine, only a special battery. She liked the tiny size because it made her feel nearly invisible. He opened the little craft's passenger door for her and helped her be seated.

She was so lucky to have found such a gentleman. Once she was settled in her seat, he shut her door then walked around to his side and took his seat. Now that he became Captain, he raised the little baby up and began the short flight back to the office.

They arrived back in The Bryton Brothers' parking garage, and Lania still was not speaking to him, not one word. He truly wondered what thoughts were going through her mind. Did she understand what the doctor told them about her memory and the Lizzard? If he needed to battle this huge Lizzard, it may require more expertise than he had. If he hired someone to do the job, he'd have to deal with loose lips, which he found completely unacceptable. People seemed to have many ways of breaking their silence, yet believing they had not. Usually, first to their best friend, thinking they'd be safe telling one person. Then the one friend does the same thing, and the secret is fully exposed.

He helped Lania out of the pretend vehicle, the name he gave it due to the tiny size, even if it did the job efficiently. Once they entered the living area, he helped her to the divan. "Do you want anything? Some coffa maybe?"

"I think I'll lay down here and rest. Okay?"

"You're fine. I have to do some research, so I'll be right here close to you. I really need some coffa first. It's still very early. I'll be right back." The moment he walked away, she laid down, and he knew she needed to rest. He quickly ordered his hot, caffeine-ridden drink, doctored it up, then returned to the info-center. He sat down and began researching the strange Lizzard the doctor talked about. It felt odd to him to be in charge of Holt's area. Another reason he missed his brothers and the help they always gave.

He picked up the sheet the doctor printed, and was glad he did since he'd already forgotten the creature's full name and a few stats. He looked at the paper, Lizzardious Eraseomus. According to what he read, that was the official name of the poison, and the Lizzard itself went by the name Lizzardious Maxamous, which simply meant the largest Lizzard known. Eraseomus happened to be the actual name of the poison which flowed from the creature's teeth when it bit anything. Lucky must be his middle name. He needed to know more about this monster if he stood a chance to live through the capture process.

He read further and took notes about what he needed to take with him. The largest and strongest cage available, extra strong ropes, and snake milking supplies. Nothing large enough seemed to have been created for such a giant, monstrous creature, so he needed to improvise using the biggest versions of what he required. Snakes and this poisonous Lizzard, both injected poison through their sharp, front fangs. Oh, what fun. He called his supplier and ordered what he needed. The size of the cage happened to be his friendly salesman's number one question. He kept asking what kind of giant mountainous catis he planned to catch.

If he were chasing after a catis, he'd feel better. At least he'd have a fighting chance, even if the feline happened to be huge. He could not admit to, or explain a giant Lizzard. No person in their right mind would ever want to trap the creature he happened to be after. He may be a warrior, yet even warriors faced limits. Time for him to get the right mental attitude about this, or he'd certainly fail. Mind over matter, always his mantra, and it mattered, he knew it did. So, he agreed with his salesman and ordered the largest and strongest catis cage they sold.

The supplies always arrived at the office before mid-sun-cycle if he ordered them early. He slipped away and walked to the underground parking area to ready his craft for the flight. He checked what supplies were on board, and everything appeared to be in order. He made sure he packed plenty of first aid supplies. Based on the circumstances he faced, he couldn't be too careful. He needed to ask Lania if she were any good at sewing up arms and legs. A thought like that certainly could not be considered positive; however, he needed to be sure all supplies and help were in place. Must be prepared.

He laughed to himself since he'd just failed with the mind over matter thing. He needed to get better fast. After a deep breath, he exhaled and repeated, "I can do this. I will not be hurt. All is well." His usual mantra. Hopefully the Universe considered it enough.

Lania woke up and felt totally lost with no idea what surrounded her. Then it all rushed back. Where had Jace gone to? She sat up and looked around, but did not find him. She stood, then walked over to where he said he would be working in the info-center. The smaller screens on the console showed different areas within the office and parking garage, and there she saw Jace emerging from the large craft. He then walked down the ramp totally in charge, a true Captain.

She loved his take-charge quality, and the way he handled responsibility so expertly. He feared nothing, a very handy trait if he were to deal with the largest Lizzard on any planet, one far bigger than him, and Jace stood large, tall and muscled, a very big man. No way could Jace possibly say this would be an easy task. Although, based on what she knew about Jace, he would be successful, like he was at every job he performed. Then they would return to the doctor's office, and in no time at all, her memory would be back. Her real, true memory. Finally.

The vid-display showed Jace about to enter from the back. The door barely shut when he walked into the room. She turned toward him. "Hello. I'm over here."

Jace walked over to Lania. "Checking things out, I see?"

"This system is amazing. You guys seem to have everything covered."

"We do. It's our job, you know. We're security experts. It's why we're called Bryton Brothers' Security."

She laughed. "I know. I hadn't seen it all up close before." She took her eyes off him and looked at the giant console in front of her. "This all just amazes me."

"You haven't seen everything it can do. I don't have time to show you right now. The supplies will be here momentarily, then we must leave to find our Lizzard."

"Getting your craft ready, Captain?" Her question brought a smile to his face.

"Yes." He checked his wrist-piece. "Let's have our mid-meal first. Remember what the doctor said." He laughed at her. "You're a good excuse. I'm really hungry and don't want to face a giant Lizzard on an empty stomach. So," he took Lania's hand in his, "let's go to the galley and get busy."

"I cannot refuse your offer, kind sir." She loved it when he took charge and led the way with authority. Especially when he held her hand, his warmth seeping into her, feeling very reassuring. He felt good, strong, and full of everything she lacked. Once in the galley, he pulled out a chair and assisted her while she sat at the table.

"What can I get you, My Lady?"

"You don't need to call me My Lady, Jace. I realize after watching the vids, I'm supposed to be called that, and I suppose they have to in the Royal Palace, but you certainly do not need to."

"I feel good saying it. It will be my pet-name for you, so you can be '*My* Lady'."

"I can't refuse when you put it so elegantly." She smiled at him and he smiled back at her. They simply stared at each other in awkward silence, the way two school kids might. Did he feel about her as she felt about him? If so, they were in real trouble. She never wanted to let him go. He would always be her security in a sea of doubt and wonder.

"Okay. What do you want to eat?"

Jace's question snapped her back to reality. "Surprise me. I really don't care." She cared about him and what he thought deep in his heart. It may be best not to know what he felt since so many complications stood in their way of having a real relationship.

"All right, but I don't want to hear any complaints."

She simply shook her head while she watched him conjure up two plates of food and carry them to the table. "It smells wonderful. What is it?"

"Simply eat it, you'll be better off. It's nothing weird. I know you ate it when you lived here, even if you never ate it in that strange place you recently lived in."

"Fine." She took a bite of what appeared to be some kind of potateble with gravy, and it tasted wonderful. Then she cut off a piece of the meat and tried it, shocked when it melted in her mouth. "This is fantastic. Really fantastic." She looked into his eyes, and they reflected a very satisfied reaction. "You're right, again. I'm sure I ate this before since it's so good."

"See, I told you."

"I need to learn never to doubt you. It appears you're always right. And I'm not used to any man being always right, believe me."

He laughed. "Don't tell my brothers, or I'm doomed to teasing which will never end."

"When will they return?"

"Soon."

"So, they might burst through the door anytime?"

"Not quite so fast."

All of a sudden, she heard the tinkling of tiny bells playing some kind of musical tune. Its purpose may be to draw attention to the lift, yet it sounded very relaxing to listen to.

"Be right back."

She watched him leave in a flash and guessed the supplies he'd ordered were here. He'd obviously rushed up to accept the delivery. This sun-cycle she actually felt very hungry, so she continued to eat while she waited for him to return. He ate too fast anyway, so she liked having a head start. He'd be ready to fly away before she knew it.

The lift door opened and he stepped out, carrying nothing. "Where are the supplies?"

"In the lift. I'll carry them out later. I wanted to finish lunch first."

"I don't blame you, it's really good."

"Glad you like it." After a few bites, he looked up at Lania. "You don't have to go with me, you know. You're welcome to stay here where you'd be more comfortable."

"Get serious. I can't let you go alone, and you know it." She groaned. "I realize you haven't known me long, but I'm not comfortable being left behind. Does that make sense to you?"

"Wow. You're beginning to change right before my eyes! I picked up a frail, missing princess, who seemed shy and quiet. Now you've turned into a strong minded, demanding woman I don't recognize."

"Jace, I'm sorry. I didn't mean to..."

Jace laughed. "Lunch seemed to do the trick for you. I love the new you, really. I'd much rather see this side of you."

"The bossy side?"

"No, only the side in control, the side which is naturally you. Unfortunately, those people took it away from you."

"I'm just glad you're not mad at me. I guess I simply spread my wings a bit after being held down for so long. It felt good. I meant nothing by it. And if I showed a bad attitude of any kind, they severely punished me, so I learned to hide it."

"I'm sure you did. I can't imagine what you went through. Again, I'm sorry you experienced such horrible treatment. I know you didn't deserve it."

"Thank you. Now, enough of the sob story. We need to get going, we have a Lizzard to find." She watched Jace quickly eat the rest of his food. He stood, picked up both of their dishes, then slipped them into the opening in the wall. He shut the clear door, then walked back to her, took her hand and helped her stand.

"Let's do it, My Lady."

Chapter Eight

Jace landed his craft a safe distance from the waterfall-fed pond high in the mountains. The elusive Lizzards supposedly liked these types of ponds the best, so he decided to begin here. He looked at Lania who sat quietly next to him. She appeared bothered by something, so he felt compelled to ask. "Are you all right, My Lady?"

"I'm fine." She shook her head. "I'm worried about you. What if the stupid Lizzard bites you? What if he kills. . .or does something worse? What will I do? I can't even fly this thing to get help. I don't know how to use your med-lab. Basically, I'm useless!"

Her statement came out of nowhere and was totally unexpected. He didn't want to think anything negative right now. "You're over-worrying." He needed to put her more at ease somehow. "I'll meet you halfway. I can't teach you to fly, we don't have enough time. I can show you the necessities." He saw tears streak down her cheeks which showed him her nervous and worried attitude went deeper than he realized. He never imagined she cared about him this much. He also realized she felt guilty since it all fell on her memory issues as to why they were here.

Jace released his safety-belt, stood and knelt next to Lania's chair and looked her in the eye. "My Lady, I will not die here. I won't do anything to put you in danger. Count on it." She turned in her chair, threw her arms around his neck, and pressed her lips against his, which gave him an irresistible invitation. He kissed her back with all the passion he'd been working so hard to deny. She kept pace with him, and he felt deep-seated feelings in her, like she loudly said she wanted him the same as he wanted her.

He slipped his hand beside her and unfastened her safety-belt, so she could stand and press her body against his. Together they rose to their feet while her warmth seeped into him, and he never wanted to let her go. If he taught her one thing this sun-cycle, this was it, how to kiss. How to grow closer. How to express her need. How to love. Love may be a difficult lesson when she was still legally attached to an evil monster named Raulf. Such a thought caused him to gently end his kiss, or did Lania kiss him? Either way, he pulled back and studied her surprised look.

He waited for a moment, giving them both time to regain their composure. "Come, I'll show you how to operate the med-lab in case I have need for it." He walked her down the hall, then into the proper room. Once inside, he laid down on the raised table. "This is where I need to be to be assessed. If you cannot get me up here, watch." He pressed a button on the side of the hard slab bed and it lowered itself to the floor."

"I see. So, if I can manage to drag you in here, I can simply roll you onto this table thing. Nice. What else?"

"I detect an attitude, missy."

"I believe you are right, mister. I do have an attitude." She pressed the button on the bed and raised it to normal height.

Jace's heart raced when Lania leaned into him. After tasting her lips once, he became anxious for another kiss from the beautiful woman a breath away. He reached up for her, surprised when she pulled back.

"Not so fast, explorer. This lesson is not over."

"Excuse me, please." He gave her his biggest smile and hoped it might lift her mood.

"You're excused. Continue."

"How formal. Okay. See the metal arm above me? Pull it down, then touch the recessed button on top, and it will begin the diagnosis process. The machine is very complex and complete, and will analyze everything, no matter how small. It will tell you everything you need to know, and more than you can understand." Jace chuckled for a moment. "Unfortunately, if I need stitches, the machine is not the best at mending wounds. I hate the way it sews, so I prefer people sew me if necessary. Besides, the machine can only sew me if you hold the wound shut, so you might as well do the job yourself."

"We'll see about sewing. I've only done a bit of mending."

"Good. Hopefully a little mending will be all I might need."

Lania frowned. "Anything else, professor?"

"Oh, you'll find a simplified, shorter version of my condition behind the small screen over there." Jace pointed to the enclosure behind them. "You can read it on the vid-screen."

"Got it. Anything else, commander?"

"Not at the moment. Right now, I need to assemble a cage." Jace looked at Lania. "Why are you calling me so many names?" She simply stared at him. "I get it. You're protesting to when I call you, My Lady. Right?"

"I believe you understand me quite well, warrior."

"Okay then. Now that I know."

"Need help?"

Jace sat up on the table then eased himself down to the floor. He stood in front of Lania. "If you want to. It's not necessary."

"I am happy to help." Lania tipped her head down. "I'm sorry, Jace. I do not mean to be so grouchy. My attitude got the better of me. I don't know what's wrong with me. I don't understand it myself."

"I think I do." Jace slipped his arms around her waist and pulled her closer to him. She rested her head on his chest, a move he craved. "You've been through six annual-cycles of horrible treatment, plus your memory has been removed, which has caused a lot of confusion and loss. I want you to remember, I'm doing everything in my power here to help you solve all of your confusion. Once your memory is returned, we can begin phase two of our plans."

Lania raised her head and looked at Jace. "What is phase two?"

"I don't know those details yet, but we'll be ready for it when the time comes."

She pulled his head down to her face and kissed his lips.

He returned her kiss, deciding it best to keep it short. Too much to do, and if he gave in to desire, he'd never leave the craft. Reluctantly he pulled back and put his hands on her cheeks.

"Follow me." He took her hand in his and led her down the hall toward the supplies.

"We have work to do." He led her back to the storage area where he'd put the trap and pulled out the large box. He quickly pushed the heavy box into the main area, opened it, then spread all the parts out on the floor so he could see them and assemble easier.

"I hate to say this, but this looks impossible!" Lania put her hands on her hips.

"Patience, patience. Nothing is ever easy." He smiled up at her beautiful face.

"Well, you must have more patience than I do."

"I have been working hard on my patience issues." He looked into her mesmerizing dark eyes. "I do have a problem with patience. Don't tell anyone." Jace laughed while he began to put the cage together. It had been a long time since he'd gone hunting with his brothers and all three of them participated in cage assembly. He'd put together many cages like this one in his youth, but none this large. Hopefully those early experiences would provide the help he required with this project.

He'd ordered the heaviest duty cage available in the height he guessed he needed. He hoped this one would be heavy enough, although he had no idea the strength of the creature he planned to battle. He'd done his homework, but until he found himself in the middle of a fight for his life, he wouldn't know the true ability of his opponent, or the cage. He hoped he'd planned properly and guessed right. The same issues held true no matter who or what he had to fight as a warrior.

Lania watched his every move, yet did not touch the cage. She seemed terrified of it, yet she knew he had to use it. She simply feared for his life, and he didn't dare disappoint her since she needed him to get back home. "You do realize, I refuse to allow a Lizzard to best me in battle."

"Easy to say. You haven't seen this creature yet. I haven't seen you fight yet, but no man is indestructible. This is not another warrior weaker than you. This is a creature capable of killing you in a second!"

"Calm down, Lania. I'll be fine. I'm going to trap him, then very carefully milk the venom."

"I'm sorry, Jace, this makes me way too nervous."

He set the tools he carried down on the floor, then moved next to Lania. He put his arms around her and pulled her tightly to him. "Listen. I need your support, and this is no way to be. You must believe we'll be successful and neither of us will be harmed. A successful warrior uses the power of positive thinking."

"My positive thinking must have flown away with my memory. Right now, I don't have either." She shook her head then looked into his eyes. "Sorry."

He felt her press harder against him, her entire body shaking, her fear palpable. He'd be rude to dismiss her, yet her negativity began to seep into him, something he needed to stop. Such a predicament. He gave her a squeeze then returned to his work. This project needed to be completed. Once he picked up his wrench, he finished tightening the last of the bolts. He then stood on top of the cage and jumped. It didn't budge one bit. With his booted foot, he kicked the sides—nothing. It seemed perfectly ready.

He opened the side cargo hatch and shoved the large cage down the ramp. It tumbled end over end to the ground, then continued a few meters more. At least it remained in one piece, which was a good sign. He only needed to fill the little tray in the front of the cage with some tasty, fresh bait. He walked back to the galley, ordered some raw beefus, put it in a bag, then headed back to the hatch. Lania waited for him, arms crossed in front of her, a tough look on her face.

"I want you to stay here. I'm only going to set this trap for our friend, then I'll be right back and we'll wait for him together."

"I can't let you go by yourself. What if. . .."

"And what are you going to do? How will you stop this creature?" She looked at him with such frustration he felt sorry for her. "I'll be right back. You can watch me through the front shield of the craft."

She didn't say a word when she turned and quietly walked to the front of the ship where he asked her to wait. He hurried down the ramp then closed it. Lania might not appreciate a visit from a giant Lizzard. When he grabbed the cage, he immediately realized it weighed far too much to carry, he chuckled to himself. It took both hands and all his strength to drag the overweight contraption across the ground toward the pond.

Once the cage finally met the water toward the center of the north shoreline, he opened the hatch door which faced where the water turned deeper. He stuffed the fresh bait in the so-called bait-trap at the front end which he'd set partly on the shore. He needed to stand on stable ground to milk the creature once it became trapped. Then Jace settled the opened end into the water where the Lizzard would likely be tempted while swimming. By the stars, he hoped the plan worked. Based on how it sat right now, he'd be able to stand and deal with the creature. This is what his contact at the supplier swore worked many times in the past for trappers, even if they weren't after a Lizzard.

He'd seen boots, and a jacket once, made out of this creature's hide. At the time he'd thought it presentable, but way too expensive. His appreciation for the hide just grew exponentially, even if they shot the thing in the head. Now he only needed to wait. He needed to get back to Lania, who he knew remained in the process of worrying herself to death before the Lizzard even made an appearance.

Did Lania worry for him, or the fact she couldn't fly the craft? No, he knew she worried for him, because if he knew her like he thought he did, she'd figure out how to fly and get herself home no matter what. He quietly chuckled deep in his chest. She was a woman in charge, which was her problem here since she had no control.

In a jog, he made his way back to the craft, and entered through the side ramp door. He hurried to the captain's area where he knew she'd be waiting since that area provided a great view of the lake, exactly the way he planned. The view through the front shield always remained perfect since it sat in a circle all the way around the front and sides of the pilot's cabin. Lania would be safe watching him from inside the cabin. Sure enough, she sat wiping tears from her cheeks, then turned and showed him a strained smile.

"You set your trap up pretty fast. I suppose this isn't your first time?"

He slowly nodded. "My brothers and I did a lot of hunting in our younger annual-cycles, even though we were out for lighter and smaller animals."

"Well, it looks effective. Now all we need is a giant Lizzard."

"To be precise, a Lizzardious Maximous."

"We must be precise since the stupid creature fits its name, the largest Lizzard existing anywhere." Lania stared at Jace. "Hope he fits in that thing." She pointed to the cage out front of the window.

Jace chuckled at the silly voice she'd just used, but it was a correct assessment. It sounded funny. He loved when she showed a bit of humor since laughter kept him going. He'd been looking for hers and he may be finding it. "The part I question is you called it stupid, and we don't know if he is. Hopefully, he is. Did you know during my research, I learned only the male has the poison we need? So we'd better hope a male decides to be hungry."

"Is this where I tell you the male is the stupid one to crawl into a cage to get a little bite to eat?" Lania shook her head. "How do we tell if it is a male? Are you going to roll it over and check things out?"

They both happily laughed for a moment, then abruptly stopped when they looked out the front shield. The creature they came to find headed toward the cage along the bank of the pond. "He's huge! Way bigger than I pictured him."

"I couldn't have said it better. And I pictured him really big. Such a monster, wow! He may not fit in the cage. Jace, what will we do if he gets away?"

"Come back with a bigger cage?"

"Don't be silly."

"I'm not. Problem is they don't make a bigger one. I bought the biggest and heaviest cage available. You're right, this guy. . .wow! I don't know."

"What does research know anyway?" She gasped and her hand moved to her mouth. "Look!"

"I see. You're right. He's stupid. He's going into the cage whether he fits or not. Oh man!"

Jace ran to the back door, hit the open button, grabbed his ropes and ran down the ramp. He needed to get to the giant before he started to back out of the contraption. The back drop door fell down as it was meant to do, but rested on the middle of the creature's hindquarters. His build proved way too big and far too long for the dumb cage. Plan B did not exist. He rushed to the front of the cage where the Lizzard's head thrashed around and beat against the sides.

When his nemesis saw him, he lunged with his mouth open, teeth protruding over the metal bars. Thank the stars he remained half-trapped inside, unable to jump out at him. The monster definitely tried to lunge in for the kill, and he thanked every star in the galaxy he failed. Hopefully it was a male.

He had to get the rope around the Lizzard's neck in order to hold him in the cage and speed became the critical issue. First, he had to maneuver the noose, but the creature kept his jaws wide open, teeth showing, with his body thrashing and lunging. It would be a complete miracle if he accomplished the task. He didn't know how the creature had the ability to move every one of his body parts at the same time, but it knew no limitations.

The cage bounced up and down, tilted back and forth, and kept moving farther away from where it began. Every time he tried to get the rope inside and around the monster's neck, he nearly lost his entire arm. This battle seemed impossible. He hoped he'd be able to wear the creature out enough to capture him. Nothing concerning this ugly, massive being could ever be called easy.

The harder he tried, the worse it became. He had no idea how to overcome this obstacle. Even though he'd done his research, nothing explained how to capture one of these giants. He'd told Lania all he knew about the species, which was basically nothing. Few men had ever even seen this creature, and probably no one had done battle with one and lived to talk about it. The teeth on the Lizzard were the biggest he'd ever seen on any animal, mammal, or any living creature. This monster defied description.

The moment he managed to get the rope around its neck, the Lizzard chomped down on one of the metal bars across the front of the cage again. This time he bit completely through a super thick, solid, supporting lateral metal bar. Jace never would have believed it could even be possible due to the thickness and heaviness of the solid metal bars.

Jace stood there in total shock. Granted this cage was for a giant catis, but what he just witnessed would shock any trapper or hunter. Thank the stars he remained stuck inside, but if something didn't change fast, this oversized-monster would escape. Jace looked up and saw Lania standing at the back of the creature.

He noticed something in her hand, but had no idea what she carried, and didn't care as long as she stayed safe from danger. The stupid Lizzard tried to bite him again and he had to be sure he didn't get his way. He struggled with the huge creature, still unable to get the rope around his rough, wide neck. He glanced up in time to see Lania stab the creature in his lower back with a giant needle. She emptied the huge syringe full of liquid and pushed the top part all the way down, then slowly pulled the needle out and stepped back.

There must be something in the syringe either to kill this thing or put him to sleep, he wasn't sure which. The groans coming from the Lizzard slowed quieted. He'd either fallen asleep, or died. Lucky for him, the Lizzard's head remained through the front opening so he quickly put the rope around the creature's neck, then tied it to the roof of the cage before he walked over to Lania. "What was in the syringe?"

"Tranquilizer."

"Thank you!" He wrapped his arms around her and gave her the biggest hug of his life. "How much did you put in him?"

Lania held out the syringe. "This was full. I have no idea how long it will last. Long enough to do what you have to do. I hope."

Jace pulled her to him and kissed her. Right now, he owed her his life. He wanted to thank her with his kiss, and so much more. His feelings for her just grew greater than he ever planned. Lania represented the complete package and she served him well. Beautiful to look at, smart in all matters, fearless, and funny. What more could he possibly want? Nothing. He deepened his kiss. He wanted her. All of her.

Reality returned and he eased back, ending the kiss which had gone way too far. He put his hands on her shoulders and guided her back. "I'm curious where and how did you find that syringe full of tranquilizer?"

"While I was waiting it appeared you were having serious problems, and you said I would need to be your doctor if you were injured. That thought made me look around for something to help, and I found that tranquilizer in a drawer in the lab actually, not the med room. But when I read the label, I decided it might help you contain this thing, and possibly save your life if necessary. So, I brought it out here to help, and sure enough, you needed my help."

"Lania, my sweet, you did a fantastic job. Wish I'd thought about that, but I was too busy thinking about this monster." He glanced at the sleeping creature. "Listen, if this thing begins to wake up, I want you to get back inside the ship immediately. I can't protect you from him. Understand?"

"Completely. I've been watching. I don't know how long this," she held up the syringe, "will last. Do you want me to get some more in case we need it?"

"Is there another syringe like that?"

"I found two, but only brought out one."

"Then get the other one because I still have to milk the venom from his front fangs."

"I'll bring the bag you need. Just sit on the rock there and rest for a minute. You must be exhausted. He gave you quite a workout."

"Okay, just hurry. We don't know when he'll wake up."

"Be right back."

Lania ran to the ship and entered through the side door he'd left on auto-open. Jace sat on the nearby rock and waited. He knew if he were to complete this mission alive, he needed to proceed with extreme caution. He didn't want to be negative, so he swore the stupid Lizzard wouldn't get close enough to him to even hurt him or get the better of him. The sleeping giant looked so peaceful right now, his eyes shut in chemical rest. He'd witnessed the monster in action, and he was the complete opposite of the sleeping, harmless creature in front of him now. After his so-called battle, the monster himself had verified he was definitely on the stupid side.

Lania's kiss filled his mind, and he'd much rather think about her. Damn. The woman consumed him and he couldn't explain it. He'd been with lots of women, kissed them, spent moon-cycles with them, yet he experienced nothing like he did with Lania. Did this mean she could be the woman for him? It didn't matter since Lania did not have the freedom to ever be with him. She came from the Royal Family, with responsibilities that did not include him. Besides, she still had a life-mate--the evil Raulf. What a joke, the evil man now had two life-mates when a lot of good men couldn't find one.

It still remained completely impossible for him to picture Lania with Raulf, plus he refused to think of them together. He did wonder why Raulf's ruthless evil had not already consumed

Lania's sweet and caring personality? The man had no conscience, or feelings of any kind, except anger if he didn't get his way. So how did they end up life-mated? A mystery to be solved when he returned home. Too bad he couldn't feed Raulf to his new long-toothed friend in the cage. He laughed at such a thought, especially the word friend.

First, he must milk this monster, if such an act were even possible. Unfortunately, he had to wait for the stupid thing to wake up. The creature's venom only flowed if he were awake and biting something. He did need to restrain the Lizzard enough to accomplish the impossible feat. One thing for sure, he refused to let it get the better of him, and he simply considered the Lizzard one more enemy to face.

If he used more rope and tied up his hind legs, securing them to the sides of the cage, it might help hold him down so he couldn't lunge. He ran back to his craft, up the ramp and inside, where he nearly knocked Lania to the floor. He caught her in his arms, and since her body pressed against him, he kissed her quickly before letting her go.

"Maybe you should run into me more often?"

"My pleasure. If I had more time, it would be way better. Right now, I need to hurry and get more rope. I hope to disable him enough to get what we need."

"Good idea. I have the special bag you asked for. I need to go get another sleep shot for our friend."

"Good. Once I get the venom, you can inject him, then we'll make a quick exit from this place."

"I like it. You get the rope. I'll get the injection."

Chapter Nine

Jace nodded then ran to the supply room. He grabbed the strongest rope on the shelf and hoped it could do the job. It took a sharp knife to cut it, and he had one in his pocket which he pulled out. He did love a challenge, even if this ranked far above and beyond anything he'd ever faced. Not having experience to draw on bothered him. His main goal was to master this creature. Plus, staying alive ranked high on his list, especially since it was his only key to success if he were to help Lania.

He returned to the living area where Lania waited for him. The giant syringe stuck out of his bag, and he nearly laughed at the size of it. He'd always known those were in the med cabinet, yet never expected to use one, ever. The size alone made him laugh.

"Something funny, Jace?"

Jace took the heavy bag from Lania and put the strap over his shoulder. He pulled out the giant syringe and held it out to her. "This is funny when you look at it. It's huge!"

"I know." Lania giggled. "It had better be huge to work the way it did." She pointed at the Lizzard. "He is huge."

"He certainly is." Jace shook his head. "I can't thank you enough for thinking about giving him that shot." He smiled at her. "You're the best, My Lady."

"So glad you think so." She smiled at him. "What's next?"

"You hang on to the sleep med in case we need it, but do not, under any circumstances, give it to him until I get the venom. We will never get a second chance. This is it. Understand?"

"Yes. Even if you're dying, be sure the venom is in the bag."

"Good. We must stay together on this."

"I'm with you. Lead the way, Warrior." She laughed. "Or do I call you Lizzard Slayer?"

Jace chuckled a bit. "I don't plan to slay him exactly, just piss him off enough to try to bite me." He put his arm around her and escorted her down the ramp and over to the sleeping giant. "I'm going to get everything ready for our friend." The first things he pulled from the bag were all the milking supplies, which he laid in front of the cage, close to the Lizzard's mouth. Then he picked up the rope and walked to the back of the cage.

The Lizzard's rear legs were too wide apart to tie together so he made sure they were each tied tightly to the sides of the cage. Then he went back to the front and did the same to his front legs. Just when he began to relax a minute, the giant began to stir and groan. Time for battle.

Two large black eyes opened and stared at him, then the monster began to pull against his new restraints, extremely angry for being tied to the cage. He then began thrashing to the point the cage nearly tipped over. His head banged into the metal in front of him and his two giant fangs hung on the outside through the hole he bit in the cage. Jace held up the milking bag. The stupid animal pulled his head away and tried to back out of the cage.

The creature, determined to free himself, kept pulling against the ropes with all four legs. Hopefully the rope and knots would hold. Jace yelled at the Lizzard to get his attention, and it worked. He lunged toward him and tried to bite him, exactly what he wanted him to do. He shoved the bag up over his fangs, then pressed himself closer to the cage so the Lizzard might believe his teeth were actually biting him.

The plan worked. Venom flowed into the bag while the creature banged against the iron restraints and pulled harder on the ropes. The crazy Lizzard somehow managed to get his left front leg free from the rope, then stuck his leg and huge clawed foot through the metal of the cage. Jace felt a sharp talon dig a deep scrape across his back. He carefully removed the bag and held it closed, then inched away from the cage. He'd moved back, but not far enough for comfort.

This thing acted completely crazy now since his bite produced nothing to taste and chew. Thank the galaxy this battle was over. He closed and secured the venom bag and hoped it would be all the doctor needed, since he would not be able to get any more from the creature. He jumped aside when a fat, front leg and large clawed foot tried to strike him again. Once was more than enough.

Jace felt warm blood running down his back, but doctoring had to wait. He looked up and yelled to Lania, "Give him the shot!"

Lania shoved the huge, over-sized syringe into the ugly Lizzard's back the same way she did before. The creature slowly ceased his movements, calmed down, then fell asleep once again.

"Thank you." Jace sank to his knees on the ground to carefully pack the venom bag and all the other supplies. First, he double checked to be sure the Lizzard had fully gone to sleep, then he reached in the cage, untied the other front leg of the giant, then freed the rope around his neck. When he straightened his stance, he noticed Lania staring at the blood on his back.

"Jace, you're hurt. How bad is it?"

"I don't know, can't see it. The pain is really bad. Have I lost much blood?"

"From what I can see, yes. Let's get you back to the craft, fast."

"Grab the bag. Can't leave the venom after all this."

He waited while she ran to the front of the cage to get the bag. He gave one last glance at the creature to be sure he completely untied him so he'd be able to make an exit when he woke up. He realized he needed to untie his back legs, so he sloshed his way to the back of the cage and untied the monster's rear legs.

All his legs and neck were now free, so he'd be ready to leave. He had what he wanted, no need to kill the giant Lizzard. He tied up the slide-down door so the crazy monster would be able to free himself all on his own when he woke up. If they weren't long gone when the Lizzard woke, they would at least be safe in the craft.

Lania walked up to Jace and put her arm around his waist. "Lean on me. You don't look well."

"You're right. I feel rather shaky."

"You've probably lost too much blood from the looks of your shirt. It is completely soaked in the back."

He gave Lania a nod. The bloody shirt felt glued to his back, but the excruciating pain from the creature's scratch made him realize the wound must be deeper than he thought. Lania led the way back to the craft, and he appreciated her help. It seemed his craft moved farther away than he remembered parking it earlier, but with Lania's support they finally made it to the side ramp. The auto-open worked and they both walked up the ramp and into the craft, and he was very thankful she was able to assist him since he wasn't walking very well.

Once they were both inside, the door automatically closed behind them and Lania took him straight to the med-lab. He unfastened his shirt and let it fall to the floor next to the scanner table. When he laid, stomach down on the cold, flat slab a shiver ran through him. Lania now had perfect access to his wound. "Well, doctor, what do you think?" It surprised him when she moved closer and he saw her clothes, covered in his blood.

"Until I get past this blood, I won't know. Where are the sterile wipes?"

"Everything you'll need is in the drawers under me." He felt dizzy even though he lay still and prone on the exam table. Not good. The room began to spin and Lania's face became a blur, then the entire room faded away and suddenly turned black.

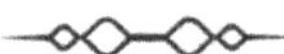

Lania kept wiping gushing blood from Jace's wound. She needed to work fast and expertly if she were to save his life. Before she could sew his wound closed, she needed to clean every tiny bit of the open area since the giant creature probably injected some of his poison on all the tissue she could see through his claw-nails. Jace had passed out, which proved a good thing since the cleaning process would seriously hurt, and he'd already suffered a lot of pain. She grabbed several supplies and chemicals from the drawer and began to work quickly to clean out the deep gash on his back, along with the surrounding areas.

The task proved far more difficult than it should be due to all the fresh blood which still gushed out of the long, jagged opening on his back. He continued to lose more and more of his precious blood. Actually, flowing blood was nature's way of cleaning out the body, so she considered it a good thing, as long as he did not lose much more. Jace was at his blood loss limit.

Finally, she finished the cleaning process and scoured the drawer where she ultimately found some clips and used them to hold the wound closed so she could sew it shut. The machine of Jace's perched over her head, might be able to fix this, but he begged her for hand sewing if required. She felt relieved she would not have to use the big machine hanging over his head with all of its buttons and controls. That machine over them intimidated her in every way possible, which made her happy she'd agreed to hand sew if necessary—and it was extremely necessary.

The ugly creature created quite a jagged wound and that made her task really difficult. Finally, her sewing task was completely accomplished, so she began to bandage it carefully, but fully. He'd be fine, but would definitely be in severe pain for quite a while. The Lizzard's claws cut very deep. The good news, if there was any, the creature's claws measured far longer than the depth of the wound. If that crazy monster had cut all the way in as far as he could, Jace would be dead.

Thank the stars for such a detail since Jace already lay in extremely serious condition. She did not have much experience in this kind of work, but she knew about the possible outcome. A lucky break for Jace, even if he didn't know exactly what happened yet. She pushed these thoughts aside because they seriously scared her, and she needed him in so many ways, but wanted him even more.

Since he remained unconscious while she sewed him, she did not have to sedate him or numb anything. One question remained, when would Jace wake up? They would be safe in the craft, but he had to do the flying, or teach her while they went. She was in no hurry, but she wanted him awake so she could ask him how he felt. The good news here was that he remained alive. Jace had a close call, whether he ever admitted to it or not.

Lania settled back in the chair next to the table he lay on, where she'd found Jace looking at her not so long ago. Now she knew why a chair was placed in such a location. Two things she'd learned about this man--how soft his skin felt, and how hard his taut muscles were to her touch. He obviously kept himself in fantastic condition. Without a shirt, she noticed he had the best shape of any man ever, and was perfect in every way. He looked like an artist's sculpture she saw in the vid he made for her.

What should a woman do with a perfect man? Keep him for herself? Of course she should, yet somehow, from what little she knew about her past, it may not be a possibility for her. They might both want each other, but circumstances would likely pull them apart so fast her head would spin. If, and when they both looked at the scar on his back, they would have a common memory to share.

According to what she knew, her future looked bleak. Here lay the man of her dreams, handsome, kind, smart, a man with all the right attributes. Yet, she still remained legally tied to Raulf, the worst man on the planet. Would she be able to detach herself from Raulf? Good question--no answer. If there were a viable way to do so, she would find it. Currently the evil idiot had her sister for a life-mate. Power-wise, she understood, but she had no idea how her sister tolerated the man. It had to be deemed an illegal life-mating once she showed up. As Jace constantly said, 'one issue at a time'.

When her memory returned, she knew she would love her sister dearly. From what she'd seen in the vids, they'd always been close, and it appeared she trusted her in all things. It also seemed when their father died, she'd grown even closer to Marna. The only thing she struggled with had to do with Marna's life-mating to horrible Raulf. The bigger question she had for Marna—did she have feelings for the evil man?

When her actual memory returned, she might be able to remember those parts of her life for real, and experience the feelings that accompanied those memories. People took their memories for granted. Why not? Fortunately, her experiences taught her never do that again, and not to give in to other people's wishes all the time.

A moan drew her attention and she looked at Jace, who seemed to be waking up a bit. "Hey sleepy, how are you doing?" She stood and stepped close to the edge of the exam table where he lay. With her hand, she gently touched the skin of his shoulder. His bare skin sent tingles to her stomach. She loved the way he felt, way too much. Of course, she needed to be extremely careful not to get near his wound.

"Did you sew me up?"

"I did. Per your request."

"Absolutely. I hate what the machine does. It leaves much bigger scars than what your work will."

"How do you know? You haven't seen what I did."

"Trust me, I know. Been in this predicament before." Jace tried to laugh. "You probably saw my other scars."

"A few of them. I mean, they don't show much, so no concern. Now, the one I just gave you will be a very different matter. I'm not a doctor, or overly handy with the needle. And your friend was not careful with his long claws. For some reason that creature did not care how long of a gash he gave you."

"I don't care. It's not on my face where everyone can see it." Jace tried to push himself up on his elbows, but fell back down. "Don't panic, I'm going to stand the hard way."

She watched him swing his legs around to the side, then slide to the edge of the table until he managed to get his feet on the floor. Then with his good arm, he pushed off the table and stood. "Better. Help me to the pilot's seat. We need to get out of here."

"Okay." While she followed him out of the med-unit, she grabbed a pillow for his back from the shelf on the wall. In the hall he slowed, and she quickly slipped up beside him. The very narrow hall made it difficult to get her arm around him, but she managed, then guided him to his captain's seat. Her arm tightened around his waist when he wobbled in his effort to sit. She put the pillow behind his wounded back, hoping to ease his extreme pain. "Do you want some meds for the pain?"

"Not until we're home. Pain meds make me act weird, or should I say interfere with my normal thought patterns. I want to be sure we get back."

"True. This is no time to crash or get lost. Luckily it won't take us long."

"Strap in and we'll get going."

The moment she sat and looked out the front; shock flew through her. "Look Jace! He's gone. The crazy monster escaped. He's free again!"

"I planned for him to escape. We got what we wanted, but he didn't need to die. All in all, he's a magnificent creature. He's just too big of a threat to enjoy."

"I wouldn't use the word enjoy. Possibly appreciate? We might be able to do so if he stayed still long enough." Lania laughed. "He would need a much better attitude for us to enjoy him. Know what I mean?" Jace started to laugh, then immediately stopped. "I shouldn't have made a joke. I'm sure laughing is painful. I'll try to remember."

"Thanks. At least let me get some drugs first." He smiled at Lania. "Right now, we just need to get home. It's the safest option." He turned his gaze on her. "First, I want to thank you for saving my life, Lania. You're an excellent doctor; in case anyone asks."

"Let's keep it our secret. Sewing people up is not fun, and I really don't plan to do it again." She smiled at him. "Only for you, my sweet Warrior, Jace Bryton."

Jace tried to laugh but stopped. "You have my sincere thanks. I know what you mean about sewing up wounds. I've done it before myself, and it isn't an enjoyable activity. I've patched up both of my brothers in the past. You do what you have to do, fun or not."

Lania fastened her seat strap then looked at Jace. "Ready to fly, Captain? Let me know if you need any help. I can move any of the switches you might have to strain your back to reach."

"I'm good." Jace started to touch one of the controls, but jerked his hand back. "I forgot my handicap. Didn't think I'd forget so easily, or so fast." Jace groaned.

Lania chuckled. "No, you're just doing your macho thing all men do when they can't admit they need a bit of help."

Jace nodded. "Please turn those top two switches over there." He pointed. "Flip them to the on position, then the three under them to off."

"Yes, Captain. Anything else?"

"I'll let you know."

"Yes, sir." She loved the way he took control. No matter what job he did he always performed as an expert. No man knew everything, but Jace certainly had it all in perfect order. She may not remember much about other men without her memory, yet she well knew Jace could not be more extraordinary if he tried. She never wanted to let him go, ever. He just risked his life for her memory and she would cherish him forever.

It didn't take long before they were in the air headed back to the busy city they left behind. The crazy Lizzard disappeared back into the wilderness, and she felt relieved to be free from the clutches of the dangerous creature, and she was sure Jace felt the same. At least they were both alive to tell the tale. For a while she wondered if Jace would survive. Thank the stars her handsome man stayed busy flying them back home. Back to what?

Chapter Ten

Jace landed the craft on the roof parking, then hit the button to lower it into the garage. He sensed his brothers might be home when they arrived, and their craft now sat parked in the proper place. Lania needed to meet them sometime, and he couldn't think of a better time. He hoped she liked them since they all belonged together, and he needed their help to straighten out the mystery surrounding her complex situation.

"Lania, My Lady. My brothers have finally come home, so prepare yourself to meet them."

"How do I get ready, my Warrior?"

Jace laughed. She used the warrior title to rebuke the My Lady title. He still liked calling her My Lady, because when he did, he felt like she belonged to him, and he wanted her to himself more than he ever believed possible. Although, he did like it when she called him, warrior since it supported his pride level. He almost laughed.

He looked at Lania. "Just know all three of us have a good sense of humor, and we joke around a lot. So don't let our stupid remarks get to you, we don't mean anything bad, or harmful by them. We simply like to laugh. The rest I suppose you'll see."

"I guess I will. Let's go meet them. I know you've missed them."

Jace unbuckled his gear, stood, then held Lania's hand while she stood. "I can't lie; I have missed them at times. Of course, since you've been with me, I really haven't missed them at all. Except, I'd have made them help me with the ugly Lizzard."

"I'll bet so. Now you can just brag about your dangerous battle."

"I can do more. The ship's vid recorded it so you can see everything we did. Gives us both bragging rights." He led the way out of the craft and over to the garage door. He looked into the lock, then while the door opened, he followed it with his arm, an invitation to Lania. "After you."

"Thank you, kind sir."

He enjoyed everything about this woman. The way she walked, talked, looked, acted, truly everything about her gave him pleasure. His thoughts about her were dangerous indeed, and he needed to push them out of his mind. She did not belong to him, and very likely never would. No one called this woman My Lady by accident. She belonged to the Royal Family.

Even worse, she belonged to evil Raulf. He didn't know what kind of problems might ensue since Raulf still remained legally life-mated to Lania once she made her appearance. Lania's sister, Marna, may have problems giving up Raulf for all he knew. He didn't really know much about Marna. This whole situation confused him and seemed impossible to figure out.

One step at a time, he reminded himself while the entry door slid open. Both of his brothers waited for him and nearly knocked him over backwards with their exuberant hugs. It took them a moment before they realized they were not alone, not to mention the grins of pain obvious on his face. "Dane, Holt, I'd like you to meet Princess Lania Sloten. You might remember her better by the name, Lania DeMorgan. However, she'd rather forget that last name, like we all would."

Jace watched Dane and Holt both bow at the waist, and in unison they both said, "Nice to meet you, My Lady."

"I'm happy to meet both of you. Jace has talked about you both a lot, so I'm glad to finally see if what he said is true. I must say, all three of you are very handsome. There's no mistake you are identical triplet brothers."

"Thank you for the compliment, My Lady," Dane said.

"Please, just call me Lania. You do not need to call me My Lady. I'm not currently in my position."

Holt cleared his throat. "All three of us are here to rectify your situation. I know Jace has been working with you in our absence. We're here now to help in any way possible."

"Thank you, gentlemen. I do require a lot of help." They all chuckled for a moment. "However, your brother requires some help right now. He has a terrible wound on his back from a giant Lizzard. I sewed him up, although his wound probably needs something I don't know about. I've been told you are both proficient in the med-unit."

"We are," Dane said. "First let's see where we're at here so we can begin our work." He looked at his brother. "How long ago did this injury happen?"

"Just a couple of time-units ago, at the most. You can run the scanner in a bit."

"Good. We don't want any problems." Holt grabbed a stool from under the counter and pushed it under Jace.

Jace shook his head. "Remind me to show you the vid of me and the giant creature. I've never seen a Lizzard of such a size before. He didn't fit in the extra-large wild, country bear cage I bought. Nothing compares. I never want to see a creature of that size again, especially not so close."

Dane stared at his brother. "So why did you decide to play with this giant Lizzard anyway?"

"I like your word play." Jace laughed, then coughed. It felt like his back injury just burst through his lungs. Most uncomfortable. "Someone gave Lania a poisonous venom injection which completely removed her memory. Our doctor said he'd be able to return her memory if I could find this Lizzard, milk its poison venom, and bring it back to him. Hence, I just played a battle game with the monstrous Lizzard."

"Wow." Holt shook his head. "You must have fought quite the battle."

"To say the least." Jace tried to laugh, but only managed a cough. "Lania saved my life doing something I wish I'd thought about."

"Don't keep us in suspense, Bro." Dane laughed. "Tell us what she did!"

"She tranquilized the monster. Put it to sleep with the giant syringe we keep in the craft's cabinet. Yes, the one none of us has ever used. After the injection, I had to wait for the ugly creature to wake up so I could milk the venom from its' teeth. The moment I finished playing with venom, Lania gave him another injection" Jace smiled. "This time I yelled for her to do it."

Dane laughed. "You two make quite the team. Wish I could have been there."

"You know we need to take you to the doctor?"

Jace nodded. "I suppose, if you can set it up. I'm not sure how long the venom stays viable. Doc told me to let him know when I got it."

Holt left the room to make the call. He lived up to his personality, usually in charge, but more secretive. Jace noticed how both his brothers looked at Lania. They gave her the proper respect, but they also noticed her beauty since she lit up the entire room. What man wouldn't notice? They weren't exactly drooling, but their faces relayed to him they were quite taken by her.

Of course, who was he to talk? He'd been the same way from the moment he laid eyes on Lania in the jungle. Currently, his reactions to her went far beyond noticing her beauty. He wanted to make love to her, although his back needed to heal first before he'd be able to satisfy Lania. She deserved the best, and he currently was not at that level.

Now he wondered when he'd become protective and jealous? He wanted her all to himself, even if it were a wishful dream. He needed to get himself together if he were to survive working with Lania. The gash on his back just turned more painful than it had been, something he didn't think possible. The doctor should be able to help. The room began to spin, and he feared what might happen next. At least his brothers were here to help. A weak and dizzy feeling flooded his body.

Lania caught Jace before he fell off the stool he'd been sitting on. She put her arm around her unconscious wounded warrior. "Holt! Dane!" Both brothers rushed over to her and grabbed Jace to keep him from falling.

"Lania, where is the venom? We're going to the doctor right now."

"In the craft we flew." Holt and Dane carried Jace down the hall to the back door, then out into the underground parking area. They'd motioned for her to hurry and join them. She ran behind the brothers to board the craft they'd flown.

"Jace has a high fever. Thank the stars the doctor can see him now."

Dane looked at Lania. "He also agreed to see you. Where will I find the vial we need?"

"Just grab the blue bag by the co-pilot's seat and bring it with you." Lania smiled at Dane. "The doctor will take care of Jace before he sees me. I insist." The ramp door opened and Jace's brothers carried him up and inside the craft. Once they laid him on the same divan she'd been on before, they secured the safety straps around him.

Dane left to get the bag and Holt settled into the captain's seat. Dane rushed back into the main area, handed her the bag, then took the co-pilot's seat, while she sat in the chair closest to Jace. Her hands shook while she fumbled with the lock of her shoulder strap.

Jace looked horrible, his face was pale-yellow, as if all the blood had drained away. Jace never looked this weak before. His high fever had caused a devastating effect on his exhausted body, and this man was no wimp. She put her hand on his forehead while the craft lifted into the sky. Jace lay paralyzed in a very bad way. While the craft flew, she desperately hoped the doctor could perform magic on the man she cared for. No, the man she loved. Yes, she'd fallen in love with this poor Warrior Man. He was *her* Warrior now.

Thank the stars they were close to the office, so the trip would be fast. Holt even piloted the craft swiftly in the heavy traffic. Obviously both his brothers were seriously concerned, the same as she was. In no time they landed on the roof of the doctor's remote building. It looked familiar, plus it did not seem to be in Holt's personality to land on the wrong roof. That thought nearly made her laugh.

Dane rushed past her, down the hall, then out the open back door. He returned in a flash with a rolling stretcher to put Jace on, a far better way to transport an unconscious man. She unfastened her strap and grabbed the venom bag while she watched the two brothers unstrap Jace and carefully lay him on the rolling-stretcher. She needed to walk quickly to keep up with Jace's brothers.

"Follow us," Dane yelled over his shoulder.

She quietly followed Dane and Holt while they pushed her ailing warrior down the ramp and out of the craft. The doctor opened the door to the private entrance and they all hurried inside. The brothers wheeled Jace over to where the doctor instructed.

She followed them and hoped she didn't make the doctor angry. She desperately needed to stay close to her warrior. She walked behind them down the hall and into the exam room where they laid Jace on the table face down.

The doctor removed the bandages. "What happened here?"

"Jace was milking the giant Lizzard when the rope holding one of the creature's front legs broke, and the creature attacked him. I cleaned and sterilized the wound best I could, then sewed him up."

"You did a fine job." The doctor looked up from his patient. "His reaction has nothing to do with what you did, or didn't do for him. It has to do with the Lizzard since he is so extremely poisonous. He may need a bit of venom himself, which will become an antidote with my additives. I'll run some tests to see."

She watched the doctor lower the scan machine for it to read the damage. It did not take long before it provided the doctor with a complete readout. He shook his head while he skimmed over page after page of information. She hoped everything written on the page wasn't all bad.

"Doc, what does it say?" Holt asked.

"Well, the creature can inject poison through its claws, but not the same amount as he can with his fangs. The poison it does inject with its claws, seeps into all the surrounding tissues and cannot be removed. That's why I said you did all you could. No one, not even a doctor, could remove it all without doing far more damage to the patient."

"Jace insisted on finishing the milking process after he received his wound. That may have contributed to his extra poisoning. He said he would never get another chance."

The doctor looked at Lania. "Of course, it allowed more time to seep into his system than we wanted it to, however; had you not cleaned it so well, Jace would be dead. So, like I said, you did a great job. Jace will need a minor dose to equalize the effect of the poison."

"I'll be right back with it." Dane started to walk to the door.

"Dane, wait." Lania pulled the container of venom out of the bag she held and gave it to him, who in turn handed it to the doctor. "He won't lose his memory, will he?" She could not help herself; she had to ask.

The doctor chuckled. "Not like you, my dear. Besides, it will all be right when he wakes up. Your case is extreme, or should I say complete and complex. Jace may forget what he had for the early sun-cycle meal, but no more. This poison is quite strange. I could find no exact explanations for any of it, although I'm sure of what we're about to do."

"I'm happy his memory will remain intact. We don't need two of us not knowing anything."

The doctor walked over to Lania and put his hand on her shoulder. "Once I give you the injection of venom, your memory will return. I can't say exactly how fast, but it will be fairly quick. I promise."

"I trust you. The brothers trust you, so I trust you." Lania looked into the doctor's eyes. "I can't believe I didn't get the poison out of the wound. I worked hard to sterilize everything, and I went as deep as the wound allowed."

"Like I said, the claws inject it and it infiltrates everything around it. Plus, even you said you couldn't treat him right away. The way you cleaned his wound held down the amount of poison available to affect Jace more. I know you did everything possible. You have no idea how much more the wound would have affected him if the job you performed on him had not been so perfect. You cleaned it exactly right at the time without injuring him more. There's medically no way you could have done any better. Like I said, and I truly mean this, without your work, he would absolutely be dead." The doctor shook his head at her. "I mean that, Jace would be dead, so never question what you did for him."

Dane cleared his throat. "We owe this lady our sincere thanks after hearing your assessment. We knew she'd helped him, but we had no idea how much. Thank you, My Lady."

"No thanks necessary. I'd do it again in a heartbeat."

The doctor nodded. "Thanks to you he still has one."

First Dane, then Holt patted her on the back, then kissed her cheek. "Don't fuss over me. Save it for your brother. He'll need all of us in order to recover."

Holt cleared his throat. "I hope we brought enough venom for both of your patients, doctor."

The doctor held up the bag containing the venom. "Plenty. I don't even need quite this amount. Although, there will not be much to spare." He smiled.

All three of them watched the doctor set the bag down, add some drops from a few bottles of his own, then load two syringes. One looked small and contained very little. The other appeared quite large and completely full. It did not take any imagination to know which belonged to Jace. The doctor gave her warrior the small injection, then put the fancy machine to work on his wound. He then turned toward her.

"Why don't we go into the other room so you can have some privacy." The doctor indicated the doorway.

"I can't leave Jace, he's. . ."

"He's fine, and he has two brothers at his side. Besides, you can return quickly."

"All right. Let's go."

CHAPTER ELEVEN

Lania settled onto the comfortable chair in the small room the doctor put her in to give her the injection. He stepped up beside her and injected her in her arm before she even realized what he had done. He told her not to stand for a few moments since the injection might cause dizziness. He also explained how the injection would work, along with possible side effects. Then he hurried back to care for Jace, for which she was grateful.

She considered him to be a great doctor. He explained to her how important this venom would be to her. The good doctor knew exactly how rare the venom was, and said little research had been done to know all the effects it might possibly have on a person's body. He told her the injection should fully return her memory from what he had learned, but she needed to be patient. He thought it should be quick, but not enough research had been done to be more specific.

She needed to allow it to work unhindered in her system. She wanted to be with Jace when he woke up, yet her memory remained of the utmost importance. Jace risked his life for her to have this remedy, and she thanked the stars and the universe he remained alive, receiving the urgent help he required.

A glance around the room indicated she must be in the doctor's supply room. She noticed a countless number of bottles labeled with one kind of med or another. They were all in an area not the same as the doctor's regular practice space. To pass time while she impatiently waited, she began to count the shelved bottles. Suddenly it felt like someone pushed her against the back of the chair and held her tightly against the leather. Then clear memories of a man she knew to be her father flew to the forefront of her mind. It felt like she could reach out and touch him right now.

Lania shook her head and tried to stand. Instead, she fell back in the chair while one memory after another flashed through her mind. Her entire life played out for her like one gigantic vid. She tried to consume the huge rush of memories that flooded her mind all at once. This memory flash made Jace's vids seem like slow motion. The doctor implied it might work this way, yet to consume it all so quickly after everything she'd been through was extremely difficult. Even her wretched life on the strange jungle planet played out in her mind's eye.

This phenomenon felt amazing and hard to believe at the same time, especially since it kept flashing before her eyes so quickly. She could barely take it all in. Confusion, wonder and excitement all danced inside her. She gained no information regarding who sent her away or why. She remembered nothing about a conspiracy, even if Raulf kept her locked in her room until he needed her for a show-piece on his arm for their public appearances. No words could describe how the evil jerk acted, or continued to act.

She felt completely relieved to know he never touched her in bed like a true life-mate. In fact, from what her memory revealed, they never even shared a bed, so she knew having sex of any kind to be a myth the public conjured up to believe they were a happily life-mated couple.

It did not matter who decided to imply they lived happily together. She still did not understand who came up with such a ridiculous story. Her memory proved she insisted Raulf never touch her in a sexual way. Of course, Raulf agreed since he only wanted the title of Supreme Ruler of Lorton and the power attached to the title. If anyone wanted her shipped away, it must have been Raulf. He took great pleasure in causing pain. Of course, it did not make sense for Raulf to ship her away, he could have simply killed her. Whether by his hand or someone he hired.

The most amazing memories returning were inside the famous cavern, doing battle against the energy with her father. Together they caught white-hot energy balls and threw them back across the cavern. They had to try to turn the angry energy into a more complacent, softer version of itself so planet Lorton could remain a balanced, safe and happy place to live. He taught her so many things in the cavern while she stood with him. It really brought him to life. She did the annual battle with him until he passed, then Raulf pretended to do battle, and Raulf did nothing. She could not function by herself since Raulf was useless. In fact, Raulf attracted and created more evil since he could not get rid of the bad energy.

She and her father did battle in the cavern until the energy level became neutral and livable once again. If the energy below the surface of Lorton was not kept in peace, it had the ability to create unrest above the surface, causing war and constant turmoil. Therefore, the energy battle had to be performed to maintain life on Lorton.

The battle actually required The Royal Ruler and his life-mate. Unfortunately, her father had been without a life-mate since she was small, hence her involvement when she was older. Her father was great at the energy battle, but he truly needed an official mate to help him since she had been too young.

The rules for the energy battle were clear, without a life-mate he could take his first-born child. The energy information he'd taught her had been critical, and she allowed it to settle within her body. When her father took her with him in the cavern, she was under thirteen annual-cycles, but since her mother had passed, he was left with no choice.

Then many annual-cycles later, came Raulf as Supreme Ruler, and he pretended to go down for battle, except all he did was hide behind the nearest rock to escape being touched by the energy. She could not do battle efficiently alone, it required two people. A person could be killed by the energy if their partner made a mistake. Since she was alone, each trip they made into the cavern only left Lorton worse off than before.

She now knew how to do the energy battle; she simply needed a partner to actually work with her. The energy battle was never about the rulers at all; it was the way it touched each and every person's life. The rulers may like to take credit and act like it was about them, but it was to keep the peaceful, happy lifestyle everyone on Lorton needed and enjoyed.

It might prove to be a complete impossibility since she did not hold The Royal Ruler position, and remained a single woman, therefore; no life-mate of her own. No way would she ever go in the cavern with Raulf. Even if she did, Raulf had proven he did not have what it took to do the Energy Battle. She needed a willing partner who was unafraid of the battle facing him.

Explaining the energy battle was next to impossible since every time proved different from the last. The energy seemed to have a mind of its own, if that were possible. All she knew was right now, she was the only living being on Lorton who knew anything about it, or had done it before. She now felt the burden of fixing the energy since it seemed quite angry with the people above always fighting and arguing, more crimes were being committed, and they were not far from all-out war which would completely destroy Lorton.

She needed to pursue the conspiracy issue since her memory returned, and there were three capable, willing brothers ready to help her. The thought brought a smile to her face. All three of the very handsome brothers were extremely competent of providing help. Of course, her heart reached out to only one, her precious Jace. She wanted to get to him now, so she scooted to the edge of the reclining chair and pushed herself up using the arms. She felt fine, so she headed back across the hall.

Her injured warrior still laid prone on the table, his back up while the doctor finished using his magic touch on his wounds. Thank the Gods the deep, jagged gashes looked much better now, no longer red and swollen. She saw his two brothers in the far corner leaning against the wall, their eyes glued on their brother. She walked over to them, hoping to learn something more about Jace's condition. "What did the doctor say?"

Holt looked at Lania. "He'll be fine in a few sun-cycles. Doc treated him with the healing machine, and the injection is taking care of the infection which caused his high fever. This doctor is good, which is why we use him, and pay him so much."

Lania knew Holt's grin verified the doctor's high compensation. "I'm so glad to hear he's going to be fine. How soon before he wakes up?"

"He's already started to wake up, so it shouldn't be long." Holt looked at Lania. "How about you? How's your memory?"

"Surprisingly good. I believe it has returned, and the four of us have much to discuss." Lania looked into Holt's eyes. "If you agree to help me. Jace already signed on and indicated you and Dane would also be willing,"

"Of course. If Jace is in, we're all in. We stick together. We're brothers first and foremost. We look out for each other and our clients."

"Your concern is real. I love your devotion to each other and your clients. You three brothers really do stick together and are truly loyal to each other. It is so refreshing to see."

Holt shook his head. "Have you never seen loyalty before?"

"No, I haven't. You'll understand when you hear my story. We'll wait until we can talk back at your place. Jace needs to be there. All there, if possible." She smiled and shook her head. "I'm just relieved he'll be okay. He really worried me."

"Us too. We know he's tough. We've all been injured before. It's never easy to see someone you love in pain."

"I agree." Jace moaned and she turned her head toward him so fast she nearly fell over. Holt grabbed her arm to steady her. "Thanks."

The doctor moved the machine away from Jace's prone body. "He's fine. He just needs a few moments to regain his bearings. Then you can take him home. Try to keep him down for at least two sun-cycles, four if you can. His bones and muscles need time to heal properly. I had to give him a few new stitches to mend vessels and muscles deep inside, and they need to settle in also. I know he's tough, but even tough guys need healing time. I don't want to fix the same things over again."

"We hear you. Thanks, Doc." Dane walked over and shook the doctor's hand. "Many thanks from all of us."

The doctor looked directly at her and she knew what he wanted to ask. "Yes, my entire memory has really and truly returned, from my earliest childhood until this sun-cycle. Thank you so very much. I truly appreciate what you have done for me."

"No problem. I'm glad your memory is back. You owe Jace thanks for the venom, and he owes you for his life." The doctor smiled. "I'm just glad I had the ability to help you both."

Lania and Holt nodded their agreement to the doctor before he left the room. She felt like an intruder. The two brothers stared at her and she sensed they wanted to be alone with Jace. She decided to ask. "I can leave if you want time alone with Jace."

"Why would you think that?" Holt asked.

"You both acted like you wanted me to leave."

Dane laughed and pointed to his brother on the table. "You may have guessed what he thinks most of the time, but you're not so good with us, little lady." Dane smiled at her. "Or should I say, My Lady?"

"Right now, I don't think I'm anyone's lady, so don't worry about it." She wanted to laugh at the shocked look on the brothers' faces. "Guess you aren't too good at knowing what I'm thinking." She couldn't stop the smile tugging at the corners of her mouth. These two made such funny faces at her she finally had to laugh at them.

"I think I know why Jace likes you so much." Holt shook his head. "You're exactly his type."

Dane stared at his brother. "Exactly what type is she?"

Lania chuckled. "Yes, what type am I?"

"You're smart, quick witted, beautiful and caring. Everything a man wants."

"Every man except the evil idiot who called himself my life-mate, and basically wanted me dead."

"That's hard to understand, especially the part about him wanting you dead. He hid it really well from the public. We're good at reading people, and we didn't see it coming." Holt shook his head. "Care to explain?"

"I will once we get back." She shook her head this time. "Just remember I'm a good actress."

Dane smiled at Lania. "Now you're using our key to victory. Talking things over, being good actors, and coming up with a really unique plan to take Raulf down. I can't wait. I've wanted to do this for a long time. I always knew something was very wrong in the Royal Palace, now we have proof."

Lania knew she furrowed her eyebrows at Dane, unable to help herself. "What do you mean, proof?"

"We have you, which is proof. Right?"

She smiled at Dane. "Anyone as conceited as Raulf leaves himself open to many things due to his greed. I despise him. My best hope is to find him dead." Lania paused and wiped a lone tear from her cheek. "I mean every word. If he's not gone soon, this planet will destruct, literally it will. The energy is so far off, I wonder why there hasn't been massive wars breaking out everywhere already. We need a plan, a really good plan if we're to succeed. This entire planet will be better off without Raulf. Plus, he cannot deal with the energy in the cavern, and neither can my sister."

"We can all see the planet is an inch away from complete unrest and upheaval. It is getting ugly. You're very right about that." Holt stared at Lania. "What can we do about it?"

"We have one option, to get Raulf out of power. Right now, no matter what you think of me, I'm the only one capable of wielding the psychic energy to balance the planet. If I don't, you're absolutely right, it will get even uglier, and completely out of control fast. And yes, we're nearly there now. Time is of the essence."

"Glad to hear you say so, My Lady. Maybe I need to say, Supreme Royal Ruler?" Dane laughed. "Sorry I laughed. You should be in power, not the evil man who's in charge now."

"I understand, believe me. You have to laugh when you talk about Raulf, except for the fact he's so evil it feels wrong to laugh. Confusing to say the least, but I feel better knowing we all agree on what we're dealing with."

"How can we help?"

"Well, we need a plan, and I don't have one. Jace told me the population of Lorton believes me to be dead, and I probably need to stay dead for now. The less the population knows before the battle, the better. Anyone loyal to the man will try to kill me before the public knows I'm alive. He's not simply evil, he's full of himself. You'll never meet a more conceited being."

"We can use that self-confidence against him." Dane paused a moment. "We'll develop a plan around his arrogance and conceited attitude. He does not believe anyone dare unseat him, and we're going to do exactly that." Dane looked at Holt and smiled.

"You two must know something I don't. Raulf is not easy to fool. He's very careful who he allows close to him, and he always seems to know if someone is trying to take advantage of him. We may all hate him, but the man is smart, and we can't afford to forget his intelligence." Lania shook her head. "This plan must be absolutely and completely foolproof."

Holt cleared his throat. “It will be, My Lady. We’re very careful and exact about what we do. We haven’t survived this long by being careless.”

Dane put his hand on her shoulder and looked into her eyes. “I don’t know what Jace told you about our business, or how we operate.” He nodded at Lania. “We’ve been at this a long time, and have learned how to deal with the Raulfs of our solar system. He’s not the first man with such a personality. However; he has more power than anyone else we’ve taken down.”

Lania took a deep breath when Dane removed his hand from her shoulder. “So, what’s your plan?”

“A good plan requires great thought, and we want Jace to be in on the plan, and you of course.” Holt looked into Lania’s eyes.

“I trust you Bryton Brothers, I really do. Everything is at risk and it is so difficult for me to even begin to explain.”

“We understand more than you think,” Holt said.

Dane nodded. “Remember, we never take a job lightly, especially one with the massive repercussions of this one. Together, we’ll do it. I have no doubt. How we’ll do it is up for grabs, but do it we will.”

A groan from the table behind her made her turn immediately. She rushed to Jace’s side and took hold of his hand. He opened his eyes, looked at her, then smiled. “How are you feeling, Warrior?”

“Much better, My Lady.”

He glanced at his brothers. “Have you been getting acquainted with those two silly beings?”

“You mean your brothers?” They both laughed. “Yes, I’ve gotten to know them a bit better.”

“Have they told you a bunch of lies about me?” Jace asked.

“You might not want to know the answer. They did discuss my case with me.” She ran her hand up and down his bare arm several times. “We have a lot of work to do, so no time for small talk.” He smiled at her and it made her stomach flutter again. For some reason he always affected her in the same way, and no matter how hard she tried to ignore it, her body always reacted to him—even in his current condition.

“I’m ready to get out of this place.” Jace sat up on the table bed and swung his feet over the side.

Dane rushed to the table. “Hold it, Bro. Let me help you. We don’t want to pick you up off the floor.”

“I’m fine,” Jace insisted.

“Just this time. The fever made you weak, so quit being mister tough guy. Be sensible for a change.”

Holt moved to the other side of him. “Dane’s right. Cooperate, tough guy. Doctor’s orders. In fact, he told us to hold you down for four sun-cycles, at least, so get used to our orders. Got it?”

Jace smiled at his brothers. “Maybe two sun-cycles?” He shook his head. “Fine. Let’s go.”

The doctor opened the door and entered the room. “Miss Lania, may I speak with you for a moment, please?”

“Of course.” She followed the doctor out of the room and into a different room down the hall. It seemed way nicer than where she sat last time. More of an actual treatment room than a storage area. She took the seat he indicated and watched him look at some kind of chart in his hand.

“So, tell me, did your memory truly return? And if so, is it complete?”

“Yes, and yes. I am shocked it returned like it did. Memories flashed through my mind, like a fast-forward vid. Everything has returned, and is still there. I’m so grateful to you. It means everything to me to have my memories back. You never know what’s important until you lose it.”

“Very true. I just wanted to verify the injection’s success. I can honestly say, I’ve never given such a concoction to anyone before. It seemed a bit worrisome to me, yet I knew if anything could possibly work, it must be the Lizzard’s venom. I am truly sorry Jace suffered such injuries in the process. At least you took care of him. I’m sure he’ll be fine very soon.”

Lania smiled at the doctor for a moment. “To the other part of your question, I can honestly say, I’ve never received such a concoction before.” She nodded. “I’m glad I did. Thank you so much, doctor.”

“You’re very welcome. And for your information, I specifically treated the poison I injected into you, so it should not have any ill effects to your system. If you feel bad for any reason, please contact me.” The doctor smiled. “You’d better hurry now. I know how Jace is, and he wants to get home.”

"You know him well." She chuckled a bit when she saw the grin on the doctor's face.

"I do. Possibly too well, same with the other two. They do dangerous work and require my services on a regular basis. All three are very good men."

Lania stood and walked to the door. "I believe you. I've seen them first hand prove their worth." She pulled the heavy door open. "Thanks again." She slipped out and hurried to the craft before it left without her. Once inside Holt shut the door and they took off before she finished fastening her seat-strap.

Chapter Twelve

They finished their meal and now they all sat at the info-center, close to the immense vid-screens. Of course, they viewed the most updated version of air read-outs, and they looked much clearer than what she saw before. Of course, she had been away in never-never land for over six annual-cycles, far too long to live such a primitive lifestyle. She planned to make the evil man pay for putting her in such a miserable camp. Next to this life-style it certainly was a camp.

Right now, they needed to create a plan to take down the evil man in charge. She needed to control her attitude if she planned to work with the brothers. Holt demonstrated why his brothers called him the info-whiz they turned to in order to organize everything. He worked fast and produced excellent results at the same time. The other two sat back and watched while he brought up a timeline of events.

Holt continued to type. "As you can see, I'm working where the six annual-cycles began, when they claimed Lania died. It's obvious the date of her funeral became the beginning of everything taking a really bad turn."

Lania felt totally amazed by what transpired since she'd been sent away. It had not taken Raulf long at all to life-mate her sister. Then again, Raulf, always worked in a hurry, especially if it involved credits, or power. If he had not life-mated back into the Royal Family so quickly, his position as Royal Ruler of Lorton no longer existed, as a result he remained connected through her sister.

Holt leaned back in his chair. “Once he life-mated Marna, and settled into his new lifestyle with her, he purchased the club we’re all familiar with. The largest moon-cycle club on planet Lorton. We’ve all been there at one time or another. Every adult has been there at some time.”

Lania cleared her throat. “I haven’t.” All three brothers stopped their work and stared at her. They stared at her and shook their heads slowly as if they didn’t believe her at all. “It’s true. I’ve never even seen the club. You must remember, my life has been very sheltered and closely monitored on a regular basis.”

Jace scratched his head. “Evidently. It’s hard to believe, although in your case, quite understandable. Guess we never gave any thought to the type of restrictions you might, or did have to live under. All the people we know, or have met, spent some time in the club during their lifetime, so we assumed you had also. Sorry, My Lady.”

“I realize other people have all the freedoms I never did. Therefore, you cannot go by me.” Lania sighed. “I’m sorry, I…. She shook her head. “I’ll admit, I wanted to be a normal young girl and woman, however; my father never allowed me such luxuries.” Lania hung her head, unable to face Dane and Holt. Jace tightened his hold on her, pulling her tighter to him. Jace, a man with compassion and a big heart, a man she had easily grown romantic feelings for. Just then Holt walked over to her, tipped her chin up with one finger and made her look him in the eye.

“My Lady, please forgive us. We did not know your background, our mistake. We should have known. We’re just in the beginning stage of our research and planning, so we often blurt things out before we think. Plus, you must realize, we’re not used to having anyone with us during this process.”

“I forgive you, but I was not offended. I realize no one has experienced the life I’ve had. I’m afraid I stand alone, although I don’t wish my circumstances on anyone.”

“Thank you.” Dane interjected. Now, give us all a hug to seal the deal of working together without offence.”

“Alright.” She hugged Holt, surprised by his robust strength. He backed off just before she lost her breath. Then Dane came up to her and reached out for a hug. At least Dane used restraint, unlike Holt, although, all three brothers were very caring—and strong. Funny thing, they did not realize how much she appreciated their caring trait. “Thank you, all three of you. I do appreciate you. Now, back to work, and do not let my presence worry you, just shout out whatever you want. I promise, I won’t take offense. Especially when you yell bad things about my life-mate. In fact, I’ll gladly join in with your insults. He can’t be insulted enough!”

Jace laughed. “Sounds like fun. I’m sure you can insult him even deeper and far better than we ever could.”

“Nothing intimate since we were never together. A few things maybe. I’ll throw out my best insults, and I have plenty to contribute.” Lania chuckled, and all three brothers joined her, and it turned into a nice bonding moment. She really adored all three Brytons, yet Jace alone pulled at her heart in a way she needed to protect. Not because of anything he did, simply because of the man he was. She could not help being attracted to him in every way possible. She viewed him as a complete package. Normally men who were as handsome as Jace were totally self-centered and not her type. Jace totally blew that theory out of the galaxy!

Jace caught her staring at him in a way she knew he might recognize. His experience in the flirting game must be quite extensive since his looks alone gave him an upper-hand most people, whether men or women, never had. She may be backward at flirting since she had no experience in her memory; however, she knew she just gave him her best ‘come-on’ look.

She doubted they could be a real couple, but she certainly liked playing the game with him since she knew she’d read the same look on his face. She could not call her life normal, and her future was seriously in doubt. It remained all too possible Jace may only be someone who helps her regain power. Nothing more. The government would never allow them to be together the way the laws currently read, and changing those laws were next to impossible.

Holt and Dane returned to their seats in front of the vid screens and continued to work more of their magic. It seemed like it took forever before Holt pointed at the floating read-out in front of them.

“Are we looking at some kind of credit read-out from the depository?” Dane shook his head.

"It is." Holt pointed at the screen again." Do you see the total in the account?"

"No." She watched while Holt moved his cursor to the correct place, then he enlarged the amount so they were all able to clearly read it. Her breath caught in her throat. "Am I reading the total correctly?"

"If you see over nine-million credits, then yes, you are. Now look at this number, it's the amount in the account when he purchased the famous night entertainment club." Holt pointed. "Twenty-two thousand credits. Raulf has owned it six annual-cycles. This means he's gained around a million and a half credits per year, after expenses."

Jace rubbed his forehead. "I'd say he's been selling more than drinks. The question is what? I know he legally sells women. I'd guess the illegal, designer drugs, the kind his clientele likes best, makes him the most credits."

Dane nodded. "I believe you're right. We need to prove it and trace it to get what we need. With so many drugs legally available in the outlets, it's difficult to believe an illegal market still exists."

Lania glanced at all three brothers who nodded in unison. "So just buy something you know is illegal, they'll sell it to you, right? Plus, drug charges are tough, aren't they? Or has it changed since I've been gone?"

"We all wish the drug laws were better enforced, but since Raulf is behind all the laws…" Jace shook his head. "No charges are ever brought against him, or anyone else selling it, at least in his club anyway. The facts in a case dictate the plan we use, better than we can. So," Jace took a breath, "we'll do all our homework and find out what he's selling, who his suppliers are, and how he washes it all to show up in the depository. I'm also thinking he may have more than one account, and or depository, and I'd guess they might contain even more than the one we saw."

"Oh Jace—I did suspect that." Holt ran his fingers over the keyboard. "You may just be right, Bro."

"We all know Jace is right concerning designer drugs. Even more so about credits." Dane shook his head. "Raulf probably has ten times the amount we saw hidden somewhere, most likely in several depositories. We'll find his stashes. You know we will. Tell her Jace. Explain our schemes to the lady while she puts you down for a rest. And don't argue with me. Holt and I are more than capable of researching, and you know it. Now, you two go. And Lania, don't let him talk you out of it. He needs rest. Doctor's orders."

"I understand. Jace, let's go. You're with me now, so march to your room. I will follow and make sure you rest."

"Yes nurse. I'll go. This time anyway. We'll discuss the future of you being boss." Jace started to walk toward his room.

Lania followed, surprised by his slower pace, indicating he needed rest far more than she realized. His brothers knew him well, and the doctor knew him better when he gave orders for him to be careful and take it easy for two sun-cycles. Jace always felt his ideas were the best, so it remained difficult to tell him what to do. In general, his ideas were usually right, except when it came to his health, then he needed guidance.

When they reached his room, he hurried to his bed and fell onto it. At least he landed laying down on one side to protect his back and looked reasonably comfortable. She sat on the bed next to him and felt his forehead. He ran a slight fever. "I need to get you some meds for your fever."

Jace smiled. "I just took some meds the doctor gave me for pain and whatever." He chuckled.

"I think those meds are messing with you right now."

"No, they're not." He grabbed Lania's arm. "Lean down and kiss me. You know you want to. Right?"

She did not have an answer for him. In all honesty, she wanted to kiss him, yet he seemed way too messed up at the moment. The pain meds had a heavy hold on him, so his actions were far from normal. Besides, she should not let him know how she really felt. Anyone she became close to might have to sacrifice their life, and no one should have to make the ultimate sacrifice. Especially not Jace. Not again. "Not a good idea, Jace."

"It's an excellent idea." He pulled her down to his chest. "Now, kiss me woman! I want you desperately!"

Dear stars! Did he really mean what he said, or were the meds still talking? Either way this. . ..

He guided her down until her lips pressed against his, and the warmth of his skin against hers made her head spin. Then his tongue found hers and she heard herself sigh along with him. The physical pull between them was far too strong to deny. His kiss became magic, just like everything else about him. He was wonderful, and she wanted him. She never wanted a man before, but Jace fell into the special category.

Jace groaned and deepened the kiss. His hand. now on her back pressed her tighter against his chest. The feel of his heavy breathing, the moans and groans they both emitted seemed too much. His brothers might hear them. Plus, this activity just flew out of control. She tried to end the kiss. He refused to allow her to move and held the back of her head with his hand.

Lania relaxed and fell into the moment she'd waited for since she met the man. Still, she could not admit to her romantic yearnings for Jace--kind, caring, helpful, and very loving. Based on looks, he ranked number one on the most fantastic specimen of masculinity ever list. Any woman who got close to him could not stop herself from falling in love with him.

Love? Love was an extremely strong word. Lust may be more appropriate, and they were both guilty of sharing that emotion. She pulled back quickly and it worked. He looked at her with a very shocked expression on his face. This had been a fantastic moment, but she doubted Jace would ever remember it took place.

"What's wrong, my sweet? Don't you like kissing?" Jace stared at Lania and laughed.

"You're laughing at me, Jace Bryton!"

"Never at you, only with you. Come on, sweet lady, you know you liked it. I felt it, very strongly too, and no woman out there can fool me."

"Really? You've kissed how many women?"

Jace grinned. "I must admit to kissing quite a few, for various reasons."

"Various reasons? Sounds a bit...aah...strange? Or just vague?" The grin on his face looked arrogant to say the least. "Care to explain?"

"I'd rather ki...ki…kiss you some more. Come closer, my swe...weeet. Please? I really wa...wa...nt you."

Jace spoke the last of his words slow and slurred. He certainly acted over-medicated. Definitely all the meds were talking, not Jace, and he did not even realize he was talking. He had no idea what he was doing, who he did it to, or why. His silly antics made her laugh. She hoped his passion would turn real.

"I wan...want...yoooooou.." He fell asleep in the middle of his sentence. Good. Best she left him to sleep it off. He had been funny, and that always enticed her. She felt overly attracted to him, and it was so very obvious to her why. One look at him, even sleeping, and he screamed of sexual energy, and still looked like a warrior capable of winning any battle. Damn, he looked so cute and sexy!

When Lania stood, she studied Jace lying on the bed. Memories of him wrestling with the Lizzard creature entered her mind. He'd done quite a job staying alive while not killing the prey. He milked the creature and saved her memory, and she'd be forever grateful. When the moment felt right, she would tell him her true feelings. Right now, too much work lay before her, and two brothers waited for her return.

Plus, her precious Jace needed his healing rest.

Chapter Thirteen

Holt and Dane both stared at her when she walked into the living area. Did she look different? They couldn't possibly know what just happened between her and Jace. Or did they? A triplet thing? The Bryton triplets had a closer bond than she had ever seen in her entire life. They thrived on their brotherly, mental intuition about each other's thoughts, and what they planned to say before they ever spoke, a quality which often got in her way. They maintained some kind of secret psychic bond that never failed them.

She had carefully watched the three of them interact with each other from the moment they were all together. Since she had always been a bit psychic herself, it was easy for her to notice it in the brothers, and realize how they used it to their advantage. She doubted they grasped what they were doing—it simply happened and they enjoyed their quiet togetherness and communication. She always wished it had been that way with her sister, but she and Marna were never close enough for such a connection. Then again, they were not even twins.

Dane and Holt smiled at her in a way that made her believe they knew what just went on between her and Jace. She felt her cheeks turn red so she looked down and sat in the chair across from the brothers.

"Did you get our brother tucked in okay?" Dane laughed. "He can be a handful."

"We've both seen him on pain meds before, and he can be quite amorous, to say the least. Did he behave himself with you, or did you have to fight him off?"

"We struggled a bit, but he's resting quietly now. Sound asleep actually." They just proved her assumption regarding their smile and what it meant. She may never get used to the way these triplets silently functioned.

Holt smiled. "Good. Now, where were we? Oh yes, Dane and I started a search to see who owns what around here. Before Raulf became entangled in government, he'd become very immersed being a successful businessman, so he had a good start. Credits bring power, and," he cleared his throat, "the man loves power. Can't live without it, or so I've seen and heard."

Lania nodded. "You heard correctly. I have no idea what all he owns. Yes, he loves his power, and constantly misuses it for his own reasons. He has never done anything for the people. Most leaders do their job and work for the betterment of their people and society. Not Raulf. He's never done anything for anyone, other than himself and his own pockets."

"You are very correct." Holt kept typing. "All the facts we presently have do show a pattern to watch for, with different angles to catch him at his own cheating games. The vids clearly show how they get their card players drunk, then stack the cards against them so the house gets all the credits. You can plainly see the dealers cheating."

Dane laughed. "I didn't need to watch a vid; I've seen those dealers in person before. All I thought at the time was I would never get in a card game there. I also witnessed women being sold to the highest bidders. Most big clubs do so, and have been since the beginning of time. They have a separate room where the women for sale gather and parade on a small stage one at a time while the men decide what they're worth. Sex has always provided lots of credits, which is why the government legalized it long ago. They wanted to collect taxes on it. That said, it also allows cheating past your wildest dreams. I suppose I should say unlimited credits in his pocket."

"I know nothing about it. Sorry." Lania hung her head, disgusted no one ever educated her in such matters. She needed to learn fast in order to keep up.

"Let's just say there is no way for the government to know how many women were paid for, or how much was paid. That leaves a giant hole to stash credits into without being caught." Holt looked at Dane. "I will dig up all the dirt on him and his cohorts I can find. I know he has to have a lot of help. Someone will certainly talk to us and most likely spill all the stars."

Lania had to tell them something only she knew. "Under the tough façade Raulf puts up and shows everyone, he is quite weak." Lania shook her head "He can't stand up for himself, so he always has his people carefully tucked around him. I've witnessed him send those men out to do jobs regular citizens would go to prison for doing."

Holt stared at Lania. "I didn't realize that about him. An interesting flaw, wouldn't you say, Dane?"

"We can definitely use that information to our advantage. Thanks, Lania. Anything you can tell us is helpful. We need to know his strengths and weaknesses. Both are extremely important. Our plans work best when we're able to use both those qualities." Dane cleared his throat. "No matter our plan, we must move slowly and carefully. We can't even border on failure. One shot is all we get. No mistakes allowed. None."

Lania nodded along with the brothers since they were right. "If Jace were here, you would have a unanimous vote. That's exactly what he said when he battled the giant Lizzard. He made his feelings regarding failure extremely clear to me many times." She watched Holt slide off his stool to stand. He looked worried and relieved at the same time. How was it possible for anyone to have two different expressions on their face at the same time? She may never know, but all three brothers would get that look on occasion.

Holt scratched the back of his head. "So, we're dealing with an egotistical maniac, who loves credits more than his life-mate. His main interest is himself and how many credits he can accumulate. I want all of us to think of a scheme we can offer him which proposes a ton of credits, with no work required on his part."

Lania cleared her throat. "You realize far more than credits are at stake, don't you? The continuance of the entire planet literally lies in our hands. The unrest on the surface will increase exponentially soon, then no one will be able to stop it." Lania looked them both in the eyes. "You do understand what I am talking about, don't you?"

Holt nodded. "I don't know if anyone fully understands. All we know is there's a ceremony about to take place which is supposed to keep us all calm, and alive. Some believe it only keeps the Royal Family happy and safe. I've never understood it all. What can you tell us, my lady?"

"I'll try to explain it so you can understand." She motioned for both brothers to join her at the table. They all sat and she cleared her mind of everything except the ceremony. "The battle is very difficult to explain. The citizens never see the energy I speak of. It just 'is'. The Royal Family's job, whether they like it or not, is to contain good energy and dismiss evil energy. Like the saying goes, 'the battle of good over evil'. It happens everywhere, except in different kinds of battles between different people, animals and even creatures. In these battles, especially animals, the outcome is very visible since the loser is either dead or bathed in blood.

"In the cavern the end result may or may not be visible. Energy does not bleed, nor have I seen it die. It can change forms, attack anything around it, even completely melt giant boulders. It is strong, which is why it can cause such unrest on Lorton."

Lania continued. "When you are in the cavern dealing with the energy, your main tool is your gut feelings. By that, I mean you sense any progress you may have made. If you don't feel success, you continue the battle. I realize this makes no sense, but it is the basis of what goes on down there that no one sees except the two people involved."

Dane frowned. "Based on what you say, it's no wonder the people don't understand anything about the battle, except it exists and must be done to continue peaceful existence on planet Lorton."

"Basically, that is true since I've done battle and must honestly say, even I don't understand the energy or what it is doing. So obviously the people will probably never grasp what happens down below Lorton. It is rather unexplainable. The energy can, and does throw itself at you, and you must catch the ball and throw it back. I know that sounds very strange, but it happens."

"Hello!"

They all looked behind them where the familiar voice resonated from. Jace walked toward them and seemed ready to go somewhere. Lania wanted to melt under the heat of his gaze. "Well, hello, sleepy-head. Feeling better?" The man could be called a very experienced player all right, and right now she wanted to play.

"I'm better. I hate being dizzy. Anyway, what's going on here?"

"Well, I was bringing your brothers up to date on the energy battle. Do you understand it, Jace?" She looked into his beautiful blue eyes and noticed a softness he had lost while battling the Lizzard, and she felt thrilled to see it return. This man really did have it all. Damn to the Universe! He could never be ignored. Especially by her.

"I suppose I understand it like everyone else on Lorton. I've never heard anyone talk about it in detail. They mostly say it's exotic, forbidden, and something regular people aren't supposed to know about, or understand. Strange how it has become such a part of our lifestyle and customs, yet no one understands it." Jace looked at Lania. "Care to explain the Royal Family's part in this ceremony?"

"I'd love to, if you all want me to." She watched the three men eagerly nod at her. "Okay then. Once every annual-cycle, the ruler and his life-mate must go down into the cavern of oneness. To accomplish oneness, absolutely no discord can be present. Oneness can only exist without opposition for a limited amount of time, and Lorton is there right now."

Holt scratched his head. "So why are we in such discord right now? They've done the ceremony every annual-cycle, yet when they're done, things may be better for a couple of sun-cycles, then in a couple more, everything seems worse and reverts back to the same crisis state of near-war. Can you explain why?"

"Yes. Whoever has been going down into the cavern to do battle does not have the necessary energy ability to change anything. Therefore, the state of Lorton remains the same and begins to turn worse. The few sun-cycles you notice peace, is simply a temporary result of people being in the same cavern. What you don't know, is that Raulf and Marna may go into the cavern but they do absolutely nothing. There is no battle because they do nothing. That is why it remains obvious nothing changes after their visits. The energy quickly recognizes the fact and returns to its angry state since no one truly calmed it down."

"How do we fix the battle to be successful?" Dane cleared his throat. "What I want to know, is if we're certainly headed for war."

Lania shook her head. "Not if we can level out the energy flow and return it to an acceptable level."

"How do we accomplish such a feat if we haven't been able to do so in the last six annual-cycles?" Dane stepped around the table and took a seat next to Lania. "I'm afraid to ask.," He nodded several times. "You know how to deal with the underground energy, don't you? That's why they kept you alive, isn't it?"

Lania chuckled. "Your guess is good and your assumption is most likely correct, however; I cannot, and will not go to an energy battle with Raulf. In fact, I won't go anywhere with him."

"Oh, my sweet Royal, I'm not asking you to partner with Raulf. We're simply asking if you will consider fighting the energy if we find the right person to help you." Jace stared at Lania for a moment.

"Absolutely, but I have no idea who you might find to help me." Dane and Holt both laughed long and hard while she and Jace stared at them. "What's so funny?" Lania did not understand why they were so tickled and laughing so much.

Holt and Dane answered together, "You're sitting next to him!"

"Now, why on Lorton are you two putting me in the battle?" Jace looked at Lania. "Excuse them. They're children who need a lot of attention."

"The two of you share a special bond. Anyone can see it. A bond I believe can calm the powers underground and even out the energy. We have all experienced some form of discontent, causing fighting and feuding. Nothing has been right since the evil man took charge of Lorton. We must get rid of him, and fast, or we'll have nothing left to worry about." Dane shook his head. "Holt, maybe you can explain it to them."

"You did fine." Holt stared straight at Lania. "You left one thing out. You, My Lady, are the only living being on Lorton who understands the energy exchanges and what is necessary to sustain life here." Holt looked Lania in the eye. "Wouldn't you agree?"

If she was not sitting, she might have fallen to the floor. Her legs felt weak and she knew if she held up her hands they would be shaking. She suddenly felt totally alone. Out of nowhere, a strong arm curled around her shoulders and pulled her closer to the warm body which just sat on the chair next to her. No need to look. She felt Jace, felt his strength and protection, comforting and warming her. Holding on to him came naturally to her now. Maybe his brothers knew something she did not.

"You're making Lania nervous. First, we need a failproof plan, no matter what." Jace took a deep breath. "We must bring down Raulf, and find a way to put Lania in charge of the ceremony, which is now twelve sun-cycles away. We cannot let Raulf and Marna anywhere near the energy cavern. So, let's put our heads together. What do you say?"

All three brothers nodded their acceptance then looked at her. It took all her strength to remain upright in the chair. She trusted these men, even if she did not understand what in the universe they might be up to. Right now, no one else even knew she was still alive. The people of Lorton believed her long gone, never to be seen again after going to her funeral. How did she get past her own death? Minor detail to the brothers. They seemed to know everything. She gave them her nod.

All three Brytons left the table and took their places in the info-center. It turned very quiet while they studied their own searches and outcomes. She did not even know what might be going on, or what they were looking for. They all appeared intently engrossed in their work so she moved to the divan where she'd be left alone to relax a bit. She had no info-device, and right now, did not want one. The brothers knew what they were looking for. Since she lived the past six annual-cycles of her life so far away, looking for anything seemed futile for her.

This complex puzzle needed to be put together with up-to-date info. Raulf obviously proved to be the beginning and end to everything they searched for. He seemed to be a complex man who, despite his evil personality, was unfortunately very smart. Plus, he actually appeared fairly good-looking, even if she hated to admit it. Not like Jace or his brothers, but he held his own. She laughed to herself since no man could compare with a Bryton, especially her Jace.

Even smart men went down like lead anchors, especially when they were so conceited they were not looking. She'd see to it herself. With the brothers' help, Raulf's downfall would really happen, and all of Lorton would know immediately. The evil man deserved every bad thing that came his way, ten times over, at least. May Raulf burn in Diabolous for eternity!

If Raulf had not been smart, he would never have made it this far. To life-mate two sisters of Royalty took guts and connections, or at least enough credits to buy who and what he wanted. Raulf was slick, intelligent, cunning, complex, all while maintaining a black heart, so dark even he probably feared himself. True evil, without one shred of a conscience, or thought of others in any way. He only thought about evil and destruction, which must be considered the absolute worst, and most dangerous kind of evil.

Lania pulled her legs up, dropped her shoes and rested her head on her folded knees. It seemed strange to have been ripped from a life of six annual-cycles and not miss one tiny little piece of what she left behind. Of course, she had no life there at all. She may have enjoyed some of the kids, but definitely not enough to make her want to do it again. Especially when every adult there treated her worse than the dirt on their feet.

One sun-cycle she may have her revenge on those horrible people. As for Raulf, he deserved nothing less than pure torture. He had to have sent her to Extram. She never considered torture, or even thought of it before Raulf appeared in her life. His evil made people do things they otherwise would never consider.

Lania had one pressing question remaining that she needed to learn the answer to; who in the government turned on her and accepted Raulf's bribe credits? Whatever she learned, she wanted to deal with those betrayals immediately. The number might be high, or simply one man, but she felt absolutely positive Raulf bought people to get rid of her. She needed to let the brothers investigate. They all had to learn who stood behind this conspiracy.

Chapter Fourteen

Jace studied Lania sleeping peacefully on the divan. She appeared a bit tangled, yet comfortable. Her beauty always seemed like a shining star to him no matter where she may be, or what she might be doing. He found her perfect, and such perfection belonged in a museum, held in high esteem.

Poor Lania, she'd been through some huge cosmic storms. At least she'd survived, a fact Raulf would learn to regret. The moment Raulf heard about Lania's survival, Jace would turn himself inside out and scream until the bats returned to the caves. It was bound to be an amazing moment, one for the history books. Nothing was better than making great history.

Every person alive knew Raulf to be a total jerk. Actually, Evil should be his real name. Any man capable of killing his own life-mate for personal reasons, like wealth and power, was no man at all. He couldn't wait to get his hands on Mr. Evil and make him suffer the same way he made Lania suffer, if such a punishment existed. Usually, the worst of men cried like babies way before it became necessary. They were cowards underneath all the blather and showmanship. They were great actors and terrible warriors, the main reason they paid other people to protect them. Not this time. He'd personally inflict punishment. No one had the right to treat Lania the way she'd been treated.

While his Princess enjoyed her sleep, he and his brothers learned something very interesting. Stupid Raulf began mining for the rarest of gems way beneath the planet's surface. The rarest gem on planet Lorton, Purple-Stone, which rested at hazardous depths beneath Lorton's surface, making it the most expensive stone sold.

Very few men were willing to go below to mine the stone due to the depths. The difficulty factor involved breaking through multiple energy layers to reach those stones, which often proved impossible; hence the rarity and price. It seemed all Raulf's clientele knew he sold Purple-Stone. What they did not know was that he started a mining company to produce it.

Very few men ever attempted to mine Purple-Stone, since nearly every minor hired would either be found dead, or lost forever in the depths of planet Lorton. The mining pay remained the highest on this, or any other planet. However; the minors seldom, if ever, survived to spend the credits they earned. He personally knew a couple of guys who went down. They never came back up. Another sad tale. Going down so deep became known as a death sentence, rather than a job. Of course, Raulf was not concerned for his miners' safety.

It took either a very brave, desperate, or a stupid man to mine for Purple-Stone. Jace never planned to go down, and he made it clear to his brothers never to go under either. Luckily, they both agreed with him. They all decided the high-risk made the job of mining totally out of the question. At least all their plans to help Lania took place above the surface. Except possibly for the energy battle.

Jace glanced back at his brothers to see why they were all excited. "What did you two find?"

"Raulf has many businesses which provide him with credits galore. Although, one stands alone and has the most value, his mining operation. He has sold more Purple-Stone since he took office than anyone has. Ever!" Holt paused and stared at his brothers. "Do you know what this means?"

Jace shook his head along with Dane. "Tell us.

"First of all, his Purple-Stone mining business doesn't show up on any system, so where are all those credits going? I think we'd all agree it's going straight into his pocket. Where else would Raulf put so many credits?"

Jace slowly nodded. "How about going after his prostitution business? We all know it's booming."

"You're right, but Raulf's club has the correct license to run legal prostitution." Dane scratched his head. "The man has too many sources of income. I really don't know how he hides it all. Purple-Stone, prostitution, gambling, liquor. Anything else?"

Holt laughed. "All the alcohol and entertainment at the club is very pricey. The problem with nearly all his sources of income is they're all legal, except the Purple Stone. Does it really matter? We simply need a way to get close to him, so I say whichever endeavor puts us in the right position is the best way to go."

"Illegal usually works best, but we would have to become very interested in Purple-Stone. Of course, that would be the most expensive way and would take about every credit to our name. But we all know credits speak louder than words."

All three of them nodded at the well-known phrase which played a major role in their business. The truth remained so evident. Jace sat on the bench and waited while Holt and Dane sat on the other side.

Dane looked Jace in the eye. "Do you have a plan?"

"I do. However, it will take a while to work out all the details." Jace took a deep breath then continued. "One or two of us will pose as buyers, and we'll flash our credits around his club. We'll gamble a lot, whether we win or lose. We make ourselves seen and known around town as the guys with more credits than brains. Then we'll work our way to lining up a purchase of Purple-Stone. We'll insist to meet the main boss so he can confirm the validity of the deal."

Holt rubbed his forehead for a moment. "You think your plan will work? Nothing is that simple. Never is. And to believe we can get Raulf to show up seems doubtful. He couldn't have gotten this far if he were a complete idiot. Besides, what will we do with him if he does show up?"

"I only know what I'd like to do." Jace stared down at the floor.

"I have to agree with Holt." Dane took a deep breath. "Plus, too many people know who we are. Triplets can't hide very well. Plus, we have no idea how many credits this plan might consume, credits that will go into Raulf's pocket. We'll never see those credits again."

Jace straightened in his chair, not because he felt tired of sitting, but due to the pain shooting from one side of his back to the other. "I believe Dane is totally correct. Credits are important, we all know that. We can't afford to lose as many credits as that plan would require, and we don't know it would even succeed."

"Dane stared at his brothers.

"Possibly if we tweak it enough and hire a couple of guys to front us." Holt looked at his brothers. "I'll take care of finding a couple of guys to help, I just want to know if you're in?"

Jace took a deep breath. "Even though I feel that the plan is very shaky, I'm in."

Dane nodded. "Let's do it."

They all smiled. Jace still wondered if this caper would work out. It sounded simple, and at face value it might be, however; nothing involving rulers, the Royal Family, or government ever proved simple. All the current buyers knew the situation, but to throw in tons of credits and purchase Purple-Stone seemed an impossibility to infiltrate.

Dane stood then nudged Holt, and they took a few steps toward the back hall. "Holt and I are going to the garage. We'll be back in a few."

Jace acknowledged them with a wave, then turned his attention to Lania. He wondered what she'd say when he told her about the plan. For some reason he felt she'd want a say about it. He needed to have a chat with her before things went too far. She might know better how to keep everything from falling apart. In the distance he watched Lania wiggle and blink her eyes open.

He walked across the room and sat down beside her. "My Lady, feel better now?"

"How long did I sleep?"

"Maybe not long enough." She squinted at him and he smiled. How could she look so absolutely cute while half-asleep? The thoughts that ran through his mind at the moment were very inappropriate, but exactly what he wanted. Her. Unfortunately, what he wanted and the reality of life were always at war.

"Are you trying to tell me something, Warrior?"

"My brothers and I have come up with a plan to infiltrate Raulf's system of selling Purple-Stone to elite buyers. We'll make our moves and advance inside his miserable club operation."

Lania shook her head. "Jace, no. Not a good plan. Sorry. I know some things no one else knows. I am more than willing to share and listen to plans. We can all decide on the better one. Understand?"

Jace hit the table next to him with his fist and took a deep breath. "Yeah, you think my brothers and I are stupid, and you're the only one who knows the right way to do it? Am I warm?"

"Not exactly. Jace, don't be mad."

"How could I be otherwise?"

"I think you're in pain and that is getting in the way of your thinking. The very first thing on our agenda is the energy battle, and what is required to return the energy below back into smooth operating order. Do you understand me, Jace?"

"What in the universe does that have to do with taking down Raulf?

"The battle must come first, no exception. After the battle we can decide how and when to take the evil man down, but until the battle is over, we do nothing."

"I'll tell my brothers what you said." He started to stand but Lania jumped up from the divan and stood in front of him.

He stared at the beautiful, dark locks curling slightly around her face while she put her hand on his chest to stop him from getting up. "What are you doing?"

"Jace, calm down, please. Somewhere between the pain and the meds you've lost your usual way of thinking. Remember our discussions about the energy situation, and how it is causing such unrest on Lorton right now? Think, Warrior, think. You realize how important that is, and time is short before it happens again."

"I still don't understand how Raulf fits into all this?"

"Maybe not, but I can show you how I fit in."

Her beautiful hair hung all over. He could not possibly think of anything other than Lania, the amazingly, gorgeous woman in front of him. He had to kiss her right here, right now, in the moment, and it needed to be a long tender kiss, the kind that lasted a lifetime. Jace pulled her close to him, put one hand on each of her cheeks and gently guided her lips to his. He then began to kiss her lightly and tenderly. Then his urge to consume her grew immensely, and faster than he thought possible. He deepened his kiss, slipped his arms behind her and pulled her down onto his lap. Damn she tasted good. He never wanted to let her go.

Lania's arms threaded behind his neck and shoulders and tightened around him. He felt the outline of her firm breasts, and they seemed much larger than when he simply looked at them. Firm, yet so soft, all at the same time. The feel of her pressed against him felt far more fantastic in reality than what he imagined, and he'd imagined a lot.

She could not mean more to him if she tried. Lania represented everything he wanted, and so much more. She lit a fire deep within him, one only she could extinguish. He needed to stop this before his brothers returned from the garage and saw something he didn't want them to see.

He pulled back and ended the kiss, not ready for Lania's look of disappointment. "My Lady, I fear my brothers will return any moment, and we might be caught in a…a…"

"Compromising situation?" Lania chuckled. "You're right, Warrior, absolutely right. So where should we start?" She stood.

Jace guided her back down onto the chair next to him. "Wherever you want. You'll get no argument from me." Jace knew he had to remain seated for a little while, afraid to stand since Lania could definitely see what she'd done to him. "Do you think addressing the three of us together is the best way?"

"Probably." Lania sat up straight in the chair and looked at Jace. "I am sorry you think I insulted you and your brothers. I did not mean to do so. I simply do not agree with that particular plan."

"I'm sorry I said you think we're stupid. I'm just frustrated and I took it out on you. So, I'm the one who is sorry." He smiled at Lania. "However, I will not apologize for a more than wonderful kiss." Jace laughed. "Even if I am a stupid man, I know the differences in kisses, and your kiss rated off of my charts."

"Oh my. I'm not sure what to say now. I think I'll just go freshen up and think about it, my Warrior. While I'm gone you can get your brothers back in here. We have much to discuss."

Jace watched Lania hurry off to the lav down the hall and he heard the door shut. He hated to let her out of his sight because he would miss seeing her beauty. He'd fallen for her, and could no longer deny it, at least not to himself. He wanted her right beside him, no matter what. His growing love for Lania might be difficult to explain to his brothers. Being the oldest, by a few breaths, meant he went first in many things, but falling in love never made it to his list of accomplishments before, nor did he expect it to ever be there.

Only time would play a part in how far he and Lania took their relationship. Right now, he felt inextricably drawn to her. He wanted her, all of her. Now and always. Enough said. He took a deep breath, glad for the reprieve, and time to regain his composure. It shocked him when he realized how fast and completely, he responded to her. He'd kissed many women, yet never was he so completely ready, so quickly before. Now he knew to use more caution when around the most beautiful woman in this galaxy and beyond. The woman he desperately yearned to call all his.

Most of his thoughts felt premature. He couldn't stop the unmistakable pull emanating from her, and those feelings totally consumed him. This sexual draw between them proved extremely eye-opening. He'd only kissed the lady, and now she'd become everything he wanted in his life. His thoughts about Lania pulled at him strongly, yet felt so right. She seemed to comfort him, not to mention the excitement and desire she stirred within him whenever he saw her, and especially when he touched her.

Jace shook his head in an effort to bring sense back to his thinking. He never acted on crazy thoughts before and did not plan to start now. He believed in the saying of, 'All in its time'. Solve this case first, then think about the lady involved in it. her name remained Lania DeMorgan, she was still legally life-mated, and not on 'the easy list,' like some called it on planet Lorton. Why did they call it the easy list? He'd found many women who were easy, but that never interested him, unless he found the woman a good match, which had never happened before. It didn't matter. He simply needed to concentrate on first things first.

Lania took her turn to shake her head. She wished her explanation could be easier and make more sense. She could not change the difficulty factor due to a lack of facts; she could only hope the brothers understood. "The man insisted on life-mating me. I wanted nothing to do with him. I thought him evil then, and I know he is now. My father, very alive then, insisted I life-mate him due to political issues."

Lania took a deep breath. "My father was all I had, and I loved him dearly, so, I agreed, on one condition, that he never sleep with me or touch me in any manner, except what we needed to show the public so they believed in us. I couldn't stop him from touching me in public without being obvious. I could only smile and pretend I loved him, which is what you saw." Lania looked down at the floor, took a deep breath then continued. "Since I hated the man, the act proved extremely difficult for me to pull off convincingly. Raulf forced me to do it well, if I did not, he said he would kill my father."

"Wow. I never guessed that about either of you," Dane said.

Holt scratched his head. "Neither did I." He looked up at her. "Your father passed quite quickly, if I remember correctly, and you still did it until the end?"

"Once my father passed, he said do it or he would kill me. Now you know why I absolutely despise the man. He is reasonably handsome, but his evil erases everything and anything good about him. My best hope is for him to be found dead!" Lania wiped a lone tear from her cheek. "Yes, I mean it. Life on Lorton would be far better if Raulf were completely out of the picture, and I mean completely. Plus, he cannot deal with the energy in the sacred cavern, and neither can my sister."

Holt stared at Lania. "It doesn't take a genius to know they can't. The planet is only an inch away from complete unrest and upheaval. It's getting ugly."

"I must add, once my father said I had to life-mate Raulf, it then went to a vote of The High Council as required. I need you three to find out who on the council he bought, and who turned against me. Right now, I have no idea. This is something you three must look into before all this is over. The men responsible for taking bribes will be dealt with, by me."

Jace hit his fist against the table. "The lady has spoken."

"We all agree with her, I assure you. We aren't getting rid of Raulf to still have a corrupted government. So, yes. We will honor your request, My Lady."

"Thank you, gentlemen. I needed to hear your agreement. Now, back to our discussion." Lania scratched her head. "The first thing we must do is get Raulf out of power. Right now, no matter what you think of me, I am the only person on this planet who can wield the psychic energy in the cavern. If I don't, you're absolutely right—it will get ugly and out of control even faster than it has already. And yes, we've nearly arrived at the point of no return. Time is of the essence."

"Glad to hear you say so, My Lady. Or should I say Supreme Ruler?" Dane laughed. "Sorry I laughed. It's where you belong. Not the so-called man there now."

"I understand, believe me. You have to laugh when you talk about him, except he's so evil it feels wrong to laugh. Confusing, even if we all agree on what we're dealing with."

"Any suggestions, princess?" Dane asked.

"How to best accomplish this is open for discussion, and I appreciate that. First, I must say we should not worry about Raulf's businesses right now. We do not need to infiltrate or worry about Purple-Stone. That said, our main goal needs to be the Energy Battle which will take place soon. This is where Raulf can be taken down. I know how to wield energy; all I need is a partner I trust."

"Feel free to pick any of us, My Lady." Holt laughed. "We all know it needs to be Jace. You two have already worked successfully together and can do so again. Right?"

She smiled at all three brothers. "Of course. However, I must ask your birth order. I realize you are triplets, that said, one of you came first, and he is the one I must work with. Firstborn has the ability the others may lack."

"Wow! Listen to her Holt," Dane said, and all three brothers laughed. "That's Jace!"

Holt shook his head. "I knew she'd pick him!"

"Absolutely." Holt looked at Dane. "We never get to have any fun." He snickered. "Then it's settled. We'll leave you and Jace to work out those details. Dane and I are free to help in any way you require. Still, I must ask about his club and all of its activities, legal or otherwise."

"Raulf will go down for his crimes, and they should not be difficult to find. I trust Bryton Security, so do your job the way you see fit. My main job for the moment lies with the energy battle. I need to teach Jace what will be expected of him to battle the energy, which is no easy task."

She waited while all three brothers laughed at her statement, then they nodded their approval, and she did the same. At least they cooperated with her, making them easy to work with. If they acted difficult about things, she would literally be tearing her hair out by now. Instead, she simply needed to learn to work with a man so distracting, it might prove impossible. Instead of teaching him about energy, she might let him teach her about other things.

How on Lorton could one man be so nice, sexy and handsome? The three Bryton brothers may be identical triplets, equally appealing to a woman, yet every part of her remained constantly focused on Jace. Her feelings for him grew more each sun-cycle. She should not be having these feelings, yet they were so strong and deep seated she could not stop them if she tried. She must work on those feelings if she planned to partner with Jace in the up-coming energy battle.

Feelings for a man were completely new to her. She never felt this way about Raulf, or any man. Sometimes the new feelings seemed fantastic, other times plain sinful, even if they were always exciting and wanted. Hopefully, she'd be able to curtail herself long enough to train Jace how to wield the energy thrown at him below the surface of Lorton. Dear stars, she hoped Jace could master how to be a true Energy Warrior.

The plus side for her was to be working with someone who cared about doing his best for the people of Lorton. She could not train Raulf since his only concerns were wealth, and what woman he could get into his bed each moon-cycle, which made him worse than a piggor! Although, she hated to insult any animal in such a way. Raulf was the wickedest of the wicked. If she never had to look at Raulf again, she would die a happy woman.

Her eyes found Jace, and she gave a sigh of relief. This man stood for everything Raulf did not, so the obstacle before her remained to train Jace. The actual training would not be easy for either of them. Becoming a true Energy Warrior took a lot of natural talent molded into a deadly weapon. He stared at her with so many questions in his eyes. She did not know if she was ready for the complicated task ahead.

Training Jace. Would he consider the tasks complicated? Difficult? Interesting? How could she handle being alone with him underground when she could barely control herself right now?

Time together may be tough for them both. It did not matter how they felt about each other, only the battle they must face together.

Chapter Fifteen

Lania studied the super handsome man in front of her, amazed by his movements. He did his best to imitate what she showed him, unfortunately men were not full of style and grace. Remarkable barely described him. He tried to follow her exact directions, even if it bordered on making him look extremely awkward. She looked away before she laughed. Most men preferred being like a warrior, at least real men did. For a man around two-meters tall he was actually quite ambidextrous.

His well shaped muscular body remained firmly planted in her mind. She could no more ignore him than a catis could ignore a mousie. When she glanced up at him, he stared at her in a strange way. As well as she knew him, she had no idea what he was thinking.

"I'm ready for more training whenever you are. I'm sure it will take me time to accomplish."

"Accomplish? Interesting word." She saw him watch her lips every time she spoke. What could he be thinking? Jace seemed to be making this far more difficult than it needed to be.

"What am I supposed to do?"

Jace proved to be too much of a distraction for her to concentrate. She shook her head and mentally kicked herself. The well-being of the entire planet lay on both of their shoulders, so they both needed to behave. "Jace, you have much to master if you're to survive and win the battle with me. This will not be easy. I want you to understand what you will be facing, and it is very difficult to explain to anyone who has not seen this type of energy before. It can, and will kill you if you are not careful."

He smiled at her. "Then how has Raulf managed to survive his battles?"

Lania grinned at Jace with her controlled, sarcastic look, which she hoped he knew meant she had no patience left. "I told you, he never really did battle, he only pretended. My sister, who now walks at his side, is also completely useless in the battle. I don't really know what they did, or how far own in the depths they went. I only know they did not battle any energy If they were successful in their battle like they claimed, planet Lorton's living conditions would be perfect. Instead, it is in a current state of disaster."

"You mean chaos?" Jace stood and walked to her side of the table. He held out his hand. "Come, My Lady, I have much to learn. Where shall we do this?"

"For now, we should be outside in the sun. Do you know of a place where we can be totally alone and no one can see us?"

"Totally alone?"

"If possible."

"Absolutely. Come with me."

Jace took her hand and led her to the elevator. They went up to the top floor where his small craft waited for them. He opened the passenger door for her, assisted her inside, shut her door, then walked around and got in on the pilot's side.

She knew they were already on the edge of town, so it only took a short time for Jace to fly them to the top of the mountain behind their place and park. He got out, quickly went to her side, helped her out, then together they walked to the flat, grassy area to their right.

He watched with interest while she walked in a circle, then spun herself around a few times. She then held her arms up to the sky and smiled with her eyes closed. Damn this work seemed so difficult with him just watching her, making her feel so self-conscious. She closed her eyes, unable to look into his gorgeous blue eyes. One swift glance later and she couldn't miss his eyes glistening brighter in the sunlight. She turned circles to the right, then to the left until she stopped and lowered her arms.

"Jace, come stand next to me and do what I do." Jace took her hand in his and pulled her to him. He put his arms around her and gave her a reassuring hug. She felt her body begin to shake nervously.

"I'll help you bring peace to our people. I promise, My Lady. Promise."

He held her tight until she quit shaking, then slowly released her. "I appreciate your promise, Jace. I really do. I'm counting on you. "She shrugged then stood up straight. "You must learn to catch energy in your hands, mold it tightly, then throw it at a target. Can you imagine doing that?"

"Of course."

Lania shook her head at him and frowned. "I mean, absolutely imagine molding hot energy, then throwing it back where it came from?" He smiled at her until she let out a small chuckle. "This is no joke, Warrior, and you must understand how very serious I am. If you are not equally serious, you'll become dead serious, which means, you will not walk away from the battle."

She stared into Jace's eyes. "And if I no longer have a competent partner, I may not walk away either. Then Lorton ceases to be a livable planet and Raulf remains in charge. Very sad story. So please, tell me you totally understand."

"I understand, Lania. I didn't mean to make light of anything to do with the battle. I'm sorry if I upset you." He smiled at her. "You must admit, we still need to maintain our sense of humor. If we don't, we may go crazy, and that is not good, now, is it, My Lady?"

"You are correct." She tilted her head toward him. "Don't become over confident. The moment you do is when the energy will attack you. And believe me, it can, and will hurt you. I am not joking about the energy."

"Understood."

She knew he probably gave her the wrong idea about him as a student since he seemed to be joking around to remain sane. His brothers all did the same kind of thing, which made it difficult for them to work with anyone else, especially a woman. The brothers were definitely not used to having a woman around.

"What's next?"

"Without the ability to be inside the cavern, it will be nearly impossible to instruct you on the exact way to work with live energy."

Jace scratched his head then looked into her eyes. "What if we can go into the cavern? I can get us inside without being seen. What do you think?"

Lania looked at him totally baffled. "Perfect. You'd learn so much faster than trying to grab an imaginary sun in your hands and dance around a field." She laughed. "It is pretty funny. Remember, you did not see me laugh. But Jace, how in the universe can you get us inside without being seen?"

"Leave that to me."

Jace smiled at her and as usual, she melted under his gaze. The sun glistened off the striking dark strands of his shaggy hair which fell over his forehead. She fought the need to reach out and brush it away. Bad decision right now. "When do you think we can get in the cavern?"

Jace had to see how attracted she was to him because she could not miss how much he wanted her. Did he realize how damn handsome and appealing she viewed him? Her self-esteem may have been stolen from her, luckily Jace had enough for them both, along with the confidence to make it all happen for them. Although, this still remained too soon to tell Jace about her past. Some details were not really necessary.

She honestly never met a man like Jace before. She knew he wondered if she trusted her own judgement and thought processes. With very little self-esteem, she did struggle with endless issues. Plus, she knew he wanted to enjoy her as a woman, and do things with her she never thought about, desired, or experienced before. Some things he taught her already, other things she would have to learn if she ever went farther with him. Simply to be in his company right now made her feel complete, happy, and alive. He stared off into the distance with a blank look on his face. "Jace? Where have you gone? I asked you a question. Did you hear me?"

"Sorry. My mind did wander for a moment."

"When can we get inside the cavern? The sooner the better."

"Let me talk with my brothers. We'll come up with a plan."

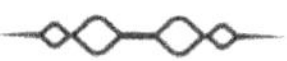

Lania stepped down onto the sandy floor of the second level in the cavern. Her mouth dropped open at the sight before her. She'd been here many times. However; it did not look like it currently did. Three monstrously huge rocks had been placed down here, probably for Raulf to hide behind. Where did they come from? They did not exist when she fought with her father, nor were they in place when she was pretending with Raulf.

“Is something wrong?” Jace asked.

“Well, this entire area looks completely different than the last time I saw it. These giant boulders were not here. The floor lay empty of all obstacles and protections. This I know for a fact.” Jace simply stared at her like she lost her mind again. “Seriously. It’s true.”

“I’m not saying it isn’t true. I’m trying to figure out how anyone would be able get boulders this size down here. They’re huge!”

Lania stared at Jace. “You’ve never been down here before, right?” He shook his head at her. “These monstrous rocks are as impossible to explain as the evil man himself. He had to have them brought down here to hide behind. Nothing surprises me where he’s concerned. He had to have done it when he was forced to come into the area with my sister.”

“I agree.” Jace glanced around. “Explain to me why these boulders might be necessary to him or anyone?”

“When you’re fighting with energy and light, they can save your life by absorbing the negative and protecting you from the burning heat of the energy.”

Jace shook his head. “Why would they throw negativity around? I thought this was supposed to be positive, and show how great the ruler is?”

“Didn’t I tell you it is not about the ruler; it is about the people and equalizing the energy balance. It does not always go the way the ruler might plan, especially considering who the current ruler is. Mr. Evil, to most of us, and I’m quite sure the energy forces see him in the same light.”

“So, how did he survive? By hiding behind these boulders?”

Lania laughed. “I doubt he’s even been this far down. If he has, the answer is yes since he doesn’t know anything else to do. He certainly has no idea how to handle the energy. I watched my father down here, and his work proved fantastic. He knew what to do, what they wanted. He claimed success, and the results of his battles spoke for themselves."

Jace nodded. "I remember well. The planet hasn't been peaceful since he's been gone. He did a wonderful job. Anyone who lives here says the same thing." He scratched the back of his head. "How did the Evil One survive? He really is the epitome of evil, and I mean every word of that statement. I can't think of one thing good about him."

Lania sat on a rock which looked like a bench, low and flat. "I cannot argue with you. Raulf is evil personified. I don't know how he lived through any of his battles. My guess is he hid well enough not to be killed." She stared at the gravel floor, then glanced up at Jace, who looked more handsome than she'd ever seen him. Maybe it was the lighting, or his perfect face. Something drew her to Jace, something she could not identify, yet that particular force pulled her closer to him in so many ways.

"Is something wrong? You're looking at me with a strange expression. One I've never seen before."

Wow, he caught her mooning over him. She certainly never meant to be so obvious about her desires. "I'm just concerned about your safety, Jace. I'm sure you understand."

"I do. So, teach me what I need to know." He nodded at Lania. "Don't forget, I'm a warrior at heart."

She smiled at him. He puffed out his chest and fisted his hands on his waist like warriors tended to do. "Okay then. First of all, as I mentioned, it is not about the ruler, or how great he is. It is, and always will be, about the energy below the surface of Lorton, and how it touches each person's life, whether they know it or not. Do not, for one second, believe it is about you or me. It is simply about the job we do so every citizen can enjoy their life on Lorton. Do you understand, Warrior?"

"When you put it that way, I understand better. I suppose until I come in contact with the real energy and begin to comprehend it, and the process we'll be doing, it may be difficult for me to completely grasp it all. I have told you I'm a warrior, and warriors need to learn about the fight and the enemy."

"I understand you well, Jace Bryton. And I know you are a Warrior; your reputation speaks for itself." She looked him in the eyes. "And I'm counting on your warrior's abilities and attitude.

Remember though, I never said the energy was your enemy." Lania stood. "Hold out your hands, palms up." The moment he did, she slapped them and he jerked in surprise. "You weren't ready for me."

"Obviously not. I should have been."

"You're right. When the battle begins you must be ready for anything and everything. Remember, there are no rules down here. You will not receive a warning of any kind, so always be ready."

"True in most fights." Jace tilted his head. "I'm sure you have more in mind."

Jace took Lania's hand and sat next to her on the bench. "Will we have more success if we do things together?"

"The power to fight nearly doubles at times when two fighters join their minds and their strength. My father and I did so at times, and we learned how it works. No one knows everything about the energy balance down here. I don't know of any other planets which require an energy battle every annual-cycle."

"Neither do I." He looked directly at Lania. "So, teach me all you know. I'm ready."

She thought he might get up, instead he pulled her to him and pressed his lips against hers and gave her a light, questioning kiss. Then he pressed harder, and it seemed his question turned into a demand. She knew he wanted her, and the way he made her feel, she wanted him just as badly.

Her feelings spun in circles, and her desire grew to intense need. Jace was the only man she ever wanted. Would making love to Jace here and now be a good idea? Here in the cavern? Her mind flipped over and over, and her answer remained, "Why not? They were under no rules, and her evil life-mate cheated on her constantly, although, she never considered, or felt herself life-mated. She had become totally ready for Jace, without further doubt. She wanted him now.

He pulled her tighter against him and deepened the kiss even more. Damn! This man was the best kisser ever. Jace may have been her first, yet she instinctively knew his kiss went beyond words. He made her body tingle and shudder with need. Before she gave herself to him, she needed to tell him something.

It took great effort for her to pull back and end the kiss. Jace lifted his head and looked at her with a rather rejected, expression on his face. “I have something I must tell you.” She placed her hands on his cheeks. “I’ve never been with a man before.” He leaned down and gave her a soft, easy, no demand kiss then pulled his head away, staring into her eyes..

“I’ll admit, I want you desperately. I’ve thought a lot about this, and I leave the choice entirely up to you. I’d never force myself on you. It is completely your choice, My Love.” He kissed her cheek. “You did not need to tell me. A man just knows.”

“How? How is that possible?”

“By the way a woman responds, her attitude, her words, her movements.” He kissed her cheek again. “You’ve done nothing wrong, quite the opposite. I knew from our first kiss, you’d never experienced a man before, in any way.”

“Oh my.” She looked at the ground and felt like an idiot. He gave her all the time she needed. Finally, she looked up at him. “Yes. I want you now. I can no longer deny my need for you to love me.”

“Very well then. I will be more than happy to love you. Only *if* you are sure?”

She smiled at him and nodded. “Very sure.”

He leaned in and began kissing her once again. His arms tightened around her, then he picked her up and laid her down on the bench. The long, flat slab did not exactly support her entire length, so she raised her feet and her knees. Jace knelt on top of the bench between her open legs. The way he looked at her made her shiver in excitement.

“You are so beautiful. You’re perfect in every way,” Jace whispered.

“You’re too sweet. I do n…” He placed a finger over her lips so she couldn’t speak.

“I’m telling you the truth, My Lady. That is exactly how I feel, and I doubt there is a man on this planet who’d think differently. Never doubt my words. Your beauty leaves me speechless.”

When she tried to speak, he pressed his lips against hers and kissed her yet again, with power, and a longing she felt down to her toes. Her own yearning grew fast and furious, and it shocked her since this was her first time. She did not know exactly what to expect while with a man. With that thought, she instinctively knew

Jace would take care of her in every way, and never hurt her. She knew him well enough to feel safe with him.

His fingers found the tassel of her zipper and he slowly pulled. The top she wore opened, and he eased it off her shoulders. Then he made fast work of her bra. Now that she lay half naked, it took him no time at all for his mouth to find her nipples. He sucked and played in a way which gave her goose-bumps all over her bare skin.

Then he reached his hand to her waist and gently tugged off her pants and undergarment in one big sweep. Damn he was good! Of course, she never once doubted his ability. Now she lay completely naked in front of him. "What about you, Warrior?" He smiled at her. "Take your clothes off and satisfy my curiosity."

"I cannot ignore your request, My Lady." He lifted one leg down, then the other and stood on the ground.

She watched him nearly rip his shirt while he pulled it over his head. The bare chest before her looked like candy to her senses. Then he unzipped his pants and shoved them down in one fast swoop and she looked at what she had never seen. What if her decision to make love turned out to be wrong? Doubts flooded her mind quickly while he remounted her on the benchlike rock. She doubted he could be more ready for her if he tried. He gently prodded at her until she felt herself open wider to him and he slowly, gently began to slide inside her.

She expected a great pain to assail her when he made his entrance. Instead, she simply felt pleasure and relief. Jace may never believe she was a virgin although nothing seemed to matter to Jace except making love to her. He truly made her feel special, and the sensational feelings he created within her went far beyond her wildest dreams. He proceeded so gently and caringly while he pushed harder and faster. It felt better and better. If this is what she had missed, she regretted every time-unit without making love to her personal warrior.

Feelings of love and satisfaction were only possible when Jace gave them to her. She may have just found him, but the wait proved well worth the time. Thank the stars her evil life-mate never touched her since he only produced pain and suffering. With Jace it felt like a total sharing, and she gave him everything within her. She wanted to please him in every way. Her heart, and now her body, belonged to him, and him only.

He carefully, kissed every part of her, but also slowed down his sexual exploration. Did he want to make it last longer? Or did he enjoy her this much? Whatever he did felt fantastic. She loved every touch, kiss and movement. The man did everything so carefully, leaving nothing un-kissed. Jace made love exceptionally, and every moment felt like heaven.

Then her body began to react and places she did not know existed. The most intense feeling she'd ever experienced took over her lower body. She shivered, unable to stop the reactions in every place female. She knew she'd found complete satisfaction with the man of her dreams.

No sooner had she finished when Jace ramped up his speed and motions and found his own satisfaction within her. He filled her with love, and the greatest sensation she'd ever felt. Now she would want to make love to him all the time. Slowly he pulled back and slid off her to huddle at her side, making sure they both fit on the so-called bench. When she fully opened her eyes, she saw a glow about Jace she'd never seen before.

He quickly dressed and so did she. When they finished, he stared at her with the strangest expression on his face. She wondered what thoughts ran through his mind. "Is something wrong?"

"You have a strange glow about you. You look like you're a bulb of light. I've never seen a person glow like you are!" He reached his hand out to touch her.

"You have the same glow about you. At first, I thought I was seeing things, but you glow like I do, I guess. I can't see myself."

"I can't see myself either so we're even." Jace looked at her face. "I don't understand this light coming from us."

Lania looked at the glow of her hand. "If I were to guess, I'd say making love in this environment increased our energy ability somehow. I can't explain it any better. We need to hold hands and see what happens. They joined hands and the glow grew even brighter. They both watched in awe when a flame flew up from their joined hands and disappeared into the ceiling of the cavern. "Oh Jace. I cannot believe this. Somehow, we created a new kind of energy. Or maybe it's a necessary kind to win the battle. What do you think?"

"You know more about all this light stuff than I do. I haven't even seen what kind of energy exists down here, or the kind we'll be fighting." Jace looked into Lania's eyes. "What do you call this kind anyway?"

Lania smiled. "Some call it the energy of the Gods, some call it evil." She lowered her gaze. "To be honest, I don't really know. I suppose it is whatever you want it to be. Like I said, no rules, not even for names."

He laughed. "You're right again. I thought you called it something simply to identify it."

She looked into his eyes. He gave a real effort in his attempt to learn in his own way, and she needed to grasp hold and move forward. "To even see what we just saw is unusual. I've not seen energy lift from anyone when not in battle. While in battle anything can and does happen." She smiled. "What we did is amazing. I hope it indicates our energy ability together is extremely strong."

"I hope you're right. Now, explain to me what happens during an energy battle."

Chapter Sixteen

Jace listened to Lania try to explain what she didn't understand. Many things in the universe went past explanation, and every planet's experiences happened differently. He'd always felt no one fully understood what happened below the surface of Lorton during the energy battle. She stopped explaining and stared at him.

"Continue, Lania. I'm listening." She gave him a frustrated look, yet she still presented more beauty than he'd ever seen. Now he could truly claim her as his.

"I have the feeling I'm boring you."

"No, My Lady. Never. Please continue. This battle means our lives, and the lives of everyone on the planet from what you tell me. I understand the energy can be used for good or evil, and it makes perfect sense, considering the current mood of our people. I suppose we have Raulf to thank. I now have a better understanding of what's going on."

"I'm glad you do. I've known for a long time; I just was not able to stop him. Until now. We cannot fail. If we do, it will be the end of Lorton."

"Your assumption is absolutely correct." He touched her cheek with his hand for a moment. "Do you have a battle plan, My Lady?"

"Please, call me Lania. I don't feel like anyone's lady." She looked up at Jace. "If you know what I mean?"

"I believe I do." He looked deeply into her eyes. "Tell me what my part will be in all this."

"Oh, Jace. If I knew the answers to your questions, I'd be a genius. All I can really say is follow my lead and directions, and be prepared for anything and everything at any time."

"Could you be any broader?" Jace shook his head then chuckled. "I'll do my best. I'm a warrior you know. I'm not trying to sound conceited, just competent, with a touch of humor."

"I understand you better than you think, Warrior!" Lania laughed.

"Keep it up and I'll make you pay for it."

"Really? How?"

Jace purposely gave her his best come-on grin and she worked very hard not to laugh at him. She looked so cute he wanted to make love to her again. "First I'll strip off your clothes, then lay you back down on the rock bench, then..."

Lania held up her hand. "Enough! We have things to do here. We don't have time for more lovemaking."

"Oh really?" Jace wrapped his arm around her and pulled her to him. "We always have time for love. Shall I demonstrate?" He lowered his head and kissed her with a passion that made controlling his urges difficult,. Slowly, with hunger for more, he pulled back and ended the kiss against his will.

"Oh my. You're serious, aren't you?"

"Very."

"Remind me not to test you."

"Then start teaching me something I need to know."

She smiled at him with a knowing grin, indicating she really wanted to make love with him again. Unfortunately, they both knew what limited time remained for them here.

"These bulky rocks can stop some of the energy thrown at you, but not all of it. Sometimes the burning energy can, and will literally dissolve one of these huge rocks into nothing. Yes, I said nothing. They can make the gigantic boulder over there completely disappear, then you must catch the glowing ball of energy in your hands and arms. Then you throw it back before it burns you. You can call it a very strange and dangerous game of catch."

"I'd say. If it will melt rock, will it melt or burn us?"

"It definitely can, and often does. You must concentrate on victory and no pain. Just hold goodness in your heart and hands at all times."

"Explain the goodness remark." She shook her head at him while he stared directly at her face, covered with wonder and fear. She didn't scare him, only made him want to kiss her.

"The energy has a way of reading you. It senses good from evil and it seems satisfied with good, and angry at evil. It reacts like any person does when confronted with either emotion. I realize that may not make sense to you right now, but believe me, it is true."

"Actually, it makes perfect sense. Go on."

"Simply hold on to good, or you can call it positive thoughts. The energy will try to anger you, and it will test you. Don't fail. Think good and positive no matter what. I have a very strong feeling you will be tested, and witness it attacking a rock or something around you to scare you. Hold your ground with positive thoughts and good behavior."

He shrugged his shoulders. "Sounds easy enough."

"Your mind must hold, think, and show goodness, love, compassion, all things considered positive and happy. It is not easy at all. Believe me. I've experienced it. For some reason, this energy intensifies every emotion within you, and makes it far more difficult for you to remain completely calm. You must hold on to the calm behavior, because if you don't, the price you pay will be very high, and don't think for a moment that the energy will not see your doubts or bad thoughts. I don't know how that happens, but it does."

"I understand what you're saying. I do, and I will behave properly, or should I say maintain my calm and think positive, happy thoughts."

"I certainly hope you do."

Lania stared at him like a misbehaving child. He could possibly fall into that description, but for her, he would do his job, whatever it took. "You can count on me, My Lady. And do not tell me you are not *My Lady*, because you are in every way possible. Understand?"

"Yes, *My Warrior*, I understand."

Jace gave her his accepting nod. She turned away from him and began to look around. His mind drifted to his brothers who made it possible for them to be down here. Making love to Lania had constantly been on his mind so long he could think of nothing else since it was so important to him. He'd be forever grateful to her for fulfilling his dream of being with her, and giving him her precious gift.

Lania was done looking around and she returned to stand in front of him. He gazed into her beautiful, dark-brown eyes, and she immediately concentrated on him. It seemed questions were written all over her face along with wonder and contentment.

Lania shook her head. "Is something wrong? You are looking at me very strangely."

"No, my sweet. I'm simply enjoying you. Okay?"

"I'm not sure what to say?" She lowered her head.

Jace tipped her chin up with the tip of his finger. "Don't look away. You're beautiful, and I love looking at you." She shook her head and looked at him with a completely embarrassed expression. "Has a man ever told you how beautiful you are? Ever?"

"No may, except you."

She shook her head in denial. He placed one hand on each of her cheeks to stop her movement. "My beautiful princess, you are the most gorgeous woman in any galaxy. Never forget what I just said, and never deny it's true. I have seen many women, yet none hold a star to you."

"Oh Jace, you don't understand."

"I'm pretty sure I do. No one has ever pampered you, complimented you, or encouraged you. Therefore, you doubt yourself, your abilities, and especially your beauty. Am I right?"

"Pretty much. Kind of…yes." She stared at the ground. "My father occasionally said a few good things to me, and he remains the only one who ever did. Plus, you know how it sounds coming from a parent, more like a 'have to tell you this'."

"Believe me, Lania. I would never lie to you, about anything. Count on me, lean on me. I'll be here for you." She looked up at him, tears in her eyes and a grateful expression on her face. After a deep breath she looked intently into his eyes and he lost control. He leaned down, pressed his lips to hers and kissed her with all the passion he felt. She stirred him to the core, and he wanted her to know how important she'd become to him. His entire world now spun in circles around Lania.

The way she kissed him back now totally sent him over the stars. He knew she put all her trust into this kiss, and he treasured her gift deep in his soul. He knew trust barely existed within her, and that she found it extremely difficult to give or receive trust. He silently vowed never to disappoint her. It scared him to think how deeply in love he found himself, and how completely he wanted her for himself in every way possible. This was true love, nothing else. He felt it, and it was a feeling he'd never experienced before.

"Lania, *My Lady, My Love*. Before we leave this cavern and our solitude behind, I must tell you something important." She started to speak. He touched his finger to her lips. "You are the most beautiful woman I have ever seen, and I've seen my share. None of them compare to you, and you know if it were not true, I would never tell you. I love looking at you. I love you. Never doubt me, or what I tell you. I mean *every* word."

When she opened her mouth to tell him something, he kissed her before she was able to utter a word. Memories of looking at her picture and finding her in the jungle assailed him. The moment he first saw her, she took his breath away, and still had it, stirring every emotion in his body. Slowly, sweetly he ended his kiss. She looked up at him in wonder, or did he see shock? "I didn't have to tell you what I just said, but I wanted you to know you're beautiful and I love you."

"Jace, My Warrior, I love you, too. More than you know." She smiled. "And the first time I saw you in the jungle, you took my breath away, and you still do. I consider you the most handsome, well-built man on Lorton, the entire galaxy, and every galaxy beyond!" She smiled, then laid her head on his chest.

"Oh, *My Lady,* and I do mean *My Lady*." He shook his head. "If only we had more time." He checked his wrist-piece. "Unfortunately, we need to leave now, but our time will come. I promise. Trust me."

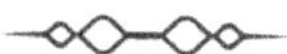

Lania woke, stretched her arms over her head then sat up in bed. She glanced at the timepiece on the table, shocked when she saw how late she'd slept. Thoughts of spending time-units in the cavern with her handsome and fantastic Jace still sent shivers down her spine. Every moment with him was complete joy. He could not be more kind, entertaining, or handsome if he tried, and he proved himself a fantastic lover! What more could a woman ask for? Absolutely nothing!

She managed to get out of bed and make her way into the lav for a shower. She stepped inside the enclosure and super warm water massaged her body. It felt so good she wanted to stay all sun-cycle, but she knew there were too many things to do. She wondered what Jace kept up his sleeve since he always had a secret hiding there. The thought made her laugh. Her Warrior, always hid a secret plan, and they would surely need a fantastic plan if they were to survive and accomplish their ultimate goal of equalizing the energy below Lorton. It remained imperative they bring peace back to the people.

Jace and his brothers worked amazingly together, a true joy to watch. Most siblings got along, yet none she knew maintained such a close bond, especially with mysterious abilities they used whenever they wanted or needed them. How exactly it worked remained a secret between them. Then again, she never worked with triplets before. They were bonded for life by those invisible ties which were impossible to break. Their mysterious connection was something to be grateful for. The brothers were blessed, and they knew it, enjoyed it, and made good use of their bond, and she planned to do the same with her warrior.

She liked all three brothers a lot, but she loved Jace—truly loved him. Yes, she loved the man. Special, important, and oh so sexy was the only way to describe *Her Warrior*. She found it difficult to be around him now since she knew what making love with him felt like. Making love turned out to be far more special than her wildest dreams. She still could not contain her thoughts about what they did in the cavern, yet she needed to concentrate on the job ahead. Or should she say battle? It didn't matter what she named it; she and Jace were responsible for saving Lorton. Jace would fight at her side and depended solely on her instructions and help.

Quickly she put her clothes on. Pants again, since Jace told her to wear them yesterday, and she was sure he would suggest the same for their adventures this sun-cycle. He said because of the climbing and other things they had to do underground; pants would be best. Once dressed, she hurried out to see the man who occupied her every thought.

She found Jace sitting at the head of the table recounting his energy lesson to his brothers, who seemed extremely curious. It made her smile at the way they shared everything. She hoped their lovemaking remained a secret. Hopefully he kept what they intimately shared to himself. It belonged to them, alone.

Jace stood when he saw her enter the room. He looked amazing in his black pants, and black shirt which hugged his ruggedly, muscled chest, and highlight the bulges in his arm muscles. What a sight to behold. Wow. He always wore the same kind of shirt and pants, but they looked so great she still had to work to keep her jaw from dropping open. He waved for her to join them, so she walked over to the empty chair he pulled out for her next to his. The only place she wanted to sit.

"I must say, I do love to see you wearing pants. They look wonderful on you." Jace smiled broadly while he pushed her chair under the table.

"Jace is right, My Lady. You look great in your dresses, but pants suit you very nicely." Dane smiled at Lania.

"I must agree," Holt added.

"Thank you, gentlemen. You are all very kind."

Jace laughed. "No, My Lady, we're honest." He looked her in the eyes. "We can't help ourselves."

Lania smiled then joined the brothers in their laughter.

"Okay, back to business. Lania tried to teach me all she knew, but you guys know how that goes. She is very knowledgeable, and I have complete trust in her. Do either of you have any questions?"

Holt looked at Lania. "I have one for you. How can you teach Jace to do all the moves if you don't have any energy to use?"

She smiled at her audience. "You're right. A lot still remains missing in Jace's lessons. Lessons are difficult, because once the white, hot, energy flows toward you, and you have to catch it and throw it back, it is truly the only time you learn the reality involved. So, all I can do is verbally prepare Jace, then hope to the stars, that when the time comes, he'll remember everything, and do battle accordingly."

Holt clapped his hands. "Very good, My Lady. We hope you're right. So much depends on both of you succeeding beyond expectations."

Lania nodded at Holt and Dane. "You are both totally correct. We fully understand, and will do battle accordingly. I can't say much else. Jace's true test won't come until he's in the middle of a battle, and we will face several, possibly countless battles. No matter what, I want both of you to know, I will take care of him. You might say we'll succeed or fail together."

Dane cleared his throat. "That's a very dangerous statement, My Lady."

She looked Dane in the eye. "It does not mean we will die, although the chance always exists."

"Too bad Raulf couldn't have been a victim of battle."

Lania nodded. "Such an outcome would satisfy many, including me. However; it has yet to happen, because he never does battle. Of course, the only proof I have is the fact he's still alive." All three brothers laughed. She smiled at them, but she did not find it quite that funny. Life on Lorton would be far simpler, and way better if Raulf fell victim to the angry energy. It always angered her the way he lied to the people of Lorton about what he did below the surface.

"Sorry, My Lady," Jace said. "You understand we mean no offense to your life-mate."

"I don't mind a bit. He deserves...well he deserves far more than he will ever receive." They all looked at her, happily she understood. Dane and Holt both stood, then pushed in their chairs.

Dane nodded at Lania. "We have some work to do on the transport. You two behave yourselves." He smiled, then left.

She watched both brothers disappear down the hall toward the underground parking area. When she turned, she found Jace right behind her and he placed a very pleasant kiss on her lips. She returned his kiss with all the feelings churning within her this sun-cycle. Jace could not be a better kisser if he tried, which made her wonder how much practice came before her. He was far too handsome and sexy not to have practiced a lot. She still wanted to ask him how many women he'd been with. Although the number really didn't matter since she just became the absolute winner.

Without warning he pulled back and took a deep breath. She looked at him for a moment, but needed to know. "Is something wrong?"

"No, My Love, you're just too tempting for me. If I don't stop this instant, I will carry you to my bed, and that is not a good idea at the moment. Understand?"

"Absolutely. So, what do we do now?"

Jace smiled. "Tell me more about the energy battle. I doubt I can know enough about it. I want to be totally prepared."

"Can't blame you, but no one is ever totally prepared because the energy has a mind of its own, if it has a mind that is. This is too hard to explain since it is so far out of the ordinary. When those white, glowing balls come charging toward you, it makes you want to run and hide until it disappears. Exactly what Raulf does. He is a coward. Something I learned while I pretended to be his life-mate. However; hiding will not win the battle. Eventually it may put an end to it, but it will change nothing, nor will it win anything. Winning is our goal."

"You're right, My Sweet. I'll be with you all the way. You can always tell me what to do even during the battle. Right?"

"Yes, but sometimes you can't speak, and other times the energy becomes so loud you cannot hear a thing. Oh, Jace. I want to prepare you better, but it's nearly impossible. To be honest, no one is ever fully ready for all the things the energy does, or is capable of doing. Even I'm not completely equipped for everything, and sometimes I get scared, something I hate to admit."

Jace pulled Lania to her feet and put his arms around her. "I'll be at your side. I'll do everything in my power to protect you and win the battle."

"And I am so very, very, glad to hear you say so. We will succeed together, I know it."

"I believe we will." He eased her back to look into her eyes. "Has anyone been killed during these battles? I can't remember."

"One ruler, so long ago no one remembers. My father told me, which is the only reason I remember. He taught me all about the history of the energy meetings, which they were once called. They were not always identified by the name 'battle'."

"Interesting. Do I know this ruler?"

"I doubt it. Have you heard of Erician Symatra?" She watched him shake his head no. "I didn't think so. He, from what my father said, seemed to have a lot of Raulf's traits. Like evil to the core with just his own interests at heart, which only lasted so long. The energy took his life after only three meetings with him. Remember, the energy can lose its temper, which increases its power at least ten-fold, if not higher." Lania touched Jace's cheek. "When the energy gets mad, you better run fast." She shook her head. "What I'm saying is, never make the energy mad. Always work with it the best you can."

Chapter Seventeen

Jace couldn't take his eyes off Lania. Her beauty simply amazed him to the point he'd never tire of looking at her like this for time-units on end. Currently he practiced the energy catch and release part she taught him. The so-called battle would take place next sun-cycle, yet his mind kept returning to a bench in the cavern and making wild, passionate love to Lania.

"Jace, you're not concentrating!"

"Yes, I am. Just not on what you want me to." He laughed and she gave him a perplexed look. "My thoughts did stray to the other things I'd rather be doing with you."

"Like what?"

"Take a guess."

"Oh."

She turned away from him too late, he already saw her cheeks turn a deep shade of red. It was impossible to miss her instant blush. Lania was so extremely shy and unsure of herself that he knew he had to work on that with her. She needed to come out of her shell and get ready for war with Raulf, and possibly several others in high places she may need to unseat. He hoped this plan worked so she'd be able to accomplish the task. "Lania?"

"Yes."

"Do you know how to regain your true power within the government?"

"I think so. I'll need help from you and your brothers. Possibly an entire army."

"There's three of us. We're not an army."

"Maybe we should hire one then? What do you think?"

Jace laughed, then stepped toward her and took her hand in his. "We may not be an army; however, we do have connections we can call any time. We might call several of our contacts, just in case." He gave her hand a little squeeze. "Do you have any friends inside the castle on the hill?"

"I really don't know. Gale, Raulf's sister was the only person who was ever nice to me, but they kept us apart. Evil does not allow friends, or anyone to be nice, especially to me. Raulf kept my sister away from me as well. I would love to contact Gale, but we would have to be super careful because he will not hesitate to kill her

"Asking Gale would prove too dangerous for her and possibly us too. It's probably best if we don't look for help from inside." Jace looked into Lania's questioning gaze. "I must ask you something, do you think we need to make love before the energy battle? I mean our energy came alive after we shared our love in the cavern. So, I thought we'd do the same thing again." She looked at him with a questioning expression. She pretended she didn't understand, yet he knew she did. "You know what I'm asking and why."

"Oh, Warrior, I do not know what to say, except," Lania stared at Jace several moments, "yes. I agree with you, and I can only hope, and wish to the stars, it will have the same effect it did last time."

"Even if it doesn't, we'll have an extraordinary time. Won't we?"

"Count on it. If we have time that is."

Lania giggled at him and made him feel like a spoiled little boy, and without a doubt he completely fit the description of spoiled. "Why are you still laughing at me?"

"No, I'm laughing with you." She wrapped her arms around Jace's neck. "You do have a way of getting everything you want, don't you?"

"Well, I…"

"I know I'm right." She gave him a quick kiss on the lips and he grinned at her. "Admit it Warrior Man, you know you do."

"What I want, more than anything, is you. I've fallen madly in love with you in case you haven't noticed."

"I've noticed." Lania grinned. "And it looks most becoming on you."

"Let's make love now. You know, practice for tomorrow?"

"Don't push it."

"You know me too well." Jace tilted his head and stared at her.

"I'm beginning to, Warrior. Now, let's get back to work so we can win this thing. We're running out of time for everything."

"Of course, you're right."

She laughed at him. "And don't you forget it. "

"I would never doubt you."

Before she could protest, he kissed her so deep, and with such passion, he felt hot all over. She tempted him to the point she had to give him anything and everything he wanted. They both wanted it badly. What a pair they made, far better together than apart. They did draw on each other's strengths, erregardless of the impending battle.

Jace wanted Lania so badly he no longer cared where they did it, or who might see them, even if they were acting dangerous and inappropriate. Still, he didn't want his brothers to find them naked someplace. He always tried to maintain appropriate behavior, so he pulled back and ended the kiss he desperately wanted to continue. "Lania," he whispered, trying to catch his breath. "This is not the time or place."

"I know." She stared at him for a moment. "I want you, Warrior. So very much."

He could not take his eyes off of her. "I care about the battle, but I care about you far more. You should know how I feel about you."

"I feel the same about you. However; we don't want to show ourselves in a compromising position since your brothers will be back any moment."

"Exactly." Jace shook his head. "I'll back off."

"I may have to call you '*Bad Warrior-Man*' all the time if you keep this attitude up."

He couldn't help but laugh with her. He liked the bad warrior man name, which he may even have earned. He slowly released his hold on her. There was a reluctance on both of their parts, and he felt relieved they were on the same star-wave. Love was strange. It made a person feel invincible at times and gave them an, 'I don't care who sees us,' attitude. Not the best way to think under some circumstances, like now, since he knew love could also become embarrassing for them both.

Suddenly Jace's two brothers emerged from the lift and made their way to the info-center and took their seats. Jace joined them without an invitation. He couldn't tell what they were aiming for here, but he knew he'd be able to see it clearly soon. Lania took her usual seat next to him at the long bar-table where the computer readouts showed in the air above.

Holt pointed to the vid-display in front of him. "There's Raulf's casino, and this angled shot," he pointed to Dane's vid-display, "shows the dealers cheating the players, who have all been served enough drinks to knock them out cold."

Jace laughed. "The dealer's slight-of-hand isn't very good."

Dane nodded. "You're right. This proves the cheating is happening on a way larger scale than we first thought. Plus, this view," he changed the screen, "shows the ramped prostitution going on. He's into everything that pays big credits, and I suspect illegal Purple-Stone sells for way more credits than anything else."

Holt shook his head. "What if we try to take him down through his casino? He's got enough illegal stuff going on in his club to put him away for a long time."

Jace stood. "Remember, we told Lania we'd hold back. She said she'd make sure this would be used against him. Just save those vids for future use. Once he loses the battle, and Lania and I survive, she'll take him out in a very humiliating way, and make him pay for all of his crimes."

"Count on it. I can hardly wait." Lania smiled.

He and his brothers knew Lania hated Raulf and found the idea very appealing. He also knew what great pleasure she'd take in destroying the man who destroyed her. Lania was not a revenge seeker. except against Raulf, her one exception. He deserved every bit of what she wanted to give him, and more.

Dane looked at Lania. "I'm sure you will. My question is, does my brother know enough to fight the energy battle with you and survive? He's been around too long now to lose him." He groaned.

Lania smiled at Dane. “You know I will do everything in my power to keep him safe. If we stay together in the fight, we’ll do fine.”

Holt nodded with a grin. “It shouldn’t be a problem for you two. You always seem very together.”

Jace could not miss how Lania’s cheeks turned bright red, as usual whenever she felt embarrassed, and Holt’s little comment did it this time. Holt and Dane laughed loud and long. Jace had to join his brothers in order to pacify them. They always felt their jokes were way too funny not to laugh. He and his brothers often laughed to cover their fear.

“Okay guys, enough.” Jace shook his head. “Now explain how we’re supposed to get into the underground before the battle begins.”

Dane cleared his throat and looked at Jace. “You’ll have to spend the moon-cycle inside the cavern since there will be too many people around from dawn until the ceremony. So, to sneak you two down there requires stealth and darkness, and we will only have it the moon-cycle before, which will be soon.”

Jace nodded. “Point taken.” He looked at Lania. “We can sleep there. We’ll go prepared.” He began to create a mental list of what the two of them should take with them. They didn’t need much, only a few items to get through one moon-cycle. If they wanted success, they also needed some rest. Of course, making love remained first on his mind. He’d have plenty of time to rest in future moon-cycles, so making love would be more than possible. Time remained short. The battle would begin next sun-cycle whether they were ready or not.

“Jace, we must pack quickly. We need to leave for the cavern.”

“You’re right. Let’s get started.”

They both hurried down the hall to their sleeping quarters. Once inside he stuffed a few clothes into a bag, along with a few other items they couldn’t live without. Of course, the cavern did not have a lav, so they’d have to make do with what he threw in the bag. He finished with a large container of water and the bag immediately became very heavy. Too bad water weighed so much. With all the magical things available on this planet, they still hadn't figured out how to make water lighter. He tossed the strap over his shoulder and stepped out into the hall.

It only took a moment for him to see Lania in front of him struggling with her bag which weighed far too much for her to handle. He grabbed her bag, put the strap over his empty shoulder and started to walk.

"Jace, that's way too heavy for you. I can carry my bag."

Jace nodded, then set her heavy bag back down on the floor. "There ya go, My Lady." He nearly laughed while watching her efforts to pick it up, and she failed miserably. "Please, allow me to carry your bag for you now"

Lania tugged on the strap of the bag. "It's too heavy, you have your own to deal with."

"Actually, it balances me out." He picked up Lania's bag, put the strap over his free shoulder, then looked at her. "Better. By the way, did you bring any blankets or pillows?"

"Yes. Did you?"

"Absolutely. We're fine then."

She quietly followed him down the hall, then out into the parking garage, where they boarded the medium sized transport since it accommodated them and their supplies, yet was able to land in smaller places. Holt sat in the pilot's seat, and the vehicle rose up into the air. This might actually be a dangerous mission. He didn't care since he and Lania would have some quality alone time together.

They would have total freedom for the moon-cycle. The time finally arrived to call it what it would really be, spending time with the woman he loved. He'd never felt love for a woman before, yet he knew he shared true love with Lania. Their bond deepened each sun-cycle, and at times, every time-unit.

While they flew to their destination, Holt took the route less traveled and it still amazed him to look below and see how much space the capitol city truly absorbed. He'd seen it from this angle before, but never for this reason. The cavern entrance they were using was a good distance from all the buildings and at the bottom of a slope, so it enabled them to sneak in without being seen. Plus, someone would need to be outside in the back of the building in order to see anything. No one ever stood out back since there were no doors on that side.

The actual entrance they used remained quite hidden by the large plants surrounding the area, plus it was relatively small. Right now, no one knew about, which was a major plus. Everything that went on below all began from the huge entry above where all the people waited and celebrations took place. The planet belonged to all the people, which became difficult to think about when the future outcome lay on their shoulders. This moon-cycle and the sun-cycle to come should prove interesting for sure.

If they won, Lania would still have to deal with Raulf and her sister. He knew she didn't trust her sister's decision to life-mate Raulf. The rumors claimed Raulf forced Marna to life-mate him. Jace knew he needed to proceed with caution concerning Lania's sister since he did not really know her. Plus, he lacked the knowledge to know if she was a willing partner to Raulf or not. He couldn't very well blame or punish her when he did not know. He needed to leave Marna completely up to Lania. However; if her sister happened to be a willing participant, it would drastically change Lania's plans and her point of view regarding her sister.

Jace put his hand on his brother's shoulder. "Thanks, Bro. We'll let you know when we're done." He watched his brother nod, then he turned his attention to Lania and pointed across the landscape toward the hidden entrance. He grabbed all the bags and followed her while she ran across the lawn area and downhill to enter into the second level. His pace was a bit slower with the heavy bags on his shoulders, but they both made it safely inside. He heard the transport take off while he secured the covering back over the entrance they used.

Jace walked over to the bench they both knew well and set their bags beside it. Before he could turn, he felt Lania slide her arms around him from behind and she held on tightly. He turned her to face him, then placed a kiss on her lips and savored the taste and feel of her, not to mention the comfort her arms provided. Not enough words existed for him to say how he felt when Lania's body pressed so tightly against his. Love. With luck, the way he felt this moment would last forever.

Slowly Jace pulled back. "I've been waiting all sun-cycle for this, My Love. How about you?"

"Of course I have, and I must say, you have already exceeded my expectations. Which means, what comes next will be even better than before."

"That's always my goal." Jace ran his fingers through her hair then placed his hands on her cheeks. "I want the very best for you, for us, for Lorton." Jace was very serious about his words.

"I know you do, Warrior." Lania smiled at Jace. "You are *My Warrior*, aren't you?"

"Yes, and I will always be your warrior. Then again, I'm not sure you can afford me." She laughed at his reply and he felt relieved to hear her sense of humor return. She needed one to put up with him. This time he laughed at his own thoughts.

"We shall see." She shook her head. "You realize since I'm the true Royal Ruler of Lorton, I can command you to work for me no matter what you want to do, and you must obey me."

"Yes, My Lady, I know. I also know you wouldn't risk my life unless the situation was extremely dire."

This time she nodded her agreement. "Dire indeed. You understand, don't you?" Lania began to back away.

Jace slid his hands down to her shoulders, then well below her waist. He pulled her back, tightly against him. "My Lady, I'm at your immediate disposal. I shall do anything you tell me to do. My job is to please you and return you to full power within the Royal Capitol of Lorton."

"I appreciate your devotion. You will be rewarded in kind."

"And you are *My Lady*." Jace lowered his head and pressed his lips to hers, knowing well she'd not stop him. Far from it. He planned to make love to her. They both agreed this might help increase their energy during the battle. Anything helpful was welcome, whether it made sense or not. Half of life made no sense, so the energy battle fit in perfectly.

Lania's caresses and kisses made him feel wonderful, one of the things about her he loved dearly. He wanted her to feel totally loved, wanted and needed, something she'd been missing her entire life. He also knew how unbearable it became for her when they forced Raulf on her; the worst thing to ever happen to her. Although six annual-cycles of slavery ran a very close second.

Jace moved his kisses down her cheek, down her neck, pressing onward toward her breasts, pausing a bit to undress her with care. When he pulled her top off over her head she gasped slightly, which caused him to smile widely. The feelings she stirred in him were glorious and he wanted to do the same for her. He only hoped she felt like a real woman, truly loved and cared for. This feeling of love may be the something he'd always secretly yearned for, yet never achieved, until now.

This woman, *His Lady*, felt too good to be true. When he removed her bra he inhaled deeply at the sight of her naked breasts. She was amazing, so very perfect. When he pushed her pants and undergarment down to the ground, he felt more than pleased this was no dream. Nothing in his dreams ever looked more beautiful than the reality before his eyes. He never wanted to be without his woman again. He loved seeing her this way. His main problem surfaced again, impatience.

He couldn't wait to be inside her, feeling all the love she wanted to give him. He had more passion for this woman than he'd ever felt in his entire life for anyone. No woman compared to Lania, anywhere, ever. He knew deep in his soul she belonged to him, now and forever. He was now *Her Warrior* forever. Nothing made him happier than protecting this precious woman. His job was to keep her safe, happy and loved, which happened to be exactly his plan.

He stopped everything, pulled a blanket out of his bag and spread it on the bench. Lania took a deep breath when he scooped her into his arms, picked her up, then laid her down on top of the blanket. In a flash he shed his clothes, something he knew she enjoyed watching to tease her senses. He knew she wanted him to take his time disrobing, but he couldn't wait. He needed her now. Lania looked truly remarkable, perfectly built, every single part of her a true work of art, exactly how every woman wished to be, all of which made him feel extremely fortunate.

His dreams were answered. Lania, the epitome of everything he desired. She may still find it difficult believing he wanted her. However; his desire burned real, rare and true. He wanted these feelings to last forever. Hopefully their feelings were so strong they'd reside within both of them until the end of their sun-cycles. The future may feel in doubt, yet he planned to make it all work, no matter what, even existing over and around the reality of her true position of Royal Ruler of Lorton. Hopefully she'd be able to change the laws regarding who chose her life-mate.

Lania's lips felt so soft and warm. He ran his tongue across them before he actually kissed them again. From sounds of satisfaction she let slip, he knew she liked what he did. His hands played with her body. Everywhere he touched she responded like magic, which said she truly loved him. He kissed everywhere possible, easing, massaging and kissing his way down her neck and arms to find her breasts. He rolled a bit so he could lay beside her, giving him a better angle to play with her breasts, an activity he enjoyed too much, and sincerely hoped made her happy. She'd do anything he wanted , and that thought brought huge feelings of satisfaction to surge through him.

Would he be warrior enough for this magnificent woman lying naked next to him? He lowered his head and whispered, "Oh baby," in her ear. He moaned, unable to find adequate words, which he hoped conveyed even more than he could possibly say. He rolled on top of her, reached down, placed himself inside her, then began to love her slowly and passionately. The slow part lasted briefly before he found his movements pushing toward frantic. Where Lania was concerned, it seemed next to impossible for him to control himself. Before he knew it, he was moving swift and hard, which sent fantastic feelings to surge throughout his entire body.

Suddenly he felt her womanhood throb against him and he knew she'd found her release, which brought him even more satisfaction. He increased his loving speed, unable to contain himself, making everything he did to her seem even more intense and breathtaking. It did not take him long to reach his climax, then fall to the side of her, breathing like he'd run a race around the entire planet. So much for lasting forever.

"Oh Jace, you're wonderful."

"No, my love, it is you who are wonderful." Jace ran his fingers through her hair. "You know I've been with other women." He kissed the tip of her nose. "I must tell you, not one of them excited, or satisfied me the way you do. You are the best, My Sweet."

When she raised her hand to touch his cheek, it began to glow. "Do you see that?"

"I do." He reached up and put his hand on top of hers.

"Now you're glowing too. Wow. This place must have the effect we want and need for the battle ahead. I don't pretend to understand. Do you?"

"If you don't, how on Lorton could I? You've been here before and seen energy in motion. You've fought it and survived. If anyone has the answers, you should."

Chapter Eighteen

Jace stood when he heard the pathetic applause. It must be the evil one and his mate making their way down below the surface toward them. Time for battle, no more getting ready. Lania stood and took her place next to him. She put her hand on his arm. Oh, how he loved this woman. He was ready to risk his life for her and he didn't care, as long as they were together.

"Jace, are you ready?"

"Yes. Tell me what to do, and I'll give it my all." This effort was for Lania more than the planet. Of course, he wanted to save Lorton and return the energy level back to some form of normal, except Lania remained his main desire and reason. He'd keep her safe no matter what might happen. He'd protect the woman he loved with his life every sun-cycle. They were finally together and it is how they would stay. "The ceremony above is beginning, but won't last long."

"I know."

"Raulf must give his speech. I've been to these before." Jace looked into her eyes. "In fact, I watched you go in with your father. I remember asking how someone so young could do battle."

Lania laughed. "I asked the same thing myself. My father only said, "Watch and learn, some sun-cycle you might be on your own. Now I understand. Of course, I never knew how important those words might be, to me and Lorton. He knew, deep within, what might happen in the course of events. Smart, effective, and so very nice. A great man to be sure."

"I hope I'm able to understand." Jace took her hand in his. "And we can reminisce about this later." The smile she gave him said it all. She seemed to feel like he did about the impending battle, but their determination drove them forward with purpose.

Once again, they heard pathetic applause over their heads, which meant Raulf and Marna were on their way down into the cavern. He wished it were possible for him to fight Raulf man to man. The necessary energy battle came first, so be it. Lania looked like she'd seen a ghost. "Are you okay, My Lady?"

"I'm apprehensive. My sister is also involved, and I'm very worried. She might easily die down here."

He smiled. "So, might Raulf."

"We are not that lucky. It's not the fool I'm worried about, only Marna. I don't believe she's involved willingly, only because of, you know."

"I do. We'll protect her best we can."

"We will. I have no doubt. If we're protecting ourselves, we're also protecting her." Lania looked at Jace. "For the first time, I'm scared."

Jace pulled her into his arms. "Oh, My Love, don't be scared. You're brave, experienced, plus I'm here with you. What more do you want?" He heard her chuckle for a moment.

"You're right, Warrior. I guess I know too much now. Before, my inexperience helped me glide through uninhibited. Now, memories fly in and out of my mind, and they scare me."

"Well, only think about the good ones."

"Of course, good thoughts fix everything." She smiled. "I believe your brothers were right when they said you were my only choice for a partner down here."

"They were that time." He chuckled about his brothers. They knew he and Lania belonged together. Then the strangest crackling sound ever begin, and it kept growing louder. He assumed the odd sound must be the energy. He still held Lania to him and she shook like a scared puppy. "Was that…"

"Yes, energy reverberation in the cavern is very noisy. I thought I told you?"

"You did. Hearing is believing. I'm sure it will be louder when our turn arrives."

"Bet on it. You won't have to wait long. We're very close to beginning our part of this battle. I really don't believe Raulf or

Marna come down this far. If they do, we could have even greater problems."

"If Raulf comes down this far, I'll handle him. Don't worry." Jace gave Lania a reassuring hug, then released her. "Remember to give me instructions. I still don't know what I'm doing." Lania chuckled softly at his statement, or was it an admittance?

"I'm sure you don't want to hear me say I don't either, so I won't tell you."

"Right." Jace looked directly into Lania's beautiful brown eyes and took a deep breath. "I know we'll be fine. I feel it in my bones."

"We need to believe in our success, the entire planet is counting on us. Plus, you and I are one of those reasons. Of course, Lorton is number one on the list. If we don't make it, neither will Lorton."

"You're such a smart woman. I really mean it, My Sweet. You are, and it's why my feelings for you..." His thoughts were interrupted by several loud cracks of energy power moving closer to them. "Where should we wait?"

"Let's wait by our bench."

"Our bench." He smiled when he looked at her face. "Of course, our bench." Together they walked to the so-called bench. They remained standing, ready for whatever might happen. When he looked at the makeshift stairway between the top floor and their location, a startingly bright light appeared and slowly moved toward them.

Lania touched his hand. "Don't be afraid. Show no fear. This energy has a mind of its own and believes it is a warrior too. So be careful."

"Got it." Jace followed the yellowish-white light-ball only with his eyes and kept his body completely still. It came close, circled around them then backed off a bit.

"Don't get too confident. It will attack."

Lania's experience made him believe her. "Do I make any kind of move? Like hold out my hand or anything?"

"This is where you can make your own decisions."

"Does it do any good to talk to it?"

"Never really tried before. My father talked to me, and I to him. We never addressed the energy in any way."

He saw Lania slowly point at the light which took its place and glowed brightly a good distance in front of them. He looked at her. "Okay then, here it goes." Jace turned his attention to the light-ball, held out his fist and took a deep breath before saying, "Do you want a fight?"

The light moved closer and bounced up and down as if answering yes. He hadn't expected such a response. "I'd rather not fight, but if we must in order to bring peace to Lorton, then we shall do so." He opened his fist and held his hand open to say come on. The light suddenly attacked his hand and arm and he felt intense heat. It literally burned his skin, then backed off. It felt like a severe sunburn all in one instant.

"Are you okay?"

"A bit burnt." He turned back to the fireball. "Nice try. I'm not leaving. We must settle this unrest before we have nothing left to fight about. You will win and we will all be gone. Is that what you want?" It really seemed strange to talk to a glowing light, even though he decided to treat it like any other opponent he'd ever battled. Lania was right, as a warrior, he was doing what warriors did. They either calmed down their adversary, or angered them more than they were in the beginning.

The light ball grew in size and headed straight for Lania. He jumped in front of her quickly so the heat did not sink into her. It burned him slightly, yet felt tolerable. "This woman has done nothing to you, nor have I. Let's stop this useless fighting and reset the energy on Lorton!"

They both watched the energy ball rise to the highest point in the ceiling of their level and hover there, like it waited to attack even harder. Still, it acted like it understood him, even if it didn't seem possible on any level. Then again, none of this made sense.

"Jace, you're doing fine. Better than I expected," Lania whispered.

"I'm not sure what you expected. I don't even know what I expected." He chuckled for a moment, his eyes still on the glowing ball at the ceiling several hundred steps away from them. "It seems to understand me. Or am I crazy?"

"No, I thought the same thing. Don't ask me how."

"I'm going to keep talking to it and hope it works. It's the best chance we have. I realize the light has the ability to burn us to death without even trying. I'm convinced it can, so why doesn't it do it to Raulf?"

"Good point. Maybe you need to ask?"

"I'm not sure I should press my luck. Besides, I haven't heard it talk."

"True, Warrior. Keep up whatever you're doing. It seems to be working."

"Is this how it acted with you and your father?"

"Not at all, so I'm on new ground here, same as you."

Jace slipped his arm around her waist, keeping one eye on the glowing energy. "I'll protect you, no matter what it takes." He looked her in the eye. "I love you, Lania. I wanted you to know in case…" She placed her fingers on his lips to stop what he wanted to say. She was right, he shouldn't think for a split moment about either of them dying.

"I'm very glad you told me. I love you, too, Jace. So don't be foolish. We'll get through this."

"Right, My Lady. I shall stay only positive." Jace turned his head when he sensed the thing moving closer, and he'd done the right thing. Unfortunately, nothing changed so he held out his hand to say stop. The crazy light didn't listen, it simply moved closer and closer, slowly. "I'll throw you across the cavern again if you attack us. Please, use your energy powers to level the energy patterns on Lorton. Save our people from destruction. Lania and I will see to it the energy force is respected and protected here. We promise."

The glowing ball danced a circle around them moving up and down, back and forth, finally coming to rest in front of them. It stopped a bit too close. The heat felt extremely strong and difficult for him to deal with. The light remained in a position to definitely burn them to death, yet it didn't, a huge plus. "What about Raulf above us? What is his fate?"

The glowing ball attacked a large boulder next to them and the tall, heavy boulder simply disappeared in a flash, leaving not one trace of its existence. He stood there, frozen in true amazement at the scariest thing he'd ever seen. Lania warned him, yet seeing completely convinced him. The extremely loud noise seemed nothing compared to the heat. "You did that to them?" The globe did nothing to affirm or deny the act. "Or is that what you would like to do to Raulf?"

Slowly the heated energy ball moved toward them. Jace held out his arm with his hand open in an effort to stop the thing, and Lania did the same. Working together proved to be a great feeling and made them far more effective. It backed up and simply hung in the air. "Either fight us or fix the problem. We prefer the problem to be fixed. Forever if possible."

Lania gasped when the glowing entity completely annihilated a rock even taller and bigger around than the one before. All it took to melt the rock was for the energy to perch on top like a bird, and the rock disappeared from the cavern. Then the fire-ball came straight at them and literally caught their clothes on fire when it passed. They both threw themselves face first on the dirt and gravel floor and rolled around to put out the fire. Their good fortune held strong, and they weren't burnt, only a tiny bit of their clothes. "Lania, are you okay?"

"Yes." She looked up at Jace. "Close call."

"No doubt. I really don't think the glowing ball wants to harm us, only teach us a lesson."

"You still act like it is some type of being with the ability to understand us, don't you?"

"Hate to admit it, but yes." Jace looked around and noticed an entrance of some type to another area. "Where does that lead?" He pointed to the dark hall behind them.

"I have no idea. I've never been so far down."

Jace helped her up and held her hand. "Well, time we found out." Together they hurried to the dark entryway and slowly stepped inside. He saw a faint light at the end, so they both headed toward the small beacon. It didn't take long to locate the source of light, which was another energy ball. It appeared effective, and most likely could grow whenever it desired, even though it appeared smaller than the one they left.

"Oh my! This is the largest cavern I have ever seen. Look Jace." Lania pointed straight ahead.

"I see. Looks like a never-ending room. It's so big my large transport could fly through here with lots of space to spare."

"I like your idea." She shook her head. "I can't believe my father and I never came down here when we fought." Lania looked into Jace's eyes. "You did this. You're amazing. For some reason it did not want to fight you. I'm still in shock."

"Well. Stay alert. We have no idea what's down here." Lania's facial expression said she truly did not know what lay ahead. She bravely moved forward with him deeper into the new, unexplored room of the cavern, which would be the third level, and obviously no man or woman they knew of ever explored this far. He wasn't sure if they were being adventurous, or plain stupid.

He stopped walking and grabbed Lania's hand to make her stop. Then he pulled her to him and kissed her with all the passion he'd held back during the earlier so-called battle. He deepened the kiss even more to tell her how much she meant to him, and how happy he felt to stand here, together, with her.

Jace hoped his passionate kiss would help calm her nerves. Of course, he wanted this woman, and he intended on having her to himself for the rest of his life, whatever it took. He'd even admitted to her he loved her, a difficult first for him. No other woman ever heard those words from his mouth. Lania was the first—and she'd be the last. Without a doubt. He ended the kiss slowly, passionately, regretting they were done. "You're good, My Sweet. Now, stay with me and we'll see where this goes."

"You're way better than good, Warrior. I'll be happy to stay with you. You make me feel safe, and I love it." Lania put her hand in his. "Let's go."

He led her farther down into the cavern, walking between rocks, and stepping over the small stream which flowed back and forth through the huge room. It seemed like they walked forever without any sign of the energy. Then out of nowhere, the thing appeared again in front of them. He held out his free hand and the ball of light bounced up and down before leading them further into the dark room which lit up nicely when the energy glowed brighter.

"My Lady," Jace stopped walking and so did Lania. "Is it okay to go farther? Or should we go back to the second level? I'm not sure what we'll accomplish if we go further. Do you have any ideas?"

"Actually, I do." She first looked up, then back down. "My inner voice tells me to continue, because we have something we're supposed to find. I don't know what, just something important."

Chapter Nineteen

Jace looked at her as if she'd lost her mind. "I meant what I said. I have strong feelings deep inside pushing me to continue further down inside the cavern. It seems like something from the beyond wants us to learn more." He still looked at her like she was crazy. "Remember, the entire planet of Lorton is depending on us and what we do down here. I have the distinct feeling we will be fine if we continue. I have a sense you feel the same compulsion I do. Right?"

"To a degree. Not as strong as you do. I'm a beginner down here, and I'm a warrior, remember?"

"How on Lorton could I ever forget?" She laughed at the frown on his face. "Come on now. Prove you're a brave warrior and lead me through this wonderful cavern. By the way, did you bring a light? It certainly is easier if we can see where we're going and what we're stepping on." She watched Jace pull something from his pocket then switch it on. The very tiny light lit the area extremely well. "Thanks."

"You're welcome, My Lady. Always."

"I think you should have brought that light out earlier." She laughed again when Jace bowed at her before he began to walk again. His large, adoring smile still gave her shivers. The smile that rated number-one on the smile o'meter. It was the cutest smile ever, on any man. Or did she simply favor Jace over all other men? She favored him over any man alive. He deserved it, and a whole lot more.

There was no trail to follow, so they simply walked toward another dark opening, going around large boulders and climbing small to medium size hills. The interior looked so beautiful with stalactites and stalagmites, along with cavern growths she always thought beautiful when the light shone directly on them. Too bad they could not make use of the areas down here. There must be something this huge room could be used for. Then it dawned on her, the glowing energy lights would never allow just anyone inside this cavern.

Lania agreed with Jace's assumption that the light seemed to know who they were, and what they came to do. Possibilities often fell by the wayside when it came to nature and the events it caused. No other planet she knew of needed to keep an underground energy system balanced, especially when it must be done by the ruler, using his ability. Lorton was always one of a kind, something which also made them unique and vulnerable.

Without warning Jace's hand went to her stomach to stop her steps. For some reason he didn't speak. Then she saw the problem and wanted scream and run away as fast as possible. Her greatest fear in life looked them in the eye and remained straight in front of them. A giant, aggressive, hostile snake named; Venomistic Biteusorous, a name it lived up to in every way.

If the snake's fangs simply touched a person's skin, they would instantly die. This snake reminded her of the giant Lizzard and his ability, close to the same kind of poisoning. With their luck the snake could not be called stupid. She truly hated snakes. With her free hand she tapped Jace's hand still on her stomach. He hadn't taken his eyes off the danger slithering around in front of them. he eased her lips to his ear. "What are you going to do?"

"If it doesn't leave, I'll have to kill it."

"Don't you dare get near that thing!" Even in a whisper her voice carried an angry tone even she heard. Hopefully he got her point. "You're not indestructible, Warrior!" She had great difficulty trying to keep her voice down when she was terrified for Jace's life, and she felt ready to go into a terror fit. Jace, the great warrior that he was, did not even look worried.

It seemed like the creature heard them and moved a bit closer. Jace pushed on her stomach to coax her to back up slowly, and she willingly complied. Jace didn't take his eyes off the threat, only kept easing her back. She backed up as fast as she dared, and he kept pace with her. They could only hope the dangerous thing staring at them stayed put. Hopefully he was not hungry right now. Jace managed to back them both up until they were safely behind a boulder big enough to fully hide them from the snake's view.

"Wait right here." Jace whispered to Lania.

She looked at him with a thousand questions she could not ask, so she watched him climb to the top of the huge rock they stood behind. He reached the pinnacle quickly, and she could barely see him now. A few moments later, he returned to her side.

"He's gone. We won't be his meal this sun-cycle." Jace smiled.

"You're making a joke? Really? My stomach is still in my throat."

He chuckled softly. "Thought a laugh might do you some good." Jace placed his hands on her shoulders. "I told you. I'd never let anything bad happen to you. Believe me now?"

She could not help smiling at the inquisitive look on his face. "Yes." The moment after she spoke, he lowered his head and kissed her. Another kiss that said it all. They were safe, they were successful, and they were in love. Yes, she truly felt the love vibe from Jace like never before. Possibly due to their narrow escape, more likely he really and truly meant his actions. It felt so right, so sensual, so real, and so difficult to control her need and him.

He deepened the kiss. She sensed he wanted to tell her what lay buried in his heart, and she also wanted to touch his very soul and enjoy the most exhilarating feeling she'd ever experienced. She'd hold on to this memory forever. Jace could not be better if he tried, and she totally and completely loved him. Forever. Nothing could ever change her love for this stunning man.

Slowly he loosened his hold on her and brought his deep, all-encompassing kiss to an end. He seemed reluctant to stop, yet they both knew the time and place were completely wrong. Soon they would be out of here, safe and close to a real bed. She could not wait, did not want to wait, yet there was no other choice. A smile pulled on her lips when she noticed his heavy breathing, and the desire in his eyes.

"Lania, My Lady." He ran his fingers through her hair. "Remember, you *are* mine. Now I know for sure. No woman could, or would kiss me like that if she…"

She placed her fingers over his lips. “I am yours, all yours. Say no more. We both know what is in our hearts.” Slowly she slid her hand to the side of his face and cupped his chin for a brief moment then let go. “Back to reality, what do we do now, Warrior?”

Jace chuckled. “I love your ability to change subjects and move on like nothing ever happened. That’s a great ability for a warrior.” He smiled. “Too bad more people aren’t like you.” Jace quickly kissed her cheek. “We still need to move forward. I saw our friend slither off deep into the cavern far away from where we want to go.”

“Lead the way, I shall follow.”

“Good. Let’s go.”

She followed Jace with a new attitude. She’d just cemented all her new feelings forever inside her memory. Although, if she ever returned to the Capitol and took her true position of Royal Ruler of Lorton, there must be a new life-mating bill created, and she would make it happen. She wanted to, needed to life-mate Jace. She would make it happen. It remained tricky business since her sister was involved in all of this. Marna would need to end her connection to the evil man, Raulf, so he could be put away forever in the darkest prison on the planet!

Raulf remained a huge problem, yet there were countless crimes and other reasons to put him away. He was responsible for many illegal activities, not to mention evil things, but putting him away still remained an official High Council task. She should have no problem convincing them of his guilt.

Then, from nowhere a glowing ball of energy appeared right in front of them. This one seemed like it wanted to lead them somewhere, with no intention of harm like the others. “What do you think, Jace?”

“Caution is paramount. We’ll follow it and see.”

“Okay.” He took her hand and they followed the glowing ball up, down, and around every obstacle in their path. Finally, they reached a dark entry. Once the glowing ball entered the area all the darkness disappeared. In fact, it became extremely beautiful with pastel colors from floor to ceiling shining brightly from the stalactites and stalagmites of the cavern’s room.

The area looked extremely huge, bigger than all the others. Then the back wall came into view. While they looked, about a thousand energy balls began to glow. They shielded their eyes when the lights grew too intense. Their personal guide-globe lead them toward the brilliantly lit back wall.

Jace bumped into something and they stopped walking. Their globe joined the others. This appeared strange. Unexplainable? Definitely. No one could possibly believe this story if they tried to tell anyone. She barely believed it herself even though she happened to be living it at the moment. Could this all be a dream? No. Reality was all around her, and when she touched the structure in front of her if felt very cool, and real.

She watched in wonder when Jace's hand moved to the top of what appeared to be a podium. He pulled something down and held it in front of her to read. Both of their mouths dropped open when they began to read the scroll Jace held.

> To the Royal explorer who finds this paper:
>
> Please know this is the end of the line. The energy found here is friendly and balanced, unlike any you may find in other levels and rooms of the cavern. If you are reading this, you are the first to reach this far since I did. Let me explain.
>
> Lorton fell into serious trouble, about to self-destruct when I made my way down here to have my first Energy Battle. I am Ruler Sommult, son of displaced ruler Sommult, my father. My father was murdered by the man who took his place, and ended up in the history books of Lorton, known as Royal Ruler Maston.
>
> Setting history aside, this is the room of power and the true energy source for Lorton. Never doubt the power of this energy, and what it can do if it feels displaced for any reason. This energy detests evil, which goes from general bad behavior of the people, to corruption of the government.

I received a mental message, given in order to save Lorton, because they considered me worthy of the process ahead. I knew it might not be easy to return everything to a good normal, but I felt more than ready for the task at hand.

Upon my return to the Capitol, I instituted new laws which stopped all the nonsense immediately. It is now up to you to decide how best to do your job. All I know, is you would not be reading this unless you were Royalty on the throne of Lorton. Return and do your best. The entire planet is at stake for destruction if you are not successful. This is my warning. Heed it carefully and thoughtfully.

You have much to accomplish.

Go now and do your job.

Sincerely,

Royal Ruler Summult

Lorton, Annual cycle: 20764

They both finished reading the words of the former ruler then simply stared at each other, trying to absorb what they just learned. Like she suspected, everything lay on her shoulders. All aspects of life on Lorton needed to be rescued no matter the level, everything needed help. "Jace? What do you think?"

Jace shook his head. "All I can say at the moment is I'm glad you are ruler and not me. What a job you have." He looked into her eyes. "Do you have any idea where to begin this process?"

Lania shook her head very slowly, then took a deep breath. "At the moment, no. However; I will work on something. I realize it must be good, and I do know the first step."

"How to get rid of Raulf?"

"Exactly." She chuckled. "You're smarter than you look!" He gazed at her with a very strange expression. "Because you're a Warrior! Strong and capable." Lania put her hand on Jace's shoulder. "You do know, warriors are not expected to be smart? Plus, you are extremely handsome, and you know what is said about handsome men." She laughed, and this time he laughed along with her. Then they both noticed the energy in the room grow to over three times its size, and the intensity became at least ten-times brighter.

"Do you see all the light?"

Lania nodded while she surveyed the room. It seemed like a light fixture filled every nook and crevice of the cavern, yet it all came from the energy globes in front of them. "I see." She looked into his gorgeous blue eyes. "It appears the energy globes like laughter. Or is it jokes they prefer?"

"I don't think what you say matters. It is simply intent. They sense us through our thoughts and feelings. Like good from bad, light from dark. Our good thoughts, our love. What do you think?"

"Oh. Warrior, you're being too smart for your looks again." They both laughed long and hard while they gazed into each other's eyes. "Well, smartie, we've been down here a long time. We don't want to worry the people above."

"My brothers are the only two people who know we're even down here."

"Right. I'm not used to such a small audience." She snickered. "I have a lot to learn, don't I?"

"I suppose you do." Jace pulled her to him.

He kissed her with passion, yet kept it short this time. He knew they were still on the move same as she did, so he ended his kiss, and once again she felt the loss when his lips left hers. One sun-cycle soon, this may no longer be a problem. When they looked around, the lights were blinking at them. "Look, Jace." She pointed at all the flashing lights.

"It seems they liked our kiss."

"No." Lania put her hands on Jace's cheeks. "They felt our love even more."

"I believe you're right, My Lady." Jace put the scroll in Lania's hand and wrapped her fingers around it. "Hang on to this. I'm sure you'll need it for proof later. Plus, much discussion may happen with The High Conference and they might insist on reading this themselves."

"Right again, smartie!"

"Don't you dare laugh at me again, even if I am a smartie."

Lania giggled, and so did Jace. Their laughter caused the light globes to flash and grow brighter. "It seems they do like laughter. Imagine. Who would have ever guessed?"

"No one, for sure. Now, we'd better go. Unless there's something you think we need to do in this room?"

"I believe we sent the proper message, and all will be well now." She followed Jace's lead along the same path areas they used before, and thankfully the globes kept their light bright for them. This entire experience could only be called sensational. From realizing she completely fell in love with Jace, to learning the main secret of Lorton. Plus, she held proof in her hand verifying what she wanted to present to the people, which might well change the lives of every person on Lorton.

Her mind suddenly screamed at her loud and clear. This secret must be kept secret. It has nothing to do with Raulf, or anything else currently happening. She held invaluable information in her hand. She and Jace were the only two beings who knew about this, and she decided every citizen did not need to know about how the energy truly worked. All the public really cared about boiled down to peace and happiness in their lives. No. The scroll in her hand must not be shared. Even those in government did not need to know. Their only interest, like everyone on Lorton, rested on the success of this Energy Battle.

They headed toward the front of the cavern, crossing through the second room which seemed the largest. It didn't take long before she finally saw their bench straight ahead. When they reached 'their bench' she stopped Jace and made him sit down with her. "Jace, I have reached a Royal Ruler's decision."

"Please, tell me, My Lady."

"I don't want to share with anyone what we learned about the energy, or what the scroll says. I don't believe every Lorton citizen should know this information. If they do, circumstances might turn on us. When you mentioned showing this to The High Council, I thought it a good idea and agreed. Then serious second thoughts flew through my mind as if someone screamed at me that this," Lania held up the scroll, "remain completely between us, never to be revealed. Can I trust you on this issue? I know you have two brothers you feel you must tell everything to, but I'm asking you, as Royal Ruler, not to do so. Can I trust you to keep this secret?"

"Wow. It may be tough where my brothers are concerned. I have no problems with the public." Jace began to nod at Lania. "I will not tell Dane or Holt, or any living soul. I respect your decision, and your right to ask this of me." He kissed her lips. "Trust me. You know you can."

"Thank you. You do know how I feel about you, don't you?"

"Tell me anyway. I want to hear it from you before we leave our special place."

Lania lowered her head, took a deep breath, then looked into Jace's dark blue eyes. "I love you, Jace Bryton, with everything I have. My heart belongs to only you, now and forever." She looked around the cavern room. "This will always be our special place, where we first made love, and admitted our love to each other."

"My sweet, sweet lady. I've loved you from the moment I first laid eyes on you. When I carried you to my transport through the miserable jungle, on the worst planet I have ever seen, I admired your beauty, and immediately feelings rushed through me. Feelings I had that sun-cycle for you, are the same feelings which never left. I realize you may not believe me, but it's true." Jace shook his head. "This is not easy to admit to, you know?"

"Same for me, believe it or not. When I first laid eyes on you, I thought you were the most beautiful man I had ever seen. Of course, the mean men on Extram were all I had to compare you to, but somehow, I knew it was true. I hoped with all I had you would pick me up and carry me to safety, away from them."

She shook her head while he studied her. "And you did exactly what I hoped for. You have never let me down. I have never been in love with a man before. In fact, I never kissed a man until you." Now he shook his head at her. "Seriously. I realize how behind I am, yet it is true. Because of my upbringing and Royal heritage. You know my life, very sheltered."

"Which turned out to be my true blessing. Since you were a virgin in every way a man dreams of, and usually never finds. Your gift to me will always remain extremely special. I truly hold your gift within me with the highest possible esteem, and I always will."

Lania sighed. "You, My Warrior, are the sweetest man I have ever known, even if you only think you are the toughest warrior on the planet!" She laughed and so did Jace. "You are actually both of those things. I am so glad you carried me out of that jungle in your muscular, sexy arms." She smiled at her warrior. "You are also one more thing, the best lover ever."

"My Lady, you are the sweet one to say so to me, however, without any comparison how could you possible know such a thing?"

"My heart knows exactly what I feel, and what is truth. I will forever hold you close." Before she could utter another word, his lips were on hers, kissing her in a way that said they would not be leaving their special place any time-unit soon.

She wanted this moment to last forever. Once they returned, they would no longer have complete privacy, and once again, life would interfere with their love. The moment the public knew she remained alive; she'd no longer be with Jace. Raulf must get out of the picture, and The High Council needed to allow her to life-mate Jace.

They kissed like lovers who might never see each other again. Exploration and satisfaction all mixed elegantly and pleasurably together. He made fast work of her clothes, then his. They wasted no time wrestling naked together to consummate a love far greater than she could ever imagine possible. It was special. It was forbidden, it was fantastic, necessary, satisfying, happy, sweet and perfect. Any words in their language that explained good, great, or out of their galaxy, described what they shared. Their love held qualities to cherish and share, forever and ever.

She loved this man from the top of his head to the tips of his toes, inside and out. Jace personified the perfect man. Made just for her to enjoy, and she *absolutely* enjoyed him. Jace knew the sweetest, most beautiful way of making love. Slow, sensual, sexy and caring. Everything a woman wanted, and never found, yet she found exactly her perfect dream. From this moment on, she refused to let him go. Jace belonged to her, forever. They were the perfect pair.

Chapter Twenty

Jace stared at Dane and Holt from across the table and shook his head slowly in an effort to get them to believe him. "Some things I can't put into words. We caught the energy balls and hurled them back. We both stood firm and gave the energy the impression we'd never quit, no matter what."

Dane squinted at his brother. "Did you act like the energy knew, or understood you?"

Jace smiled. "The energy didn't know me, but I did feel it understood me. It certainly acted like it did when I talked to it. Don't ask me to explain the unexplainable. It may have been my assumption. I'm not exactly sure."

"Your story seems strange, then again, we've never heard exact details regarding the battle before. All that is usually reported is how hard it was and how successful they were, and that coming from whoever did the battle. Of course, you know that same as we do." Dane shook his head. "But it is very interesting to hear the details for sure." He looked into Jace's eyes.

"How far did you get?" Holt asked.

"We got very far down. I know this is hard to believe, even Lania was shocked, but we got to the back wall of a third cavern room. Possibly it was the fourth, I kind of lost count."

Holt slapped the table top with his hand. "I don't think anyone has ever been there before, and I mean all the Royalty that fought before you."

Jace smiled. "Probably not. We never found a path, only boulders and a sandy, rocky floor. Nothing else. By the time we entered there, the energy balls began to leave us alone. I don't know why. They sort of bounced around and simply lit our way so we could see where we were walking." He watched both his brothers nod with wide eyes. They seemed extremely happy and satisfied with what he told them. "Did I tell you how the energy ball completely destroyed, I mean melted into nothing, a gigantic boulder right next to us? Then they did it again. I suppose in case we missed it the first time. It was amazing and scary at the same time. I guess they were trying to make a point, not really sure.

Dane shook his head. "Very interesting story, for sure. I realize you were new to this. What did Lania say? Had she been there before? Had she seen a boulder melt before?"

"No, it was her first time to be that far down. She had seen boulders melt before. She'd told me about it, and warned me not to be scared, and not to make the energy mad since it could do the same thing to us." He nodded at his brothers. "We did everything we could possibly do, and I expect change to happen very soon."

Holt nodded. "I truly hope you're right. Lorton certainly needs help. Maybe we'll all survive now." He chuckled.

He joined Holt and Dane in their laughter. It certainly felt better than the other emotions that wanted out of him. "Please, do not discuss anything I've just told you with anyone. Not a friend, not anyone, please? This comes from Lania, who has every right to ask, and we have the responsibility to obey her request. Okay?"

Dane and Holt both nodded their acceptance to him, and he felt relieved when they did. "Listen, we need a plan to put Lania back in control. How can we introduce a dead woman back into power? She's been gone over six annual-cycles, yet she belongs in power instead of Raulf."

"She does need to be in power." Dane took a sip of his drink. "What about this monocycle? It will be the People's Celebration Party. Raulf and hundreds of others will be present, and the rest of the population will be watching on the planet-wide vid. What do you think?"

Holt smiled. “Not bad. It’s a good idea. What do you think, Bro?”

Jace smiled back at his brother. “Who am I to argue with a great idea? We do need an audience so Raulf can’t dispute it and take action against Lania and us. We are all extremely vulnerable if we unseat a Royal Ruler, even if it is Raulf DeMorgan. If Raulf has his way, he’d eliminate every one of us in front of all those witnesses. Raulf does love an audience. We must make it so he will be unable to do anything, at least not then.”

Dane nodded. “Exactly. We’ll call for his immediate arrest, and I doubt anyone will argue. He’s not well liked.”

“Total understatement, Dane.” All three of them snickered under their breath. They all hated Raulf and anxiously waited to see him locked up forever. The entire planet would be happy to celebrate along with them. He felt positive of their reaction. “This sounds like the perfect way, especially since every attendee wears the same mask to prove all citizens are equal. So, no one will know Lania until she makes herself known, with us standing behind her.

“Right.” Holt stood. “I’ll get on the computer and notify all our friends and working partners. I’ll tell them they must attend and to be prepared for a giant surprise. They need to fit in and go along with everyone at the party and to take their cues from us. What do you think? We need to be sure someone, if not everyone is behind us.”

Dane slapped Holt on the arm. “You’re good!”

Jace nodded. “You’re both good. I’ll go prepare Lania for what’s to come and get back to you guys. I’m sure she’ll be fine with the plan.”

Dane stood. “Okay. I’ll help Holt with the notifications.”

He watched his brothers hurry off to their info-center. Both of them were the best he knew of at their jobs. All three of them maintained about the same abilities and thought processes which proved invaluable in their line of work. They accepted jobs involving nearly everything going on. There were many issues on Lorton a new ruler needed to change and things were about to change big time when they gave Lania back to her people.

Although his abilities in the info-center were more than acceptable, he’d much rather deal with the beautiful Lania Sloten, Royal Ruler of Lorton. She may not be in charge at this moment, but hopefully this time next sun-cycle, Lania would be able to claim her rightful position in the government as Royal Ruler and become fully engulfed in her new position.

Lania knew well what her position meant, the people's expectations, and everything the job commanded. He wasn't surprised Lania had not shown any apprehension at the immense tasks before her. His woman was truly amazing.

He walked down the hall to the bedroom she stayed in and touched the knock tab on the door. A moment later it slid open and he found the woman of his dreams in the easy chair by the high window. "Hello there. Feel better?" he asked while he walked over and took the chair next to hers. "Much better. A good rest and a hot shower really work wonders." She stared at him a moment. "Is something wrong, Jace?"

"No, something is right. You'd better get ready for this announcement. You will be returned to your government position this moon-cycle, and our Mr. Raulf, will be arrested." Lania looked entirely shocked, even her mouth dropped open a bit. He smiled at her, and for some reason she did not smile back. Her curiosity shot to high-level.

"What are you talking about?"

"This moon-cycle is the People's Celebration Party, and we are all going. When the time is right, we'll make our appearance on the podium, announce who you are, then you can make a speech." She still looked totally in shock. "What do you think, My Lady?"

"I'm not sure what to say. What if this turns against us and we are arrested? How can we stop it?"

"Dane and Holt are contacting our numerous business contacts and asking for their support. Most probably planned to be there anyway, but I'm quite sure they'll all cooperate, especially since they all hate Raulf. Raulf the Evil."

"Strong words. You're sure of this? How many are you talking about?"

"We have hundreds of contacts who will gladly offer their help. We're not telling them about you, only to expect a big surprise, and for them to go along with us, and they will. I'm sure they'll take delight in helping with this takeover."

Lania shook her head several times then looked Jace in the eye. "I trust you. You know I do. This is a major undertaking with horrible ramifications if anything goes wrong. You do understand, right?"

"I do. We figured our success might be extremely high if we did it in front of the entire planet. You know the people who are unable to attend watch it on their vids We couldn't get more witnesses if we tried. This is exactly what we want since you'll be in charge of all of them as their Royal Supreme Ruler. With countless witnesses, Raulf doesn't stand an ounce of a chance to stop our plan. Now," Jace checked his wrist-piece, "you'd better get ready since you have a party to go to. Should I purchase a dress for you?'

"I suppose. I certainly don't have one."

Jace rose from his chair and moved to the small desk along the wall and turned on the small info-center which displayed a large readout on the wall. He pressed several buttons, then looked at Lania. "See all the dresses? Pick the one you want, click send, and it will be at our doorstep within this time-unit. You'd better hurry or you'll be late."

"Yes, My Warrior, I will hurry. What about you? This is a formal affair, you know?"

"My brothers and I are more prepared than you could ever imagine. We'll be fine. It may be difficult for us to decide which formal evening-suits to wear." He laughed while he headed for the door. "Hurry. I'll bring it the moment it arrives. Have you found the make-up drawer yet?" She shook her head. "Third drawer on the right side of the mirror, beside the desk part and chair. I know you're beautiful the way you are, My Sweet, but make-up is necessary for an evening formal, even though you will wear a mask during the beginning. You do have a public speech to make with all of Lorton watching. Don't you?" He saw her nod, almost with a frown. "So, make yourself more beautiful than you already are, if that's even possible." He smiled very happily at her.

"Thanks for reminding me. Like my nerves needed more to worry about. I do not have a speech ready. What will I say? I was a babysitter for six annual-cycles?"

"That's good for a start. I can't believe you're nervous? You're the most composed woman I've ever known. Now, go find and order your dress. Can't have you up there in front of all of Lorton naked! Besides, that's only for me, your warrior." With that statement he got up, walked to the door, then looked into the slide-reader. He left the moment he found the space.

Special was written all over this moon-cycle, and the party would be transcribed into Lorton's history books to be remembered forever, and remain available for every Royal Ruler and member of The High Council that came after them. Making history might be fun! He laughed to himself while he headed to tell his brothers Lania fully agreed. For the most part anyway.

When he walked up behind Holt he paused for a moment. "Wow. You two have been busy. Am I seeing what I think I'm seeing? Over two-thousand will stand behind us? Hope there's room for everyone."

Dane glanced at his brother. "Yup, and we're not done yet. With a bit of luck, our plan will go perfectly."

"How did you manage that?"

Holt laughed. "We didn't tell anyone about Lania. We did mention Raulf might not like the surprise, and they didn't need to hear anything more. You know good and well, no one stands behind the Evil One."

"Everyone's basic answer, 'anything Raulf doesn't like, we do! We're in!' And they really meant what they said as you can see!" Dane laughed. "It's really been easy. They'd be there in an instant if I told them Raulf will be arrested!"

"Well, I'm certainly glad to hear the good news. You may have to come up with a plan to get everyone into the celebration. Think about it. Thanks guys. I really appreciate your help." All three of them slapped their hands against the other in celebration.

"How did Lania take it?" Holt stared at his brother.

"She's nervous and naturally had some reservations, mostly due to the surprise, and the fact she doesn't have a dress or a speech ready. She's ordering her dress, and she'll think of something to say. She knows how to do her job. Plus, we're right behind her to back her up in case something comes up, or she forgets her words." Jace nodded. "This is going to be sweet." Both his brothers smiled at him. "Now, if you two are done playing here, you'd better get dressed for the party, it's coming sooner than you think and we need to look good."

The door alert went off. "Dear stars, that was fast!" He knew it must be Lania's dress, so he hurried to the lift to go to the upper level. The moment he arrived he found the fancy box and knew exactly which vendor she purchased it from, the most expensive seller on Lorton. He didn't care. She deserved the dress she desired, and far more. He may still have a heart-attack when he received the bill.

He picked up the box, entered the elevator, and rode back down. His brothers turned to look at him when he stepped out. "She needed something to wear this moon-cycle."

Dane and Holt both laughed before answering together, "We see!"

Jace held up the box and laughed. "Nothing is too good for the First Lady of Lorton!" His brothers laughed even harder. "Actually, The Royal Ruler of Lorton!"

They both knew the store she'd picked since they'd all been with women before who seemed very fond of the outlet, especially if someone else paid for it. Finding a duplicate somewhere else always provided a cheaper way to go, yet it never worked since all women knew a knock-the-same when they saw one. Besides, this moon-cycle Lania had to look the part if she planned to take over the entire planet and become the Supreme Royal Ruler of Lorton, so his credits were well spent.

He hurried down the hall to her room and knocked. She told him to enter. He stepped inside her room and handed her the very light box he carried. She sat in the chair by the window and opened the package like a child on holiday, fast and furious. He found the smile on her face priceless, and knew she loved it. "It's beautiful. Made exactly for you."

She jumped up, ran to the mirror and held the garment up in front of her like she wore it. He couldn't wait to actually see her in it, and he wouldn't have long to wait. "You'll look extraordinary in that dress. Now, it's getting late. I'll let you get ready."

When he turned to leave, she stopped him by throwing her arms around his waist. In a flash, he turned to face her and she kissed him quickly. It still happened to be a kiss that melted his heart and awakened every part of his body.

"Thank you! I'll wear it with pride since it is a gift from you."

"You're too sweet." He so wanted to make love to her right now, passionately, slowly, completely. The time, once again, being totally wrong, pulled them apart. Some sun-cycle he would be able to remain at her side, every time unit, and every moon-cycle after that as well.

"You are the sweet one. Thank you. Now go, I have a lot to do. And you'd better get yourself ready."

"I'm fast. Men never have all the problems women do. I know the suit I'm going to wear, and a shower does not take me long." He looked her in the eye. "Unless you're in the shower with me." She laughed at him and he took a step back. "You wouldn't be laughing if I pinned you in the corner of the shower, kissed you everywhere, passionately touching you, making you moan with pleasure." Too bad he couldn't make that a reality. Her cheeks already turned quite red and he knew exactly how she felt. "I'll leave you be. Simply come out when you're ready."

"Will do, Warrior. Don't worry."

Jace nodded, then exited fast, before he changed his mind and kept her from getting ready. He could not stop his thoughts from visualizing Lania in his shower and making mad, passionate love to her again and again. She was amazing, everything he ever wanted. His ideas may not be practical right now, but they were damn good ones!

No time to dream. He needed to picture what might happen at the party this moon-cycle. With so many people, what they wanted to do might be pushed in many different ways. Like the new saying went, "The more the merrier." Hopefully the majority of the people who attended would be their invited friends who promised to back them up. The thought of all the help did a good job of holding down the dangerous factor, not to mention his personal worries.

He hoped for the perfect moment to make the ultimate move up on stage to announce the living, breathing, Lania Sloten, Royal Ruler of Lorton. He refused to use her legal last name. Technically, she remained life-mated to Raulf, even if her sister now held the title. He laughed while he shed his clothes and stepped into the shower. Hot water always felt so good on his back, and everywhere it hit his body. It actually itched his newest scar, which still seemed a bit sensitive even though it was mostly healed. Too bad he couldn't get rid of Raulf as easily as the soap he'd rubbed all over himself.

Personally, he'd love to end the evil man's life, although putting him away, never to be seen again, would count as second best. Lorton maintained an excellent reputation for having the strictest detention centers on any planet in the galaxy. They gave detainees no leeway, ever, and no prisoner ever escaped any of Lorton's facilities. Exactly what Raulf earned for himself.

Right now, he preferred to concentrate on Lania, the woman who belonged to him, not Raulf. Thank the stars Raulf never touched her in a sexual way. If he had, Raulf might not live long enough to go to prison. Jace finished his shower, grabbed the towel and dried off. He planned to dress in a flash since he wanted to be in the living area when Lania made her grand entrance.

CHAPTER TWENTY-ONE

Lania slipped her shoes on, then took one last look in the full-length mirror and decided she looked pretty good. She picked the bright red dress to highlight her dark hair, and the black face-mask. The government somehow decided if they all wore the same masks it made them all equal. What a joke. Everyone knew a lie when they heard it. The rich and famous always ranked higher on every list, followed by the high-ups in the government. The government liked to play games, especially big ones like this moon-cycle.

Once Raulf became ruler he considered himself a man on the high list, which made Raulf the biggest joke on Lorton. Thank the Universe everything Raulf stood for ended this moon-cycle. He'd never be put in charge of anything again, including himself.

At the same time, every woman in attendance tried to out-dress the others. It seemed more like a fashion show, and every woman would stare at her as if they were all in competition. The only times she ever missed these after-battle parties was while she was on the miserable planet of Extram.

She remembered well the crazy way each and every woman pranced around, then flashed sideways looks at men. She used to believe those women to be loose, because they begged any man they could find to take them. All the younger women, and even the young girls believed that nonsense, although it did remain close to the truth, some women were always making very obvious passes at men.

To her, this party was always a bit strange, probably because of the way some women acted. It made her angry. She feared if a woman pulled such a flirtatious routine on Jace she might punch her in the face, then shove her to the ground. Fine, she harbored a bad case of possessiveness when it came to '*Her Warrior*'. He was special, and he was hers, without question. She hoped he would never fall for anything that obvious from another woman. Somehow, she completely believed in his loyalty to her.

She tried to tug the top of the gown up a bit to hide her cleavage a little better. It didn't work. The bodice was created to enhance every curve on a woman. Nearly every appropriate gown for this party was similar in design, with few differences. She tried to pick the one which covered the most. Try being the keyword. Another silly trick to really hook a man.

After one last glance in the reflective glass, she opened the door and stepped into the hall. What will Jace think of her? She could only walk slowly since the heels she wore slowed her down. At least they were shiny, glittery, real silver shoes which were decorated to brightly say, 'look at me'. She felt the slight wobble in her step and hoped her nervousness did not appear too visible.

Plus, her dress was quite tight and did not fan out until past her knees, so she hoped running would not be required this moon-cycle. She giggled to herself, because if running were required, Jace would have to carry her, and that was something he might actually like to do.

The moment she reached the living area at the end of the hall, three Brighton Brothers jumped up from their chairs and stood at attention with smiles on their faces, however; Jace's expression went far beyond words. His eyebrows nearly disappeared into his hairline, and his deep-blue eyes opened so widely they looked several shades lighter. His mouth remained slightly open and displayed his beautiful, white, perfectly shaped teeth. If his smile became any larger, she truly believed the corners of his mouth might split open.

Without a doubt, all three brothers thought she looked good, yet it seemed Jace wanted to tell her something more, and she knew she would hear about it if, and when they were able to speak privately. She smiled back and gave them a big thank-you nod.

Jace took a step forward then stopped. "Lania, My Lady, you look absolutely stunning. Perfect. Amazing!"

"Thank you, Jace." Heat grew in her cheeks to a point she needed to splash water on them. "And you are obviously wonderful, so masculine, neat and perfectly put together. I love your look."

Holt moved to stand between his brother and Lania. "I think you two are overdoing this. You both are making me nervous!" He laughed and Dane joined him.

When Dane quit laughing, he looked Jace in the eye. "And not for the reason you think, Bro."

This time Lania laughed along with the three brothers. It felt good to relax a bit, and let some of her stress flow out with the desperation she felt, along with her feelings of being scared and worried. These brave men always took good care of her and made sure everything went perfectly. Failure was not an option if planet Lorton wanted to survive. It was all up to her, and she knew Jace and his brothers insured her safety and provided all the support necessary to enable her to stand up to the evil Raulf and have him taken away to prison.

Jace stepped up to her, offered his arm, which she gladly accepted. Together they walked to the hall, then down the narrow way out to the parking garage. Dane and Holt walked right behind them. At the moment, she felt secure, and hoped this feeling lasted the entire moon-cycle. The job ahead scared the Diabolous out of her.

Once they were all out of the house, they walked to the transport, then up the ramp. Dane took the pilot's seat, Holt took co-pilot while she and Jace made themselves comfortable on the divan in the main passenger area and fastened their safety belts. All kinds of thoughts assailed her. Most seemed horrible since they focused on the evil man she couldn't get out of her mind, Raulf. She enjoyed her time without a memory, only because she was free of evil Raulf.

Jace leaned toward Lania. "Remember, I love you, My Lady. Never forget." Jace tipped her chin up with his finger. "Never forget." He bent his head and kissed her.

Lania melted into his arms and kissed him more passionately than he kissed her. She feared their next chance may never come. If they were alone right now, they both would take it much farther, still, this kiss said it all. Love, and more love consumed her, something she desperately wanted and needed to feel.

Slowly she ended the kiss and put her lips to his ear. "I love you so very much. Now and forever, I am yours." She kissed him deeply to strengthen her words. Without hesitation he kissed her back with even more passion, and if they did not stop now, they would certainly become a spectacle for both of his brothers. She forced him to end the kiss, even if he did not want to let her go.

"I want this over so we can be together," he whispered in her ear.

"Me too." There may never be a 'together' for them once she moved into her pending position of Supreme Royal Ruler of Lorton. She planned to make demands to The High Council that Jace be allowed to life-mate her. Although she had to pass two new Lorton laws to make it possible, with no guarantee she would be successful. Whatever it took, she would become *his warrior*, which meant she would fight to the end for the love of her life. She did not tell him because it might deeply hurt him to think for one moment they may become separated with no chance of togetherness.

Dane cleared his throat. "We're landing now."

She knew what he meant when he cleared his throat. His brothers never missed a thing. It was an admirable trait since they did security work, but a big pain for her and Jace at times. The craft descended easily, and glided to a perfect stop in front of the gala's parking entrance. An attendant arrived to park their craft in the proper size lot. Dane gave the young man a warning look and Holt did the same, even though they presented him with a large tip. Predictable brothers.

Jace exited first, then held his hand out to assist her exit. He easily saw all the trouble she went through simply trying to walk since the skirt of her dress held her back, not to mention the heels. He'd seen her walk at the house and should realize why she was so slow. He probably thought she only tried to impress him. He looked at her and smiled, even though her pace remained way slower than normal. Luckily, Jace did not seem to care, he simply changed his walk speed to match hers. He was a true gentleman who would do anything for his lady. Nothing about this moon-cycle felt normal. The young man who waited at the bottom gave each of them a mask they gladly put on for security, at least for now.

She enjoyed being helped by Jace, especially when it required him to touch her. Soon he would be taken away from her, and she hoped to the stars it would not be for long. If she had her way, Jace would be back with her so fast it would be like he was never gone. However; she spent enough time in and around government to know how the best plans often fell apart, and excuses would be all she heard. She also knew how slow they were to accomplish anything. First, she needed to be accepted as ruler, then pass two laws. Not much to do. She smiled, which seemed appropriate at the moment.

At least no steps stood in her way into the fantastic palace garden area where the party took place in full swing. They all adjusted their masks before they joined the other guests in the public area. Immediately Jace pulled her to the dance area and engaged her in a sexy slow dance. At least she felt it sexy since Jace's body pressed tightly against hers, moving ever so slowly, revealing exactly how he felt.

Luckily the dance lasted quite a while, which gave Jace time to adjust and survey their surroundings, same as she had "When will the main event happen?"

He smiled at her. "At the right time, and not before."

Jace made her give him a silly grin. "And you know when this 'right' time is?"

"I will."

"Guess I'll have to trust you. In the meantime, should I be doing something?"

"Just enjoy yourself."

Lania looked over his shoulder and saw both brothers engaged in dance, each with a very beautiful woman. "How do your brothers do it?"

"Do what?"

She forced him to turn around. Once he did, he chuckled softly then turned back and looked her in the eye.

"The Bryton Brothers have a reputation with the ladies."

"Too many ladies here." Lania couldn't help a small laugh, especially when he gave her his purposeful look of innocence even the mask could not hide. Jace spun her around with the sweeping music and continued the dance without missing a beat. He was good, she'd give him credit. Good at everything she'd seen him do, including wrestling giant monsters. He performed even better while making love.

Jace leaned down and nearly placed his lips on hers—but the music stopped. He quickly lifted his head and they both looked around. A man walked up on the podium and tapped the voice-device to draw attention. Once everyone stopped what they were doing and turned toward him, he began to speak.

"As President of Public Affairs, I would like to welcome all the equal guests this moon-cycle. I'm sure you all know, we are celebrating the successful Energy Battle, performed by our illustrious Supreme Royal Ruler, Raulf DeMorgan, and his life-mate Marna, our lovely First Lady. I know you are all anxious to hear how the battle went, so I will now introduce your Supreme Royal Ruler, Raulf DeMorgan!"

All the attendees clapped and welcomed Raulf. They didn't have a choice, plus he obviously invited his closest allies. She wanted to stop all the applause. He didn't deserve an ounce of it.

Jace leaned toward her ear. "I instructed all my allies to go along with current happenings, and they are."

"Have you seen them?"

"They're all over. In fact, the majority of people here belong to us, which certainly works to our advantage."

"Very true. You've seen to everything, My Warrior." Her comment made Jace smile. She could barely watch evil Raulf take the stage in the center of the large garden. Hopefully Raulf's reward waited right around the corner. Instantly would be her first choice. He stepped up to the podium and began to address all the citizens he cared nothing about, except for their credits of course, the only reason they were still alive.

"Welcome citizens of Lorton. I'm excited to have you here this moon-cycle to celebrate my success once again! I believe you've already felt some of the marvelous effects of my triumphant victory. As always, I've taken care of you and made Lorton a far better planet to live on."

Lania nearly lost her mid-meal over Raulf's words. His innate ability to make people sick really showed, yet the attendees behaved the way they were instructed and gave Raulf the applause he demanded. He held his arms up in the air, asking for even more than the audience gave. He truly acted like the jerk everyone knew him to be. She knew well what a greedy, self-centered maniac the man was, and she knew he loved putting on the act he currently presented to the public. Nothing could change Raulf, he remained evil to the core

Most people exhibited at least a partial good side to compensate a little for their bad side. It may be extremely rare to find a person with absolutely nothing good about them, but Raulf was that person. Raulf lowered his arms and the applause faded.

"The First Lady and I found the battle to be extremely difficult." Raulf paused and Marna joined him, "But as you all know, we were completely successful!" He took Marna's hand in his and they raised them high in the air.

More applause broke out and Lania's stomach really turned this time. She got sick simply looking at her previous life-mate. Or was he still her current life-mate? She did not know how the law viewed this current situation. She would end her legal ties to Raulf, even though the legal status of their life-mating had already turned confused when Marna life-mated him. Now her sister currently held legal claim as First Lady and Raulf's legal life-mate. Of course, the public did not know she stood here very alive, but they were about to find out. Jace took her hand and gave it a squeeze to reassure her, something she desperately needed.

Raulf began his explanation of the Energy Battle and she shook her head Jace joined her in disbelief. They tried not to be obvious since they both knew firsthand what happened. Raulf must live in a child's storyland to make up his story of success. He certainly spoke like he knew precisely what happened, and he came across to the audience as very convincing that what he said was the absolute truth. She'd never known anyone who could lie like Raulf and be so persuading in the process.

Jace leaned down toward Lania's ear. "Be ready. Our time will be soon."

"What about his guards? Won't they stop you?"

"We'll be fine. Trust me, My Lady."

"You'd better be right, or we are all dead."

"Don't worry, I'm right."

Jace sounded very sure of himself, and he remained so calm, both facts forced her to trust him. What choice did she have? None. Her life lay completely in the Bryton Brothers' hands, whether she liked it or not. There was no time for self-doubt, her only job now required her to wear her brave face and have a convincing, ruler's attitude. Jace now moved her toward the podium.

Raulf's self-indulgence finally came to an end, and she knew their move would come before the crowd returned to dancing and drinking. Her mouth parted when several guards, and men dressed in fancy suits, took the stage behind Raulf and Marna. She nearly laughed when the evil man's mouth dropped open, shocked when he noticed something he did not plan.

Then Dane mounted the steps and moved right next to Raulf. "My Ruler, I have a surprise for you. One that will shock you." He waved at his brother who mounted the steps with Lania on his arm. They walked up to him. "My Ruler, let me introduce Lania DeMorgan! You may recognize her as your life-mate. She has a few words to say."

At his announcement she removed her mask and looked Raulf straight in the eye. "As you can see, you failed to murder me. I have come back to haunt you, and claim my rightful place on planet Lorton." The moment she finished her statement, the guards behind Raulf, grabbed his hands, pulled them behind his back and put on restraints.

"I speak as the real, lawfully entitled Royal Ruler of Lorton, and I hereby order the immediate arrest and public trial of Raulf DeMorgan, for attempted murder, and the illegal take-over of Planet Lorton's Rulership, among other crimes he has committed." She took a deep breath. "Guards, take him to his cell. Anything he may say now will be a lie, and we have heard enough of those!" Applause broke out at an overwhelming level. Every attendee appeared to be on her side. Thank the stars!

The guards removed Raulf quite roughly. "Guards," she said to the men behind her. "Please take Marna and detain her for questioning. Not in a cell, just in a palace room under guard. Thank you." She couldn't help the smile tugging at her cheeks while she watched Raulf being treated like the garbage he was. He deserved everything he received. So far so good. Now she needed to tell the public something. She held up both of her hands and the applause slowly diminished. "I appreciate that you are all happy to see Raulf DeMorgan leave." She pointed toward Raulf, and crazy, loud clapping began again. She held up her hand. "Please, allow me to finish before you show more approval."

When silence finally fell over the crowd, she began her speech to her anxiously, awaiting public. "Citizens of Lorton, I could not be more excited to be back. I am also relieved to have survived a horrible ordeal. First, I was given a toxic poison which totally erased my memory. I did not even know my own name." She heard members of the audience gasp while she spoke.

"Then I was taken off this planet and flown several galaxies away to Extram. They were supposed to murder me, then dispose of my body. However, they needed someone to care for their children. Therefore, I became their nanny-slave for the six annual-cycles I have been gone. Then Jace Bryton, of Bryton Brothers' Security, miraculously found me in the jungle on the day I finally decided to make my escape. Mr. Bryton brought me back to Lorton, and seriously risked his life for me to regain my memory. Then the Bryton Brothers brought me here this moon-cycle to claim my rightful place as Supreme Royal Ruler of Lorton.

"I expect Raulf to be found guilty of multiple crimes I have learned of, although I am not at liberty to explain now. I must be sure the law is followed to the letter. We do not want the evil man to be freed due to legal mistakes." She surveyed the crowd and noticed nothing except nods and smiles looking back at her.

"I have my full memory back, and from this moment forward, at least for the foreseeable future, I will take my place as the Supreme Royal Ruler of Lorton." Applause broke out even louder than before, and she loved it. Their clapping belonged to her and her alone. It felt great to know the public supported her so enthusiastically. She absorbed it all until the crowd settled down.

"One more announcement, you should all see an energy improvement on Lorton since I conducted the energy battle with a partner. Raulf has never performed the battle, he does not understand how and is not capable. I believe the results I was able to bring will be felt soon if not immediately, and as your Royal Ruler, I will do them every annual-cycle as required." She allowed the applause that could not be stopped if she tried.

"Please, all my loyal citizens, let the real party begin!" More applause. They were going to have sore hands in the morning. For now, the sounds of the crowd sent thrilling shivers through her body, and she loved every moment of the sound.

Jace offered his arm and she willingly accepted. He escorted her off the podium and down to the dance area. He led her in a dance, then about everyone in attendance joined in the merriment which resonated in every area of the garden party. She could now claim to be the happiest woman on planet Lorton, especially when her lover held her so close against him.

Chapter Twenty-Two

Jace's heart raced while he held Lania in his arms. He now danced with the Royal Ruler of Lorton! He never dreamt such a possibility could ever happen, yet here he danced, in real time and place. Jace wasn't dancing with the Royal Ruler, he danced with the woman he was madly in love with, and no longer cared who knew. Although, revealing how they felt about each other fell totally into Lania's territory since she just became the person in charge. The secret now belonged to her, along with the timing for the revelation.

He loved how everyone supported her. Their plan worked perfectly, at least so far. It always remained possible for something to go wrong. He refused to think about the negative when he felt so happy and blessed at the moment. Only positive thoughts for the future. Lania finally gained her rightful position, so without a doubt, everything from this moment forward looked promising. The dance ended and he stared at his partner. "Do you think you have anything you need to do right now, my Royal Ruler?"

Jace's words forced her to smile. "I'm sure there is. I'll have time next sun-cycle."

"My Lady, I must leave you here this moon-cycle, and I need to be sure you'll be okay." Jace looked into her eyes. "And completely safe."

"Understood. I got wrapped up in this moment with you." She grinned at Jace. "Let's go inside and I'll give you a tour."

"Fine, as long as we take guards with us. Not all the workers inside know, or understand what's going on right now."

"You're right." Lania smiled. "As always My Warrior Man."

"Count on it" He smiled broadly. "I do love it when you call me that."

"That's because you are exactly that and you well know it."

He nodded at Lania, then waved to four of his comrades and both of his brothers, pointing to the building to the right of them. They all made their way through the crowd, basically unnoticed, especially since they all wore their masks once again. Of course, everyone now recognized Lania since her bright red dress gave her away in every direction. The thought made him want to laugh. He felt glad to be through the open gate to the entrance where they all made their way up the stairs and through the archway.

"Lania will lead the way, and I'll be beside her. Follow us to be sure all is well. Not everyone inside will know what just happened. They won't be expecting a new Ruler to be their boss."

"We're all with you," one of the men said.

Both of his brothers gave him the nod which said 'carry on'. He knew he'd always be able to count on Dane and Holt, no matter what. They knew what to do under any circumstances put before them, even if this proved to be a first, and hopefully a last. "Let's go then."

He raised his elbow for Lania to take his arm, and she did so very willingly. Oh, how he loved her, truly loved her. A new feeling for him, and one he would never take for granted. In fact, he planned to propose to her when the right time arrived. First, she needed to assume her Royal position. It might take him a while to get used to her new title since he considered her his lover, not his ruler. He'd have to find new ways of doing many things from this point on and into the future.

They entered one of the numerous main halls where several staff members worked due to the party outside. Jace walked up to them, Lania on his arm. "I want to introduce you to your new Royal Ruler, Lania Sloten."

Jace carefully watched their reactions, ready for battle if necessary. However, all the people in this room were women, so he didn't expect any retaliation. In fact, they all bowed gracefully the expected way when meeting a Ruler. Then in unison he heard them say, "My Lady," the typical, acceptable greeting.

Lania tapped his arm with her free hand as if she were saying thank you to him. She deserved all the respect they could give.

There wasn't a person around who wouldn't consider her far better than Raulf.

"Please rise and return to your duties." Lania looked at Jace. "Continue please. Mr. Bryton."

He led her out of the room and down the hallway. While they walked, he leaned his lips down to her ear and whispered, "I wasn't sure how to introduce you. Do you prefer DeMorgan or Sloten."

"You did perfect. I far prefer Sloten. We'll stick with that, especially since my sister remains First Lady DeMorgan."

Jace smiled at her while they continued down several hallways. Finally, they paused and the men behind them also stopped. "Where do you want to go, My Lady?"

"To the main Ruler's chamber. I need to put a call out to all current employees and make my announcement. One more time will be plenty."

"Which way then?"

"Straight. I'll show you."

Jace let Lania guide him by leaning against him or tugging on his arm. Four halls later they entered the room he'd become familiar with, even though he'd never entered from the hidden door in the back. Lania sat in the Ruler's seat which contained touch-commands all over one arm. She pushed one, and before he decided what it might be for, workers rushed into the room. He moved behind Lania and stood quietly at attention.

Once they all gathered inside the chamber, Lania stood and looked across the accumulation of people. He knew she planned to introduce herself, yet for some reason, he sensed a strange feeling of unease present around him. He watched her stand and take several steps forward to the edge of the raised dais area.

"Welcome. Since all of you have been inside working, I'd like to make an announcement. I am Lania Sloten, previously DeMorgan, and I will be your new Supreme Royal Ruler. Raulf is under arrest for my attempted murder, and many other crimes which have surfaced. My father, Romond Sloten, was the previous bloodline ruler, and since I am his first-born daughter, that now makes me your official Royal Ruler."

When Lania paused, the entire audience unanimously said, "My Lady," and bowed at the waist. She truly was the center of attention. Every soul residing on Lorton now knew Lania was alive, taking her place as official Royal Ruler, and the basics of what happened. When Lania finished her explanation of events to these last workers, she dismissed them back to work, and they ended with the usual, "My Lady," the proper statement of praise expected from anyone having an audience with their Royal.

Protocol always proved necessary, and they all showed proper respect for their new Supreme Ruler. Of course, he wanted to show her all of the normal respect, unfortunately, there was far more on his mind. His desire for Lania rose higher the longer he watched her. He never imagined any woman would ever hold so much control over him. He loved it, and he loved her. She was the woman of his heart, and he expected their love to grow even deeper each sun-cycle.

He allowed her the control. He loved her, and he did not give love or control easily. Never before had he given his love, trust, and control to anyone, except his brothers. He smiled and it worked well since the workers smiled their greetings to him while they passed on their way out of the large hall. He wasn't used to being in the public eye this much, and it made him a bit uncomfortable.

If he were going to be with Lania, he'd better get used to public appearances, and people eyeing him up and down when he stood with their Ruler. He didn't care, just so the beautiful woman's hand resting on his arm belonged to Lania, right where he wanted her to be. In his bed always remained his first choice. Some things must simply wait for the appropriate time and place. Several legalities stood between them at the moment, however; he knew Lania planned to change those issues quickly.

Jace began to move off the podium and take Lania with him when four guards and one woman entered the hall. He recognized the one woman, Marna, Lania's sister. Lania ran to her. She quickly grabbed her and pulled her into a big, sisterly hug before guiding her into the nearest empty room.

Jace waved off the guards who remained at the doorway where Lania and Marla entered. Before he went inside he told the guards to wait outside the door, then he quietly closed it behind him. The two sisters both let out screams and hugged each other tightly for the longest time. Somehow Lania looked happier to have this reunion than Marna did, although they both hugged and danced circles around the room. He felt invisible to them both.

His gut told him not to trust Marna. No particular reason, however; being life-mated to evil Raulf stood out enough to make him worry. He trusted Lania and her feelings for her sister, except her six-annual cycle absence gave Marna plenty of time to completely change. They finally stopped squealing and hugging then simply stared at each other.

"Oh, Lania, I've missed you so! I thought you were dead. Everyone on Lorton thought you were dead. What on Lorton happened to you?"

"Well, someone drugged me, and erased my entire memory. Then, they sent me to a very far away planet where I took care of children. Until Jace Bryton found me and brought me back."

"It's a miracle, sister! Not just anyone returns from the dead, you know?"

He carefully listened to both women laugh, and without a doubt, Lania's laugh sounded genuine, while Marna's laugh came across strained, with a totally fake tone to it. Obviously, he wanted to find a reason not to trust Marna. He didn't even know her laugh, so making assumptions could be wrong. He needed to get a grip on himself. His feelings were against nearly every person in the government, except for Gale, the woman who hired him.

Hopefully he'd find Gale somewhere in one of the massive buildings on the Royal Grounds. If he did, then he'd at least know she survived, remained safe and no one knew she'd hired Bryton Brothers' Security. He knew she'd been careful, yet the chance of being caught remained extremely high when going behind the backs of very important, well-known people, not to mention evil. She must truly hate her brother, even more than everyone else.

It may be odd to hate your brother, yet when evil ran so deep, it obviously left her with no choice. He must have treated her horribly in order to give her those feelings. He'd love to delve deeper into the relationship between Gale and Raulf, except he needed to find her first.

"Marna, are you okay? I mean, since you are life-mated to Raulf. I fear what he has done to you."

"I'm okay. It hasn't been fun." She looked at Lania's face. "I've survived. At least he hasn't beat me, or hurt me physically."

Lania nodded. "I'm relieved to hear you tell me that. Of course, you are aware of how Raulf is since you've been with him the past six annual-cycles. It must have been horrible. I'm so sorry, Marna."

Jace watched Lania give her sister a short hug. He also noticed Marna's reluctance to accept the gesture. Lania must also have sensed it because she let go rather quickly. Something did not feel right here, and he wasn't sure what, or why. Was it possible Marna picked up Raulf's way of doing things? Did she truly hate him? Or did she have feelings for her life-mate? Only time would reveal the truth. His gut told him Marna told nothing but lies to Lania. He trusted his gut, not Marna.

"Marna, you do know Raulf has been taken into custody and locked up. How do you feel about his arrest?" Lania stared at her sister.

"Too soon to know." Marna shook her head. "I suppose I'm relieved. It hasn't exactly sunk in yet."

Lania nodded and looked into Marna's eyes. "I understand. I have experienced many strange and different feelings recently, and my memory hasn't been back long enough for me to sort everything out. Sometimes I still have memory flashes which are hard to explain."

"Please try. I've worried about you, mourned you, missed you. Now I want to hear all about, well, everything I missed." Marna smiled at her sister. "I want to learn about everything you went through."

Jace saw many strange emotions in Marna's smile while he watched the two sisters chat and catch up on each other's experiences while apart. It seemed Lania revealed far more than Marna. What did she want? She might well be a control freak and want to stay in power, or she may truly be interested in Lania's experiences. Marna made it difficult to assess since he really didn't know her. He barely knew Lania well enough to be sure of what he was seeing, hearing and believing.

Then they both turned toward him. Lania walked over to him, took his hand, then together they went over to Marna. He'd go along with Lania, even though meeting with her sister felt completely strange to him.

"Marna, I'd like to introduce you to Jace Bryton. This is the man who found me and brought me back to Lorton. He works with his two brothers at Bryton Brothers' Security."

"Nice to meet you, Jace Bryton." Marna held out her hand."

Propriety said he must kiss the back of her hand, even if he didn't want to do so. He found it extremely difficult to bend his head down and give a quick kiss to her outstretched hand. He forced himself to be polite and proper so he quickly kissed the back of her hand, very glad it was now over. "Happy to meet you, My Lady." He was also forced to address her current position, whether she deserved it or not.

"Thank you, Mr. Bryton." Marna smiled at Jace. "You certainly are a handsome devil."

"Thank you, My Lady." She gave him a slight nod, then went back to chatting with Lania. He'd much rather observe than be a part of their conversation. There were a ton of questions he wanted to ask Marna, but he knew she'd never answer truthfully, so he didn't bother to ask. And for the love of planets, she'd called him handsome in front of Lania. Of course she didn't know about them, but still it caught him off guard.

For some odd reason, Marna's actions pushed him into a deep, forceful, and extremely protective mode for Lania's sake. He wanted to grab Lania and get her out of this place. It felt as if Raulf's evil had permeated everything. Or maybe Marna simply absorbed his evil and accepted it into her personality. Maybe all her, 'Dear Sister', stuff was a total act? His gut confirmed his feelings were right, even without justification or proof. He must have been in the security business too long, because he couldn't shake the doubts rampantly attacking his mind.

Where were his brothers? He assumed they'd be here to back him up. Hopefully everything outside this hall progressed better than in here. He certainly couldn't leave Lania alone with Marna. He remained the only person available to protect Lania from Marna and Raulf, if circumstances necessitated.

He held on to hope at the moment. Hope that Raulf's prison stay proved to be forever, a place where he couldn't hurt anyone. He also hoped in the process that Marna did not become a problem for Lania. That may be pushing it, he knew, yet he also knew how much Lania loved her sister, and he'd hate to see their relationship fall apart.

Since the sisters were busy talking again, he walked back to the wall, where he watched and listened. He only remained leaning against the wall here to protect his precious Lania. He loved the woman who held control over him, the woman he intended to spend the rest of his life with. However; he had zero control over these two sisters. Lania may require his help here to remain becoming The Royal Ruler of Lorton. His future with Lania now lay in the hands of fate.

Lania. Her name now permanently engraved on his heart.

Chapter Twenty-Three

Lania stared at her sister and wondered where their closeness went? She no longer felt like a sister to Marna. Since there had not been a conversation between them in over six annual-cycles, she wanted to ask Marna thousands of questions. Hopefully her sister's answers were honest and true, although she sensed a reluctance in Marna and wondered if Raulf held influence over her.

The Bryton Triplets flashed in her mind. Three men attached to each other in ways she never thought possible. conversations without speaking, and here she was having difficulty trying talk to Marna. She always wanted to feel like a twin sister to Marna, but they were never truly that close, something she now realized. Her previous assumptions had been so very wrong. The close bond between herself and her sister was only what she wanted, not what they actually had.

"Marna, please tell me about life-mating Raulf. Did he force you?" Her sister stared at her like she did not believe she even asked the question. She could only wait for an answer which Marna did not want to give.

"Well, aaah...forced is a harsh word." Marna shrugged her shoulders. "Not really, but at the same time, I did not exactly have a choice."

Lania shook her head. "So, he forced you." Her sister simply stared and shrugged her shoulders a couple more times and tipped her head back and forth. Strange behavior. Marna never acted this way before, at least not that she remembered. "So, which is it? You can be honest with me."

"Oh, can I?" Marna shook her head. "I'm not sure. You come marching up on the podium, taking control, arresting Raulf and shoving me into a room like a prisoner. Now you say be honest?"

"I'm still your sister." Lania looked into Marna's eyes. "Talk to me. I'm here for you, you know I am." She watched her sister take a deep breath while she contemplated her answer.

"Do I?" She shook her head. "I don't think you are. You've already shoved me back so you can take my place, or whatever you're doing. There's never been a woman in charge before, so good luck with your plan."

"My first plan is to put Raulf away for the rest of his life. You have yet to tell me your true feelings about him." Her sister stared at her, then gave her the strangest looking smile, one she never saw before.

"Really? Wow. You sound like a conceited bitch." Marna groaned. "They used to call me, 'My Lady' and you just stole my title from me. You also stole my life-mate and threw him in prison. Then you saunter around and pretend to be my dear sister with my best interest at heart?" She shook her head. "I don't think so!"

Her sister's voice was so loud they probably heard her three hallways down. This conversation had really taken a bad turn. "Marna, I am very sorry you see it that way. I.."

"Sorry?" Marna laughed.

Her sister's sinister laugh sent horrible chills through her body. Simply talking to Marna had turned difficult, something she never remembered. They may not have been as close as she thought, but they never had problems talking to each other. "Marna, you are only an annual-cycle younger than me. I always thought of you like a twin sister." It seemed Marna totally changed in her absence. Oh, she expected changes in her sister, but never this much.

Marna walked closer to Lania. "I can't believe you're here. You were supposed to be dead! We went to your funeral! What a joke!"

She shook her head. "It sounds like you wanted me dead. I'm sorry to disappoint you."

"How did Mr. Bryton find you?" She glared at Lania. "I guess I should ask the stupid man himself since he's still standing over there in the background." Marna looked toward the back wall. "Well, Bryton, how did you find her, and know to bring her here?"

Jace took several steps toward her sister, and Lania thought he might want to kill her for calling him stupid. Instead, he stepped up, took his place beside her, the way he always did. He cleared his throat and shook his head

"I am not sure how to address you. For now, I will simply call you Marna. I went to Extram on behalf of a client, which is all I can say. Then while walking through the jungle I ran into your sister, Lania. I recognized her from all the vids, however; she did not know her own name. I then made an executive decision to bring her here when I completed my assignment."

"Well, aren't you Mr. Right!" Marna laughed. "Were you hoping for a reward? Bringing back a dead woman should pay something. Right?" She laughed harder.

Jace backed up. "I shall leave this to you two ladies."

Lania wondered why Jace did not attack her sister. It appeared he felt these issues should remain between sisters, and he may be right. Jace did not know any of the answers to their sisterly disagreement, but she also knew who he protected. Plus, the ugly look on Marna's face was enough to send anyone away. She nearly laughed at her sister's horrible grin.

"What's the matter, Mr. Right, can't handle me?" Marna giggled. "Guess I need to call you stupid again!"

Marna literally yelled the last statement at Jace. Never had her sister acted this badly and disrespectful toward anyone. Then it hit her, before Raulf. "I suggest you hold your tongue, if you know what is good for you."

"Fine. Tell me again what you did there, on Extram, for six annual-cycles?"

Her sister stared at her as if she were her worst enemy. "I took care of children."

"I see. So, you just took care of kids for over six annual-cycles?"

"I took care of young children for the remote community. They treated me horrible. They made me feel like a piece of trash. They barely spoke to me, unless they wanted to reprimand or demand. Never a nice word." She hung her head and stared at the floor. "I endured far worse than horrible." She looked up and saw complete confusion on Marna's face. "They barely fed me. They would throw me a slice of bread and give me a glass of water, if I were lucky. Once in a while a bit of protein, but not often. I barely had enough strength most of the time to walk with the little children to the play areas. I guess they figured it would keep me from escaping."

Lania reached out and took Marna's hand in hers. "We have always been close. Didn't you ever feel I might still be alive?" She gave Marna's hand a gentle squeeze. "I believe if I'd had my memory, I'd have felt you still."

Marna jerked her hand away from Lania. "Well, I didn't feel you, and we have never been close. That's what you wanted, not me. And as for babysitting," she laughed, "you were supposed to be dead. Raulf saw to it, or so he said. Too much confusion going on at the time, and everything happening around me. After that injection I gave you, I assumed you'd be killed without remembering a thing. We sent you away to die, not babysit!"

Lania looked deeply into her sister's eyes. "Finally! The truth. You never planned to see me again. Well, I'm here, and if you saw me when I first arrived, I looked dead. I stood skinnier than that pole over there." Lania pointed to the wall across from them.

"I see you all right. You should be dead! Instead, you came back here, and now my entire life is ruined! I'm not happy about any of your antics. Not one bit. And if I have my way," she rushed up to Lania and shoved her shoulders backwards, "none of it will happen!"

Lania stood still and tried to regain her composure. "Don't be so upset!" Marna rushed up to her again and shoved her shoulders even harder this time.

"You show up from the dead, take away my life-mate, my power, then have the audacity to tell me not to be upset?" She laughed in Lania's face. "Really?" She pushed her . "You've got to be kidding, bitch!"

Marna's last push was hard and she almost fell backwards. When Lania looked behind her, she saw Jace moving closer to her, and she feared what might happen next. He could kill Marna so fast she would never know what happened.

Jace glared at Marna. "Touch Lania again and you're a dead woman, and never doubt a stupid man."

Lania saw his hands fisted at his sides and she knew what he wanted to do, but she also knew Jace respected women. Even if they demonstrated horrible behavior, he would not beat a woman, especially not her sister. He might remove her in a manner she hated, but she would still be in one piece.

"Wait a minute, dear sister of mine." Lania stared into Marna's mean eyes and decided it was past time to be tough. "First of all, Raulf is still my legal life-mate, so technically, you are not life-mated to Raulf. Plus, your power belongs to me!" Lania nodded. "I realize how wrong I was to think for a moment that we were close and shared an intimate, sisterly love bond. "

"Finally, you get it!" Marna laughed. "Never thought you were so slow." She continued to laugh.

Marna's laugh became so loud and evil the entire building probably heard it. She could only shake her head at the sister she once loved. "What has happened to you?" Lania wanted to cry. Her sister continued to laugh in her face, and she somehow knew she'd lost her forever. Plus, she now knew Marna played a huge part in her disappearance. "You called me a bitch? How dare you?"

"You are, right now, and I want nothing to do with you. Neither does anyone close to me. Especially Raulf!"

"Really? Raulf isn't close to anyone!" She ducked and felt the breeze of Marna's fist when it barely missed her face. Her punch would have hurt, Marna now rubbed her knuckles since she hit the wide, very solid, support pillar behind her. Lania could not stop a small giggle, even though it made matters worse while Marna wiped her bloody knuckles on her skirt. She stood up straight and looked Marna in the eye. "I stated a fact, and you try to punch me? What has come over you?"

"You have, bitch. If you want me on your good side, let Raulf out of prison right now!"

"That is *not* possible. He's committed a long list of crimes and must pay the price for his actions."

"Really? You'll have to prove all those 'so-called crimes', and I doubt you can." Marna stepped back.

Lania noticed her sister wanted space, especially since Jace now stood at her side. Truthfully, she wanted Marna gone. "Just so you know, I want nothing to do with your life-mate, except to put him away forever."

"Well, you're living up to your new name, bitch!"

"You can call me any name you like, but it changes nothing. My biggest regret is you're no longer my sister. You're definitely not the sister I once loved and trusted."

"Regret? You don't look like you regret anything. You're power hungry and want revenge against me for taking Raulf away from you!"

"You couldn't be more wrong if you tried! I never wanted the monster in the first place. You on the other hand..."

"Stop right there! You have no right to call him a monster! Did he ever hit you? Hurt you? No, he didn't. So, you need to rethink that name, and do it fast!"

"He never physically hurt me, but he did murder our father. Think what you want about him. His life is in The High Council's hands now, where it needs to be."

"So, you say. You might be sorely surprised."

Lania stared at her disillusioned sister. Or did she have council members on her side? It sounded like a warning she should carefully remember. She no longer felt trust, or anything good between them. Raulf must have gotten to Marna, without a doubt. Before Raulf, Marna never acted, or talked like this. Lania felt as if her heart had been viciously ripped in half. The half she'd given to her sister now forever gone.

"Too bad you'll never know what you missed. Raulf is fantastic in bed! So good you'd never believe it. Thank the stars you rejected him because he couldn't take his hands off me! We made love so many times no person could count that high! Every time fantastic. You have no idea what you missed, bitch!"

"That's the best you can throw at me?" Lania shook her head. With her previous world completely shattered, she tried to wrap her brain around the 'new Marna'.

"I regret your memory returned. I was promised that drug removed it forever! Unfortunately, they were wrong!"

"I assumed someone close to me gave the injection." Lania took a deep breath. "I never really suspected you."

"Of course not. That's why it was so easy!"

Marna laughed so loud it hurt her ears. How had she been so naive about her sister and her deep-seated evil personality? At least she would never make that mistake again.

"Nothing to say, bitch?" Marna continued to laugh. "What could a rejected virgin say about sex anyway?" She laughed louder.

"I have one thing left to say." Lania waved at the guards who Jace already let in and now stood behind her. "Arrest this woman immediately, and securely lock her in the prison." She stood motionless while Marna's hands were secured behind her back. The guards then began to escort her out of the room, except Marna continued to laugh and kick her legs wildly in a miserable attempt to cause as much trouble as possible. She even threw her body around in her continued effort to stop the guards from dragging her across the floor while holding her arms.

The poor guards were forced to drag her since she refused to walk, or cooperate with them in any way. Due to Marna's lack of help, the guards still managed to maneuver her out of the room and through the double doors on the far side, across from where they stood. She felt sorry for the guards due to the difficult time Marna gave them. Soon Marna would cry the blues and try to get someone, anyone, to release her. Once she legally gained her position as Royal Ruler, Marna would spend the rest of her life in a cell where she obviously belonged.

Now that Lania thought about it, her sister had not changed completely. In her younger days she still had a wild and crazy temper at times, which had grown immensely since the last time she had seen a demonstration. Marna never accepted defeat without crying and making a huge fuss. She always pled her case, and insisted she was right about everything, especially when she was wrong.

Marna was no longer right, or in charge of anything. She had completely defeated Marna, and she would never call Marna her sister again. Warm arms wrapped around her and she recognized Jace's consoling hug, and she turned into his embrace. "Close the doors first, please."

"Yes, My Lady." He hurried to the door, shut and locked it, then returned to Lania. "Are you okay?"

"No." She shook her head and looked into Jace's soothing blue eyes. "Maybe. I don't know. Part of me wants to cry my eyes out, and the other part only wants revenge. I'm still absorbing what just happened." Jace hugged her tightly for a moment then eased her back. “It reminds me of eating some of the moldy bread I was given in that horrible place.”

“It always hurts when someone close to you betrays you. It’s something you may never fully get over, and that’s okay.” Jace looked into her eyes. “The person you loved dearly just stabbed you in the back and ripped your heart out. You’re entitled to cry if you want. I’m here for you.”

“Oh, Jace, my love. Thank you. I can always count on you.”

“You can, I promise. I will never hurt you. You can trust me, My Love. You can always trust me. Count on it.”

She hugged him tightly and savored the feel of his warm body.

“You’re shaking. I’m so sorry this happened. You know what you must do, My Lady.” He squeezed her tight. “I love you with all my heart. There is nothing more you need to know right now.”

Tears rolled down her cheeks. She’d held them back too long, now they had a mind of their own, flowing out without her permission. She felt his hands on her shoulders guiding her back. He pulled a small wipe-cloth from his pocket and began to dry her cheeks. She looked up at him. “I don’t know what I would do without you.”

Jace smiled. “I hope you never have to find out.”

Chapter Twenty-Four

Jace took a deep breath. "By the stars! You have no idea how badly I wanted to punch out Marna. She was horrible to Lania and to me. That woman sure does have a mouth on her!"

Holt groaned at his brother. "Jace, you realize Lania is no longer your lady, she is literally, My Lady now, and we're the ones who helped her return to her position. I'm glad you followed rules and behaved yourself.

"It was no easy task, Bro. You should have heard what she was saying. Everything she said was disgusting to say the least."

"What did Lania think about her sister?"

Jace could not help, or stop shaking his head. "She no longer has a sister. Her words, not mine."

"Wow. Must have been bad for sure. But you need to let it go. Lania will contact you, if and when she needs you."

"I understand. I do." He stared at Holt. "Can't I at least see her?" Jace stared at both of his brothers who were not madly in love with anyone. Love did strange things to a man, a fact that just sank in firsthand, and very painfully.

"She hasn't even been gone twenty time-units yet." Dane shook his head. "You'll be able to see her again. I'm sure. In the meantime, you have to adjust. I know you remember how you felt before you fell for the beautiful princess, don't you?"

"I don't know what you mean, Dane, I haven't fallen." Dane laughed at him and so did Holt. He never could fool his brothers, no matter how hard he tried, it always proved to be a huge waste of time. "Okay, fine. Maybe I have."

"Maybe?" Dane slowly shook his head at his brother. "You don't have to apologize. If I were in your shoes, I'd have fallen for her, too. What's not to love about her? You're one lucky man. We're trying to tell you to quit pretending you two are not in love. We know better."

"I have to right now if I want to be with her. It doesn't seem promising at all, and you both know what I mean." Jace looked at his brothers sitting across from him and smiled. "You're right about one thing; nothing is bad about Lania. Except now she's untouchable."

"Hey! How long have we worked together, Jace? You know how we believe nothing is impossible where the Bryton Brothers are concerned. We'll help you find a way to be with your woman." Holt knocked his knuckles against the tabletop.

Jace took a deep breath. "This is different, and both of you know it. We've never dealt with the rulers of Lorton in this way before. Plus, none of them hired us, remember? Lania may have been the object of our endeavor, but we were hired by someone else."

"Well, the government of Lorton should be extremely grateful to us for returning Lania to her rightful position. Not one person liked Raulf, including himself!" Dane interjected.

Holt nodded. "You're both right, not one citizen on Lorton liked him!"

"Except Marna." All three brothers chuckled slightly, and it felt good. "Having two brothers like you guys, who are so honorable, loyal and talented, always proves to be a pure and perfect blessing to me, and I'm glad you're both here to help me." Jace shook his head while staring at his brothers. "I know, you guys never thought I'd say such a thing." He smiled. "I also know if anyone can help me see Lania, it's you two."

"Count on it." Holt stood, walked to the info-station, grabbed his portable, then returned to the table and sat back down. "Okay. Let's hear some ideas I can put in here and test run. You know how it goes. We've done this before for our clients."

Dane smiled at Jace. "Remember one thing, Jace. If I fall in love and need help with my woman, promise you'll help me?"

"Same for me, Bro," Holt added.

Jace smiled while he nodded at his brothers. “You both have my promise.” He looked each of his brothers directly in their eyes. “I’m not exactly a client, yet I certainly need your help with Lania.”

“We know you do, and we’re well aware of how you feel.” Holt stared at Jace. “The procedure is still the same. Now, let’s discuss a plan.”

“I can’t think right now.” Jace scratched his forehead. “I suppose I need to make an appointment for an audience with the ruler.” Jace thought for a moment. “Make it for our firm, rather than me, an individual. It may sound more important, and less personal. We have to clear the booking criteria. You can’t very well say, I love her and have to see her.” Jace laughed.

“Of course not. Fine. Bryton Brothers will book an appointment first thing in the sun-cycle. What will be the nature of our business?” Holt asked.

“Good question, Bro. We need to think of the perfect reason.” Dane leaned back in his chair. “What if we say we need to settle the final details of our service? We might throw in we have information concerning Raulf which Lania must hear immediately. Sorry, Supreme Royal Ruler, Lania DeMorgan.”

“Must we use that name?” Jace asked, even though he knew the answer.

“You know good and well what we have to call her, especially since we want a formal audience,” Holt said.

Dane leaned forward. “Jace, this is the time to tell us about who hired us to find Lania in the first place. You never said, and it is something which has never happened in our firm before. I know you realize it.”

“You’re right. She might be a key to everything.” He looked at both of his brothers who stared at him with questioning looks on their faces. He’d never mentioned the woman’s name to his brothers, and if he wanted to succeed, there could be no secrets. “The woman’s name is Gale.” He listened while both brothers gasped. “I know. She’s Raulf’s sister, but she’s nothing like her evil brother. She hired us, and paid us well, so we have no problems with her.”

“The question is,” Holt paused and took a deep breath, “why?”

Jace tipped his head sideways. "She feels the same as everyone. She hates her brother and would prefer to be brotherless. She also wanted Raulf removed from power. We owe Gale a huge vote of thanks for returning Lania to her rightful place, which helped us get rid of the evil controller."

Holt scratched his head. "Nothing about this job has been simple, or even made sense most of the time. I wonder how Gale even knew Lania might still be alive?"

Jace was so busy finding Lania and bringing her back, he hadn't really thought about Gale's knowledge. "My best guess is she may have overheard a conversation she shouldn't have. Does it matter? We completed our mission and returned Lania to Lorton."

"You completed the mission. Holt and I didn't do anything except go to the ball with you and offer our support. You did all the hard work, Bro."

"We're still all in this together. I have a really strong feeling that we must check on Lania. I sense something is desperately wrong. I don't know what. I feel something bad has either happened, or is going to happen."

"I feel that, too." Dane stood and began to pace, then stopped and looked at Jace. "What do we need to do?"

"Request a meeting with Lania. We'll think of a reason, but we need to find out first-hand if everything is okay. She won't be able to contact us if anything goes wrong. Until Raulf and his life-mate are out of the picture for good, and safely put away, Lania will remain in severe danger."

"I'm in," Holt said.

Dane nodded. "I'm in."

"Good. We'll petition for an audience right away and see what happens. The worst scenario is we're rejected, and the best is we proceed."

"You might be right." Holt stood and walked to the info-center.

Dane chuckled. "We kept him from his keyboard too long."

"I suppose we did, but he's tough. He can't be away very long or he has withdrawals. Most addicts go for therapy." Jace laughed. "There's no help for Holt's problem." They both laughed. Holt looked over at them and shook his head. Holt well knew he and

Dane always joked about him and his info-center addiction, even if it wasn't totally true. They did need Holt there since he truly functioned better there than either of them. It would always be Holt's specialty, even if they did have to do their part occasionally.

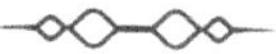

Lania listened to the next group of men who came to see her. They wanted the capitol to purchase weapons from them for protection. Not anytime soon at the prices they asked, so she politely dismissed them. She hurried through the next group, then her heart caught in her throat when the Bryton Brothers walked through the entryway and up to the podium all three exhibiting their masculine, sexy strides while they toward her. She wanted to run to Jace and throw herself into his arms. If the possibility for him to hold her tightly the way he'd done so many times before were possible, she'd be so elated no one could stop her.

They were asking for a private hearing due to the complexity and significance of the matter. She willingly granted their request, and they all retreated into the smaller, private meeting room behind where she sat, next to the comfortable area. It just felt good to get out of the oversized chair. She walked to the head of the table, then excused the guards in the room on the basis of privacy. They all quietly waited for them to leave before they took deep breaths to relax a bit.

"I am sooooo...happy to see you three!"

Jace put his arms on the table and leaned forward. "Is everything all right? Are you having any problems?"

"Well, my sister turned against me, and I ordered her arrested, which you already know, Jace, since you were there. I hope the guards are on my side and not Raulf's, or the problems will be great."

Dane cleared his throat. "My Lady, do you have any reason to believe someone is working against you?"

"Mainly Marna and Raulf. Marna is the one who poisoned me to erase my memory. She played several parts in my fate. She even threw it all in my face, like I deserved it. She probably would have killed me if the guards were not there, and of course you, Jace. I don't really know what else to say. Something with my sister drastically changed, or at least it seems like it did. I suppose it's too early to tell who's on whose side at the moment. I believe the three of you understand."

Holt nodded. "You're correct, My Lady."

Jace tapped the table with his thumb, then looked up. "My Lady, we are all so very sorry about your sister." He cleared his throat. "Of course, I filled my brothers in on Marna." He shook his head. "I always felt very uneasy about her. I just never told you since I had nothing to back it up. Now I understand why."

Holt looked at Lania. "Do you have a way of contacting us should you need our help?"

Lania took a deep breath then exhaled. "I really don't know. I suppose not, unless I go through channels, then I have to count on everyone doing their jobs the way I expect them to, and not take Raulf's side over mine. If they do, then my message will fail."

Holt reached into his pants pocket, pulled something out and laid it on the table. He pushed it toward Lania and it rolled into her hands. "That My Lady, will alert us immediately if you need us. Keep it in your pocket and press the button on the end, and we will come running instantly."

"Trust him, My Lady, he knows what he's talking about." Jace smiled at Lania. "Holt's tiny little toy object there will alert our system, and we'll know you're in trouble."

Lania chuckled slightly when he called Holt's device a toy. He and Dane and did love to tease Holt and she had fun watching them do it.

"If you press the top of the," Jace smiled, "toy, it will go off and we'll find you. It has a homing device which shows us your exact location. Never fear, the Bryton Brothers are here." Jace nodded. "You already know our silly saying, don't you?"

"I, for one, never call that saying, 'silly', and yes sir, I understand it very well." She wanted to throw her arms around Jace and kiss him madly to thank him for being here. She forced herself to maintain proper protocol, especially since the guards watched them through the soundproof glass, not to mention his two brothers. "I thank you from the bottom of my heart, I truly do. I hope this little thing works. Hopefully, I will not need it. Just in case, I will keep it on me at all times."

"Please do, My Lady. You must stay safe." Jace leaned back in his chair.

Lania felt upset by the anxious look on her lover's face. His expression probably matched hers, neither of which was good. She wanted to be intimately in his arms the entire moon-cycle, and every sun-cycle of her life. She loved the man. She had to find a way to have him accepted to be her life-mate. Jace still needed to make the choice about her and ask her, of course. She so wanted to co-rule Lorton together with Jace. She might be dreaming, but if she had any authority in the government, she planned to use it to make her wishes happen the way she wanted.

"My Lady, please tell us if you have any needs right now. We'll be happy to help in any way possible." Holt looked Lania in the eye. "You will tell us, won't you?"

"Absolutely. I trust the three of you completely. I owe you all my life. I would not be here had Jace not found me and brought me back home. Don't worry. I'll ring for you if I need help. You can count on me, my handsome gentlemen."

"Great." Dane leaned forward. "Handsome, are we?" He chuckled. "We are identical triplets of course." He tipped his head from side to side. "Is there anything we can do before we leave?"

"Not unless you can get Raulf executed immediately." Lania smiled at the men before her. "Just kidding. I realize I should not joke about Raulf, or his execution. When it comes to the evil one, I cannot help myself. He is a complete unacceptable joke. Although what he has done is no joke. I also don't know if he still has any people on his side, people who could free him. You understand, I'm sure."

"We do, My Lady." Jace stared at his Ruler.

"That, My Lady, could become a very serious problem should there be any truth to the thought," Dane said.

"Gentlemen, I have no proof, nor have I heard anything. It is just one of those feelings that drive a person insane and never happen."

Holt leaned closer on the table. "Just remember my device if such a time should come. We will be here for you, we promise."

Jace nodded. "That we will, and you know you can count on us, My Lady." He smiled at Lania.

Oh, how she loved his smile. Unfortunately, it made her want to kiss him passionately, even more than before. However, kissing could not happen now, or anytime soon. This situation felt impossible, and she wanted it to end fast, like this very moment. "I really do appreciate your device," she held up Holt's toy, and I will keep all three of you near and dear. You have helped me beyond my wildest dreams. From getting my memory back until now. You three are the best. The very best." She laughed. "Although," she smiled at them, "I believe you already know that, don't you?" She laughed again.

Now all three brothers laughed with her, and it felt good. At least she could trust these three capable men, who she knew would never let her down. Needing them on a moment's notice had been on her agenda before. At least now she knew they remained close and ready. She found it extremely difficult to keep her distance from Jace when she wanted him so desperately.

By the stars! The things she wanted which only Jace could give her. "Well, gentlemen, I do love having you here with me, but I do not wish to raise suspicion. So, I shall end this meeting before we have too much fun. I have your device and will keep it close. Rest assured. Thank you again for the visit. Really, there is no way I can thank you enough. Seeing you three has been a huge help to me. I must say, I have missed you Brytons."

Lania stood and began to walk out of the room. From the corner of her eye she saw all three brothers rise from their chairs and stand at attention the way they were required to do when a ruler left the room. They followed protocol perfectly, for which she remained grateful. The one thing she truly needed to protect was her intimate relationship with the Bryton Brothers and play like they were simply men doing business with her. She feared that someone, anyone in the Royal quarters, or close to her, might find out, or suspect she was close to the Bryton's. Especially her relationship with Jace. Her two assistants aside, they were safe, she trusted them with secrets many times.

All three of them stood so handsome in front of her, although her heart belonged only to Jace. He represented everything she wanted in a life-mate. As a man, Jace presented the most attractive specimen, ever. The only possible comparisons would be his brothers. Yet she felt Jace had special qualities that pulled her to him. He satisfied her in every way she could think of, and he cared deeply and passionately. He wanted her the same, or more than she wanted him.

She felt very sure of Jace and counted on him for nearly everything in her life. The High Council must accept him as First Man of Lorton. She wanted him to be her co-ruler, although experience taught her long ago to fight one battle at a time. Although, she could never call him a co-ruler to anyone except him. That made her chuckle.

She walked down the long hall toward her personal quarters because she needed some time to relax, and to get Jace off her mind. It may not be possible, even though she needed to give it a good try. At the moment, his handsome, sexy face filled her mind. She shook her head. There were a lot of issues put before her this sun-cycle she needed to concentrate on and find solutions to solve. Her problem was her every thought turned to Jace and not her duty. She decided she needed to go to her room and be alone for a while and concentrate on everything requiring her attention, not simply one man.

Chapter Twenty-Five

"I think things went well with Lania. Don't you guys?" Jace looked at his brothers and wondered why they grinned at him the way they were. "Oh, come on." Now they laughed at him in an overly knowing way. They usually knew what he was thinking, or what they imagined he was thinking. Either way, they'd be right. His thoughts were about Lania, and were very specific to them both, and he refused to share with anyone, especially his brothers.

"We realize what you're thinking, Jace." Dane couldn't stop laughing.

"I'd rather you didn't." He wanted them to stop. "Can we get down to business?" He waited while they stopped their laughing and sobered up enough to talk. "Fine. Now, did you notice Lania did not seem like herself?"

"What exactly do you mean? You know her way better than we do." Dane stared at Jace.

Holt leaned toward his brother. "Dane's right, you know. Explain, please."

"Well, she looked worried, and seemed overly nervous. She even admitted there could be a plot floating around against her. Remember?"

"Yes, she did, but she's in a position she's never been in before, so it seemed normal for her to be nervous and having strange thoughts." Dane tapped his fingers on the table. "I did sense some severe unease in her though."

"You're right." Jace couldn't help shaking his head. "She seemed overly worried about Raulf and Marna. She's bound to be stressed, yet she seemed way different to me. More like she feared something about to happen. I don't know. Maybe I'm too close to her." Jace stared at the floor a moment.

"No. You're right. She seemed the same way to me." Holt tilted his head to one side. "What do you want to do?"

"There's nothing we can do until she rings Holt's gadget. By the way, I'm very glad you thought to give her the little device you made. Thanks, Bro."

"You're welcome." Holt shook his head. "You're too busy thinking about Lania which is messing with your brain."

"Yes Holt, you're right. Now get off my case." Jace stared at his brother until they smiled at each other.

"Fine, I'll step back." Holt chuckled softly. "You know I love to tease you."

"I know. Your teasing is just too close to home right now."

"Sorry. Bad habit."

"Maybe I need to teach you some etiquette, brother dearest."

Holt raised his hands. "I'm sorry. Okay?"

"For now." Jace looked at Dane. "Teach him some etiquette, will ya?"

"Be happy to. Are you going to hold him down for me?"

Jace smiled. Dane tried to lift the mood, and he did make a funny comment. If life were easier, possibly his comment might be really funny. Of course, their business had been built on large problems requiring complex solutions. He only hoped they didn't get another job too quickly. Lania's safety came first in his book. It didn't matter how hard he tried, he seriously worried about her safety, and getting her back. She looked so beautiful at their meeting this sun-cycle. Too beautiful to ignore. How long could he possibly keep this up?

"No, I'm not holding him down. You're on your own. I have other things to do."

"Well, it's getting late, guys, and I'm tired, so, I'm out of here." Jace stood, pushed his chair in then walked down the hall to his room. Time to dream about Lania, which was his only way to get close to her. If he couldn't hold her in his arms in real time, at least he could dream he held her while he slept away the moon-cycle. Alone.

Lania sat in her room, her mind totally on Jace. She felt fantastic thinking about him, even if she needed to stop. She hadn't heard a word about her sister's arrest. Of course, she wondered how she was doing. On second thought, based on the way Marna acted, she had no reason to care. It was obvious by Marna's behavior and words she wanted to get rid of her, fast. Her sister hated her, and she despised the idea, even if it was true. Plus, she would never dismiss or forget what happened between them. Unfortunately, the horrible memory would now be buried in her very soul forever.

Understanding why, or how, Marna had feelings for Raulf remained completely impossible. She did not even try to hide the fact she loved the evilest man on planet Lorton, even if loving Raulf was totally incomprehensible to her. Were Raulf and Marna two of a kind? It seemed like it based on the way Marna acted toward her. Marna got her out of the way once before, and the last time they met, she acted like she wanted to do it all over again. Possibly even kill her. Had Marna always been so unfeeling and she simply never noticed? Too late to wonder. Nothing would change Marna's mind set now. To even think it possible would prove a fatal mistake.

The moment she decided to take off her official robe, her door burst open. She screamed when four men rushed in, grabbed her and officially apprehended her. Cuffs were clamped tightly on her wrists, then they shoved her out of her room and into the hall. "Where are you taking me? Let go of me this instant!" She wrestled against the cuffs They weren't coming off. "I'm your Ruler! Let me go! Now!"

"You're nothing. We listen to the real Ruler, Raulf DeMorgan! Now shut up, bitch, and do what we say!"

Lania didn't believe her own ears. Raulf must have escaped, and she feared her sister too. She just entered a complete nightmare. Then she remembered the Bryton Brothers gift to her. No, she'd wait till she was alone somewhere. Probably when they threw her into a cell. At least Jace would have the ability to find her. Thank the stars for his reliability. Not many women had the pleasure to say their man saved them twice from strange circumstances. Of course, she had to wait until her next rescue took place. At least the device was safe in her pocket.

Raulf's guards walked so fast she couldn't keep up and lost her footing. The moment she faltered and fell, they grabbed her and simply pulled her by her arms down the long halls, then out of the building, bouncing her off tiles and cement and every stair, to the bottom of the staircase in the dark moon-cycle. She knew exactly where they planned to take her. Prison. It occupied the building they headed for. Her underarms hurt where large, strange hands gripped her so tight, their fingers dug into her skin, all the way to the bone. These men were muscular and huge. They didn't care. She had become their enemy.

They dragged her through the open doorway, down the prison halls, through locking gates until they finally reached the rooms along the end of the hall. It was where they put the most hated detainees. Prisoners who lived in these tiny little rooms basically received no attention, ever. They truly did want to forget about her. Just then something tingled on the floor.

The guards immediately stopped and nearly jerked her shoulders out of her body! When she looked down, she saw one of the guards pick up the small device Holt gave her. She could not say anything since she knew they would never give it back to her. The ugly man put it in his pocket, then they continued to drag her to the last cubicle, shoving her inside, locking the door behind them.

She began to panic since she could no longer contact the Bryton Brothers. Her future looked far more dismal than a moment beforc. More like impossible. Even if they permitted her to live, she might never see Jace again, and the thought scared her to the core, especially since she wanted and needed him so badly. What should she do? One glance around the tiny room revealed an area smaller than the closet in her own room, plus it seemed even darker inside. It felt like her old home for the past six annual-cycles. Totally unacceptable.

If she ever got out of this mess, her priority would be to make someone pay, and she knew exactly who, the evilest man alive, Raulf! She also knew her adoring sister played a major part in her abduction. She now knew Marna's true colors, so she really was alone. Only one person on Lorton truly cared about her, and she could not get to him. Jace may never know what happened to her.

Surly if Jace loved her the way he claimed, he would come looking for her when he failed to hear from her, but she had serious doubts about him having any success. How had things gone so terribly wrong when nearly every single person alive hated Raulf? Who set him free? Last she heard, he was safely locked away, like she was right now. Obviously, someone lied.

Chapter Twenty-Six

Jace paced behind his brothers who worked in the info-station. It had been twelve sun-cycles without one word from Lania. He had no idea what she might be doing. The gadget Holt gave her was quiet and constantly put her in the same location. Holt said she'd obviously taken it off her person and left it sitting on a shelf somewhere. Right or wrong, the device indicated a warehouse of some kind, they were not exactly sure, but the location was close to her quarters. Too much time already passed without a word, and his worry grew moment to moment.

Lania's lack of communication bothered him. He feared someone took Holt's device from her. If the device were still in her possession, she'd have sent some kind of message by now, and the device would indicate she moved to many different locations. It was obvious to him she couldn't call for help. He'd only heard dead silence. If nothing else, she would have had her assistant contact him. She would do something, instead he received nothing.

This new situation drove him to incessant worry. Neither of his brothers truly felt anything was wrong, they simply thought Lania simply became too busy and didn't have time to send a message. That was a remote possibility, yet the strong, nagging feeling deep inside him kept screaming something very bad had happened to Lania. It came from the rare connection he and Lania shared. They were on a different level, but connected all the same.

Without a word from Lania, he needed to guess what may have happened in the Royal Palace. Why? Why? Why? Not a word. He'd bonded with her on a level he couldn't explain any better than the bond he shared with his brothers. He felt deep in his soul something huge had happened. She claimed to love him totally, and completely, yet she couldn't take time to send him a small message? It made no sense for her to pull away like this. He'd move planets and galaxies to send a message to the woman he loved. In fact, he'd done exactly that, yet received no answer.

Could it be possible her feelings were not strong like she claimed? He'd told her the truth about how much he loved her and wanted her. Had she simply been stringing him along? He shook his head. The Lania he knew was not like most women, and she'd never do such a thing to him. Then again, one never knew until the planets crashed. He had to wait since a woman in Lania's position maintained all the power and control. At the moment he had none.

It seemed Lania just turned into the perfect example of why he'd kept his heart safe all these annual-cycles by never becoming involved with anyone. Yet, he willingly gave his heart to her, honestly and completely. Now it could be time to lock it back up tightly once again. No woman could be worth so much stress. This sun-cycle he'd force himself to think of anything except Lania.

If she no longer loved him, or cared, then neither did he. He'd force himself to forget her faster than he fell for her. Not what he wanted to do, even though it may be the only thing he could do for them both. He owed it to his brothers to be an active member of the Bryton Brothers' Security team, and he knew he hadn't been doing his part.

"Dane, Holt, I need to apologize to you both. I've been shirking my duties, and I'm sorry. I'm back now, and stronger than ever." He smiled at the two faces who stared at him in shock.

"It's okay, Bro, we totally understand." Dane shook his head. "We know you're upset about Lania, and her lack of communication. We're sorry you've had to go through this."

Holt nodded. "You know we're here for you anytime you need us."

"Thanks. I appreciate you two. You're both the best." Jace nodded several times. "You also know I always need you both. We're inseparable. And I'm eternally grateful for our relationship."

"We feel the same, Bro. You know we do. So, back to work. We'll just watch Holt work his magic."

He and Dane laughed together, while Holt only flashed them a quick smile. Holt always showed the least amount of emotion between all three of them. He chatted with Dane and they both watched Holt work his info-center magic. Time passed, which only made him more nervous. His brothers were not the reason he'd heard nothing from Lania. She'd pulled away and he had no idea how to fix the problem. Women. They were a pain he needed to avoid from this sun-cycle forward.

"Dear galaxy! Look at this!" Holt pointed at the air-screen in front of them. "Raulf is free, has been for some time. He claims a group of misfits and outcasts set him up to unseat him. He's saying he'll execute Lania for unseating him and interfering with planetary business. He's calling her a traitor! By the stars! What's going on?"

"Look at him! He really thinks he's something, doesn't he? We have to stop him!" Dane yelled.

Jace slowly stepped toward the screen and read every word printed about the evil man who had unfortunately returned. "Look here, it says he's having a big celebration this moon-cycle." He glanced back at his brothers. "Do you think we should try out our serving abilities once again?"

An evil threesome laugh penetrated the air of their home. They'd done the waiter gig many times before with great success, so why not? "Can we match the caterer?"

"Yeah, no problem. In fact, it's exactly the same one we did last time, so we're good."

"Of course. Leave it to Raulf to waste the people's credits. He's good at it." All three of them groaned since they knew the truth behind the particular caterer they spoke of, which was the most expensive on the entire planet. There were so many others, equal in quality which charged far less. The evil one didn't care. Jace looked at Holt. "What time do we need to arrive to be part of the group?"

"Around six. We won't have much time to fiddle with the masks and wigs so we'd better get going." Holt stood and headed to his room; Dane did the same. Jace loved it when the three of them worked together on a case like this. They liked having fun, dressing up like people they were not, to go undercover and learn secrets. Dinner parties were famous for revealing more secrets than anyone could possibly count.

Jace opened his work closet door where he kept every type of costume, uniform, and disguise for every company on Lorton. He searched through the ton of clothes that hung in front of him that he'd used at one time or another. He took out the waiter outfit for the required expensive catering business. It went well with the grey wig and old man mask.

Most waiters fell into the older category. Young men never wanted to wait on people. They couldn't handle being bossed around the way waiters always seemed to be. He put on his mask, attached the wig and spent a lot of time adjusting it to look perfect. The Bryton's didn't dare risk being recognized, or embarrassed, so they all dressed the part to fit in perfectly.

All three of them were ready about the same time and looked each other over in the hall in front of the back door. They'd see any mistakes and straighten them out immediately. This time they'd all done a great job, everything looked perfect. They walked across the parking area and hurried to board their little four-person transport. Dane piloted, he and Holt went along.

It only took a brief time to arrive at the caterer's building, park, then blend into the crowd of cooks, waiters and dishes. Once the motorcade finished loading all the food and drink necessary, all the workers boarded the extra-large, truck-trans and headed toward the Royal Capitol Building, very close to where they were now. The dinner would be held in the main hall, which seated the most people and still left room for entertainment and dancing.

The other employees did not seem willing to talk, which was fine since he wasn't in the mood for idle chit-chat. They were lucky and fit comfortably into the employee transport with extra space to spare. He reminded himself to get in the mood to be the older waiter, and tune into conversations, hoping they might lead to Lania's whereabouts. She had to be held somewhere close by. Walking the halls and opening doors never worked well. Someone always leaked something or saw something they shouldn't. He and his brothers must find a way to get the information they needed.

He helped while every employee set up the dining area with tables, chairs, and all the finery necessary for an elite dinner. It took them all since this was a huge event, way larger than most. His heart raced at the thought of Lania attending this event, then he quickly calmed himself. If she were being held against her will, she'd certainly not be here. Dreaming again. Time to quit. This rescue was required for the planet, not for him personally Lania belonged on the Ruler's throne, and The Bryton Brothers' duty was to return her to her rightful position.

Gale might attend the dinner, after all she happened to be the evil Ruler's sister. He didn't dare expose her part in any of this since it meant her life. Gale worked hard to maintain her goodness, even though it seemed an impossibility for her to accomplish under the circumstances. Hopefully he'd catch her alone somewhere and have the opportunity to ask her about Lania.

The large hall looked like an intimate party of gigantic size, if such an event were possible. He wished he could sabotage the Ruler's seat and place setting. Especially his food so the man would drop face down, dead. That would be great.

Holt told him all of their support team had been notified and were standing by to offer help. They needed it, without a doubt, if and when they removed Raulf. How did the evil man return, only to be removed a second time? Had he no shame? Could he be so stupid or conceited? Damn to the galaxy and back! Now he believed it was their fault for not keeping an army of guards at the Royal Palace and at Lania's side.

The official guards swung open the large double doors and swarms of people streamed inside, looked for their placemark, then took their assigned seats. They all waited for the moon-cycle of food, and entertainment to begin. Once everyone settled down at their appropriate tables, the brass instruments sounded the arrival of the Ruler himself. Sure enough, all the people immediately stood at attention, and in walked Raulf and Marna. He couldn't miss how attached to the evil man Marna actually was, walking with her arms around him and his around her, both looking super happy. It made sense now why she'd turned on Lania.

Did Marna know where they put Lania? Of course, but she'd never tell. Jace had a pretty good hunch where they put Lania, yet he could not go barging into the prison cells unless he was absolutely sure, especially about which one she had been put into. Jace surveyed the room looking for Gale, searching all the nearby tables, but didn't see her. He expected her to be located close to the head table since she was family, instead, he spotted her far away, seated at one of the last tables in the back of the room with several very old women. Raulf must really hate her to seat her so far away. A couple more steps and she'd be out in the hallway.

If Raulf knew Gale hired Bryton Security, she'd be dead, sister or no sister. Raulf would dispose of her faster than the daily garbage. He really needed to talk to Gale. To do so he got back in the serving line. He didn't dare assume the old women at her table to be too senile to know what they talked about, so he needed patience, no matter how difficult it was for him. He needed to approach her slowly and carefully and to find out if the women at the table were with the program or not.

Jace saw his brothers standing together by the far wall and made his way over to them. He stood in front of them and acted like work was the center of their discussion. It didn't hurt when he pointed backwards and circled his arm a bit, pretending to say they needed to attend to the people behind them. "See the woman dressed in blue in the far back corner with the old ladies?" He waited to see them nod, which they finally did. "Well, that is Gale, Raulf's sister, the woman who hired us. I will try to approach her if I can. Hopefully one of us will be able to achieve a conversation with her."

"You got it. We'll keep an eye out and help you however we can."

"Thanks." Jace walked away at a rapid pace. He wondered if he looked like one of the supervisors? He slowed down a bit when he remembered how old he pretended to be. All the workers meandered into the kitchen and waited while the cooks presented the first course dishes to the wait-staff. They each took a tray with their share on it, and each tray had a table number assigned to it. He needed to work it right and get Gale's table, the only one he wanted.

It certainly helped that he and his brothers had done this many times before because they fit right in with their job performance and wait-staff looks. The odd thing to them seemed how management never noticed three extra helpers. Thirty or forty workers did the job, sometimes more. No wonder they lost count, like this moon-cycle.

They continued to serve the tables in order. Finally, they stood in line and were five tables away from Gale's. He needed to be at the end of the line, so he waved Holt in front of him to get his food tray. Jace started a fight with Dane, then waved two guys to go in front of them. Then he stopped harassing Dane and stood nicely. He now waited perfectly in line for Gale's table. They'd done the fight thing before and it always worked. Gale's food tray now rested on his arm to be delivered.

It took a few moments to reach her all the way in the back, and he noted a shocked look on Gale's face when he reached her table. She looked up at him, almost like she recognized him. "Good evening, ladies. Hope you are all doing well? I've brought your salads to begin. Please tell me what kind of dressing you'd like and I'll be happy to provide it for you." He had six different kinds lined up on his tray and he pointed to each and announced the various names.

The first lady just stared straight ahead without saying a word, so he chose for her. The second lady wasn't much better. The third lady simply pointed at all of the bottles and mumbled something unintelligible. Again, he chose for her and she seemed happy. Now it came down to Gale, the only one left. He stopped beside her, she told him what she wanted and he complied. He leaned close to her ear. "Do these women understand what is going on?"

"Not really," Gale whispered.

"How on Lorton did you recognize me?"

"Expecting something from you soon. I knew by the way you walked I suppose. Not exactly old. Plus, you are way taller than the other old men.

Jace nearly laughed at her comment. "I kept forgetting who I pretend to be. Do you know where Lania is?"

"She's in the worst section of the prison. Been locked up since the end of the sun-cycle you Brytons were here to see her."

"Dear stars!" He stood straight. "You certainly have you ways of knowing things."

Gale chuckled. "I have my ways, and they're good. I can't reveal any more."

"Understood." He lowered the serving tray to look like he was working. "Thanks for the info. I'll be back shortly." Gale gave him a slight nod. He then walked back to the kitchen, cursing himself.

Of course, Lania couldn't contact him. This information explained everything. Someone must have found Holt's device and shoved it up on a shelf in the warehouse. He always knew Lania wasn't there, but it certainly explained her silence. Lania no longer had the device on her so she couldn't use it. Now he felt horrible for his constant blaming and lack of trust he'd felt. He should have known she'd never desert him, or stop loving him.

Wow. He'd been a total fool. At least Lania couldn't see or hear his bad behavior. He failed to trust her. He'd always found it difficult to give women trust. Obviously, he had a lot to learn about the male/female relationship. First, he needed to figure out how to get the love of his life out of a very secure prison. No easy task.

Where there's a will, there's a way. At least that's what he'd always been taught, and the time to put the old theory to the test seemed to be right now. He knew from past experience anything could be possible if a person wanted it enough. He'd seen his brothers do miracles, and he'd also done some himself. However; this required all three of them, possibly more. Whatever it took, they'd succeed.

Time to proceed. No matter what he would free Lania. She didn't deserve this kind of treatment. She was a true lady who wanted to serve her people and make life easier for every citizen of Lorton. Bryton Brothers' Security must free the missing princess, who was missing once again. This time he refused to leave Lania alone. He'd sleep on the floor outside her door to keep her safe. This could never happen again. Ever!

Chapter Twenty-Seven

They managed to get themselves back to their office and now all three of them sat at the table and discussed possible scenarios to free Lania. They'd talked about and dissected every possible idea they could think of, yet nothing pointed to the exact route they should take, so they still had no plan. They only knew failure was not an option. The old saying always popped up.

"Well," Dane began, "I suppose I need to call all our friends on Lorton who stood by us the night Lania took her rightful place. I know they'd show up again if we needed them."

Holt stared at Dane. "I don't believe we require so many, but I'll contact a few of them."

Jace nodded. "The more men we involve, the more conspicuous we'll be. I need to go in and get her alone. Two of us leaving the cell area may not be a problem. A bunch of men would definitely be an alarm signal. If I carry one of Holt's devices, and you put a few of our friends on standby, I could be in and out fast. What do you guys think?"

"You're probably right." Dane nodded. "Do you know what you're doing, Bro?"

"I think so. I'll go in as a guard, I'll wear the uniform and even a partial mask and I'll maintain the premise until I escape with the Princess."

Holt nodded several times then looked up. "I like it."

Jace took a deep satisfying breath. "Then it's settled. Now we need to decide when." He looked both brothers in the eyes. "I say the sooner the better. No sense making her suffer any longer than necessary."

"I agree. Let Holt and I do our homework. I'm thinking you could go in during a shift change. Hopefully you will only have one guard to disable. Holt will let you know what time."

"Are we settled then?" All three of them bumped fists over the tabletop and smiled. "This is an important job, and I appreciate your help."

"No problem." Holt rose and walked to his info-center and began to work.

"You know we stick together." Dane got up and pushed his chair under the table. "Especially when the job is this crucial."

Jace stood, "Don't mean to be mushy, but I'm lucky to have brothers like the two of you. Thanks again."

"Don't mention it. You'll owe us, and don't forget!" Dane laughed and both brothers joined .

"We're quite the trio." Jace loved his brothers, and they performed their very best together. This rescue meant far more than any job he'd ever done. To him personally and to all of Lorton's population. His brothers understood completely, and totally supported him. Holt and Dane were good at planning; he remained best at the actual operation.

"Hey guys, we need to get going fast," Holt called over his shoulder. "According to what I found, Raulf plans to move Lania to the place no one will speak about. You know where I'm talking about. She'll be moved before next sun-cycle begins. You'd better get dressed Jace. We're about out of time."

"I'll be right back. Print me up a schematic of the prison, inside and out so I can take it with me."

"Gotcha," Holt said.

"Get going!" Dane hollered.

Holt and Dane both yelled while he hurried down the hall and into his room where he threw open the work closet doors. Thank heaven he had the right uniform hanging in wait. He grabbed it and the boots that went with the uniform and hurried to get ready. Once the complete outfit was on, he'd be able to concentrate on the little details he might need.

A partial mask hung on the closet door in front of him that would change his looks enough not to be identified. Mainly it wrinkled his forehead and made him look partially bald, but it did have a short, dark beard on the face. Change enough. He filled his pockets with several of the small weapons he preferred, ones that did the most, or the least damage, covering about any situation he might encounter.

He must be prepared for all situations since he had no idea what faced him. He would not kill innocent guards though, only if it became necessary to protect Lania's life, or his. Innocent people did not deserve to die for doing their jobs. He hurried back down the hall to his brothers. Holt raised his hand in submission which made them both laugh.

"Before you holler, here is the help device, and here are the two schematics you requested."

"Thanks." Jace looked over the papers, satisfied he'd memorized the layout. He mainly needed to know how to get in and out fast, plus Lania's location. "Do you know the exact cell she's in?" He folded the papers and pushed them in his back pocket, just in case.

Dane shook his head. "While you were gone, we tried to get the number. Couldn't locate it. Think like Raulf. Look in the farthest, nastiest place and you'll find her there."

"Good idea." He patted both brothers on the back since they were sitting side-by-side at the work area. "Thanks. Ready?"

"You have all the weapons you need? Insta-sleep?"

"I need some sleep. Love that stuff."

"I'll get you a couple," Dane insisted. "Meet you in the transport."

He and Holt went to the lift and rode up to the top floor then got in the small craft. They'd barely set foot inside when Dane came running up behind them. He handed him the sleep spray.

"Ready."

"So are we."

This time Holt sat in the pilot's seat, something he and Dane didn't want since he usually flew too slow for their liking. Up they went. This time, Holt hit it hard and they flew at record pace to their destination. They had to let him off in an inconspicuous location, so he wouldn't be noticed while he infiltrated the masses. This procedure always served as their norm, and he felt grateful for all their past experience.

Rescuing the love of his life played on his nerves more than he wanted to admit. Did she miss him? Did she think he would come for her? What did she think right now? Did she still love him? So many questions with no answers. Once they made their escape, they'd be able to talk, kiss, and do whatever they felt like. Would Lania want to make love? Or simply return to her duties? It depended on her current feelings for him. Those feelings might be from one extreme to the other. Or her feelings may be exactly and how his were. Confusion raged within him where he and Lania were concerned.

He had zero time to over-examine feelings. He simply wanted to share with with her when they were alone, and be ready to talk about their relationship. If they still had one. For a while he'd dismissed his feelings, since he decided she no longer wanted him. If what he'd learned so far proved correct, he'd been so very wrong. It all depended on Lania now, and he should leave it up to her.

They arrived where he was to get off. He jumped out the back hatch door while Dane held it open. They paused in the brushy area so his presence wouldn't be noticed. He headed straight for the fence and scaled one side then hopped over quickly before a guard or anyone saw him. Of course, this moon-cycle he dressed like a guard to blend in, an absolute necessity. According to the schematic, he needed to enter from the guard's side entrance in order to gain access to the portion of the prison where he thought Lania's cell might be located.

When he circled around and came up the proper way to the entrance, the door guard stopped him, and he wondered how he should play this out. He decided to march up as if he'd done it thousands of times before.

"Hold it right there, buddy."

Jace froze at the man's order and held his hands up a bit to say he was harmless.

"This your first time here?"

"It is. You got a problem?"

"Well, you're not wearing the proper badge."

"Don't have one yet." Jace hoped he gave a proper answer.

"Let me go get 'ya one. Hold on."

Thank the stars it worked. The man stepped inside a small office-like room to the side of the entrance for a moment then returned and handed him a shiny, gold badge, the same kind all the guards wore. He quickly attached it to his uniform over his right shoulder area where it went. The man nodded at him then opened the arm-gate and he entered.

"Ya need any help or directions? This is a big, complicated place."

"I think I'm fine. Thanks." Jace walked in and turned right toward the isolated cells. It seemed like the longest walk of his life since he headed for his love, his woman, his sweet Lania. He still wondered how Raulf was capable of transferring her to the frozen sector For extra punishment some prisoners were kept in unheated cells, leaving them there until they froze to death when the cold climate hit. Prisoners there were treated like dirt on boots, and not cared for at all.

Once a prisoner was sent there, they didn't last long, ask anyone on Lorton and they'd tell you the same story. Cruel Raulf kept proving his evilness over and over again. It also made him wonder what happened to the caring public—but he doubted they even knew. Raulf was not known for telling his evil secrets.

He reached the end of the long hall and arrived at the check-desk. The man behind the counter wrote down his badge number then pointed in the direction for him to go, down the hall to the right. He walked slowly, pretending to be on patrol. Some prisoners heard him coming, got up and grabbed the rails that covered a high window on the door and tried to see him. They had a weird system, since men and women were kept in the same area, although not in the same cell.

Women in prison acted out less than men, remained quieter, and were fewer in numbers. He expected Lania to be off by herself if possible. Then he noticed the hall to his left, the exact one he'd been looking for. Isolation. He stepped into the dirty, dreary hall. Just then someone grabbed the back of his collar and pulled on it, jerking him backward. Jace immediately turned and faced the perpetrator. "What are you doing?"

"Checking you out!"

"I work here. Let go of me this instant!"

"Bossy, are ya?"

"You have no idea. Now, let go!" The man tested his patience so Jace slugged him in the stomach and smiled when he buckled over in pain, unable to catch his breath. To finish him off, he brought his fist up under his chin and hit him as hard as possible, pleased when the man fell backwards down to the floor, unconscious. He reached in the man's pants pocket, took out a set of keys, then put them in his own pocket.

Jace picked up his pace since he now had a victim who could easily be found. He hurried to the end and turned left where three cells sat in a row. He peeked in the first one, empty. The second cell had an open door. When he looked in the third cell, he saw Lania curled up like a small child in the far corner, sitting on the floor, knees bent, her arms around her legs and her head on her knees. She appeared to be asleep, yet he knew better. He pulled the keys from his pocket and proceeded to find one that unlocked the door.

A faint voice from the back corner said, "Leave me alone. Please!"

He walked the few steps to her and stopped. "Are you sure you want me to, My Lady?" It seemed she refused to look up or answer. She looked very weak and dehydrated. "You are My Lady. Don't you know by now, Lania?" At his statement she looked up and stared at him with big brown eyes, full of tears. "Do you recognize me?"

Lania tried to stand. He had to help her before she fell and hurt her obviously frail body. It appeared she'd been treated very badly to be in her current state of health. She probably had only been fed one meal a day, if that much, and looked skinnier than she had the first time he saw her in the jungle. Of course, it didn't take long under these circumstances to appear so badly and look quite sick. Lania now stood, so he slipped his arm around her and walked her to the cell door.

"I am glad to see you, Jace. I...I...arely saw through your ugg...ugggly mask."

"Don't try to talk. I'm going to get you out of here. Understand?" She nodded and he relocked her cell door, then headed back up the hall until he saw his own personal roadblock. Four men dressed exactly like him, all four physically bigger than him. He was no slouch, but these guys were huge and he felt quite outnumbered.

This might be difficult, but he had no room for failure. He had the sleep spray, though he needed to be careful not to inhale or he'd be lying unconscious right next to them.

He gently placed Lania against the wall and helped her ease down to sit on the floor and prayed she'd be out of the fracas. He let go of her and headed toward the two men coming down the narrow hallway toward him. If it had been wider all four men would have attacked him at the same time.

Jace grabbed one of the men, bent his arm back and down he went. He proceeded to put pressure on his airway in exactly the right place so he couldn't breathe, then the man fell unconscious to the floor. The other giant tried to jump on him. Jace ducked and the man kind of lumbered over the top of him, then landed hard on the rock floor. These men obviously did not use hand to hand combat much. A lucky break for him.

Then the other two came straight at him. While they rushed toward him, he readied himself for more hand-to-hand battle. They each grabbed one of his arms so he couldn't hit them with his fist. They faced him, each with one arm outstretched. They grabbed him and held him off the ground so he bent his knees and shoved his hard booted feet into their groins, right where every man's weak-spot resided. His quick action sent them both backwards, forcing them to let go of him while they doubled over and fell to the rocky floor. He then rushed forward, put one foot on one man's chest and gave him a close dose of sleep spray, then did the same to the other man.

On his way back to Lania, he carefully gave the other two a dose of sleep to be sure they didn't get up anytime soon to follow. He shoved the small cylinder back into his pocket then helped Lania to her feet. She remained way too wobbly, so he picked her up in his arms and carried her down the hall toward the exit. Hopefully he'd only have to face one guard at a time. Good thought, but unlikely. Two guards walked toward him and stopped right in front of him.

"What are you doing with the prisoner?"

"Taking her to the med-unit."

"You don't do anything without written directives." The guard shook his head. "I know you don't have any because none passed by me, and I always know first. So put the bitch down. Now!"

Jace turned around and sat his love on the floor, her back against the wall. Then he faced his next opposition. "Are you in charge here?"

"At the moment I'm in charge of you for sure. You're too new to have any pull with anyone here!"

"Correct, but if this woman doesn't get med help immediately, she'll be dead and Raulf won't be able to have any fun with her."

"So be it. He didn't give no orders, which means we all do nothin'. Hear me newbie?"

"I do, however;..." He quickly turned, swung his leg around in the air and hit the man on the side of his head with the toe of his boot. The grouchy man went down fast. The other man pushed forward and he did the same maneuver with his other leg. This time he had to follow up with a couple of fists to the head. Then they each got a dose of sleep before he picked Lania up and left the building.

The guard who first stopped him did not appear at his station, a true blessing. His arms were full with his beautiful woman, and he was tired of fighting. He wanted to get Lania out of here and into his bed where he'd be able to protect her and nurse her back to health. With a little luck, he'd spend the rest of his life doing exactly those things, especially the watching her part.

She was a joy to watch, her beauty nearly blinding, and he loved it. He loved her.

Chapter Twenty-Eight

Lania opened her eyes and wondered where she was. Then it hit her. She was in Jace's bed. When she turned over, she found him sleeping in the chair by her head. She wanted to reach out and touch him. He looked so peaceful and handsome, but she did not want to scare him awake. Of course, she'd always thought him handsome. The last time she saw him, peaceful did not come close to describing his actions.

She remembered watching bodies fly through the air, then ending up lifeless on the floor. Jace was a remarkable warrior. He fought four at a time like he was on vacation! He had truly been *Her Warrior*. Thank the stars he was so very good at his profession. Although all of his fighting, and what he did for a job no longer mattered to her personally. Their relationship had ended, and she knew she had to move on. He obviously had, so what made him save her?

It would be difficult to let go of her feelings for him. Her memories in the cavern, and even in this very bed seemed impossible to forget. Especially when part of her never wanted to forget those experiences, or the man responsible for them. She rolled over to her other side.

Looking at the overly desirable man now only caused pain. This situation had turned into a heartbreaking dilemma she wished never happened. Being The Royal Ruler, she should be more than capable of dealing with every problem that came her way, including Jace.

What had gone wrong? This situation she found herself in needed to be rectified immediately, and she required the Bryton

Brothers help once again. Did she dare hire them? If they returned her to the Ruler's position, she would have enough credits to pay them. She did not want them to work for nothing. She wanted to be fair with them. She would have to think about this before she made a solid decision. Then she heard his voice.

"Hello sleepy. How are you feeling?"

Lania rolled back over to face him. "I'm fine. How did you know I was awake?"

"I could tell. I know everything about you, My Lady."

He smiled at her which had its usual effect on her. Luckily, she was lying down. "Thank you for freeing me, Jace. I do appreciate it." She started to get out of bed, then realized she only had her underwear on. "Where are my clothes?"

"Your prison garb is on the chair in the corner. There are clean clothes in the closet in your room you're welcome to wear." Jace pointed down the hall.

"Thank you. Now, if you'll please leave. I need a shower and I must get dressed. I'd appreciate the privacy. So, if you don't mind…."

"Lania, why are you being so aloof and formal? I thought we'd moved way past friendship."

"You thought wrong. I understand how some men are."

Jace grinned at Lania and shook his head. "So, I'm some men? That's really how you think of me? Like some men? Why, My Love, why? I thought I was far more to you than some man."

"You shouldn't need to ask me. You know why. Don't make something out of nothing. I get it. And anything you do for me, from here on, I'll pay for. Don't worry."

"I'm not worried about credits, only us. Any comment?"

Was he for real? "Us?" It was her turn to shake her head. "There is no us. You well understand. Now, please leave. I must get ready."

Jace chuckled. "I'm not leaving. I have a private audience with My Lady, and I intend to use it. So, tell me what happened to 'us'?"

"You left me without a word and never came back until last moon-cycle."

"Is that what you think?" Jace inhaled slowly. "You couldn't be more wrong."

"You dare call me wrong?"

"You're not my ruler at the moment. You're the woman I love, and we're having an argument."

"You call this an argument? It's more of an affirmation we don't belong together. You have already made your feelings and intentions perfectly clear. Now, let me get dressed!"

Jace glared at Lania. "You think getting dressed is more important than us?" Jace stood and stepped to the end of the bed. "I'll gladly give you what you want." Jace shook his head and stared at Lania. "I'll leave." He stared at her a moment. "I hope you think long and hard before you write 'us' off completely. You're talking about the rest of our lives, not just this moment. I'm here for you, if you want me. Your choice. Think carefully, My Lady." Jace walked to the door. "Remember, I love you." He took a breath. "I gave you my heart the moment I saw you, and have never taken it back. It's yours, and yours alone."

She watched in trepidation while the door slid open. The moment he stepped out into the hall, her heart literally broke in two and pain flew through her body. What did she want? Really want? A question she never truly answered. In fact, she had never asked herself, since she had no choice in decisions pertaining to her rightful position in the Lorton government. Jace insisted she think about their relationship, and it seemed way past time she did so.

What had Jace done? He had not broken up with her, he simply disappeared. She decided in prison it had been his choice. All the guards, and even the prisoners in the neighboring cells told her about Jace and his women. They said he never really cared about any one woman, and especially not for her. They pounded it into her mind, sun-cycle after sun-cycle. How could she not believe them? They even told her women's names that he'd been with while she remained locked up in the disgusting cell.

Although circumstances kept them apart, and she was the recipient of constant stories about Jace and his women. Had she been a fool to believe the bad stories? Or was she now being a sensible woman who finally realized she had trusted the wrong man? How could she even know for sure?

He told her he loved her. They said he did not. Did he truly mean what he said? Now she shook her head, trying to sort through her own thoughts. Reality slowly began to creep into her thoughts, and it was not a pretty picture.

While in his arms she'd totally believed him, so why not now? Had she believed the lies told to her while in prison? They'd been extremely mean, and they only wanted to anger and hurt her. Why had their lies rang so true to her at the time? They laughed because they insisted she was now completely alone, and no one loved her, or even cared what happened to her, ever. They said he had been having sex with several other women, and enjoyed them completely.

Life always got in the way of her plans, and this seemed no different. Her duty as Supreme Ruler did not include Jace, at least not at the moment. Raulf had horned his way back into power, leaving no room for her, and definitely no room for Jace, a man of high standing in the community, a handsome man no woman could ignore. Her heart pounded hard at the thought of Jace with his shirt off, and if she kept thinking, she'd pull him back into her room and they'd make wild, passionate love.

Those thoughts made her realize why she believed the stories told to her in prison. If she thought about nothing else except Jace and loving him, that's what all the other women thought as well. Of course, but how could they possibly know about her and Jace, or the other women he had been with before? Mystery for sure, but they did, and she had believed them. It all required a lot of thought she did not have time for right now. Or was it a conversation that was desperately needed?

Jace touched her heart like no other man or woman ever had. So many people expected things from her. Jace had no expectations, except for her to be with him and love him. They had been great together, when they were together. So why did she have doubts and second thoughts about the 'us' he kept talking about? Nothing seemed wrong with the relationship of 'us' when both parties felt the same.

Did she believe the tales of criminals, or did she believe her own heart and mind? Why did she think Jace would turn his back so quickly? Did she think desertion might be a good reason? Circumstances constantly flared between them. Now that she thought about it, they had not actually lost love, only time together.

She couldn't have contacted him even if she wanted to since Holt's device went into one of the prison guard's pockets. Plus, the people around her obviously kept him from contacting her. They did need a long talk to settle this. Hopefully it wouldn't take a long discussion to produce the outcome they could both be happy with. Life could be extremely cruel. She wanted to be happy for a change. He did say he gave her his heart when he first saw her, and she knew such a personal revelation did not come from Jace easily. He was a Bryton, her Jace, her love, her Bad Warrior-Man.

Everything had a time and a place, and she needed to put those things in proper sequence. For once she decided to put herself first. Her happiness did matter, even if it remained tied directly to him. Jace was a fantastic lover, who adored her in all the right ways. He convinced her with his sincere statement regarding his heart and she believed him.

It was her job to make The High Council allow Jace Bryton to become her life-mate. If they did not, she needed to leave the 'us' in the past. Yet it remained next to impossible for her to never see Jace again. He was special, perfect, and oh so mesmerizing. She really wanted to throw herself into his arms, and let him take care of her. She trusted him, she loved him, she wanted him. The main problem now was finding the right time to settle their differences. Then they could both enjoy the kiss and make-up part.

Did Jace want the kiss and make-up part, or was it only her thought? She wanted to slap herself for all her back-and-forth ideas. The answers must wait for their face-to-face conversation. This time she'd put it on him. It seemed right anyway. Dear stars, she debated herself once again. Did love cause self-doubt for everyone? Anxiety? Plus, a list of other things ten-meters long?

A knock on the door stopped her. At least she'd managed to shower and get dressed while she continued to confuse herself. "Who is it?"

"Jace. My brothers and I are waiting for you so we can make a plan."

"I'll be right there. Thank you." She ran the brush through her hair then went to the door. She hurried out of the room and down the hall. Hopefully they could talk and settle this problem quickly and easily. Not the 'us', only returning her to The Royal Ruler position once again. The three brothers were seated at the table, and they left one chair for her, next to Jace, as always. It made her smile. "Good sun-cycle, gentlemen."

"Good sun-cycle, My Lady." Dane smiled. "We're here to create a plan to put you back where you belong. Where we truly want to see you. We're open to suggestions, especially since you know the inner-workings far better than we do."

"If you run your ideas past me, I can tell you if they'll work or not." She looked into Dane and Holt's eyes. They both looked even more tired than she felt. They would all feel better, and happier when this exhausting work ended. If it ever did.

Jace picked up the paper in front of him. "My Lady, my brothers and I have discussed several ideas. We've narrowed it down to three. I will read them and wait for your opinion. All right with you?"

"Absolutely. Please, continue."

"Okay. First idea, is to go in with lots of men, hundreds if necessary. Second, maybe twenty men or so, third, only the three of us. What are your ideas? Who is behind this, and who are we ultimately fighting?"

"First, no. Hundreds of men are not necessary and way too obvious. It could even turn into an actual war of sorts. Not good. Third, the three of you may not be enough. The second is the most likely to succeed. Having men on standby is the best idea."

"Good. We assumed the same. We're not sure how many to begin with since we don't know how many enemies will be waiting for us." Holt scratched his head. "Your thoughts, please."

"You're exactly right." She looked around the table. "Bryton Security is known as the best around, and I totally agree. In short, someone freed Raulf and Marna, and they took back the power of the high office. We all know from past experience, Raulf and Marna are not the most popular. The palace workers are terrified of them. But I am quite sure there were many of Raulf's men left behind to wander the halls and do whatever was necessary for their credit payments." Lania took a deep breath. "I do know a few men who are loyal to only me. It is a very short list, loyalty is a fickle thing, and often depends on credits. Some people can be bought, but those loyal to me cannot."

"Well, your loyal people will need to be contacted. Quietly, of course. The last thing we want is to draw attention." Holt nodded.

"I can contact them if you tell me who to get in touch with and the best way to accomplish the task."

"Sounds good. Give me a bit of time to create a list. It won't take me long."

Jace looked at Lania. "What about contacting one person and letting him, or her contact the rest? I'm sure the most trustworthy person knows who best to trust. Possibly even better than you, My Lady, since you haven't been around those people for quite some time. A few contacts may have changed. You never know. So, pick the most trusted of all for Holt to contact, or at least to begin with."

"You make an excellent point. I will think on it." She stood. "I need to think alone."

Jace watched Lania elegantly leave the room. He found it extremely hard to sit next to her and not touch her. He desperately wanted her. Now and forever. For some reason, he could not guess what was going on in her mind. She seemed cold and uncaring toward him, acting in a way he'd never seen before. Her warmth and sincere smiles totally disappeared. Where did they go to? He had no idea. Now he dealt with Lania, the Supreme Ruler of Lorton, all business, and overly serious.

Returning Lania to power would be extremely difficult, yet it was of the utmost importance. It had seemed so easy when they simply removed the old and put in the new rightful heir, even if it was a woman. They did exactly that, and thought all was well. They forgot to look into who Raulf paid and left behind when they put him in jail. Could Lania's problems have anything to do with the fact she was a woman? Many things needed to change. The old ways were truly old. Change needed to occur immediately.

He didn't know how to approach Lania's cold demeanor. Possibly, if he knew how and why it appeared, he'd be able to attack it. The most logical reason was her prison stay. Did they do something to her there to cause this reaction? Some of the ideas about the men who worked there flashed through his mind. The things they may have done to her made him so angry he wanted to scream and take revenge. Hopefully nothing sexual happened.

He needed to work with his brothers and fix the current problems facing Lania, and hope they were right about everything. The well-being of the entire planet lay in their hands as always it seemed—and remained a huge responsibility. It may be Lania's problem, yet she'd put it all on Bryton Security. This became too much all at once, to save the government, return Lania to power, and get his woman back. All the issues were extremely important, yet the one most important to him remained personal.

"Jace? Dane calling Jace?"

When he heard his name, he mentally shook himself and looked at both of his brothers, who stared at him in total confusion. "I'm here. Go on."

"I've been talking for a quite a while, and you haven't replied to one thing! Where did you go?"

"Sorry. Thinking."

Holt laughed. "You've never been a good thinker!"

All three of them laughed this time. A sense of humor still held high value and remained imperative to them. If they didn't all laugh at times about their jobs, they'd lose their minds, quickly. Besides, right now they'd tease him until he gave in. "You guys got me here. Now, let's get busy and create a plan."

"First," Dane began, "Holt and I want to know what's going on between you and Lania? Something's up and we need to know in order to make any necessary adjustments."

"Nothing is going on."

"Jace, come on, Bro, we know better. We're not blind, or deaf. We know, so be honest. Okay?" Holt sighed.

"I'm being honest! *Nothing* is going on, even though it should be. Know what I mean?" His brothers both lifted their eyebrows and cringed at him. They both knew very well how it went with the ladies. "I don't know much more than what you observed. Lania and I need to talk, unfortunately we have not had a chance and we need to." He looked into their eyes, relieved to see understanding while they nodded slightly at him. He moved his stare to the papers in front of him. "I'll let you know if anything pertinent surfaces. Okay?"

"You got it, Bro." Dane shook his head. "Now, who should we partner up with for the take-over?"

"A tough question. All those contacts from the last job did really great. Let me check and see who has around twenty-five members. Then when we contact them, we'll ask for their entire group's assistance since they employ the number of men we decided to include." Holt pressed keys on his info-system, searching for answers. "One group has exactly the right number. And they're one of our preferred contacts, so they'll work perfectly." He looked up at Dane. "You know their leader best. Want to contact him and check availability?"

"Sure. 'The Lorton Protectors'. They're a great group of men, who really do support putting Lania back in power. Of course, they hate Raulf and his group. They'll be more than cooperative if they're available. I'll speak to their Captain of Operations. I don't see a problem."

"Neither do I. We always work well with them," Holt added.

Dane nodded. "I fully agree."

Jace looked up at Dane. "Credits?"

Dane chuckled. "I assume once Lania is returned to power, she will ensure payment to all of us." He looked at Jace, "Right?"

"Of course." He smiled at his brothers until they began to laugh. For some reason laughter made everything seem good, and they really needed it right now. When their laughter died away, Lania returned to the table and took her seat next to him.

"Gentlemen, after great consideration, I chose Representative Joehend Rickmond. He was loyal to my father, and has proven his loyalty to me also. I believe we can fully trust him, plus his connections will help immensely. He will also know who we can and cannot trust. Here is his information." She slid a piece of paper to the center of the table. "He is The High Council's Chairman. The highest man in the High Council, except the Royal Ruler, of course. Since he's in charge of The High Council, he will be the main person to go to for whatever you need. He knows me well. That is a completely personal contact number for him."

"Thank you." Holt picked up the piece of paper. "He'll be perfect." He stood, then walked to the info-center.

Jace watched his brother begin inputting information. Once he started, things happened fast. He was an expert at his job, which always played a huge part in their service. Their planet, and every planet he knew of, relied on information stored in all the numerous systems available. Most of the time it proved extremely helpful, although in some instances, what they learned defied explanation.

"Jace, are you coming?"

"What?" He stared at Dane like he just woke from a nap. His mind tended to wander these sun-cycles, at least this time it was not on Lania. He was trying to keep Lania out of his thoughts, because for some reason she took over every single one, then he became completely lost. "Sure." His brothers shook their heads at him. Dane and Holt both knew what was going on, whether he told them or not. He normally thought about Lania, and they both knew it. Triplets shared many of their inner thoughts and feelings telepathically. Only during a few rare times did their thoughts belong only to them.

They usually read each other like books, which had become extremely helpful, and they depended on that special communication in their business. At other times, knowing too much about your brothers often got in the way. He'd suffered through his brothers falling in love, or believing they'd been in love many times. If one brother told another brother the woman he'd fallen for was bad for him, he usually refused to believe it. They'd never told each other any woman was good for the other one. He sincerely hoped it changed in his case.

Triplets could never have secrets.

Chapter Twenty-Nine

Lania finished dressing, not sure if she chose the right gown to wear. If everything went according to plan, she'd be back in control of Planet Lorton this sun-cycle. She must look the part of ruler if she wanted to be respected in that position. A woman never served Lorton as ruler before, and she was determined to be the first. Even the council seemed in favor. She already discussed two of her most wanted decisions with The High Council before she was so rudely removed and put in prison!

People like Raulf had no excuse. Evil or not, he could only be called a horrible being. Raulf put credits above people and she hoped The High Council would give him the worst punishment possible. She planned to insist on the absolute worst. Death.

Just then the door announced a visitor, and she knew it had to be Jace. "Come in," she called. She secured the belt in back then turned to see Jace standing before her looking more appealing than he ever had. He wore the black uniform of a palace guard, just like his brothers wore this morning. She'd seen them leave on the cam-screen. She also knew the plan.

"I hope you don't feel left out since you had to stay here with me." Jace simply stared at her and she truly wondered where his thoughts were. "Nothing to say?"

"Not at the moment. Right now, we just wait for the call. Hopefully it won't be long."

"It must be tough for you to stay with me and not do all the fighting stuff you like."

"This is not a matter of like, it's a matter of survival, and accomplishing my job successfully, nothing more." Jace shook his head at Lania. "What makes you think I like fighting?"

Jace acted nervous. Did the big job today have him overly worried? Or did she do it to him? He'd never been nervous around her. Not that she knew of, so why now? Although it might be a stretch to think he cared enough to be so nervous. "I saw you at the prison. You fight extremely well. I just thought you liked it."

"It's a necessity at times. That's all." He started to walk toward the door. "Jace, wait a moment, please. I was wondering exactly what Joehend Rickmond had to say?"

"He told Holt that Raulf and Marna were freed by Raulf's paid men. In order to put you back in power it will be a simple case of arresting Raulf, Marna, and all Raulf's paid employees. Unfortunately, that was our mistake last time. We only knew about half of his men, he obviously had more than we were aware of. Rickmond knows who they are so throwing them all in jail this time should be easy and prevent all problems for you. You should be able to just walk in and take your place. Simple."

"Thank you. I appreciate you telling me."

'You're welcome, My Lady." Jace hurried to the door and the moment it opened he started to leave, but stopped. "Whenever you're ready, we can wait in the main area where there's more room."

She watched him disappear from sight. He seemed in a big hurry to get away from her. What a change. Before he could barely wait to be with her. She shook her head. When love left, it must really be gone. Obviously, her love still remained with her since she did not want him to leave. In fact, she wanted to talk with him before they became separated forever, a thought she refused to have.

She needed to go wait with him. For some reason all she wanted to do was put her arms around him, have him hold her close, and tight. She loved the feelings he gave her when he held her safely and lovingly in his arms. Protected and happy, the result he left her with, and she treasured every millisecond of it. She no more had the ability to forget the happiness Jace gave her, than to forget the evil living in Raulf.

The door slid open and she left her room to join Jace in the main area. He sat in the upholstered chair, tapping his foot on the floor. More nervous actions. If she took the time to admit it to herself, she did not feel nervous, she felt terrified. Scared to death, with no one to comfort her and tell her everything would be fine.

She took a seat on the end of the divan closest to Jace, whether he liked it or not. If she reached out, her hand would be on his arm, and she wanted to feel him in the worst way. His muscles were always so tight and dangerous under her fingers, and those feelings made her stomach twitter. Even now Jace continued to have the effect on her which made her stomach turn inside-out.

Jace looked directly at Lania. “You’re ready if we’re called?”

“Yes.” What did he think? She didn’t dress like this every day, only for certain occasions, like taking her new job as Royal Ruler of Lorton.

“It shouldn’t be long.”

She smiled at him. “How do you know?”

“Guessing.” He turned his head away from her. “Just want you to be ready.”

“Jace, we need to talk. I…” The alert sounded from Holt’s info-center and Jace jumped up from his chair so fast it nearly tipped over when he stood. It simply showed her how anxious he was to get away from her. He obviously didn’t want to talk. She watched him head to the lift, so she followed. At least everything would soon be over. If it ended between the two of them, so be it. Time always proved to be the true test, and hopefully love prevailed between them.

She followed Jace in silence, and remained so during their flight to the Royal Palace grounds where he landed, then helped her exit the craft. Jace offered her his arm so she could walk with him. Her man never lacked manners, or proper protocol. She accepted his arm and allowed him to escort her up the main steps and into the great hall at the top of the stairs.

When they entered, she saw Holt, Dane and High Council Leader Rickmond standing between them. All three men gave her a slight nod while Jace walked her closer to them. Like a true gentleman, Jace escorted her to Leader Rickmond and presented her hand to him. He then turned, stepped back, and stood beside his brothers. She laid her hand on Rickmond’s arm, the same as she did Jace's and waited to see what Rickmond might say. One thing stood out clearly to her, Jace's arm felt so much better to her touch, and she had not wanted to let him go.

One by one, The High Council Members walked into the hall and took their regular places. They all faced the dais and stared up at her as if she were on fire. She hoped they were happy to see her back, and from their changing looks, they were, which remained of the utmost importance since they all played a part in her decisions and ruling ability. She felt quite happy to work with them.

The Lorton Government only remained a good one when they held the peoples' interest at heart, something she greatly appreciated. The government must be for the people, at least it was like that while her father and his priors ruled, and she would do the same.

The only space left in the huge room was a tiny bit of standing room, and even that quickly disappeared under the men's feet. The chamber had filled way past capacity. She could honestly say it was the largest group ever seen in this chamber at one time for a meeting.

Every High Council Member and every person who ever held a title came to see her. The turnout was truly amazing, and all for her. Or so it seemed. Possibly simple curiosity. She knew they all wondered what she had in mind for the future of Lorton.

Her time was now. So many important and complex issues lay heavy on her mind, yet she did not prepare a speech of any kind, never thinking she needed one. She had not really thought much about what all might happen this sun-cycle.

Councilman Rickmond stepped up to the enhanced podium and held up his right hand, since her hand was still on his left arm. She watched Rickmond's expression, which at the moment was a wide smile, an expression rarely seen on a man of his importance. He lowered his hand and the room fell silent. Now her nerves made her feel like fainting, a horrible sign to give all these men regarding the first woman ruler. The thought nearly made her laugh, which would be even worse.

"Ladies and gentlemen, esteemed Council Members, and all attendees this sun-cycle." He took a deep breath. "We have finally, and completely accomplished the task of removing our previous leader. All I will say, is that he, and his life-mate, are safely put away where they will never escape, or bother Lorton again."

A huge, extremely loud applause erupted at his statement. Everyone hated Raulf and obviously her sister as well, both evil and unlikeable, a tough lesson she still dealt with in her own way. The clapping seemed to go on forever. Councilman Rickmond simply nodded and let them express themselves. They slowed down and the huge room grew quiet once again, so Rickmond continued to speak.

"As you can see, I have, My Lady, Lania Sloten, here at my side." He looked at Lania.

Applause broke out again in a vigorous and loud manner, which took quite a while to slow down. At least they seemed to want her, which provided a gigantic relief and sent a shiver down her spine. Hopefully she would give a memorable speech. She smiled. Not because she was expected to, but for her people and how very special they were to her. Councilman Rickmond raised his hand to try to stop the applause since he looked ready to continue.

"May I present, My Lady, Lania Sloten." He released her hand from his arm and stepped back to stand behind her.

"Thank you, High Councilman Rickmond." She faced her audience and soaked in their long and appreciated applause. The poor people must be tired of clapping by now even though it was their only way of showing emotion and support. Bit by bit it grew quiet, and she took a deep breath to steady herself.

"First, I want to thank you all for attending this sun-cycle. I am here as Your Lady, soon to become Royal Ruler of Lorton." They started to clap again so she held up her hand and they immediately stopped. They must obey her right now. "I know there has never been a woman Ruler before; however, I believe it is past time Lorton did." The applause broke out again. This time she allowed it since she loved the show of faith to her by the High Council members. She gave them their time and gratefully smiled.

"I want all of you to know," silence covered the room, "I am a ruler of the people, and for the people. That is what this government is for, to make the people's lives easier, provide sensible laws to live by, and show kindness whenever possible. I believe every citizen is equal, and all citizens deserve the same treatment." More loud applause, so she paused. She gave them her best smile and 'thank you' nods.

"I also propose a new law that states The High Council can no longer choose who the Royal Ruler must life-mate. That is a personal choice, the same as it is for you. The Royal Ruler needs to have the freedom to choose their own life-mate." Clapping began again, although this time she wanted and needed their support on this issue. She refused to allow The High Council to dictate her life-mate. "I may be the first Ruler to life-mate someone of my own choice, but I guarantee it will be a good choice." She waited happily on this applause.

"The man I choose will be honorable, proper, and more than capable of serving by my side. I plan to choose someone who can listen to me and give advice." She smiled. "Should I ask for it." She waited for the chuckles to die down. "Of course, I will always rule according to my duty, the laws of Lorton, and especially for you, the people. Everyone needs a capable confidant, and I deserve to choose mine." More applause meant they agreed with her, which sent satisfying chills down her spine.

"I'm sure I don't need to remind anyone of the recent past, or some of the difficult times we have all endured. That means changes are in order, and I will make those changes." The clapping began to annoy her. She wanted to finish this speech and then relax. The pressure of it all began to weigh heavily on her. "We all know about the numerous issues which require attention, and I want to reassure The High Council, I will do my duty and take care of everything. However; I found the paperwork that proves the previous ruler neglected everything during his term of power. Which means I will take care of all the people's business as quickly and properly as I am able to do. I promise you, I will take care of every single issue, one sun-cycle at a time." The applause gave her a moment to catch her breath and think how to end this gracefully.

"I give every citizen credit for going through the last few annual-cycles peacefully. I am sure it was not easy, and I guess you all wanted to do something you knew you should not. I think we all experienced those same thoughts. Someone sent me off to a remote planet, but they removed my memory before I left Lorton. Thank the stars my memory has returned so I'm capable of helping my beloved citizens now." She bowed her head and waited for the applause to calm.

"Before I close, I must thank Bryton Brothers' Security for their undaunting, continuously excellent work to make my return possible. I believe you all know the story. I also would like to add that I personally went underground and fought the energy battle Raulf and Marna were not capable of doing. I hope you will all see big results soon, the kind that makes life exceedingly easier for everyone!" The applause could not be stopped; they even gave whistles and nods this time.

The moment the applause slowed down she raised her hand. "I will not keep you any longer. I only wanted to explain my intentions, and the direction I hope to lead Lorton. Every good thing about this planet will be maintained, and what requires to be fixed will be repaired to satisfaction. Of course, everything depends on The High Council allowing me, a woman, to become Supreme Ruler of Lorton."

More applause went on and on. Grateful as she felt, the emotions took their toll on her and her lack of strength caused her to be completely worn out. Time to end this. "Thank you all for coming, and for your adamant attention." She bowed her head, the Ruler's way to show thanks to their audience, and she did want to thank them properly.

Just then Jace stepped up beside her, and offered his arm, which she gladly accepted. He escorted her back down the same steps they used before, then through the hidden door panel set inside the back wall which led to the private lounge, where speakers were left alone to relax, before and after an appearance.

"Would you like a drink, My Lady?" Jace asked.

"That sounds wonderful. Thank you." Jace's tone still sounded far too business-like. She understood, considering the way she'd treated him. She walked across the thick carpeted floor and took her place where the Ruler usually sat while in this room. It felt fantastic to finally be off her feet and sitting down, which told her she had been far more nervous than she believed possible. Obviously, she used denial to avoid situations, like giving speeches, and how to deal with Jace. Back to one step at a time. One sun-cycle at a time. One...

"Here, My Lady. Your drink."

Jace handed her a crystallick glass with an icy-red liquid in it. "Thank you, Mr. Brighton. I appreciate it more than you know."

"You're welcome. Please enjoy."

When she glanced up at him to say something, he'd already turned and walked across the room. He took the farthest chair from her, obviously talking was not on his agenda. What was he afraid of? What did she do to him? She viewed this situation as totally ridiculous. The man seemed to be playing some kind of game with her. Should she waste her time to pursue Jace's lack of interest in her? He did not want to speak to her, and he made it very clear he did not want to. What was going on in his mind remained a mystery to her.

How could it be possible for her to know what Jace thought when she did not even know her own thoughts? She wanted to find out. That said, she could not wait for him. She could not wait for any man. Of course, she just entered totally new areas with The High Council, and that alone created a bit of calamity. Her choice of a life-mate must be perfect, and the man she chose had to agree with her, and Jace did not. Not anymore.

It seemed clear as sunlight to her now. They were done. No more 'us'.

Chapter Thirty

Holt stared at his brother. “I thought you and Lania were going to work this issue out? Do you even know what it is?”

“I’m not sure.” Jace shook his head. His brothers always knew if he lied. “I wanted to work it out.” He took a breath. “She seemed cold, and totally into her Ruling responsibilities. Besides, until she can choose her own life-mate what’s the point? Until The High Council decides she has the same rights every other Lorton citizen has, I don’t have a chance. At least I hope she’d choose me. Then again, I have no idea at this moment.”

“We can go talk to her if you want?” Dane looked Jace in the eye.

“If necessary, I’ll be the one to speak to her. I’m sure you understand. Thanks for the offer.” This problem with Lania belonged solely to him. His brothers couldn’t help in the same way they always did, only he and Lania could solve their problems—if there was even a solution to be found.

Dane scratched his head. “Are you up for more jobs? At the moment we don’t have anything requiring all three of us, I only wondered in case one comes up.”

“Of course. I’m a viable part of this business. I’ll always do my part.”

“Just checking,” Holt added.

“I realize I’ve been a pain lately, and I’m sorry. We’ve all been through this before. I suppose someday we’ll all succeed at finding the right mate. Until we do, we’re the same threesome we’ve always been.”

Dane nodded. “We like the sound of that, Bro.”

They laughed together like in the past. He knew well what it meant if any one of them found a life-mate. The 'trio' relationship would change; it had to if their life-mating were to succeed. Adding anyone to the trio mix seemed to be a challenge none of the brothers wanted to take, which is probably the reason he felt the way he did toward Lania.

Jace the brave, felt afraid of what a woman would do to his relationship with his brothers. The three of them lived together since birth, and not one of them could possibly imagine changing the dynamic trio. A woman in the mix had the power to change the trio in many ways. They were each afraid to be the first to make such a change, yet each of them knew it would happen one sun-cycle.

All three of them wanted to leave an heir behind, whether male or female, yet each of them backed away from being the first. Plus, with Lania, the mating responsibilities would become far too demanding to do this job with his brothers anymore. He couldn't stand at the ruler's side and still work with his and their clients.

It felt impossible, even if The High Council answered her request and allowed her to choose her own mate. He might still find time to work this job, yet Lania could need him on a moment's notice. Definite conflicts would arise between the two assignments.

Life seemed strange, and one never knew what the stars had in mind. Destiny. Until he might have a clue what to do, he'd simply continue being one of the mighty three Bryton Brothers.

"Jace? Are you, alright?" Dane asked.

"Fine. Why?"

Dane and Holt laughed at him. He knew he'd been daydreaming again and decided he truly needed to pay closer attention. "Sorry. I'll do better. I promise. It's over now, and over it shall stay."

"Whatever you say, Bro. We're with you," Holt said. "Now, we must get down to business. We have many things to clear up. So, are you two up to a business meeting for Bryton Brothers' Security?"

"Bring it," he and Dane both said.

Lania stood at the podium in front of The High Council and lowered her right hand. They just finished swearing her in as Supreme Royal Ruler of Lorton, a position she always doubted would be hers. They passed a new law that said it no longer mattered if the Supreme Ruler was male or female, as long as they were in the Royal Family blood line and qualified to lead.

Many issues she wanted to confront still remained, including choosing her own life-mate. She felt now might be the right time to address the main issue of all and finish her agenda. "If I may, I want to address The High Council at this time regarding their choice of my life-mate. I say it is time to change that law. I am more than capable of choosing my own mate, and if I am not, I do not deserve to hold this position of authority."

"My Lady," High Councilor Joehend Rickmond began, "We have discussed this issue during our sessions previously. However; we have not reached a cohesive law or decision. We are considering your request." He picked up his notebook. "If there is nothing else requiring immediate attention, we will continue our discussion on said matter, and summon you when we have come to a vote. Will you agree to allow us such time, My Lady?"

"Very well. I have many issues to attend to. I'll await your summons. Thank you all for your consideration. I do appreciate your time and thoughts on the matter. Again, thank you." Lania gave them her 'thank you' nod, then turned and left The High Council Chambers. It wasn't a bad place, just too formal and stiff for her liking. Although, formal business always went like it just did, and business was business.

She did not wish to upset The High Council, since so far, they were very accommodating, and she hoped their attitude continued through the life-mate law request. Even if it did, she had no man waiting to present. At one time she believed she knew the perfect man, not now.

Jace changed so quickly. There must be something she missed, yet if it happened, she should know since she would have been there. Obviously Jace meant what he said to her, there was no more 'us' to their relationship. Not the kind of 'us' she needed since she must find the perfect, permanent 'us' to life-mate.

Now she needed to figure out how to find that man. If The High Council agreed with her, they would want her to life-mate very soon. For some reason, they felt a woman incomplete if she had no life-mate. Since Jace fell out of the picture, she no longer had true motivation to even look for a man. Although, if she had to, she at least wanted to be the one to choose and present him to The High Council. No more forced pairings, not for her, not for any future Rulers.

She needed to consult with her two advisors, the two women on Lorton she knew the best and completely trusted. They would tell her how to go about this and remain inconspicuous. Whatever she did, required her to maintain low visibility. She did not want to advertise the fact she searched for a life-mate. That promised disastrous results. Men would line up for her attentions, wanting a position of power. That scared her to death.

Or did she not want to alert Jace? Probably. Whatever his problem, she no longer cared. True love did not work that way. True love always took care of situations all by itself. True love should always be honest and real. Not like this stupid game she and Jace somehow created. She would consider her advisor's input. They both knew her very well and had worked with her for sun-cycles on end, so they would have great ideas for her.

Most likely they'd suggest a party with every single, good-looking man on Lorton invited. She cringed. All three Bryton brothers came to her mind. They were probably the best-looking men she'd ever seen on Lorton, or anywhere in the galaxy. She'd make a point not to invite them. Done. She decided on her plan, meet men at a gathering, dance and be merry. What more could an eligible woman want?

The only problem with the dance-party plan was she would be making herself very obvious, exactly what she did not want to do. At the same time, how else could she meet a lot of men quickly in order to find the perfect life-mate? Getting all the eligible men inside one room did make a lot of sense, obvious or not. She had no choice.

Once inside her quarters she rang for her advisors. The moment they arrived she told them the idea. Even they raised their eyebrows at her. "What?"

"My Lady," Allisone began, "you know who you want, why are you playing games?" She bowed her head. "Sorry. You did say..."

Lania held up her hand. "I know. I'm the one who is sorry. Jace and I came to an impasse we are unable to cross. Sad, yet true. We may still have feelings for each other, although it will never come to a life-mating, so no need to press the issue. I want a willing life-mate, a man who loves me for who I am, not what position I hold. Do either of you think that is possible?"

"Well," Connita began, "I don't know. If you need a life-mate, and The High Council is willing to allow you to choose, then you had better make it count. They will not wait forever for your choice. You know they won't."

"I fear she's right, My Lady," Allisone added. "Not to rush you." She shook her head several times. "You do know how necessary it is for you to find the right man. Your life-mate will have his own responsibilities, the same as a First Lady would have." She looked Lania in the eyes. "I don't need to explain this to you. I'm sorry."

Lania smiled at her advisors. "It's fine. I understand. We're discussing and debating. That's how it goes, it is what we have always done." She nodded at the two women. "I am grateful to have you both. Really, I appreciate both of you, more than you know." Lania looked down at the floor. "I'm not sure how to erase Jace from my mind so I can move on and make a great choice. Do you ladies understand?"

Both women nodded at her, then answered in unison, "We do, My Lady."

"Well, we don't have to decide this moment. We'll have to find a way to make this work, and work well." Lania nodded. "The responsibilities are piling up rapidly, I fear. If we proceed on a party event, you will need to order a perfect gown for me. Pale orchid will work fine."

"Yes, My Lady," Allisone answered. "It will be gorgeous. You will need several gowns to be made since you will be expected to make many appearances."

"Yes. Take care of ordering those for me, please. I'm not in the mood to order dresses." Lania shook her head. "I will leave the invitations to you also. However you choose to handle those will be fine. Just one request: do not invite any of the Bryton Brothers. That would be like inviting trouble and I do not want trouble." Lania looked her two assistants in the eyes. "Understand?"

"Yes, My Lady," they both said.

"Now, I think I'll rest for a bit, if you don't mind."

"Of course. We'll be available whenever you require our services. In the meantime, we'll begin preparations." Allisone and her friend both bowed, then walked to the door. "Rest well, My Lady."

"Thank you." Lania heard the door close behind her advisors. She viewed them more like friends. Her position frowned on making friends with hired help since they were all supposed to act very business-like, and it usually worked out for the best. If things became too casual, friendly issues became unduly influential, a fact The High Council knew very well.

The term, 'life-mate' suddenly became a term with too much meaning, one she no longer wanted to say, and definitely did not want to think about. As the one surviving Royal, she must leave behind an heir to continue the official Royal line of Rulers. Such responsibility at one time seemed like a great thing, now, not so great. Oh, how life could change in mere moments.

Enough of this nonsense. She needed to list the people's needs and set an agenda to address them all. She served the people, and the people were just the distraction she needed. Landing sites for crafts of all sizes had become an ongoing problem in several main terminal areas. She needed to devise a plan to add and expand them, and this particular project could keep her busy longer than she might like. Just listing all the current places requiring expansion, and new areas to consider, might take many sun-cycles, and moon-cycles. Exactly the solution for being lonely.

Chapter Thirty-One

"So, Councilman Rickmond arrested twelve High Council Members, bought by Raulf to put Lania in prison. Raulf's twenty-eight personal guards, or whatever he called them, released both Raulf and Marna, then took the government back over." Holt shook his head. "It seemed he had this plan all along, like he expected it to happen one day. That's what they got from the guards that were more willing to talk, guards looking for a deal to stay out of jail."

Jace took a deep breath in an effort to assimilate what Holt just told him. "I'm glad to hear it's finally over and everyone is incarcerated this time." He shook his head. "It doesn't surprise me he planned ahead. He's evil, not stupid."

Dane nodded. "It's a relief. We all knew there had to be several people involved, we just didn't know who they were, or where. Lania was correct, Rickmond is very loyal to her, a fact we can be extremely grateful for."

"You're right, Bro." Jace nodded several times at Dane. Holt was at his info-center as usual, so he and Dane were conversing about a lot of issues resting heavily on the Bryton Brothers' agenda.

Holt rushed over to Jace. "This message just came in. I know you're not watching, so here ya go."

Jace read the message. "Of course, tell her to come here and I'll speak with her."

"You got it." Holt rushed back to his info-center.

Jace couldn't believe one of Lania's official advisors wanted to speak with him in private, signed by advisor Allisone Cammira.

Puzzling to say the least. She didn't indicate why. Probably to keep him hushed about his relationship with Lania. He'd willingly comply. He was never a kiss and tell type, and hated men who practiced such underhanded slander. Private affairs needed to remain private between the two parties, and never for public review.

Whatever her reason, it would be his duty to cooperate, especially since he knew Lania was now the Official Royal Ruler of Lorton. The news spilled out to the public while the swearing-in was still in progress. Part of him wished he'd been with her. At the same time, he didn't want to upset Lania if she saw him.

Allisone's note indicated she needed to meet very soon, and he knew Holt told her to come now, that's how he operated. At least he asked first this time, a bit unusual for Holt. Jace decided to keep going through the stack of papers in front of him until Allisone arrived. He knew she'd be here soon, but he worked on anyway.

Jace got through several pages before the buzzer sounded. He knew who it must be, so he went to the lift to greet the arrival. He rode up to the top level, and when the lift door opened, he found a short, well sized woman of middle-age, who must be his guest. "Ms. Allisone Cammira, I presume?"

"My, my. Aren't we formal, Mr. Bryton? Yes, I am Allisone, and we need to talk. Is there somewhere private?"

"Of course. Follow me." Jace led her into the lift and together they rode down to the main level, and he then led the way around inside, behind the lift and into the reception office they used for new clients and privacy. He pulled a chair from under the four-seat table and held it for her. Once he made sure she was settled, he took his place across from her. "How may I be of help to you?"

"I'm here, unbeknownst to Lania. She'd definitely kill me if she knew." Allisone chuckled for a moment. "You are Jace, right?"

Jace chuckled. "I am. My identical brothers are busy at the moment, or I would introduce you."

"That's fine. I'm here because My Lady must choose a life-mate, as I'm sure you're aware. What you may not know, is she is still very much in love with you."

"Aaaah. I no longer know what to think."

"Take my word for it, she is. And I do know. I'm with her nearly every waking time-unit of every sun-cycle. She is miserable, to put it plainly."

"I did not realize. And why do you believe she is in love with me?"

"Mr. Bryton, please. Do not play games with me. I know love when I see it, and I know My Lady very well. I've been a second mother to her. I advised her father in the finer areas when he needed a woman's touch. I also cared for Lania in his absence, and he seemed to be gone a lot. You might say I've been a substitute mother to her, especially since she never really knew her mother before she died. I did it willingly. I've always loved Lania. She's a very sweet person, always has been. And you should also know that very well."

"I do. Yes, you're correct."

"So why are there problems between the two of you?"

"To be perfectly honest with you, I don't know. I only know she quit speaking to me and has done her best to ignore me for some time now. I wish that wasn't the case. It began when I rescued her out of prison. She thanked me, but would never really talk to me. I have no idea what happened in there, or why she won't talk to me. That's all I know. What else can I say?"

"For starters, you can say you love her!"

"Wow, you don't mince words, do you?" He laughed. "If I told her I loved her, it wouldn't change her mind about anything." Jace shook his head and looked into Allisone's eyes. "I told her that the last time she actually spoke to me, that's when she was here. At this point she considers me dead to her. Before anything can change between us, she must be willing to talk, and I have not seen that happen, even though I've tried several times. She only ignored me. She's very good at that, in case you don't know."

"Oh, I'm very aware, Mr. Bryton. What I'd say right now, is you're one stubborn man, and she's a very stubborn woman. Together you make a stubborn pair!" Allisone chuckled.

"I believe you're probably correct."

"Not probably, Mr. Bryton, I am correct. And you well know it!" Allisone shook her head. "Again, if Lania even suspected I came here, we'd both be crumbs on the table. Do not tell her. Promise?"

"I promise. Although, I really don't know what you want me to do, or how to do it. Lania is very busy these sun-cycles. She has no time for me."

"Well, there may be a party you're *not* invited to, on *My Lady's orders*. You know why. She doesn't want to face you, for whatever reason. I'll let you know when and where this event will be, and I expect you to attend. I will see to it you have an official invitation delivered here. I'll send a currier with it."

"I don't think it's a good idea. I don't want to embarrass, My Lady, or complicate her life. You understand, I'm sure."

"I do not. You two must work things out, whether you have a future together or not. You will speak with her and make this misunderstanding go away forever. Do you understand me?"

Jace took a deep breath. This woman refused to take no for an answer. Was he being stubborn? Should he talk to Lania? Could this be a misunderstanding, or something far more? He wasn't sure, and hadn't been since this crazy situation began. Well, if he were ever to figure it out, he would need to talk with her. Good idea, or not, it must happen.

"Ms. Allisone, I will agree to go to this event you speak of. I do have one request of you. I need to know My Lady's reaction. By that, I mean you play a game with her and say, 'What would you do if Jace Bryton showed up?' Then contact me with exactly what she says, and how she physically reacts. I always read into her by her body's reactions. Sometimes she'd shake, or her voice might quiver, you know, those kinds of things. I need to know. I need all the ammunition possible if I am to face her successfully. Okay?"

"Yes. I will tell you everything, because I have faith this relationship is right. You seem even more relevant than I thought."

"Really? What exactly do you mean by that?"

"Well, you're a lot like her. Two eggs in a nest. You need to be together. I believe you're very good for her, and will be a huge help with her decisions in the future."

"Well, there's still the law stating The High Council must choose her life-mate, and I doubt they will choose me. I have no title, nor am I the type of professional they recognize. Understand?"

Allisone laughed. “My Lady has already asked The High Council to void that law and create one stating the Supreme Ruler has the right to choose their own life-mate. Of course, you would have no way of knowing that, and do not reveal to her you know.”

“I won’t. You can trust me.”

“I hope so. If I can’t, I’ll lose my position, and probably be executed for treason, or something equally as bad.” She smiled at Jace. “I assume you get my point?”

“I do.” Jace shook his head at Allisone and rolled his eyes. It was all he was able to do to relieve the tension she’d put him under. “You certainly have a way of making your point. And forcing me to go along with what you ask. Do you know that?” She nodded at him. “I can see why you’re her advisor. And I see how she would rely on your judgment. You’re very organized, honest and to the point.”

“After what I’ve told you, you call me honest?”

“You came here on her behalf, with her best interest at heart, and to me, your actions are commendable.”

“Thank you. I certainly appreciate your compliment because...” she lowered her gaze and stared down at the table, “I had many second thoughts regarding this visit. Not one clue if it was a smart move or not.” She looked up at Jace. “I must say, I’m very impressed with you, and I believe this is for the best, exactly the way I hoped.”

“I’m glad you feel that way. I don’t want to let you down.”

Allisone chuckled for a moment. “It isn’t me you’ll let down; it is you and My Lady’s future happiness which is under inspection. You’re smart, you know you are. I don’t need to tell you.”

“Correct as usual.” He saw her make a move to stand so he rose and hurried to pull the chair out for her. She stood then turned and smiled at him.

“Thank you, Mr. Bryton. You’re so very polite, and I must say so very handsome.”

“You are most welcome, Ms. Allisone. I believe every man needs to mind their manners when around a lady. As for handsome, thank you for the nice compliment.”

She chuckled. “I wish it were a fact that all men were polite these days. Not enough men seem to care anymore. I don’t know why." Allisone laughed. "I knew there was far more to you than your good looks. So happy to learn I'm right!"

"So am I." Jace smiled at her then walked to the door and opened it. "Allow me to walk you out." He escorted her to the lift, then rode up to the parking zone with her. Her craft sat in the guest area, and he ushered her to it. The entry opened upon her approach and she hurried up the tiny little ramp. "I'll wait to hear from you."

"Thank you for your attention. Good sun-cycle, Mr. Bryton."

Before he could say another word, she'd climbed inside her craft and the door closed behind her. He backed up to clear the way for her take-off. One thing for sure, she left him with a lot to think about. Allisone just convinced him to do what he'd wanted to do for a long time. No matter the outcome, he needed to talk with Lania, Supreme Ruler of Lorton. The only woman he loved, ever.

Lania—truly his love—the only woman he would ever love. It was now or never, and he knew it. Allisone was right. The only way to handle this situation was to talk it out. He hoped for the best. It sounded simple, yet it wasn't, and he knew it. If it were so easy, the conversation with Lania would have happened long ago.

Nothing was easy in love and war, as the ancient saying went. He finally understood the meaning first hand. War was simple compared to loving a woman, especially one as complicated as Lania. Leave it to him to pick a woman out of his reach, a woman who must be told who to life-mate. Even if The High Council changed the archaic law, they'd have their say in the matter somehow. Enough influence to mess up plans, if not break up plans.

At this point he desperately needed to have a talk with her, and with luck, it might go somewhere. It still remained best for him not to have expectations under the circumstances, and he refused to get his hopes up, simply to be let down yet again. No, this would be on Lania. Totally. She was the Royal Supreme Ruler, and compared to her, he was nobody, with no pull and no say in anything. He remained out of the flow as always, at least that's what his brothers always said, and he had to agree, for the moment.

He also knew he wouldn't hear from Allisone about Lania's possible reaction to seeing him at the party. If she asked Lania, it would give her visit away somehow. Lania was always good at putting two and two together and a suggestion from Allisone, like what he'd asked, would give everything away—then nothing would work and he would probably be stopped at the door.

Only time would tell.

Chapter Thirty-Two

Lania admired her new lavender dress. It was cut lower in the front than she liked, and there would be no time for adjustments. Allisone told her to try it on three sun-cycles ago to see if any changes were necessary. She'd been too busy with the peoples' business to bother with a silly dress. Since she put business first, she could now spend all night worrying about who might look down the front of her dress. She would try to be comfortable wearing it. Most men saw more than she wanted them to see anyway, that's how men were.

Oh well. She was supposed to impress men tonight, that was the entire purpose of this stupid party. Now it barely seemed like a semi-good idea. She feared this moon-cycle would be laced with potential disasters waiting to happen.

What did it matter? She must find a life-mate to serve at her side and be loyal to her. What man was even capable of taking the back seat? None she knew. She couldn't believe Allisone asked her what she'd do if Jace Bryton showed up at the event. Actually, she wasn't sure. She decided it was over, yet she truly wanted him back.

Men loved to be in charge, maintain the lead, and always have complete influence. That meant she would be continually unhappy in any relationship she found herself in, whether it was her choice or not. This moon-cycle would be an eye-opener for sure. It might be better if she kept her eyes closed. She laughed to herself. Bad jokes were all she had to entertain herself. A man in her life had become a complication she would rather live without. What a laugh since this party was hers, and her idea, now she wanted to call it ‘stupid’.

At least she didn’t have to life-mate this moon-cycle. She would only be required to dance with a myriad of men, and pretend to be having a fantastic time. How hard could that be? She shook her head, hard. All the people around her seemed to have great expectations, and they would ask one question after another. Hopefully most of the questions would not come at her until next sun-cycle. By then she would have enough believable stories to keep them all happy. Everyone except herself.

She opened her drawer and pulled out the appropriate jewelry for her outfit. Nothing could ever be wrong with her crystallinius stones which reflected light so brightly and looked marvelous, not to mention the Purple-Stone heart in the center. This necklace better look fantastic considering the cost. Nothing was too good for The Royal Ruler.

Actually, the jewelry she wore this moon-cycle once belonged to her mother who passed when she was a small girl. When it became hers, she kept it locked up because it was her mother’s, and due to its value, her father insisted. Wearing it to this event would certainly add to the royal appearance she must present. She wished she could have seen her mother wear this necklace. She would have looked fantastic based on the pictures she always admired in the album. Unfortunately, jewelry and pictures were all she had to remember her mother by.

It seemed she appeared ready now. Ready for what? The time had arrived to leave for the event so she headed out of her room and stopped in the hall to wait for her escorts. They should be called by their job title; guards. They did make her feel safe, and after her uncalled-for internment on another planet with no memory, plus being thrown into prison here, safe was positively a good thing. She now had two guards in front, one on each side, and two in the back; no one could get to her now. She laughed. Where had they been when she needed them?

They all walked down the long hall and paused at the ballroom entrance. One guard in front stepped inside to tell the announcer The Royal Ruler was at the door. No big deal, but they certainly liked to make it one. At events like this, all attendees were announced and made to feel special. Although this moon-cycle, she did not feel special. She felt on display for every man to examine and decide who would be the ultimate taker. Where did this stupid idea of hers come from? If anyone else had thought of this she would strangle them!

The royal horns played and the dance music stopped. The main doors opened and her front guards led the way to the special area set-up for The Royal Ruler to sit, relax, and enjoy the evening. Right. The words enjoy and relax needed to be deleted this moon-cycle. She took a seat at the provided round table while her guards took their appropriate places along the wall behind her. Too late to run.

Now she only needed to wait for some unknown man to ask her to dance. She would be tired later. At least she wore her comfortable dress shoes. Most heels felt horrible from the moment she put her feet into them. These were perfect for the duration, and that remained the reason for needing a lavender dress since they matched her shoes.

A man approached her table, walked up to her and stopped. He bowed, then offered his hand to her.

"My Lady, would you honor me with a dance?"

Lania took his hand, stood, and together they walked the short distance to the dance floor, which was basically in front of her table. "May I ask your name, sir?"

"I am Mauerie, My Lady."

She wasn't able to pronounce his name the way he said it, so she simply nodded and allowed him to put his arm around her when they began to dance, like everyone else on the crowded dance floor. Luckily, people did not usually talk while dancing, and she loved the small plus. There were a few people who talked, yet most remained quiet.

Her partner was a good dancer, and whirled her around for the crowd to see, which seemed important to him. It did not matter to her as long as he was nice and maintained good behavior. Maureie was quite handsome, but not really her type, whatever that was. Warrior was the word that came to her mind, and she knew why. The dance seemed to go on forever, then finally it ended. He walked her back to her seat and thanked her for the honor.

"You're welcome. You're a very good dancer."

He gave her a really big smile, which told her he loved her compliment. Then he turned and quietly left her. Lania took a deep breath, happy to sit out the next dance that just began. Wait, she was not that lucky since another man walked up to her, bowed and offered his hand.

"My Lady, may I have this dance?"

She took his hand, stood and walked toward the dance floor. "What is your name, kind sir?"

"My name is Nicromb. Everyone calls me Nic."

"Nice to meet you, Nic." At least she could pronounce his name. They danced till the end of the song, then he walked her back to her table. This same thing went on over and over until she wanted to scream. She needed a drink in the worst way. Her fingers rested by her temples and she unconsciously rubbed her head. A strong drink might help her headache. When she looked up, her mouth dropped open and she nearly fainted.

Before her stood Jace Bryton, a drink in each hand, and one happened to be her favorite kind, red fruit and ice all mixed together, with the alcohol loudly calling to her.

"My Lady, do you mind if I sit with you and share a drink for a few moments?"

"You are welcome to sit with me, Mr. Bryton. Please, join me."

"I brought you a drink. You look like you need one."

"You know me so well. Mr..."

"Call me Jace, please. This is no time to remain formal. If I call you by your name someone will definitely come over and slap me." He smiled at her.

Oh, how she loved Jace's smile, especially this moon-cycle. It may be difficult to admit, but she wanted this man so badly. It may not be proper, or right to have those thoughts, but she could not help herself. It simply felt too good to have him here. "To what do I owe the pleasure of your company?"

"My Lady, I felt it was time to speak with you about 'us'. If you agree, of course. I do not wish to overstep my boundaries with you."

"Please, Jace. Say what is on your mind. I do wish to hear what you want me to know so badly."

"My Lady, I wish to begin by saying, I love you. I always have, and I always will." He looked into her eyes and took a breath. "I'm sure you were not expecting me to tell you I love you. It's what I needed to say, before anything else. We have much we need to speak to each other about, and I'm not sure this is the time or the place. I truly want another chance with you, and we need to put whatever has happened between us, behind us. Do you think that's possible?"

She studied his expression carefully. The blue of his eyes shone brightly in the subdued light, highlighting his handsome features from overhead. More importantly, it allowed her to see he was telling the truth. Jace's eyes always looked exactly the way they were this moment when his sincerity went beyond measure. "I want to believe we could at least try."

Jace smiled widely. "Then believe it, My Lady. I speak the truth to you, now and forever more. No secrets, no lies, just truth. I promise."

"Oh Jace. I believe you. I do. We have so many things to work out, and explain to each other before we can move forward. I truly hope we can."

"I know we can. I have no doubts, especially in myself. What you're thinking, I don't know. I only know I can do this." Jace took a deep breath. "And I still have total faith in 'us'." Jace looked around, then back at Lania. "Like I said, this may not be the proper moment to confide in each other. You have many male admirers here this moon-cycle. I need to take a back seat." Jace shook his head. "But first, I must have at least one dance with you. I need to hold you in my arms so badly. They ache for you. Truly, they do."

Lania took a sip of her drink and let it slowly trickle down her throat. "I feel the same, so of course you may have a dance with me, Mr. Bryton." She laughed. "I must call you by your proper name in order to keep myself from saying something revealing. Of course, you might like those other names better. However; it would be completely inappropriate, especially coming from The Royal Ruler of Lorton."

Jace laughed, then stood at Lania's side, bowed and offered her his hand. "My Lady, may I have this dance?"

Just then the orchestra began a new song. She took his hand, stood and allowed Jace to escort her onto the dance floor. He slipped his arm around her and pulled her body tightly against his. She leaned in toward his ear and whispered, "Dance away, bad Warrior-Man." That put a huge smile on his face, and she felt his strong muscles tighten. Even more importantly, she felt his readiness to take this embrace to the next level. Of course, acting on their desires remained totally out of the question. At least she knew he spoke the truth when he said he wanted her still.

They twirled around the dance floor like two teenagers, with all the zest and energy they were able to muster, and their exuberance overflowed through their actions. Other dancers on the floor saw them coming and quickly moved out of their way. She and Jace certainly presented a huge spectacle, and she felt every eye in the Celebration Hall fixed on the two of them. The entire room could not miss how well they functioned together. Thank the stars only she felt how badly he wanted her. She was also glad he wore the beautiful jacket which stopped far enough below to keep their secret.

The music finally slowed, and the wonderful, sweet song came to an end. While Jace escorted her back to the table, applause broke out all around the room. Everyone clapped for them, including the players in the band. Oh my, such attention. An embarrassed flush washed over her cheeks, and she knew the entire crowd saw her reaction. She'd never been proud to be the center of attention like this. It felt far different than business attention, and this adoration all happened because of the most handsome man in the room, *Her Warrior,* Jace.

She made Jace bow to the crowd with her before he helped her to her chair. He then made a move to leave. "Jace, please stay a bit longer." No way did she want him to leave, at all, or ever if possible.

He turned on his heel and faced her. "If that is your wish, it is also mine, My Lady." Jace took the chair next to Lania.

She loved the way he looked in his formal black suit. Black always suited him perfectly, which nearly made her laugh. Quickly she sobered. "Jace, I'm sorry for the way I've been acting. I'm not even sure why I've been so mad at you. I've been scared. I realize it is not an excuse." She looked down, then back up at him. "It is the truth. I've worried since the beginning we could not stay together due to the stupid laws in place regarding The Royal Ruler and life-mating. I'm trying to change those laws, and hopefully The High Council will vote my way. If they don't, well, I..."

"I completely understand. I've worried about the same thing. Every citizen is aware of the archaic laws present on Lorton. The High Council needs to amend the life-mating law immediately. I doubt anyone can remember how it even came into existence. Better yet, why would anyone ever believe such a stupid law was necessary?"

"It's a long story that does not matter right now." She saw Jace's hand on his knee under the table, so she reached down and took it into hers. He was warm, and he grasped her hand, and held it very tightly in his. His grip seemed stronger than she ever felt it before, like he feared if he let her go, she would never return to him. She desired never to leave Jace for any reason, ever again.

"You know, My Lady, if I stay here, no other man can come dance with you, and the line of possible suiters has grown extremely long."

He pointed to a large group of men on the far side of the room. "They're all leaning on the bar with mad and anxious looks on their faces, very impatiently waiting for their chance with the most beautiful woman they have ever seen, and they're losing what little patience they have left very fast."

"Good. I really did not have the strength to dance with them all, nor do I want to. "Jace, let's dance again, okay?"

"My pleasure." He stood, offered Lania his hand, helped her stand, then walked her to the dance floor.

When he took her in his arms, she gasped for breath, since he managed to take it all away from her. When he held her like this, her life felt complete, and nothing mattered except Jace. She'd missed him. Really missed him, way more than she ever realized. Being held tightly by the man she loved was the best thing on the entire planet. Lorton was a great place, and it became fantastic when she twirled around the dance floor in Jace's arms. Secure. Loved. Safe. It did not get any better.

Chapter Thirty-Three

Jace still couldn't believe he held Lania in his arms, and they twirled their way through the numerous dancers all around them. Lania was perfect. The most beautiful woman he'd ever seen, and she was now finally his. All his. And he well knew she was. He also knew Lania would never cheat on him. It simply was not in her nature, since her personality thrived on honesty and caring. She was also very loving and showed him she wanted him badly, but he wanted her even more, right now!

If they were able to find privacy at the moment, they'd be doing a completely different kind of dance. The kind two lovers did behind closed doors. Yes, he wanted that to happen, yet they could not make love anytime soon. Every possible law surrounded The Royal Ruler in order to keep her safe and happy. At least Lorton's laws were supposed to do so, even if those very laws failed in several areas before. Time for big changes, changes only Lania could make happen.

Lania, now a woman of high standing, also meant moral standing, and she was forbidden to be with a man she was not life-mated to, whether it was right or wrong. Some laws were good, others needed to be revised so The Royal Ruler could make their own decisions. Not all decisions could be called good, but a great Ruler would make the best ones.

It seemed the music heard his thoughts because it slowed, then stopped. He walked Lania back to the table, returned her to her chair and helped her sit. He lowered his head to whisper in her ear.

"By the way, My Lady, your dress is exquisite, even if you are showing all those other men what is mine." He smiled at her and saw an instant blush creep across her cheeks. "I'm sorry, did I embarrass you, My Lady?"

"A bit, I fear. I am too self-conscious about the front being so low-cut. I suppose all men notice those things, don't they, Bad Warrior-Man?"

Jace laughed "Bad-Warrior-Man, really? I'm afraid you may be right. Curiosity is what all men have, I suppose. Or I think it is. For me it is. Well, maybe not. I don't know. I think I made a mess of my answer. Men are known for bad behavior. They see what they want to see, for the most part. That's about all I can say. I can only speak for myself. However; I'm not all men."

"And what does that mean?"

"That I look down the front of a woman's dress just because I can. If I might be interested in her maybe, especially if she's gorgeous, like you. If she's not my type, I'm not going to pay much attention at all. See what I mean? I suppose this is the 'men will be men' thing?"

"Why Mr. Bryton, I do believe you're digging yourself a very large hole here, so you'd better stop while you are half-way ahead." She laughed at Jace.

"You're right, My Lady. And I will take your warning as my cue to leave you for the moon-cycle. You have other suitors impatiently waiting their turn." He picked up her hand, raised it to his lips and placed a small, perfect kiss on the back. "Good moon-cycle, My Lady. It has been a true pleasure for me."

"For me also, Mr. Bryton. Good moon-cycle to you."

"Remember, we're far from done." Jace turned and walked away, his stomach immediately turning into a painful knot. He didn't want to leave her. He didn't want her dancing with more men, because he wanted to punch all of them in the face and knock them flat to the floor because he knew exactly why they were here to dance. He'd done exactly that for less reason before. He wasn't in the Royal Palace itself when he did that, only the palace prison. He laughed for having such ridiculous thoughts. Now at the Royal Palace, at a party for the High Ruler, he wanted to dictate what he could, and couldn't do. Very funny indeed.

He returned to the area where all the eligible men waited their turn. When he made his way to the crowded bar, all the others swiftly moved away from him. At least they verified what he'd guessed while he spent too much time with Lania. They did not mind showing they hated the time and advances he'd given to their leader. Little did they know about their past together. If they did, he'd surely be hung from the highest light fixture in the building. He'd been a very bad warrior indeed. His fault, not Lania's. Men would be men. He'd heard that at least a million times, which simply got him in laughable trouble with his lady.

Jace came ready to ask Lania to become his life-mate this moon-cycle while he spent time with her. Somehow, this did not feel like the right time. They needed privacy, not a huge audience. Lania never seemed to find privacy very often these sun-cycles. She seemed to have an audience wherever she went, and they all needed something from her. He needed her more, although they were a couple on a completely different level. They had to make their relationship work.

One question bothered him; did she have time for him? Time to be a good mate? Time to love and be together with him, no matter what? Time to become a mother? So many questions and so few answers. They needed to have a long talk. He wanted to propose to Lania first. He didn't want to set rules for their life-mating, only work out problems due to her position.

The entire situation fell on The High Council to change the rules regarding her life-mate. Why couldn't this be simple? First The High Council needed to decide if they would allow Lania to choose her own life-mate. Back to first things first.

The eligible bachelors obviously wanted nothing to do with him, and he didn't care one space-hole what they thought. He planned to get exactly what he wanted, and soon. This situation must be settled fast and not stay in limbo any longer. He'd spent more time than he should have with the Ruler this moon-cycle, and from the looks of the line in the lounge area, he would have no more time with her. He hated to go home and not finish what he'd started, yet the time needed to be right.

This meant he would have to make an appointment to see Lania, and that might prove difficult for him, a basic nobody. He may be someone she knew very well, yet on the Royal Scale of

Importance, he had no rank. He knew how it worked, so he'd follow the rules, since the hierarchy expected him to act like everyone else on the planet. He'd check with Holt and have him do it through his contacts.

Holt always knew the fastest and easiest way to accomplish those kinds of tasks, so he'd have him do it. Plus, since Holt did all the info-work, he knew things and people neither he nor Dane knew. Each of their jobs led in different directions at times. He and Dane seemed the closest at their job since they both basically left the info-center to Holt, the true master.

One possibility he'd nearly forgotten about, Lania's assistant. She'd help since she begged him to come this moon-cycle, insisting Lania still loved him. Well, she'd been absolutely right. Lania still loved him, and he was inextricably surprised in his own way. At the same time, he hoped and expected her to still be attracted to him in every way, since they shared a special and unique bond.

He ordered a drink from the bar and drank it slowly. His temper grew while he watched six different men dance with Lania. Every time the orchestra played another song, she danced with another suiter. Watching other eligible men hold his ever so beautiful woman became dangerous fast. He had to say, the men all appeared fairly handsome, and most were good dancers. His temper grew worse with every song, and he realized the time when he could no longer control his temper had finally arrived.

Before he smacked some man in the mouth, he decided it best to leave. He knew for sure she had no more time for him. It only took a moment to chug the rest of his drink, leave the ballroom and step into the hall.

When he turned Allisone approached in a really fast run, at least for her. She was desperately gasping for breath when she reached him so he put his hands on her shoulders; afraid she may faint. "Are you okay?"

"I'm fine." Allisone took several deep breaths. "I must ask you to follow me, if you don't mind. I can't say any more."

"Lead the way, please. Slowly so you can breathe." She took off and walked the hall in front of the ballroom. A bit strange, and he had no idea what she wanted. He continued to follow her while she wound her way from one hall to another, through one room, then another. No wonder she'd been out of breath if she'd come from this far away. When they reached a small reception area he'd never been in before, Allisone stopped.

"Sorry for the long walk. I didn't want to be followed. My Lady will be with you in a moment. I assume you don't mind waiting?"

"Not at all. Thank you." Jace nodded at her. "Allisone, I must also thank you for the visit you made to me. You did know what you were talking about." He laughed.

Allison looked Jace in the eye. "Thank you for realizing I was right." She giggled. "I am so very happy things worked out for you two." She looked down, then back up at Jace. "Did you get my note inside the invitation? I told you she rolled her eyes, then started coughing, like she was gasping for breath. Then, after a few moments, she calmly said, with no emotion, you would not show up where you were not invited."

"I read your note. Thank you. Thank you for the note, and for coming to see me. We wouldn't be talking if it weren't for you, my dear Allisone."

"You are so very, very welcome Mr. Bryton." She laughed. "I was going to say 'you handsome-devil', but I didn't want you to think I was flirting with you. It's just a compliment, but it doesn't sound right." Allisone chuckled a moment. "Now, I must go and tell My Lady you're here waiting. Good luck. Hope to see you a lot around here!"

Allisone giggled while she ran out of the room. That woman needed to slow down before she fell over. He laughed while he took a seat at the end of the long divan in the empty room. The silly thing could seat twelve people if necessary. Everything at the Royal Palace felt too formal, especially since he preferred simple and comfortable.

This area belonged to the hierarchy and their esteemed guests. He felt uncomfortable. No matter how difficult waiting here may be, he wanted to see Lania now, right now. All his patience disappeared long ago, so he was at the end of his ability to behave himself. The woman he loved needed to be in his arms and no place else. He knew he'd wait forever for the woman he loved if necessary, so wait he would.

Half a time-unit passed and he'd become overly anxious. Just then the door on the back side of the room opened and he rose from the divan so fast he nearly lost his balance. He just laid eyes on the most beautiful woman, ever. Words evaded him when it came to Lania, and since she wore what she did this moon-cycle, he simply stuttered, unable to speak. His heart raced so fast he thought he might need a doctor.

"Jace, I'm sorry to keep you waiting," Lania began while she walked closer, "It took longer than I thought since I couldn't let anyone know we were going to meet this eve. However; I wanted to catch you before you left. That's why I sent Allisone to bring you here. I hope you don't mind?"

He stepped closer to her, pulled her into his arms and kissed her deeply and long. The taste of her was so exquisite he thought he may never stop. It had been far too long since he'd enjoyed his woman, and he truly wanted way more than a kiss. Once again, he'd picked the wrong time and place for love, which was the story of his life recently. True love, the kind of love he had for His Lady. She kissed him back with passion, too much passion for him to handle when his entire body wanted her and desperately needed her.

Slowly he eased her back and smiled. "That was very nice, My Lady." He shook his head. "Too nice."

"That it was, and I want many more of those, if you're willing?" She lowered her eyes then looked back up at Jace. "We have not had our talk yet, so I'm not sure how you feel."

Jace dropped down with one knee on the floor, the other bent. "My Lady, Lania, will you do me the biggest honor on Lorton, and agree to be my life-mate?" He pulled the ring he'd bought for her out of his pocket and presented it flamboyantly, the way a perspective life-mate should. She smiled, and he considered that a good sign. Now for the answer. He waited and she simply stared at the ring between the fingers of his right hand.

"Jace, I don't know what to say. I...I..."

"Just say yes, you'd be happy to life-mate me. If it's your desire to have me."

"Oh, my love, my Warrior, yes! Yes, countless times yes!"

He slipped the ring on her finger, then stood, pulled her to him and gave her another passionate kiss. Now this was worth waiting for. He'd done it, she was now officially his. The thought ended his kiss and he eased her back. "Does The High Council approve of a mating like ours? That was part of what we need to talk about. There was something I wanted to ask you first, for some silly reason."

"I'm working on it, and I believe they'll see it my way for a change. Normally this kind of thing takes a long time. I told them I wanted an answer soon. And I must confess, I asked them before I even knew about this moment."

"Really? That seems odd, My Lady."

"No, because I wanted this from you, and somehow hoped to make it happen." Lania smiled at him. "Now what do you think?"

"Frankly," he paused and looked at her to tease her. He quit when she began to look worried. "I love you so very much, and deep within my soul, I always believed you loved me too. I also sensed, deep within me, there was still an '*us*'. There always has been, and there always will be." He reached for her and pulled her against his chest. She giggled and pulled away. "What are you doing?"

"You said you couldn't keep kissing or something might happen. I was trying to save us both from total embarrassment." Lania laughed. "I always have to look out for you, don't I?"

This time he pulled her to him and kissed her, gently and quickly. "I suppose you do, and that is exactly why we must be life-mates. However, not another heavy-duty kiss this eve. I really can't take such a kiss without," he moved his lips to her ears, "throwing you down on the floor and having my way with you in front of every vid-device in this place."

Lania put her lips to his ear. "You're a very smart Bad Warrior-Man, Mr. Bryton. So, for now, I will leave. A recording of us together will not be necessary to convince The High Council to give me free reign in certain areas." She looked into his eyes and smiled. "Understand?"

"I certainly do, My Lady. I certainly do."

"Jace, I have one question for you. How did you know about my impromptu dance?" Lania looked down, then back up at Jace. "I gave strict orders for the Bryton Brothers *not* to be invited. So how did you know, and how did you get inside?"

"I am sworn to confidentiality is all I can say, My Lady."

"Really? That's it?" She shook her head. "That is no answer at all."

"I'm afraid that is the only answer I can give you. Now, if you'll excuse me, I'll be on my way. My business here is through. I do not wish to overstay my welcome."

"You could never do that, Mr. Bryton, but leaving is a good idea for now. Good moon-cycle, Sir." She turned and left the room.

Jace stood alone and stared at the open doorway where Lania exited. She was amazing, beautiful, fun, and so damn sexy she drove him completely insane. He couldn't wait to be officially life-mated to her. One thing remained, telling his brothers what he'd just done. He hoped they'd forgive him. This mating might end his affiliation with them forever. If he were expected to always be at her side, he could not be part of Bryton Security. He'd deal with the confusion when it presented itself, just not this moon-cycle.

There were still issues to talk to Lania about, and he now knew they could easily work everything out together. Lania could not be more special, and not just to him. An entire planet looked up to her now as their esteemed Royal Ruler, the largest, and most amazing responsibility any one person could have. He'd gladly share those responsibilities with her and consider it an honor. He would, however, sincerely miss his brothers. He'd miss them more than he could say.

They'd never been apart in their entire lives. Born, raised and lived like the triplets they were, and sharing the close bond between them, the bond they could never explain to anyone. They'd always been closer than any person believed possible. Twins might know. Yet as a Bryton, he had the privilege of one more to include. They worked so well together, and he felt like a criminal since he would be the one to break up the perfect trio.

Could he do such a thing? They always knew one of them would be the first to make this type of move. It hurt him deeply to be the one taking that first step in the inevitable breakup. All three of them always knew the importance of life-mating. They'd simply thought they would always be able to continue Bryton Security. They thought they could live close to the office with their life-mate and everything would still be very close to the same.

Part of him still thought he may be able to work out some time for this job—he'd be lost without at least some part of it. His problem would be his responsibilities to and with Lania as her official First-Man—if that's what they decided to title him. He chuckled at that thought since there had only ever been a First Lady. It would be fun breaking new ground in the history books, and possibly his brothers could be a help.

Their business could survive with two of them. They'd have to take easier jobs than some they'd done lately. Something about the combo of three brothers together worked perfectly. Not one client ever expected a trio, unless they were told in advance. They looked enough alike they could fool people easily if necessary. He laughed to himself, thinking how many times that trick worked while undercover. Hopefully his brothers would understand, or so he hoped. Next sun-cycle he'd find out.

He was worried, yet both his brothers knew how he felt about Lania, and had most likely guessed he would propose to her if and when he could. A triplet thing. He'd tried to fool them regarding his feelings for her and failed miserably, so he was quite sure they anticipated his life-mating. First it all had to be officially worked out and legally accepted. They would be ready for his news, he knew that for a fact since they both waved good-bye to him and wished him good luck this moon-cycle.

Their good luck wish was for him to work things out with Lania. They may not expect an accepted proposal so fast, or possibly they did. He knew how his brothers were, and with Lana, they always seemed one step ahead of him. They would wish him well, and he would work with Lania to find the most time possible to being with Bryton Brothers Security. She knew how important his brothers were to him, and she knew first-hand the work they did. Without the three Bryton's she would still be a babysitter. What a horrible thought!

Chapter Thirty-Three

Lania stood tall and straight while she addressed The High Council. The business this day had been long and tiring. She'd been sitting most of the time, now she needed to stand in order to speak about her life-mating freedom. One chance would be all she had, so her request needed to be convincing enough for them all to agree and get the job done. Each member had probably already made their decision regarding the matter. Still, she wanted to present one last request so they would consider her case in the best way possible, and she wanted to ensure they would vote in her favor--definitely worth a try since she had a lot to lose.

"High Council Members, before I leave, I must ask you, one more time, to pass a new law allowing me the freedom to choose my own life-mate. I am more than capable, and will certainly never choose a mate the likes of Raulf." She paused while the audience snickered at Raulf's name. "I absolutely swear not to do so. However, I did not choose that evil man, it was the consensus of The High Council, prompted by circumstances. That disaster demonstrates how decisions can rapidly turn into misjudgments, which then turn into reality. No one can be positive about the success of a life-mate, although, some choices are far better than others.

"My choice will be a man of high standing, well educated, and more than capable of making decisions on behalf of the people of Lorton, the same as I can. It is no easy matter, nor an easy process to find a man with all the proper and perfect attributes necessary. Plus, I hope my choice will also be a man I can, and will love, since every single person alive knows love is a critical part of any life-mating success."

Lania paused and grazed the room to get a fix on the mood of the council members. They all kept their overly-professional demeaner in place, and not one of them gave away their feelings or opinions in any way. This would indeed be a new law for the books they needed to discuss in private, without more input from her. Most subjects were debated and voted on in front of her. Unfortunately, anything concerning the ruler's personal life would be done by The High Council in private. Not one member of the Council wanted her to look down on them if they voted against her. This way it remained a secret, more or less.

"You are all aware, I am more than capable of making this decision, if that freedom is awarded to the ruler's position. This law needs to be written for either male, or female. It is past time this new law is written and instituted immediately on planet Lorton. The past is the past. Some laws hold true being necessary and current, some do not. It is our responsibility to upgrade whenever necessary, and you are all aware, we have been delinquent in some of these areas.

"I will close my remarks and allow you to discuss the new law and the wording for the books. My request is you do create, and approve this new memorandum for The Royal Ruler of Lorton quickly. Thank you all for your attention to my request." Lania bowed her head slightly in thanks, then turned, went down the steps and left the room through the door behind her. At least the ruler had a few perks, like special entrances and exits all around the Royal Capitol buildings and grounds.

Her entire future now lay in the hands of The High Council. If they did not approve a new law, she and Jace could not life-mate. She wanted him in every way possible. Basically, everything about Jace pleased her. He was super handsome, kind, sweet to her, strong, a fantastic protector, and very smart. Everything she wanted in one excellent looking and loving package. She had thought it before and now knew it as a fact, no man compared to Jace, a perfect man in every way a woman could dream of, and more. Plus, after being with all those other men on the dance floor last moon-cycle, she had lots of men to compare him to, and as always, Jace easily won the comparison contest.

Both of her personal assistants rushed up to her with their apparent anxious looks, wanting to know how it went. She held up her hand. "I wish I had an answer for you, unfortunately, I have no idea. I made my case, again, quite well I might add. I just don't know how convincing I was. Hopefully, I accomplished my goal."

Allisone stepped forward. "My Lady, just know we hope you will receive the answer you're looking for. I for one know how much it will mean to you." She giggled. "Especially since you have that beautiful ring on your finger now."

Lania held her hand up and wiggled her fingers, especially the one with the large, sparkly ring on it. "Oh my, how did you ever notice?" All three of them laughed.

"We are thrilled for you, My Lady, you know that, I'm sure." Allisone nodded.

"Thank you both. I appreciate your support. Now, I need to go to my office. Call if you need me." She turned from them and began to walk down the long hall. When she reached the wing containing all the royal offices, she turned and walked to the one at the end.

She was pleased to have her very own, totally private office where she would be left alone to work. Sometimes too many people wanted an audience with her and would throw fits if they were made to wait a sun-cycle or more, and that behavior annoyed her to no end, especially when she needed to work on so many things piled on her desk. It seemed during her busiest moments, someone would sneak into her main office out of nowhere and begin their request. Someone in her entourage was usually forced to stop them and usher them out. Perfect did not exist.

Once inside her plush little office she made her way behind the desk in the back corner and sat in her comfortable chair. It felt great to sit and have her back supported the way this chair did. It felt like magic, and she needed magic right now. She wondered how much time The High Council might take to discuss her request, write a law and vote on it. Had she asked and expected too much? Probably, but she really wanted, no needed an immediate answer, even though she knew it might well be an impossibility.

If ever their decision might be hurried, she wished it would be now, over this issue. Her patience was gone, and she felt like breaking something, something big! A helpless feeling gushed through her, which was a feeling she truly hated no matter when it happened. Waiting for other people to do their part was never her strong point, and she needed improvement in the patience area. Their decision affected her entire future. Didn't they realize? Did they have any idea what they played with? Probably not since they rarely created or voted on a bill which affected The Royal Ruler in such a personal way.

It nearly made her laugh when she thought about Jace's main bad habit, the one they shared, a lack of patience. They truly were alike in more ways than she remembered. Speaking of Jace, where was he? What was he doing? He may be lying around relaxed, or he may be worried just like her. Damn to the stars and back! She hated this wait with a deep passion. She always thought when she became The Royal Ruler, she would never find herself in this position. Yet here she was, ready to tear her hair out by the roots.

It was time to get something done, and she needed to accomplish a lot based on all the issue-filled papers piled on her desk. It would help keep her mind busy, instead of thinking about Jace, and how they needed to be together. She pulled a stack of papers in front of her and began reading. This may be a long sun-cycle.

Time-units passed slowly. Lania felt happy she had accomplished so much while she waited. Jace barely came to mind, until now. She finished one pile of papers, yet there were many more piles waiting. At least she eliminated one, and it felt good to have at least one pile gone. This work proved to her, without a doubt, Raulf had done absolutely nothing for over six annual-cycles. The evil man was far too busy being evil, stealing credits, and taking women to his bed to do any required work. Oh well, she would fix the problems, just not as fast as she liked.

The alert light on her desk went on calling her back to stand before The High Council. At least the wait was over, one way or the other. She notified her guards who escorted her back to The High Council Chamber which she had left several time-units ago. This time the walk felt like it took forever, even though nothing had changed. She now stood at her podium in front of The High Council and waited to be addressed.

"My Lady," High Councilman Joehend Rickmond began, "thank you for being so prompt." He looked directly at The High

Ruler and gave a nod. "We have made our decision, and we believe you will be pleased. You will be allowed to choose your mate. However; we reserve the privilege of final approval, and that should satisfy everyone." He smiled. "Hopefully."

"My question is what does this man have to do to pass inspection by The High Council?" She tipped her head sidewise while she looked at Joehend Rickmond. "And what if a certain man is a love match, and The High Council simply decides they don't like him?"

"The approval process will not be so difficult a man cannot easily pass. We simply reserve the right to reject a certain type of match, like the most recent one. We reserve the right to object to someone who might be obviously detrimental to the Lorton people. I'm sure you understand, My Lady."

"I understand very well."

"May I ask if you have someone in mind to become your mate?"

"I do."

"Good. Bring him before us as soon as possible so we can all move forward."

"I will check with him to see what his schedule is. I'm sure he'll be happy to appear quickly. Will I be allowed to stay during his questioning?"

"As long as you say nothing and allow just the candidate to answer."

Lania wanted to laugh at the title of candidate. Could this be the Planetary Fair and no one told her? That thought really made her want to laugh, instead she simply gave them a nod. They knew she understood. She would be a terrible ruler if she did not understand something so simple. Since her frustration level had reached its peak, she hoped this meeting would end and she could leave. She desperately wanted to see Jace and tell him the news. The High Council must be able to see her anxiety. "Is there anything further the council wants to say?"

They all stared at her like she was a statue, rather than a person. This building contained enough statues without adding her. Maybe they did not see her at all. The High Council looked the same way they always did, all business, gruff and grouchy. By their expressions, they all looked like they wanted to bite her head off. Not a good sign when she waited to present her *'candidate'* to them. They might bite Jace's head off. She needed to stop these thoughts. Hopefully her overly sensitive thoughts were wrong.

Since she was sworn in, she felt on display for The High Council to judge since no woman had ever held this position in all of Lorton's history. How could she feel any other way? It made her wonder if the council had the ability to simply remove her from her position? She shook her head. Of course, if they didn't remove Raulf, why in the universe would they remove her? She'd never do anything close to what that monster did. Evil never crossed her mind. Besides, she was the only person on the planet from the Royal blood line.

"My Lady, there are several issues to discuss, although I suspect this is not the time. So, for now, we are done. Go see if you can find your prospective life-mate and return with him. If it is not possible this sun-cycle, please alert us and we'll schedule another time. Is that agreeable with you, and your schedule?"

"I believe it is. So, if there's nothing further at this moment, I shall leave the chamber. I will, of course, keep The High Council informed of the future appointment. My thanks to all Council Members for their attention to this matter, and for their positive vote and show of confidence in my judgement and abilities." She gave them her 'thank you nod', then turned and left the High Council Chambers. She headed back to her office, her guards surrounding her like always. She wished they did not have to be with her all the time, yet she preferred safe.

When she arrived at her office, the guards took their places outside the single entrance. She wanted to laugh. Could she do anything they didn't know about? A scary thought. She picked up her messages and read through them. Luckily one was from Jace to contact him. That was exactly what she needed to do, but it was better to do it the formal way since everyone around here seemed to prefer the way of pomp and circumstance for the planetary good.

Her assistant rushed in at her request. "Allisone, please summon Jace Bryton to appear to me immediately in my office. Also, tell him to dress for a High Council Meeting." She bowed her head in acceptance of the task. "Thank you, Allisone."

"No thanks necessary, My Lady. Happy to help."

"By the way, Allisone, do you know who it is I need to thank for inviting Mr. Bryton to the Formal Dance? I know what I said, but it put us back together, and for that, I am eternally grateful." She stared at Allisone for a moment and watched her squirm while standing in front of her. "Well, do you know who I need to thank?"

"Sorry, My Lady, I do not. I'll go contact Mr. Bryton now."

Allisone rushed off so quickly she nearly fell on her face. Lania laughed. Obviously, she ran off happy, guessing why she needed to summon Jace. Allisone earned her job as main assistant due to her intelligence, a critical attribute she used perfectly every sun-cycle. She also knew her number one assistant was the person who invited Jace, since she was likely the only person who even knew they were a couple, or had been a couple. She also knew they separated, and knew about the party. There was no one else who could possibly have known all the things Allisone knew, or would have gone against her will, behind her back to give her and Jace a chance to make-up and get back together. Thank the stars she did her job so well!

Lania picked up her pile of papers and began to work. More like try to get her mind off Jace and the questions he would face because he loved her. Was it wise for her to be with him? Maybe he should decide?

Either way she would remain close. This entire matter fell out of The High Council's norm, and hers. She just broke new planetary ground with her request and service. First woman to be ruler, and first to choose her own life-mate. She was making history fast, and she felt giddy and excited her plans were working. She still worried about the questions Jace would be forced to answer.

Anything could go wrong. So much to worry about, so little time. She still wanted to break something. Maybe she needed to in order to feel better. She picked up the large glass vase from her desk, and just when she leaned back to throw it, the buzzer sounded.

"Yes, Allisone?"

"Mr. Jace Bryton is here to see you."

"Show him in, please."

Lania stood behind her desk while Allisone opened the door for Jace. Damn to all the planets! The man could not be more handsome if he tried. She wanted to attack him where he stood, kiss his lips long and hard, then rip off his clothes. He looked at her with those dreamy, deep blue eyes of his and she felt herself melt even more than she always did.

"My Lady, you summoned me?"

"I did, Mr. Bryton. Thank you for being so prompt."

"May I ask what this is about?"

"Oh Jace, I want kiss you right now."

"Not nearly the way I want to kiss you."

Lania smiled, speechless for a moment. "We both want the same thing, however; you're here because The High Council has decided I may choose my own life mate. That said, it can only happen if they approve him. So, they want to question you this sun-cycle."

"Do you have a clue what they will ask?"

"Wish I did. We're all breaking new ground here, so even The High Council does not know what they will ask." She shook her head. "However; I've seen you in action and I am sure you will be fine. You can handle them."

"Considering all the business I've done before The High Council; I've testified only once over all the annual-cycles Bryton Brothers have been in business. They'll probably remember me since I accompanied many of our clients who were called to testify. I never said anything. I only stood with them for support in case they needed it."

"Right now, you are your own client." She laughed. "I know. That sounds strange, right?"

"It does, but it doesn't make me want to kiss you any less."

"Don't start the love talk or we'll never get to the council and accomplish our goal. So, if you really want to be with me, get yourself together and be ready for any questions they may have for you."

"I will not tell them about any intimacies; in case you wondered."

"The thought did cross my mind." Lania nodded. "You must stay truthful, or they will see right through any lies, they always do."

Jace smiled. "Very true. At least in my experience."

"Mine too." The buzz on her desk went off. "It is The High Council. We are being paged. Are you ready?"

"Yes, My Love, I'm ready. Ready for you, not really for The High Council." He nodded. "We need to put this behind us."

Lania answered the page from The High Council and told them she and Jace were on their way. "Very well, Mr. Bryton. Follow me. My guards will follow you. And if you value your life, do not touch me. They will kill you."

"I know."

She heard him chuckle under his breath. He immediately stopped when the door opened. He fell into step behind her, and she led him into the hall, then down several more until they reached The High Council Chambers. The door opened and they both stepped inside, her guards remained right outside the door. She looked at Jace and whispered to him, "Do you want me to stay?"

"Absolutely, My Love. I have no secrets."

Lania stepped up to the podium with every council member's somber gaze on her. High Councilman, Joehend Rickmond pounded his gavel. Now or never. "Esteemed Council Members, I would like to present to you my choice of a life-mate, Mr. Jace Bryton, of Bryton Brothers' Security, a business I am sure you are all aware of. I am also sure you know Mr. Jace Bryton is the man who found me, brought me back to Lorton, and restored my memory. Without Mr. Bryton's extreme efforts, and risking his life, I would not be standing in front of you right now. I owe him a lot. That said, I have strong feelings for him, and wish for him to become my life-mate. With your approval, of course. I now present, Mr. Jace Bryton."

Lania stepped back from the podium and turned it over to Jace. She took her seat, the one that seemed more like a throne than a chair. Well, she was The Royal Ruler. It still seemed strange to be sitting in what she considered her father's throne. She listened while different council members asked questions. It seemed they all wanted to know something about him. Poor man. No other potential life-mate had ever been put through any kind of questioning before. Jace must love her indeed. She would remember this for future reference.

Jace answered question after question. Most concerned his business. He answered the best he could, but there were many things he could not answer in order to maintain his clients' privacy. The council understood, but kept asking anyway. Jace stayed true to his ethics, and she assumed they would consider his answers a good asset, especially since he would have to maintain many secrets if they life-mated.

This new process with Jace seemed never-ending. Why did they need to know so much about him? Too bad Raulf didn't have to go through this kind of ordeal. One more reason women needed to be allowed on the throne, so to speak. If she and Jace produced daughters, she'd like to believe her firstborn would inherit the rulership. If she'd been allowed to inherit her position from her father, her people, and the entire planet would be in much better condition.

Raulf drained the government's credits, along with wreaking havoc everywhere he went. She understood why the council had so many concerns about Jace and his intentions. Jace was nothing like Raulf, and she wanted to believe the council already knew that fact since they researched all businesses they dealt with professionally. Hopefully he would convince them of all the facts she already knew to be true and valuable.

Every one of his answers sounded perfect to her, until the questions became personal. They tried to pry into his romantic past, and she found it difficult to hide a smile. His answers were perfect still, yet he revealed nearly nothing. Jace sounded better than perfect. If she had to choose a man again, Jace definitely would be her number one choice.

No man could be better than Jace. Surely The High Council would agree with her choice. If they didn't, she'd give *them* no choice. She'd life-mate him anyway and cause all the trouble possible, and it would be no laughing matter.

Then the questions boiled down to the two of them. She sensed he'd become a bit nervous when so far, he'd been very calm and collected. When they asked him about being intimate with her, she took a deep breath and held it. Jace's answer was brilliant! He stuck to the job, yet admitted he had feelings for her, yet revealed nothing about any of their private moments. They asked if he loved her, and without hesitation he said, "Unconditionally."

They couldn't ask much more at this point. Too many questions asked were already redundant. Councilman Joehend Rickmond dismissed Jace from the podium. Jace stepped around her large chair and stood alone behind her.

"My Lady, if you will give us a brief moment, we will call you back. It should not take long."

"Very well. Thank you." With a large thank you nod she turned her head when Jace stepped up to her and offered his hand to help her stand. She gladly accepted his support while they turned and left the chamber together. He knew to keep a proper distance, but she sensed his anxiousness to get out of the formal chamber. She led him to the private royal waiting area where they both took a seat next to each other. "I'm sorry you had to go through that."

"No problem. It's over now. Hopefully I persuaded them I'm worthy of you."

"If you didn't, I'll never be life-mated!"

Jace laughed. "I'm honored you feel that way, My Lady."

"I seriously meant every word too. Not one man I know could answer all those questions better than you did. So, I am not worried."

"Thanks for your support."

"If they don't like you, I'll life-mate you anyway." Lania looked him in the eye. "I love you with everything I have, My Warrior."

"I love you more, and you know it, My Lady." Jace smiled broadly at her. "I even slayed a monster that nearly ate me. Just for you!"

"Don't make me laugh right now. We must remain serious. Don't get me wrong, I do love laughing with you. Especially when you kiss my. . .." The door opened and in stepped the announcer.

"The High Council requests your immediate presence."

The announcer held the door open and they both returned to the podium and waited to be addressed.

High Councilman, Joehend Rickmond took his place right in front of the podium. "My Lady, it is my pleasure to report that we, The High Council of Lorton, have unanimously approved Mr. Jace

Bryton to be your official life-mate. We wish both of you the very best."

She could no more stop the smile on her face than she could a space transport. Pure joy surged through every part of her body, and she gasped for breath. One glance at Jace and she saw their words affected him the same way. She took a deep breath and settled herself in the center of the podium. "Mr. Bryton and I want to thank The High Council for seeing to this matter so quickly. We both appreciate your diligence. Now, we have plans to make, and we have you to thank."

"You are both very welcome. May this life-mating be the best ever. We will be here to watch." The High Council members all began to clap their hands in approval.

The members slowly began to laugh and cheer, putting her more at ease. Even Jace joined them, so she gave in to the current lack of formality. It felt wonderful to have this jovial moment after all the recent trauma. Nothing would ever be able to compare to good news and love mixed together. The very best part, she now had the man she loved at her side, knowing he would always be with her.

Jace leaned toward her and she heard him whisper they needed to leave. She nodded. "I want to wish The High Council a good sun-cycle." She gave the council her usual 'thank you' nod. When she turned, she felt the heat of his body directly behind her. If she stopped fast, he'd literally run her over. He made her laugh, and that made her happy since a life without laughter was no life at all.

The moment they arrived outside of the chambers, he bent to her ear and whispered to her once again. "My love, we need privacy. Now. You must know where we can go. Do you have a place? Please tell me yes."

"In fact, I do. Follow me."

"Anywhere, my love."

It tickled her tummy when he called her his love. It was not possible to love him more if she tried, and she knew he returned her love even more deeply than she gave it to him. The way to her office seemed to take forever. Once inside the main area, both of her assistants rushed up to her, like they weren't allowed to do. She understood their hurry.

"Allisone and Connita, hello." They kept shouting questions. "Calm down and I'll tell you. The High Council has given their permission for me to life mate Mr. Bryton." She pointed to Jace, who nodded.

"We're so happy for you both!" Connita said.

"Congratulations. Absolutely. I couldn't be happier! I love it when laws come together!"

Allisone giggled at Lania in a way that said she felt her happiness. She knew how her assistant loved Jace in her own way. "Thank you both, so very much. Now, I must ask a favor of you two. Jace and I need some time alone since we have not had a chance to even talk to each other. So, if you don't see me, tell whomever is looking for me I'm not here and did not tell you where I would be. Am I clear?"

"Yes, My Lady. Very. Got it," Allisone said.

"Thank you. I appreciate it. I may have to give you both a raise. They all laughed while she and Jace entered her private office, and he closed the door behind them.

Jace glanced around then stared at Lania. "Nice office. Although, with all that glass, I wouldn't call it private."

Lania walked behind her desk and touched a tiny button. The windows became completely blocked and they both heard the click of the door lock. She then pressed another button, and a panel beside the bookshelf swung open and revealed her private quarters. "This way, Mr. Bryton." She indicated for him to enter through the opening.

"This is good, my love. Very good." Jace pointed to the bed.

"I agree." She closed the open panel, then pressed a button on the top of her bedpost and the door to her private quarters closed and locked. Then she sat on the bed and patted the space next to her. He slid beside her in a flash, his arms threading around her, his mouth finding hers. She savored every moment of his sweet kiss. Damn he was a fantastic kisser, the one thing she could compare and declare him a number one winner.

Jace slowly pulled back and placed a hand on each side of her face. "You know we still have several things to talk about before we life-mate."

"Fine." She touched his cheek with her hand. "Except first we need to make mad, passionate love to each other."

"I do like the way you think, woman." Jace chuckled.

"I learned from you, silly!"

"I'm glad you did. I taught you well, didn't I?"

"You did. Now I want you to love me well."

"I can't think of anything I'd rather do."

Jace slid his hands under the shoulders of her gown, then eased the fabric down to her waist. He laid her flat on the bed, and kissed her with all the love a man could have for a woman. She felt his love filling her completely until she could barely breathe. He always amazed her, and she never wanted to let him go. He pulled back, ending his kiss and looked into her eyes.

"May this moment last for the rest of our lives. I never want to be away from you. I love you so very much."

"This moment will last, because we will last. I love you more." Lania smiled.

Jace became extremely passionate, his lips returning to hers to place a deep, hard, kiss on her mouth, his need pressing, and so very overwhelming. Her heart filled with joy, happiness, and Jace. The man she would love every sun-cycle of her life. She knew they could never get enough of each other. A love like theirs was total and complete. Nothing would ever get in their way. Nothing they could not overcome, and end up stronger for the fight.

He was hers. She was his. Nothing else mattered.

About the Author

Born in Michigan, raised and married in California, Kathleen is now a thirty-nine year resident of Missouri. She currently lives in Springfield, MO, with her big-baby, a 110 lb. Lab mix, and stays busy with her son, and three fantastic grandkids.

Writing is Kathleen's passion, which she became serious about in 1987 when she joined Ozarks Romance Authors. Always a fan of sci-fi and romance, she loves combining the two elements into stories of passion and adventure in another time and place. She has written five futuristic romances which are available on Amazon. She will be releasing a trilogy about three identical triplet brothers in a couple of months.

Other Books By Kathleen

www.ingramcontent.com/pod-product-compliance
Lightning Source LLC
LaVergne TN
LVHW020703110826
845149LV00012B/2087

* 9 7 8 1 9 7 0 5 6 0 2 4 4 *